Robert Edric was born in Sh... novel, *Winter Garden*, won t... Memorial Prize and his second, *A New...* runner-up for the 1986 Guardian Fiction Prize for its 'austere and unsentimental comedy'.

Also by Robert Edric

WINTER GARDEN
A NEW ICE AGE
A LUNAR ECLIPSE

IN THE DAYS
OF THE
AMERICAN
MUSEUM

Robert Edric

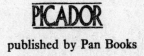

published by Pan Books

First published 1990 by Jonathan Cape Ltd
This Picador edition published 1992 by Pan Books Ltd,
a division of Pan Macmillan Limited,
Cavaye Place, London SW10 9PG
Associated companies throughout the world
1 3 5 7 9 8 6 4 2
© Robert Edric 1990
ISBN 0 330 31820 9

Printed in England by Clays Ltd, St Ives plc

For
Sara A &
Sara S

Few men in civil life have had a career more crowded with incident, enterprise, and various intercourse with the world than mine. With the alternations of success and defeat, extensive travel in this and foreign lands; a large acquaintance with the humbled and honored; having held the preeminent place among all who have sought to furnish healthful entertainment to the American people, and, therefore, having had opportunities for gathering an ample storehouse of incident and anecdote, while, at the same time, needing a sagacity, energy, foresight and fortitude rarely required or exhibited in financial affairs, my struggles and experiences (it is not altogether vanity in me to think) cannot be without interest to my fellow-countrymen.

The story of my life is blended with amusing anecdotes, funny passages, felicitous jokes, captivating narratives, novel experiences, and remarkable interviews – the sunny and sombre so intermingled as not only to entertain, but convey useful lessons to all classes of readers.

If this record of trials and triumphs, struggles and successes, shall stimulate any to the exercise of that integrity, energy, industry, and courage in their callings, which will surely lead to happiness and prosperity, one main object I have in yielding to my friends and publishers will have been accomplished.

From the preface to
Struggles and Triumphs or
Sixty Years Recollections of
P. T. Barnum
including his
Golden Rules for Moneymaking
Illustrated and Brought Up to 1889
Written By Himself

Time strips our illustions of their hue,
And one by one in turn, some grand mistake
Casts off its bright skin yearly like the snake.

Byron
Don Juan

I

IT WAS ALMOST midnight in the American Museum, and on the third floor Hackaliah Cherry was making his final round of the booths and galleries, ushering ahead of him the last of the day's visitors and securing the more valuable of the exhibits still on open display. He mumbled to himself as he went, occasionally whistling a few notes of a field song or spiritual along the darkest corridors, frequently stopping to listen to the succession of creaks and groans which followed him as the building, devoid after seventeen hours of its human load, settled back into its original shape, like a giant sponge squeezed dry and then released. It pleased and amused him to identify each sigh and tremor of this letting-out, and having accounted for those in the gallery through which he now passed, he moved on.

He stopped again at a window overlooking Broadway, where directly opposite him the brilliantly lit offices of the *New York Herald* revealed the flickering brass and steel of its vast machinery, which even then, in the very heart of the night, was rolling out fresh news of the war against the Confederacy.

In the street below, the last of the expelled visitors joined the growing crowd, all eager to be told of the latest developments. Hackaliah Cherry wished he were among them, knowing that it would be half an hour yet before he was free to take his constitutional walk and learn for himself what they were now hearing.

It was the third summer of the war, and it seemed to Hackaliah Cherry that for every person who grew weary of the fighting, for every mother who lost her son, every wife who lost her husband, every sister who lost her brother, then there was always someone else ready and willing to step right up and become enthusiastic about the bloodshed in their place. What did not occur to him, however, was that mostly they stepped right up and became enthusiastic about it at the doors of the *New York Herald* and not the recruiting offices.

At that distance, secure within the confines of the Museum and its never-changing routine, Cherry took a great interest in the war: blood was being spilled on his behalf and he considered it his patriotic right and duty to do so. He peered down, but could make out little of the wording on the news-seller's hoarding, hindered both by the barrier of his own puzzled reflection in the glass and by his inability to read.

Satisfied by the cheering that tomorrow's news was good news, Cherry moved on into the gallery ahead. The skulls of reconstructed dinosaurs swayed and clicked above him on their slender necks, and rhinoceroses and other equally improbably designed creatures moved in and out of the shadows to take a better look at him as he passed through.

At the end of the room was an animal pointed out to all who stood before it as the Missing Link between the chattering idiot apes and intelligent, reasoning Man. It was a dark and hairy creature, with broad leathery lips and perplexed, inquisitive eyes – eyes which made it look as though it might have been killed and then preserved in the very act of contemplating its own unique and vital position in the evolutionary chain. It stood upright but hunched, one hand stroking its chin in a gesture of contemplation, the other pointing directly at the visitor standing immediately before it – just as it might have pointed at the man who stood before it and shot it, about to cry out 'Wait!' and thus create an even more momentous occasion of its discovery and immediate dispatch.

Hackaliah Cherry passed quickly through this gallery – as other men might pass quickly through a graveyard in the night – whistling and keeping his eyes to the ground, his swinging lantern casting a kaleidoscope of shapes and moving shadows all around him as he went. Ahead of him, a clock struck twelve, and as the last note died it was answered by the calls and screams of a multitude of animals and birds, just as a gunshot might be answered in the depths of a previously silent forest.

*

Two floors below, Anna Swan climbed down from the low stage upon which she had been exhibiting herself. She was tired, and rubbed the ache from her legs.

Zip arrived to offer his assistance – as he arrived to offer it at the end of most days – and in return she sat on the edge of her booth, held him and kissed his glistening pointed head.

'Is that the last of them?' she asked, watching as the final visitors filtered reluctantly through the door at the end of the corridor, above which hung the sign, its lettering in the form and colour of flames, announcing the unbelievable half a million exhibits yet to be seen and marvelled at in the galleries and halls ahead. In truth, there were little over half that number, but the claim had been made by Barnum in the certain knowledge that no one would ever come to know his Museum well enough ever to count them or to be genuinely disappointed by what they saw there; and in the unlikely event of anyone actually daring to challenge this boast, he would point to his 'antarium', the large glass-fronted case in which a colony of ants was on permanent display. These, it was claimed, had been brought to the Museum at great expense and even greater risk all the way from the darkest jungle of the Amazon, having Eaten Alive one of their captors in the process. A lithograph of the man being attacked by the ants was displayed beside the case in which they now flowed along their narrow tunnels, none of them still for more than a second. Only the man's terrified face, his chest and frantically waving arms could be seen above the feverish cone of creatures striving towards his eyes, which, the notice beneath the lithograph pointed out, were the ultimate prize, a true delicacy in that Savage and Primeval World where Pity was neither Demanded nor Given. Beside the awful scene was a poorly reproduced portrait of the man taken a year before his expedition to secure the ants, his sole aim, it insisted, being to enrich the lives of all those eager in their quest to discover something of that Distant and Terrifying World.

Looking from the ants to his face, to his thin unsmiling mouth and full moustache, many of the female visitors to the Museum were predictably shocked, and their fascination with the mass of tiny creatures accordingly increased. At certain times throughout the day a bag of live grubs and butterflies was released into the top of the case and the ants emerged to give battle. Once gorged, their bodies resembled nothing more than droplets of fresh, glistening blood, and this too was made clear to those few whom it might have escaped. Everything in the Museum gave Complete Value for Money, but the attributes of some of its exhibits had always been deemed more worthy of this kind of forceful illustration than others.

In truth, the ants and their nest had not come from the Amazon, but had been brought to the city by a failed farmer living outside

3

Danbury, Connecticut, who, in 1845, had been the original challenger of Barnum's claim to possessing half a million exhibits, and who had then, for a price, presented him with this simple solution to any future challenge. Neither of them had been able to count the ants, but it afterwards became one of Barnum's jokes among his acquaintances that he possessed both the most expensive and most profitable insects in the country. His reasoning over the rewritten history of the ants was typical and simple: who wanted to see something they might squash in their hundreds every day on the sidewalk, when they could gaze upon something that had stripped the flesh from the bones of a handsome young man in a place where none of them was ever likely to venture? It made perfect sense. People believed what they wanted to believe. They believed the warning telling them not to put their faces too close to the glass in case it cracked under the great pressure of the rapidly multiplying bodies within. Then they believed that the glass was the strongest ever manufactured, that it was made specifically for this task of containment, and that it had been imported at great additional expense all the way from France. They believed that Barnum had organized an expedition to retrieve the young man's bones and return them to his grieving mother. They believed that she was proud of her son's achievement in setting such a spectacle before the American public, and they believed that she personally had drawn aside the curtains on the day that this world in miniature had first been revealed. After all, what was there in any of this for them *not* to believe?

No opportunity was missed by Barnum, no connection, however tenuously or indirectly suggested, ignored. It was this, this longing to transform the everyday into the spectacular, the unbelievable and unimaginable, and to be acknowledged and hailed as the supreme showman of the age that drove him, that lay at the very core of his being.

Back on the edge of her booth, Zip waited before answering Anna, listening as the distant slamming of doors echoed through each of the five storeys. 'The last,' he said. He took a silver flask from his pocket, drank from it and handed it up to her. She wiped the sweat from her face and shoulders with a napkin.

Up on the fourth floor, Blind Tom could be heard playing the piano, surrounded by the voices and the occasional laughter of others beginning to relax after the demands of the day, a communal letting out of breath.

'I'm leaving soon,' Zip said, avoiding Anna's eyes. 'I've been

4

offered work anywhere I want it.' Dropping to the floor, he began to unfasten the hooks of his monkey suit and peel it from his almost naked body beneath.

'We could all leave,' Anna said softly, understanding him perfectly. 'Move out into the country. I could go back to Nova Scotia, build a house, take you with me, take you all.' She rose to her full height of seven feet ten inches and stretched her arms.

'I'd terrify the natives,' Zip said, struggling with the elasticated waistband and the padding around his chest.

'I'm a wealthy woman,' Anna said. 'I've got a fortune stashed away.'

'In here?'

She nodded. 'Enough to build a house and keep myself and any family for the rest of my natural.'

Anna was one of the better paid of Barnum's exhibitors, and he respected her judgment, her common sense and clear thinking. She spoke for the others when they wanted their feelings on some issue to become known to him, and without her, life for many of them within the confines of the Museum would have long since become unbearable.

'Then do it,' Zip said, finally free of his costume, kicking it free of his legs and swinging the cramp from his arms.

They were distracted by the noisy arrival of the Aztec children, who ran to Anna and clung to her. She responded to their unintelligible remarks as though she understood everything they were trying to say, which, on many occasions, she truly believed she did. Bartola pressed her face into Anna's skirts, and Maximo leapt and snatched at the flask she still held. Zip, angry at their intrusion, shouted for silence. The pair of them stopped for a moment, looked from him to Anna, and then resumed.

'They could feed the chickens at your house in the country,' he said.

Maximo pulled the discarded monkey-skin up to his own waist and mimicked the way Zip sat, his face in his hands.

'He doesn't know any better,' Anna said quickly, forestalling Zip's response.

'I know.' He regretted his earlier outburst and pulled the costume up to Maximo's shoulders and fastened the straps. The small man tried to dance, but caught himself in the loose folds and fell, standing and falling again almost immediately. Bartola, his 'sister', pointed and laughed at everything he did.

Zip watched them for a moment: the two perfect halves of the same small world, unintelligible but perfectly matched, sharing their

5

every emotion, miserable one moment, deliriously happy the next.

'How much do you think either of them understands?' he asked Anna, but she avoided the question, standing and extinguishing the lamps on either side of her booth.

This sudden onset of darkness silenced the children, and Maximo quickly freed himself of Zip's skin. Zip retrieved this and brushed the sawdust from it.

Along the corridor an unseen automaton struck the hour in an elaborate sequence of chimes, and when it had finished the silence was complete, an almost tangible presence in the building which throughout the day had been filled with the voices of a thousand people, all of them moving from one exhibit to another, testing their incredulity and stupidity, moving back and forth across the thin and shifting line which separated their amusement from their disbelief.

Zip said he was tired and left them.

A moment later, Anna Swan slid from the low stage, lifted the children into her arms and followed him into the darkness. She began to sing, her voice rising and falling as she stooped to negotiate each doorway, and then fading almost completely as she turned into the narrow staircase and began the climb to her own private quarters.

2

THE FOLLOWING MORNING Barnum was in the basement, supervising the installation of his third aquarium, moving briskly from workman to workman, castigating them, repeating his instructions, demanding that they understood exactly what he wanted. It was four days after his fifty-fifth birthday, and the first time he'd been in the Museum since that auspicious occasion. He spoke with a cigar in his mouth, and smoke rings ran along it like hoops along a carney's cane before dropping to the ground and bouncing away. Of everyone in the basement he exerted the most energy and achieved the least.

Standing apart from him were John Greenwood and Henry Butler, his two assistant managers. They repeated his orders to the joiners, glaziers and plumbers, and when called upon to agree with a decision regarding the metal supports, the feeder pipes or the attachment of the entire structure to the basement wall, they did so immediately. When Barnum was present they were forever busy, constantly moving around the Museum, encouraging the public to move on and marvel at everything there was yet to see and drawing their attention to the more recent acquisitions. When Barnum was absent they relaxed, Greenwood in particular spending a great deal of time away from the Museum, leaving its occupants to organize themselves, but always threatening to return unexpectedly and report the slightest infringement or indiscretion to Barnum, thus establishing a power over those beneath him equal to that exercised by Barnum over himself and Henry Butler. It was Greenwood who appeared the most active and concerned in Barnum's presence now. Henry Butler had long since accepted his own unofficial relegation to third position in the Museum and was content to stay there.

'Mr Butler, the pipe,' Barnum shouted above the noise of hammering. 'Does that look to be of a sufficient thickness to you, bearing in mind the colossal quantity of water which is shortly to pass through it each and every day?'

Henry Butler held a section of the pipe to his eye. It was clear from Barnum's tone that he himself did not consider it up to the task it was about to be called upon to perform. Barnum strived for excellence, expedience and excitement, but he strived even harder to achieve any or all of these as cheaply as possible. The workmen in the basement, despite their own claims, were not of the highest standard.

One of the plumbers began to explain that the bulk of the water held in the tank had little or no bearing upon the rate or pressure at which it would pass through the pipe when filling or emptying the aquarium.

'Ridiculous!' Barnum shouted, releasing the word through a wreath of smoke. 'Mr Butler?'

'Ridiculous,' Henry Butler said, glancing at Greenwood, who was clearly enjoying this display of subservient discomfort.

'Certainly it's ridiculous, Mr Barnum,' Greenwood shouted, coming forward and snatching the pipe from Henry Butler. 'Double thickness, I would have said. If this is to be the most magnificent aquarium ever on view in this city, then –'

'In this continent,' interjected Henry Butler.

'Then it is only common sense that the pipe by which the water is given means of –'

'Continent!' Barnum shouted. 'Gentlemen, nothing less than the finest indoor aquarium in the entire world is expected of us, of *me*. The finest in *five* continents, the most spectacular on the planet itself, unique in all its features, an extravaganza of glass and living creatures unequalled in the history of Mankind.' He paused to catch his breath, pleased with his declaration, wondering if he ought to shout for pen and paper to write it down before it was forgotten. 'Greenwood?'

Greenwood understood and held up the small notebook in which he began to write.

'The Aquarium of the Age,' Henry Butler said. 'A contrivance unequalled in this or any other century.'

'Get it all, Greenwood.'

Grudgingly, Greenwood added Henry Butler's words to Barnum's own.

Turning back to the plumber, Barnum asked him if he had any idea of how many pounds of pressure per square inch would be exerted on the walls of the tank when it was filled to the brim.

8

The plumber was uncertain, but knew that the figure was unlikely to live up to Barnum's expectations. Around him, the others stopped to make their own uneasy calculations.

'Per square *inch*,' Barnum repeated. 'Not per side, not per square yard, not even per square foot, but inch, gentlemen, per square *inch*.' He made the distance between his thumb and forefinger and held it against the glass. A broadside of conflicting guesses was fired at him, and realising that few of them had any basis in reliable mathematical calculation, he called for silence and ordered everyone back to work.

Several hours later the aquarium was completed and in place. Standing beside the tap by which it would be filled, Barnum gave a short speech, beginning by reading from Greenwood's notebook everything he had said earlier. Then he turned the tap, the water flowed, and the workmen applauded.

The aquarium, Barnum boasted, was large enough to house an entire family – a man, his wife and two or three small children – an idea which had occurred to him many months earlier after the failure of his previous aquaria in which his exhibits – tropical fish, seahorses, seals, sea-lions and mermaids – had invariably perished. It was Henry Butler's secret belief that nothing could survive for long in the rank and airless Museum basement, and that whatever was exhibited now in the new tank would succumb equally quickly.

The water fell, splashed and frothed against the bottom of the giant tank, and everyone watched anxiously for the first sign of a leak, which, if not quickly sealed with molten lead, might have had catastrophic consequences once the tank was filled to the brim.

Barnum was hypnotized by the foaming water, holding his palms and face to the glass. Henry Butler and Greenwood stood close behind him, feeling the vibrations as the water continued to pour, rising to knee height in only a few minutes. A trickle appeared, no more than a glassful, from a join at the base of the tank, and picking up a hammer, Barnum swung at the head of the offending rivet, only inches from the glass. By the time the glaziers had shouted to stop him it was too late; the task was done and the trickle had ceased. 'Action, gentlemen,' he said. 'Action rapid and decisive.'

The aquarium measured approximately thirty feet across, by twelve high, by fifteen from front to back.

'Gentlemen, behold,' Barnum announced. 'Our every expectation and anticipation is fulfilled.'

Inwardly, both Henry Butler and Greenwood groaned. Several of the workmen applauded again.

'Tell me now,' Barnum said to the plumber, 'how many thousands of cubic feet of water will this magnificent contraption hold?'

The plumber stepped forward, took off his cap and wiped his brow. 'Thirty by twelve by fifteen. that'll give you five thousand, four hundred cubic feet,' he said, pronouncing the figure slowly in an attempt to make it sound somehow more impressive than it actually was, and nearer to the figure Barnum clearly wanted to hear; he had, after all, already printed his handbills announcing the aquarium.

'Five thousand,' Barnum said disbelievingly. 'As li. . .' He stopped himself, his back still to the crowd. 'Could that not be an error? Should that figure not be *fifty* thousand?' Unseen by any of them, a gleam came into his eye and the cigar rose in his smile.

'Thirty by twelve by fifteen,' repeated the plumber, uneasy at being the bearer of such indisputable and disappointing news.

Greenwood stepped forward. 'Mr Barnum, by my own calculation that is no fewer than nine *million*, three hundred thousand cubic inches.' Even he was surprised by this sudden turn in their fortunes.

This new figure pleased Barnum, but only for the moment it took for the figure to register. 'It's still inches,' he said. 'Inches are for measuring small things. What is required here are feet.'

As he considered the dilemma, the water in the tank rose with a creamy froth to the height of his head and he turned to peer into it. Calling Greenwood back to him, he told him to dismiss the workmen. Then he stood and watched in silence as the water lapped to the brim of the tank and stopped flowing.

Seeing the workmen out of a side entrance, both Henry Butler and Greenwood bemoaned Barnum's decision to remain the entire day in the Museum. Over the previous months his interest in it had started to wane, and they both now believed that a good offer for the lease of the building and a reasonable price for its exhibits, living and otherwise, would secure for them the means of making their own fortunes rather than merely adding to Barnum's own. Greenwood in particular was eager to confront him on the matter. They stood for a moment out in the alley, grateful for the chill April air after the warmth of the basement. Ahead of them, along Broadway, they watched the line of people queueing to enter the Museum.

Returning to the basement, they found Barnum sitting on a chair, contemplating the brimming aquarium. He waved for silence, making it clear to them that he had yet to come up with a solution to the miserably small amount of water now on display.

He was thinking back to his previous claims, regretting the fact that, despite its almost slavish willingness to be deceived, the public was finally beginning to question the facts and figures placed before it. This did not unduly concern him; he had long since discovered that every disputed claim doubled his takings as people either came to the Museum for the first time to see for themselves the cause of the controversy, or as those who had already seen whatever it was came back a second time to re-examine it in the light of the allegations being made – allegations which were more often than not made at his own anonymous contrivance.

In a previous, much smaller aquarium he had displayed a live turtle amid a school of sea-horses. That the turtle had then proceeded to eat the sea-horses had been an unfortunate oversight, but no less of an attraction to the crowds who had been urged to view the creatures before they were all consumed. The additional and ever-present fear that the turtle itself might die shortly afterwards only added to the sense of urgency, and consequently the basement was seldom less than filled to capacity.

This aquarium had been a great success, and when its original occupants were all finally dead, Barnum sent one of his agents to scour the Debrosses fish market each night and return with something unusual to put on display. Squid, giant eels and strange-looking fish were suspended on wires in the murky water and a notice attached to the effect that the creatures on show were no longer living in an attempt to ensure the safety of the viewing public. When the novelty of these exhibits began to wear off, a woman was paid to enter the basement, choose her moment and then scream, quickly leaving as the crowds above began to move down to investigate. (It was one of the unwritten laws of the Museum that its visitors should not be encouraged to stand still for longer than half a minute in front of any exhibit. Those who wished to rest were directed to the Lecture Hall or Theatre, where they might sit and listen to a reading or watch a brief play, thus simultaneously relieving both the ache in their legs and the congestion in the narrow corridors around them. In its varying forms, the screaming-woman ploy had been used to good effect in the Museum since the earliest days of Barnum's ownership.)

Approaching Barnum, Henry Butler said, 'If I might make a suggestion . . .'

Greenwood followed him, angry that he himself had not yet come up with an acceptable solution to their problem.

'It's so pitiful small,' Barnum said miserably. 'So pitiful, pitiful small.'

'It's still a contrivance unequalled in this or any other century,' Greenwood said quickly.

'But still so pitiful, pitiful small.'

Henry Butler cleared his throat, looking pleased with himself as he waited for their attention. 'My suggestion,' he said slowly and confidently, 'is that we add *nothing* to the water.'

'Oh, bravo,' Greenwood said, applauding, but knowing a moment later by Barnum's spreading smile that he was acting a little too hastily.

'Nothing, Mr Butler?' Barnum turned in his seat.

'Nothing. Nought.' Henry Butler made the shape with the thumb and forefinger of both hands.

Barnum had been right in his guess. 'And nothing added to five million is –'

'Fifty million,' Greenwood said dejectedly.

'Butler! An example of harmless and yet ingenious legerdemain unequalled . . . unequalled . . .'

'In this or any other century,' Greenwood said beneath his breath.

'I learnt everything I know from you, Mr Barnum,' Henry Butler said.

Greenwood tasted something sour in his mouth.

Cheered by the possibilities of this solution, Barnum went back to the tank. 'And if we give the back wall some perspective, gentlemen, perspective to disguise the actual configuration of the dimensional capacity and thus –' He moved his arms and then his fingers in a series of calculations.

'And where the tank is attached to the wall,' Henry Butler went on.

'Aquarium,' Greenwood corrected.

'Go on, go on,' Barnum said eagerly.

'We contrive to conceal the actual conjunction of wall and glass by two hollow pillars, and, if possible, by the insertion of a looking-glass along the surface of the water.'

'Cast-iron palm trees,' Greenwood said.

'Thus suggesting in the mind of the viewing public that the aquarium is double its true size by virtue of the singular fact –'

'That it is partially concealed *within* the wall.'

'To allow whatever creatures are on display the necessary gloom peculiar –'

'To their own natural habitat.'

'Recreated here to –'

'Ensure their absolute comfort and safety.'

'Along with that of –'

'The members of the viewing public. Perfect, perfect, perfect.'

Greenwood and Henry Butler stopped their verbal leapfrogging together, the suggestion of one or the other already confused in Barnum's own mind. It then occurred to them both that, even pretending the tank was double its visible size, this would still not account for a tenfold increase in the volume of water it was now supposed to hold. Neither of them put this realization into words.

Barnum paced the room and applauded himself. He paused beneath the cabinet holding the remains of his Feejee Mermaid, and looking up, asked her what she thought of the proposition.

Henry Butler and Greenwood shared a nervous glance. Above them, the sound of tramping feet grew momentarily louder in the silence.

'Will they believe it?' ventured Greenwood.

'Who cares? That's what they're going to be told. I'll have their twenty-five cents in my pocket before they even get the chance to start thinking about it.'

'Bravo, Mr Barnum,' Henry Butler said.

Barnum bowed stiffly and swung both arms in a flourish. Then he left them, climbing to the ground floor and then up through the Museum to the inner sanctum of his own third-floor office and salon, insisting that he be left alone for an hour to consider the details of their suggestion. He also asked them to be ready to accompany him later on his tour of inspection before he left for home, a function he performed as regally as befitted a king passing among the loyal and dependent subjects of his realm.

'That'll be popular,' Greenwood said when he and Henry Butler were once again alone, referring to the deteriorating relationship which now existed between Barnum and many of the exhibitors currently under contract to him and living in the Museum.

'It's still leaking,' Henry Butler said, indicating the base of the tank where Barnum had hit the rivet.

'What did you expect?'

The two men sat beneath the Feejee Mermaid and contemplated the wall of water. It was Barnum's intention to install a hippopotamus as the first of his new attractions, and eventually to have several dolphins or even a small whale in the tank.

They were joined a moment later by Hackaliah Cherry, who arrived with a pail and a mop and stood in wide-eyed bewilderment in front of the tank.

13

· 'Holy Mississippi!' he said. 'There must be just gallons and gallons in that thing.' He stood at mop's length from the small pool of water and soaked it up. 'Where all that water come from?' he asked suspiciously, inspecting the narrow pipe which led from the tank to the wall.

'More to the point,' Greenwood said, 'where all that water *go* when the glass finally shatters under the strain?'

Cherry took fright at his suggestion and moved away from the tank to where the two men sat.

'Holy Moses!' he said, unaware of how appropriate and fitting this exclamation might be were disaster to strike in the manner predicted.

'How's business, Cherry?' Henry Butler asked him.

Cherry cocked an ear to the ceiling. 'Treading its dirt down to the bottom and up to the top. They excited at the war. Good news always gets them tramping round in here.' He then pointed with disbelief to the trickle of water already filling the small puddle he had only a moment ago cleared.

*

Upon being offered the preserved body of the Feejee Mermaid, Barnum had invited Sir Marcus Villiers, the eminent British naturalist then visiting America, to examine the mermaid and to verify publicly that this indeed was what he now possessed. Villiers' word, he knew, would triple his receipts. The first question he asked Villiers before making any public announcement was if he believed the creature to be real, or if, as many suspected, it had been manufactured purely for profit. The naturalist examined the mermaid and assured Barnum that he could find no evidence of a hoax, and that there was no *visible* sign of the creature's manufacture. 'But if there is no indication of a hoax, then why do you still insist that it is manufactured and not the remains of a creature which was once alive in the warm Feejee seas, from whence it came to me?' Barnum asked him, perplexed. 'Because,' replied Sir Marcus, 'I do not believe in mermaids, and nor do I wish to have my beliefs altered.'

Despite this initial setback, Barnum had acquired the mermaid and concealed her until he could come up with a way of presenting her to an equally disbelieving public. Their scepticism he did not mind, but the possibility had existed that they might also feel justified in demanding their money back. All this had happened

14

twenty years ago, when he was not yet sufficiently convinced of his abilities as a showman to dismiss such demands out of hand. Even he had to admit that the mermaid was not the most spectacular of creatures, and visitors expecting to see a fully formed, slender-waisted and blonde-haired beauty with a tail of shining silver scales were unlikely to be impressed by the three-feet-long, shrivelled and distorted half-monkey half-salmon with which they were eventually confronted.

The head was undoubtedly that of a small monkey, dark with age and with glass eyes staring out of shrunken sockets. The skin of its cheeks and neck were drawn tight, revealing a grimace of terror, two rows of sharp yellow teeth and the stiff and twisted root of a tongue. It possessed the slender arms and chest of a child, and small but fully formed breasts, immediately beneath which began the fish tail which all too obviously resembled that of a salmon.

The Mermaid was well travelled before she finally came to Barnum, having been reputedly caught in the sea off North China, coming via Calcutta and Europe to America.

Barnum's problem in showing the Mermaid was one of credibility, and the desire, following his public humiliation with the hoax of Joice Heth, George Washington's nursemaid, to avoid a repetition of any such event. He regretted more than ever Villiers' unreasonable and impregnable conviction. Consequently, he avoided all mention of his own name in connection with the imminent arrival of the Mermaid and instead he set about inserting anonymous notices and articles in the New York and New England newspapers announcing that the curiosity was now being shown *privately* by someone else. He demanded to know when it would arrive in New York and why it was being kept from the public gaze if, as claimed, it was such a genuine and spectacular discovery. Others took up the call and Barnum left them to it, each day privately inspecting his exhibit to reassure himself of the strength of his own growing conviction. Eventually the time was ripe and Levi Lyman, his collaborator in the Heth hoax, announced that the mermaid was to be exhibited for one week only at Concert Hall. The public flocked to see her, and when no overwhelming voice of dissatisfaction or dissent was raised, she was transferred to the American Museum and exhibited by Barnum himself.

Pamphlets and posters advertising the Mermaid showed her to be half a normal woman with long hair covering her naked breasts, and with a tail folded at the knee. When people complained that the actual exhibit in no way resembled this, Barnum agreed with them, pointing out to them that if he had wished to perpetuate another hoax then surely he would have contrived to create a creature resembling more closely that of their expectations; instead, here was an animal more monkey than woman – which did they believe to be the more credible? The blonde-haired women among his audiences, he noticed, had always been the first to agree with him.

Thus was public opinion swayed, his reputation saved and money made. Now, twenty years on, the Feejee Mermaid had long since succumbed to the stale atmosphere of the basement, sometimes cracking at the seams, and occasionally erupting like a ripe bullrush as she blossomed in the warm, moist air.

3

FRANKLIN, AT SEVEN hundred and twenty pounds reputedly the
heaviest man in America, was helping Zip to shave his head,
drawing the razor up from his neck to the topknot Zip cultivated
at the peak of his cone. Zip read aloud from the *Tribune*, and others
passing Franklin's room paused to listen and to ask questions about
the events Zip described to them.

Zip shaved his head daily, initially under instructions from Barnum
to emphasize its shape and the supposedly imbecilic and savage
thoughts it harboured, but more recently because he had grown
proud of his appearance. He was pale coffee-coloured and, because
he oiled his skin, he shone in the lamplight of his booth. He had never
known his parents, but his appearance suggested that at least one of
them might have been a Red Indian – possibly of the Mohawk tribe,
Henry Butler had once suggested to him, intending the remark as a
compliment. He was tall and powerful, with dark eyes and a prominent, hooked nose, and had cultivated a manner which, but for the
shape of his head, would not have been considered out of place in
the highest of New York society – a tall unsteady ladder up which
thousands were even then clambering for position. He had been at
the Museum ten years, and the more he learned of the world beyond
it, the more he chafed at the regulations and restrictions imposed upon
him. The topknot was an indication to everyone who knew him of
his growing independence and restlessness. He was also considerably
more intelligent than the vast majority of the visitors who stopped to
gaze upon him in fear and pity every day, but this too was concealed
from them upon Barnum's instructions.

'Sounds to me,' Franklin said, referring to the news of the armies
then massing around Atlanta, 'like we just about burned and chopped
to dust everything they had left down there.' There were notes of both
sadness and excitement in his voice.

'They feel justified in their acts of retribution because the word itself has been handed down to them by the politicians and other warmongers,' Zip said, turning the page, oblivious, like any man in a public barbershop, to what was happening behind him.

'As you know, I'm a Kentucky man myself,' Franklin said. 'I didn't mean nothing by it.'

'No.' Zip flinched as the razor scraped the skin behind his ear.

'No blood,' Franklin said. 'Fact is, I used to make my way in the county fairs as the Fat Boy King of Kentucky. Had my own wagon and exhibition tent.'

He'd told them all this a hundred times before, but for any of them to have been critical of these tales of previous lives would have been considered a great discourtesy among the inhabitants of the Museum.

'Grant's getting ready to cross the Rapidan, wherever that is,' Zip said.

'I lost a dirt-farm uncle and four cousins,' Franklin said sadly. 'Volunteers. Mountain men. Doubt they knew what they were all volunteering for, though. Probably thought they were just going to protect their own little patch of dirt.'

'That's the outside world,' Zip said. 'War or no war, we were never part of it. It isn't likely to come rushing in here and claim us. The lunatics are running the asylum, always have been.'

'I couldn't shoot a man, I know that much. You think a musket ball would get through all this?'

In the mirror before him, Zip saw Franklin run his free hand down over his overhanging stomach, the heavy bag of which sagged between his knees, its sides supported upon his broad thighs. His biggest crowds always collected when it was time for him to eat, which he did every second hour, heralded by a boy who ran through the halls and galleries shouting 'Fat Boy Feeds! Fat Boy Feeds!' at the top of his voice. In his booth was a painted chart listing what he ate, and at the top of this his latest weight to the nearest pound. It now stood at 720 pounds, and when this fell by a few pounds, as it invariably did with the onset of the warmer weather, the figure was left unchanged. On the occasions when he gained weight, the increase on the board was doubled. Every few weeks Franklin was accompanied by either Greenwood or Henry Butler to the wholesale meat market on Fulton Street, where his weight was publicly checked and announced. The reinforced carriage in which he travelled was always followed by a crowd of cheering children, just as Barnum intended it to be.

'My own folk are dead, too,' Franklin said, having completed his task and now rubbing scented oil into Zip's scalp. 'My pa would have joined up if he'd been alive. Ma, too, most likely. They were both fond of killing. Anything that moved in the woods around the farm, they'd kill and butcher it. There wasn't barely nothing we didn't get set before us at the table.'

In the room around them were the framed photographs of Franklin's family, most of whom, his five sisters included, were almost as fat as he was.

'That's Mary Belle,' he said, indicating the largest of the girls, her calves appearing from beneath the frills of her skirt like two sacks of flour.

'She's a good-looking girl,' Zip said, his attention half on Franklin, half on his newspaper.

'Was,' Franklin said. 'She died. Didn't I tell you she died? I'm sure I told you.' That Zip might have forgotten upset him.

'You did,' Zip said. 'I forgot. Mary Belle.'

'They all died,' Franklin said. 'All except Daisy, and she's a invalid, can't leave her bed. Pushing 490 when last I heard.'

'She's back home in Kentucky, right?' Zip said.

'In her bed. War's been coming and going around her for three years now.' Franklin took Daisy's picture down from the wall and looked at it affectionately. 'I never saw none of them after the county shows. They were all good-looking girls, always had plenty of gentlemen callers.' As he spoke, his already waxy face seemed to bubble, pockets of air pushing out his cheeks and jowls, tightening them momentarily and then leaving them slack and quivering. He repeated the story of his father's death. 'Died in harness at the plough, pulling it with three horses. Just sunk to his knees and died there and then, turning the earth, and them horses dragged him to the edge, turned right around and walked him back again in a good neat furrow before someone saw what had happened and hollered out for them to stop. There's still a long straight line where they took him back the full length. He entered the Kingdom of Heaven somewhere along that furrow, yes sir, his eyes and nose and mouth filled with good Kentucky dirt.'

'What was it killed him?' Zip asked.

'Pure fatness,' Franklin said proudly. 'They finally got the doctor up there and he took one look at him and told Ma right off that he'd passed on as a result and consequence of pure fatness. And I'll tell you this – I don't believe that man ever regretted one solitary day of his entire life.'

There was a short silence, during which Hackaliah Cherry appeared, listlessly pushing his broom into the room, checking that no one outside had seen him enter, and then sitting on a chair hidden behind the door.

'Quick, quick, quick,' he said, indicating Zip's paper. 'What news of this almighty conflagration that tearing apart our proud and mighty nation, turning brother 'gainst brother, father 'gainst son, mother 'gainst daughter, and . . .' Here Cherry faltered, either having run out of breath or having forgotten the remainder of the short patriotic speech, of which he made several during the course of each day.

'Same as usual,' Zip told him. He read out the headlines, which Cherry repeated with relish.

'So we ain't free yet?' he said. 'The proud and mighty nigger ain't yet risen up and cast off his chains, a proud fist clenched to his manly chest declaring his equality, his freedom, his rights to be considered in the eyes of the Lord as an equal with all his white brothers and sisters?'

'Not yet,' Zip said.

'Oh.' Cherry deflated. 'Well, any mention of when that day come? Beginning to feel like a mighty long wait.'

'Soon,' Zip told him.

'Been saying that for three years now.' From where he sat, Cherry pushed his broom over the floor around Zip's chair.

'How do I look?' Zip asked him.

'Like you always look,' Cherry said.

'It's a beautiful head,' Franklin said, running his hands once again over the cone and pulling upright the tuft of black hair and stiffening it with oil.

'Barnum says you got room for more brains than a average human in there,' Cherry said, 'but that they ain't no use to you on account of the way they all piled up to a point. My own personal opinion is that it's mostly hollow space. What you need all that much brain for if all you goin' to do with it is sit round in a monkey suit looking savage all day?'

'You tell me,' Zip said. Cherry had meant no insult by the remark.

'I heard tell,' Franklin said, waiting for their attention, 'that the Chinese put small children into vases and seal them up while their bones are still soft. They make a hole for air and food and such like, and another for whatever has to come out, and then they leave them there to do their growing.'

'Inside of the vases?' Cherry said incredulously. 'Holy Cuyahoga!'

'Right inside of the vases!'

'And then what?'

'Then when they reckon the child's done growing and his bones have all set into shape, they smash open the vase and haul him out.'

'Holy Susquehanna!' Cherry said.

'End result: one vase-boy. I heard tell they got giant teapot boys, too.'

'Holy Missoura!' Cherry said, his eyes growing even wider, his mouth hanging open.

Zip smiled to himself, but said nothing. He folded his newspaper and tucked it into his waistband. 'They could make up a whole dinner service,' he said.

'That's the Chinese for you,' Franklin said, pleased with the way his story had turned out. In the Museum, the journey between distant rumour and verifiable fact was seldom further than the distance between one man's lips and another's ears.

Disappointed at the news of the war, Cherry pushed the dust and shavings back into their original position.

Señor Vivalla passed the open doorway, leading Lord Byron the educated pig. Byron was dressed in his maroon velvet jacket and breeches, through which the twist of his tail protruded. He'd been scrubbed clean, and despite his bulk, he walked daintily past with the same smug, self-satisfied grin on his snout he wore when sitting in his booth with his cigar, glass of port and bookcase of leather-bound volumes of poetry.

Vivalla paused and looked in. 'Everybody's getting into position,' he said. 'Byron here was telling me he expects a larger crowd than usual in today.' He manoeuvred the pig into the room with his boot, whereupon the animal made immediately for the splashes of oil around Zip's feet and began to lick them up. 'I think he's going to be reading from Shakespeare this morning if any of you gentlemen have half an hour to come along and improve your education.'

'Hamlet, no doubt,' Zip said, and despite them all having heard the joke countless times before, they all laughed.

'Yesterday he gave us the Declaration of Independence in its entirety, word perfect, and the day before that he played a mandolin.'

'I hate that animal,' Cherry said, pushing Byron away from him with his broom. 'Somebody ought to teach him some house training.'

21

'He's upset,' Zip told Vivalla. 'On account of how the niggers haven't yet managed to –'

'Ain't yet risen up and cast off their chains, ain't yet –'

'I know the rest,' Vivalla said.

'Byron write any more of his pig poems?' Franklin asked.

'Wrote one right this morning,' Vivalla said proudly. 'Goes something like this: "Oink oink oink oink oy-ink, oink oink oink oink oy-ink".'

'Beats most of the rubbish he's been reading lately,' Zip said.

In the pocket of Byron's waistcoat was a spectacle case and a line of pens. When the curtains of his booth were drawn, he would wear the spectacles and the anguished look of a tortured porcine soul. The poems would be spread across his desk, along with any recent thoughts he might have had which he considered worthy of public consumption. People were free to reach out and take these and then read them aloud to the assembled crowd.

Zip was almost unseated as the pig pushed under him to get at the last of the oil. Vivalla kicked it and it squealed, withdrawing and turning to face him.

'I ain't ever heard it say nothing worth listening to,' Cherry said.

'That's because he only speaks to Barnum and his bankers,' Vivalla said.

'He's spying on us,' Franklin suggested. 'They've all got mean little eyes. Mean as weevils, you ask me. I for one don't trust him.'

'Me neither,' Cherry added quickly, again prodding the animal with his broom.

Señor Vivalla steered Byron out of the room. Cherry followed them, whistling as the three of them made their way along the corridor.

'Do you think any of them really believes it?' Franklin asked Zip.

'Of course they don't. Barnum just uses it to get a rise out of the Irish.' Around Byron's booth were posted jokes and comments comparing the intelligence of the animal to that of the countless Irish visitors to the Museum, many of them only recently arrived in the city. Most took the jokes with good humour, and when it became more profitable for Barnum to turn the joke against the Italians, or Poles, or the Russians, then they in turn would suffer. Franklin said he'd spoken to a butcher in the Fulton Street market who had offered to pay Barnum ten times the worth of Byron as deadweight flesh.

Anna Swan appeared, and with her Beautiful Elizabeth.

'How's it look?' Zip asked them, turning his head.

Anna stooped in the doorway, held his chin and turned his face from side to side. 'Aren't you that ignorant monkey-man we see jumping up and down on the first floor?'

'Screaming for his monkey mama someplace back in the jungle,' added Beautiful Elizabeth.

'The very same,' Zip said, presenting his cheeks for a kiss from each of them.

Franklin moved from one side of the room to the other and stood panting for a moment. Of them all, he had the shortest distance to travel to his booth.

'You all right?' Zip asked him. Both Anna and Elizabeth watched anxiously as Franklin regained his breath.

'Fine,' he said. He inspected his vest for signs of Zip's oil. Anyone appearing at less than his or her best in their booth at the start of the day would be reprimanded by Greenwood and might also be warned or even fined by Barnum during his next visit to the Museum.

'I heard Thumb and Lavinia are due to pay us a call next week,' Anna said. 'Barnum's going to bring them in to say their piece to us all and then they're going to stay with him for a while in his new house by the Park.'

No one expressed any pleasure at the news.

'I heard tell they're living out there someplace in a scaled-down mansion,' Franklin said. 'With carriages and servants and a steam yacht.'

Tom Thumb the midget had been the first of Barnum's exhibits to acquire him a fortune beyond his imagination or his dreams. Upon marrying Lavinia, Thumb had left the Museum, had travelled abroad with Barnum and had been fêted and richly rewarded at his every appearance. Now he was wealthy enough in his own right to have retired and to lead the other life he had chosen.

A distant bell sounded, and then another, signalling to everyone in the Museum that its doors were shortly to be opened to the public.

'Ten to seven,' Zip said, checking his pocket watch before leading them all out of the room.

*

Barnum, too, was interrupted by the ringing of the bells. Unseen by anyone, he had arrived an hour earlier and gone directly to his office.

'Ladies and gentlemen, it is my aim, nay my duty, to amaze,

23

to astonish and astound, to saturate every perceptible sense with the wonder and delight of this never-ending cornucopia of riches, ceaselessly and selflessly putting before you, before *you*, the American public, a thousand myriad and ever-changing . . . ever-changing . . . ever . . .' The sentence faltered on his lips, and he was aware that he had somehow lost control of it, that it had taken on an unmanageable life of its own and had turned upon him ready to strike him to silence. He slumped back in his seat and let out a long and weary sigh of defeat. In the past he had extemporized anything up to a dozen loosely connected clauses; now, however, he felt the need to practise before presenting himself, and it was partly because he had finally acknowledged this small decline in his abilities that he appeared publicly in the Museum less and less frequently. He regretted this enormously. He let out a second, more resigned sigh and consoled himself with a cigar and a salute in the direction of his own bronze bust, which, in his mind's eye at least, returned the gesture.

The bust had been presented to him by the grateful City Commissioners at the ceremony celebrating his recent birthday and was now his proudest possession, an enduring symbol of all he believed he stood for in the eyes of the City Fathers. It shone like gold on the night he was presented with it, but in the poor light of his windowless office it had already lost some of its lustre. He kept it with him in the Museum rather than in his new home because he believed that only he truly appreciated both its remarkable likeness and the genuine nature of the sentiments with which it had been presented to him; and because he knew that Charity and his daughters would only ridicule his affection for it and refuse to have it sufficiently prominently displayed in a household filled with their own rapidly growing collection of feminine ephemera.

In truth, the cheerful countenance flattered Barnum: it gave his cheeks and nose a firmness they no longer possessed; it reduced the number of his chins and suggested a manly determination and resolve which the real flesh had long since been unable to match. The eyes in particular captivated Barnum, and he felt them upon him wherever he went in the office, not in a threatening way, but rather in an approving manner, a gaze which confirmed the validity and wisdom of the few decisions he was still called upon to make.

It stood opposite his desk and was flanked by the two other personal possessions which he never tired of gazing upon: a portrait of Lincoln, solemn, chin raised, staring into the middle distance, his lapels firmly clenched; and the picture of the dying Wolfe, mortally wounded on the Plains of Abraham, surrounded by his officers as the battle against the French was about to be won, and beside him the smoking hole of a shell crater which was about to become his grave.

Every time he arrived at the Museum the first thing Barnum did was to clean the face and broad shoulders of the bust and wipe from its brow the sweat of condensation from the kerosene lamps. No one else was allowed in the office unless he was present. Greenwood and Henry Butler performed their own daily functions in an outer room, entering only when summoned.

'. . . a thousand myriad and ever-changing, ever-delighting, ever-surprising amusements. Amusements designed not only to thrill, not only to titillate, but also to educate and inform, not only to captivate, but to – to –' He faltered again, tiring at the end of his long race through the obstacles of the sentence. He wasn't even certain if the second half of what he was trying to say meshed comfortably with the first, but this was only a minor cause for concern. His major preoccupation now was to reassert himself, and alone, in front of the bust, he began to feel that he was at last achieving this. He knew there was unrest among the inhabitants of the Museum and that Greenwood was hatching plans of his own to take over the running of the place from him. He also knew that he was fighting the battle on two fronts, that Charity and his three daughters would be greatly relieved if he consented to hand over his responsibilities to Greenwood, thereafter to retire and to follow more gentlemanly pursuits, reduced to anonymous oblivion in their midst. His show-manship and the vulgarity of his methods embarrassed them as they strove towards their own separate goals, moving further and further from him the more excessive his boasts became.

If Barnum had one regret concerning the bust, then it was that the City Commissioners had not seen fit to make it fuller, perhaps to have included his chest, or even an arm and a hand with its customary and familiar cigar; but this he considered only a minor oversight, and one that might easily be put right in the future if a suitable sculptor could be found to make the necessary additions.

Pausing only to listen to the dim but growing cacophony all around him, he sat back and began again his speech announcing the opening of the aquarium.

*

Some time later there arose a commotion centred around one of the ground-floor booths, and upon hearing this both Henry Butler and Greenwood left their desks to investigate. Briefly inspecting each other's appearance, they made their way down through the crowded galleries.

Hackaliah Cherry greeted them at the bottom of the main staircase and, grabbing Greenwood's sleeve, pulled him towards the booth in which Beautiful Elizabeth sat and looked calmly down at the crowd passing beneath her, her feet level with their heads, just far enough back to be out of reach of their outstretched arms.

'It's one-eye,' Cherry shouted above the noise. 'She's doin' it again.' He urged them both to move faster, creating a considerably greater sense of urgency than already existed, and pleased at his ability to do so; or so it seemed to Greenwood, who shook himself free and pushed ahead of him.

Arriving at the booth, it was immediately clear from the laughter of the crowd that the situation, whatever it was, was not as serious as either of them had at first feared. Cherry resumed his role as guide and cleared a way for them with his broom, shouting louder than anyone until Greenwood, restraining him, climbed up on to the low stage and turned to face the crowd. He signalled to Henry Butler to stand at their rear, ready to support him with a cheer or applause should the need arise. He glanced at Elizabeth, who, after returning his smile, turned her serene gaze back to her audience, most of whom were now silent.

Since her arrival from Minnesota six months ago, Elizabeth had been one of the Museum's greatest attractions. When her appeal eventually declined she would be moved from her ground-floor booth to one on the second or third floor, but until then her popularity would be both respected and rewarded.

Greenwood asked her if she was all right, if she'd been hurt in any way. Physically hurt, he said. Elizabeth told him she was fine and continued to gaze down at her audience. Someone in the crowd cheered her, and this she acknowledged with a slight bow. Another man whistled at her, and this, too, she rewarded with a smile.

'So what's the trouble here?' Greenwood asked, holding out his arms.

Hackaliah Cherry pushed forward and started, unintelligibly, to explain, stamping his broom for emphasis.

'Not now, Cherry,' Greenwood told him, but before Cherry could respond, an Italian woman pushed herself forward, propelling her small son ahead of her.

26

'I'll tell you what's wrong,' she shrieked. '*That's* wrong, *she's* wrong, that's what's wrong. She is evil. She has no place here. Look-a.' She jabbed firstly in the direction of Elizabeth, and then at the face of her small son, upon whose grubby cheeks the clean tracks of recent tears could still be seen. 'She makes him cry with her evil eye. She is evil, wicked, she should not be here.'

'So you said,' Greenwood said beneath his breath, and waited impatiently for the true nature of the woman's complaint to become clear to him. Behind him, he heard Elizabeth say, 'Perhaps she's right,' and then laugh gently.

Beautiful Elizabeth's full title was 'Beautiful Elizabeth, The Cyclops Woman of Wisconsin'.

Nine months ago Barnum had received a cable from one of his agents telling him he'd found a one-eyed woman, and that in addition to this singular attraction, she was also one of the most beautiful women he had ever seen. He had then sent on a sketch of Elizabeth in which her central, enlarged eye was prominently displayed. At first, Barnum refused to believe him. He showed the drawing to Greenwood and told him to go and see her for himself; naturally, the agent had been eager to earn his commission. Equally, Barnum was aware of the need to present his public with more 'home-grown' attractions now that his supplies from elsewhere were proving harder to sustain. Greenwood visited the agent, and despite being refused an audience with Elizabeth he was convinced by the man's sincerity of the value of his find. A month later a contract had been written and Elizabeth was on a train bound for New York. Barnum, still not entirely convinced, sent Greenwood to meet her and bring her to him. If, as he believed, he was about to become the victim of someone else's hoax, then he was determined that Greenwood too should suffer.

She was dressed in black and wore a heavy veil drawn over her face down to the level of her mouth. She was almost six feet tall and walked in slow elegant strides from the railroad car to Greenwood's waiting carriage. In response to his inquiries, she told him that her real name was Elizabeth Pederson, that her parents had come from Norway and settled in Duluth, Minnesota, and that she had been born two years later. (Wisconsin had afterwards been substituted for Minnesota on purely alliterative grounds.)

Because her face was covered, her mouth became the focus of Greenwood's attention as he rode with her in the carriage: full, dark, wide-lipped and frequently and seductively open to reveal perfect, shining teeth. She asked him questions about what they would pass on their way to the Museum, and entranced by her voice he arranged a detour to include several of the city's more recent attractions. He was worried about Barnum's likely reaction to her: Barnum still wasn't entirely convinced by the claims for her beauty.

Still in the carriage, Greenwood broached the subject of whether or not she fully understood why she was there. She said she did, but added confidently and with a smile that she doubted if her own goals and those of Mr Barnum coincided in every respect. He then told her that Barnum was expecting a slow, lumbering farm girl with heavy hands and pig-tails.

'Ah, if that's what he wants . . .' she said. She turned her hands palm upwards and he saw that they were as perfect in every respect as her lips and teeth. 'You want to see under the veil?' she asked him. He told her he was under strict instructions not to look, to save that honour for Barnum. She laughed at the word 'honour'.

They had driven along Fifth Avenue on a clear day in late fall and she had looked out with pleasure and fascination at everything they had passed. She showed Greenwood a photograph of her parents and their home. They were worn-out farmers and she was their only child, their proudest possession and only hope for the future.

Arriving at the Museum, Greenwood took her directly to Barnum. Upon being called in to him, he started to leave, but Elizabeth held his hand and asked him to stay with her. He knew even before Barnum saw her that he wished she were not about to submit herself and that she were on her way back home to Minnesota.

Standing over Barnum at his desk she raised her veil with both hands and folded it across her forehead. Greenwood stood behind her, and saw from Barnum's face that he had found what he'd been looking for. Barnum beckoned and he went reluctantly, diverting his gaze until the last possible moment before looking directly at her.

The agent had been telling the truth all along. Her cheeks and nose were as perfect as her mouth and hands. Her chin was firm and narrow, and her neck fell in a smooth slender curve to the lace of her collar. She was smiling again – not as she'd smiled in the carriage at the sights of the city, but a broader, fuller grin, something someone standing at a distance from her might see. Mesmerized, Barnum repeated the word 'Perfect' over and over. Greenwood had seldom seen him so excited at a find.

Then Greenwood lifted his gaze past her chin and mouth and

nose to the single eye at the centre of her face, and seeing it, he gasped. This she accepted as a compliment and her smile took on a new warmth.

It was true what the agent had suggested – in some inexplicable way her single eye *added* to rather than detracted from her beauty, and when she was facing you her gaze acquired an unavoidable directness, as though you were the only person she could see or wanted to see; as though her entire attention, her whole *being* were devoted solely to the subject of her gaze. And when she turned her head to look around her, the clear blue crystal of her eye followed slowly after.

She'd drawn a dark line around it and had skilfully applied a little colour to her upper and lower lids. When she blinked her face took on a perfect symmetry, and a new balance was created between her closed eye and her lips. Greenwood could sense Barnum's growing excitement. Barnum approached her and held her shoulders, congratulating her, assuring her that her fortune was made. Greenwood saw her tense slightly at his touch, and she immediately lowered her veil and took a step back from the two men. She was almost a foot taller than Barnum and he began to quiz her about her measurements, each of which she willingly supplied. Her perfection, it seemed, knew no bounds. 'Beautiful Elizabeth,' he said, and because she did nothing there and then to disown it, the name clung to her and became hers.

She was immediately popular, developing a close friendship with both Anna Swan and Zip, and she willingly accepted responsibility for the Aztec children, becoming their surrogate mother and living in rooms adjoining their own on the fourth floor.

After a moment of silent contemplation, Barnum had asked her to tell both Greenwood and himself how her single eye had come about. Again Greenwood tried to leave, and again Elizabeth asked him to stay, which he did, sitting beside her as she began her story.

Her mother had almost died giving birth to her, a full month later than the date guessed at by the local doctor. Her father, anxious for the life of his wife, had eventually delivered her of the child by force, ready, he afterwards told her, to sacrifice the child should a choice between the two of them need to be made. She spoke of all this calmly and with a practised precision, and took no offence at Barnum's repeated urging for her to go on, for her to embellish upon these details. 'I think *you* will do that, Mr Barnum,' she told him, and then waited silently before resuming her history. Barnum was unaccustomed to being treated like this, especially by his employees, and Greenwood enjoyed witnessing both his discomfort and the ease with which Elizabeth exercised her power over him. When Barnum protested, she simply drew back her veil and stared at him.

Her head, it transpired, had been damaged by the brutal circumstances of her birth, although with the obvious exception of her eye, the injury was in no other way still apparent. The doctor had arrived shortly after her birth, and believing such young flesh and bone to be more malleable than it actually was, had attempted to remedy the damage while her father comforted his wife after her exertions. The result of this 'remedy' was as though someone had held the two halves of her face and had somehow twisted the top out of alignment with the bottom, so that one eye moved towards the bridge of her nose, the other sitting above her cheekbone mid-way between her nose and her ear. This second eye had then shortly afterwards become infected, and realising the enormity of what he had unsuccessfully attempted, the doctor had assured her parents that there was nothing to do but remove it completely, stitch up the resulting hollow and pray that the infection did not spread. This he did, fastening the loose lids firmly together and leaving only a slight depression which, as the child grew, became increasingly less noticeable and even appeared to fill from within. Her parents thanked God that her remaining eye had been spared, and they were reassured by the doctor that as she grew, their daughter's vision would be only slightly impaired, if at all. In their ignorance, gratitude and relief they believed him, and after that they never saw him again. Elizabeth was a one-eyed child, and in the way a new and struggling community in a strange land accepted most things, so it accepted her.

'And the remaining eye increased its own powers to compensate for the loss?' Barnum said excitedly, wanting to be told that this indeed was the case.

'If you like,' Elizabeth said.

Of the two men, only Greenwood saw how quickly she had learned to pitch her answers according to Barnum's need to know.

Barnum asked her to show him the vestiges of the redundant vanished socket, and he leaned close to look as she held aside her long hair. Seeing this, he repeated the word 'perfect' another four or five times. He asked her how old she was and she told him twenty-one.

All that had taken place six months ago. Now, facing the restless crowd, Greenwood took control. The Italian mother with her son was growing increasingly vociferous, demanding to have her complaint heard and attended to. Few among the spectators actually supported her, but all were happy to stand and witness the confrontation, thus creating a blockage in the otherwise fast-flowing arteries of the Museum.

'I demand to see Barnum,' the woman said. Her son, clearly unhappy with the way her complaint had turned out, tried to pull away from her and lose himself among the legs of the crowd.

'Mr Greenwood here is the ass-is-tant manager,' Hackaliah Cherry told her. 'He the one you got to deal with.'

Henry Butler pulled him back through the crowd by his collar and told him to attend to his duties elsewhere. Cherry, however, having been their guide to the confrontation, considered this unfair and moved away only slowly.

'See how Barnum treats his poor nigger employees,' the woman shouted. The crowd, aware that her original complaint was losing its focus, did nothing to encourage her.

'Madam, if you could elucidate, if you could just make a little more specific the nature of your complaint, I will endeavour to do my utmost to rectify it.'

Behind him, Greenwood heard Elizabeth's gentle applause.

'Well?' he asked the woman, who immediately pulled the small boy back to her side.

'She made him cry, that's what,' she said, again pointing accusingly up at Elizabeth.

Greenwood crouched down. 'Did the lady make you cry?' he asked the boy. The boy, uncertain, looked up and down and then nodded once.

Rising to face the woman, Greenwood asked her if she had read the notice above the entrance to the gallery warning against the unsuitability of some of the exhibits for children of tender ages and adults with weak or sickly dispositions.

'He's thirteen years old,' the woman said, as though this in some way exempted him.

The child was skinny and looked little older than nine or ten.

'Throw her and the kid out,' someone shouted from the back. 'Let's get moving.'

'Yeah. I only come to see the dog and his mouth organ.'

'Me, too. I got an uncle with one eye. Poked it out with his own finger for a wager and couldn't get it back in. What happened to hers?'

The woman, realising her argument had now also lost a good

deal of its entertainment value and original momentum, demanded to be given her money back.

Greenwood felt his heart skip a beat lest the cry be taken up by others, and was relieved that Barnum was not there to witness his handling of the situation. He shared an uneasy glance with Henry Butler.

'I'm afraid I can't do that, madam. Apart from which, I still haven't satisfactorily ascertained the true nature of your complaint. One eye is advertised, one eye you see.'

'One *evil* eye,' the woman shouted, flicking her teeth with her thumbnail in a gesture few understood.

'And people have travelled the length and breadth of the continent to be gazed upon by that one single solitary eye. Is it not a perfect eye in its form, colour, shape and all its functions? Is that your complaint? Is it insufficiently centrally located? Indeed, is it not a most complimentary, not to say hypnotic, feature of an otherwise flawless beauty, personality and intelligence? Madam, speak to Elizabeth for yourself, ask her anything you choose. I guarantee an answer within seconds, sooner. Quiz her on the great capitals of the world, upon the succession of great men to the political and artistic pantheons of this nation, in short, upon anything. Please, be my guest.' He stood aside to allow the woman to face Elizabeth.

At the back of the crowd Henry Butler applauded and was joined by several others.

'That's not what I want, that's not what I want,' the woman screamed, her voice rising with each word, angry in her defeat. 'She *spelled* him. She put a spell on him with her evil eye and now who knows what's going to happen to him.' She added several further sentences in Italian.

Turning to Elizabeth, Greenwood asked her if she could enlighten him as to what had actually happened.

'She held him up for a better look. I believe she even wanted to sit him upon the stage.' She was clearly amused by what was happening.

'Is that all?'

'I told her that *I* was the exhibit here, and that despite her son being the ugliest child it was ever my misfortune to set my eye upon, I doubted if people would consider him good value for money when they could walk right past him in the street and laugh at him for free.'

'You said that to her?' Greenwood fought to restrain his smile before turning back to the woman.

32

She was now holding her son by his ears and tears were again flowing down his cheeks.

'Hell, she's right,' someone shouted. 'He *is* an ugly little runt. Make her an offer for him. Just shut her up and let's get moving. I seen the hairy woman six times already and I want to see her again.'

Seeing that public opinion was now almost wholly against her, the woman began to stamp her feet and insist that she was not moving. Most of what she said was now in Italian.

Irritated by the fact that she was not now likely to listen to reason, Greenwood smiled coldly at her, indicated to her that he wanted to lift her son on to the stage, and then took him from her and did just that.

'I'm afraid, madam, that I concur with public opinion. He *is* a particularly ugly specimen of a child, and I cannot entirely dispel from my mind the notion that you might indeed have brought him here with the deliberate intention of profiting by his appearance. Perhaps you believed that we would make you an offer for his services.'

By now the crowd was in an uproar of laughter. In her rage, the woman began to stammer and then to curse.

'Note his cheeks,' Greenwood went on, indicating the child's broad face. Unseen by the boy's mother, Greenwood then whispered to him, winked, and tucked a dollar note into the pocket of his shabby jacket. Touching a finger to his lips, he turned back to his audience. 'Tell me, child,' he said loudly, 'is it your belief that you are in part descended from some species of frog or toad?'

The crowd burst into even louder laughter.

'Crouch down and croak for us. There may yet be a place for you in this marvellous place of variety and wonder.'

The boy dropped down into a squatting position and croaked loudly, clearly enjoying himself and excited by Greenwood's proposition. He made several awkward leaps in the direction of Elizabeth. When he was close enough she reached down and stroked his head.

To his mother, Greenwood said, 'He appears to have overcome his fear, madam. Might I now suggest that you keep a very tight grip on him.'

The small boy, enjoying all the attention he was now receiving, continued in his guise of a frog back to the front of the stage, whereupon his mother reached up and pulled him down, losing her grip and letting him fall to the ground. He began to cry. Other women in the crowd castigated her and someone helped the boy to his feet.

'Ladies and gentlemen,' Greenwood announced, 'I fear our little impromptu performance is over. However, I feel certain you will appreciate this opportunity to express your gratitude for the entertainment we have been afforded.' Taking a coin from his pocket, he flicked it to the boy, who caught it and swiftly added it to the note in his pocket. Several others responded in a similar fashion, and afterwards the crowd willingly dispersed.

Elizabeth brushed her hair, drawing it back from her forehead to more clearly reveal her solitary eye. Greenwood remained with her, exhorting new arrivals to look upon her and be amazed.

'To be gazed upon by that eye is to be the instantaneous recipient of the greatest good fortune,' he announced. 'Indeed, only a short time ago an unbelievable fortune was amassed in this very hall by someone – someone, I might add, who did not believe in the power of that transcendental and omnipotently luminous gaze – someone who came in a poor man and left with a wealth beyond his dreams. So gaze up in wonder and then move on. The stare of a single second is sufficient to guarantee your fortune for life.' He climbed down from the stage and passed through the crowd to join Henry Butler.

Hackaliah Cherry returned, still bemoaning the fact that he had been excluded from the proceedings.

'Your day will come,' Henry Butler told him. 'The war's nearly over.'

'It surely is, sir. And on that proud and auspicious occasion –'

'Just sweep, Cherry,' Greenwood told him.

Cherry said, 'Yes, sir,' and moved away, still murmuring his dissent.

4

BARNUM AND HENRY Butler sat together in the Museum theatre and watched as a succession of acts auditioned before them. After the first few hopefuls, it became only too clear to Barnum that he was going to see nothing today that he hadn't already seen countless times in the past, and that neither he nor the Museum were likely to benefit by employing anything he now endured. Occasionally, when prompted by his manager, he applauded loudly and called out 'Bravo, bravo'. Henry Butler was more sympathetic, frequently suggesting to Barnum that a little more encouragement from him might be appreciated by the performers. This, however, Barnum regarded with contempt. 'Encouragement, Mr Butler? I think not.'

Henry Butler called for the next act.

Greenwood, aware of how unbearable Barnum could be at such close quarters over such a period, had volunteered to prepare the applicants backstage, alternating novelty or specialty acts with those who simply had something to sing or recite. He too knew that there was little here that was likely to attract Barnum's attention. It had been a poor season for auditions.

A man arrived onstage carrying a dozen lighted brands and began juggling with them. This caught Barnum's eye: no one was more aware than he of the possibility of a fire in the Museum, and as the man finished his first act and extinguished each of the brands, Barnum rose and shouted for him to get out and never return. The juggler stood his ground and began to protest.

'Is he deaf, Mr Butler?' Barnum said loudly.

In response, the juggler threw down his smouldering brands and took from his bag a dozen dinner plates.

'Plates!' Barnum shouted. 'He's come to show me – *me* – that he can juggle plates! Get him off, Mr Butler. Time is precious. There

35

may yet be something to see that might raise a flicker of interest in these tired and weary eyes.'

Adamant, the juggler refused to leave the stage, and regaining his composure he threw the first three plates into the air, adding to them until he was turning all twelve in a wide circle above his head, giving them the appearance of being joined in a single piece.

'We are no longer watching you,' Barnum shouted up to him. 'Mr Greenwood, send on the next.'

Greenwood appeared at the side of the stage and approached the juggler. Distracted, the man lost his rhythm, the circle of plates lost its momentum, wavered and collided, and one by one they crashed down around him and shattered. Dodging them, he was on the verge of tears.

'Ask him to pick up the pieces before he leaves, Mr Greenwood,' Barnum said, settling back in his seat and smiling.

The juggler left the stage and Greenwood kicked the pieces of broken crockery after him.

Behind Henry Butler and Barnum, half hidden in the gloom of the auditorium, sat Anna Swan and Captain Bates. He was an inch taller than her and the same distance short of eight feet. They held hands and shared a cigar.

Captain Bates had arrived at the Museum after Anna, and had recently been absent for a month, attending his mother's funeral and helping out at the Ohio smithy his father ran. It was their intention to marry and to leave Barnum when they had saved sufficient funds to do so. Both had been happy in the Museum, but now Anna's contract with Barnum was coming to its end and she was anxious, having met and been courted by Captain Bates, for them to leave and marry and live together elsewhere – to return to that 'other life' of which everyone in the Museum spoke and dreamed. In the past it had been Barnum's practice to arrange for such marriages between the members of his 'family' to take place within the Museum, and, after negotiating a fee with the couple, for a public spectacle to be made of the event. Anna and Captain Bates, however, had been determined from the start to avoid this. Henry Butler knew of their plans, but he had been sworn to secrecy.

Bates had returned from Ohio earlier that same morning, and so far the couple had spent the day together, sitting in the peace and calm of the empty theatre until Barnum arrived to conduct his auditions. They rose to leave, but he told them he was happy for them to remain, that he respected their opinions. He had given Anna the day off in honour of Captain Bates's return, secretly fearing that without her he might have been tempted to remain in Ohio.

'He wants to make sure we know just how lucky we are,' Bates whispered to her. They were both content to sit in the semi-darkness, holding hands and watching the succession of unsuccessful performers parade before them.

A one-legged man in a leotard bounded on to the stage, hopped on the spot for a moment and then threw himself upwards, attempting, but failing, to execute a somersault. He landed awkwardly, hopped until he had regained his balance, and then bowed, expecting applause. Henry Butler clapped once and his arm was immediately clasped by Barnum.

'Where are you from?' Barnum called up to the acrobat.

Pleased with this response, the man bowed again, and said proudly, 'Why, Mr Barnum, from right here in New York City, finest city in the entire –'

'If you say so.'

'Why do you ask, sir?'

'Simply to satisfy myself that you haven't wasted your life savings on the railroads to get here, or that –'

'I hopped here, sir.'

'You hopped,' Barnum said with a sigh. 'What else?'

On stage the man began hopping again to build up momentum prior to executing another part of his act. This time he threw himself sideways, turned on his outstretched hand and landed upright again. He stood panting, but this time there was no applause.

'Next, Mr Greenwood,' Barnum shouted.

'Has my meagre display of talent brought you even the slightest degree of –'

' "Meagre" and "slightest" are the words which spring to mind,' Barnum said. 'Sir, have you ever had the misfortune to visit Cincinnati. No – I can see that would be an exhausting, not to say fatal, journey for someone in your unhappily reduced condition. Well, sir, in the town of Cincinnati it was once my misfortune to witness an acrobat with neither of his legs still intact, and with only one arm upon which to support himself and a family of seven small children. You, no doubt, have eight or nine or even ten.'

'None,' the acrobat said unhappily, already tasting his failure.

'Then your loss is not so great. This Cincinnati man demanded an audience and sought to impress me, and never, in over forty years of professional showmanship, have I witnessed a spectacle so pathetic, so humiliating or so degrading. Imagine, if you will, a drunkard with his knees bound. Imagine this spectacle of human misery and hopelessness.' There Barnum stopped. He could see that the man had no real idea of what he was telling him.

Greenwood walked on to the stage and touched the acrobat's shoulder. Unprepared for this, he fell over, rose, and fell again. When he had finally understood and hopped away, Barnum turned to Henry Butler and said, 'Did you note the ring of the phrase "Over forty years of professional showmanship" Mr Butler? It sounded mighty fine to these ears.'

'Yes, fine,' Henry Butler said, quickly calculating the extent of the exaggeration.

On stage, Greenwood coughed for their attention. Beside him stood a young woman in a long evening dress, wearing a necklace and white lace gloves which reached to her elbows.

'This is Miss Mercy Faith Désirée,' he said in a tone which did little to disguise his disbelief.

Barnum's attention was immediately attracted and he leaned forward in his seat.

'It's not my real name,' the woman said, in a voice which caused Greenwood to wince. 'I picked that as my *stage* name.' She smiled down at Barnum and took a deep breath, holding a hand to her chest. 'My real name –'

'No – don't tell me,' Barnum told her. 'Let me think of you as Miss Mercy Faith Désirée. Please, proceed.'

'I'd like that,' Mercy Faith Désirée said. 'I'd like that a great deal, sir.' She fluttered her eyelashes and inflated more of her bust.

While Barnum was distracted, Greenwood caught Henry Butler's eye and shook his head once.

'And what do you have to present before us, Miss Mercy Faith Désirée, although to this old and weary man, worn down in the service of his fellow countrymen, your simple presence is already sufficient.'

'You aren't old,' Mercy Faith Désirée said immediately, adding, 'I sing. I saw that Jenny Lind when you brought her over to the Castle Garden. I heard her, and ever since then I've set myself to follow in her footsteps. My friends all call me the Brooklyn Nightingale.' She brushed at some invisible dust from her exposed shoulder, surreptitiously lowering the line of her dress by an inch.

Greenwood raised his eyes and left her alone on the stage to perform.

Behind him, Barnum heard the whispered conversation and muted laughter of Anna Swan and Captain Bates, and called for silence.

'She's certainly a beauty, Mr Butler,' he said, his eyes never leaving Mercy Faith Désirée's smiling face. 'Would a voice to match be too much to ask for?'

Probably, Henry Butler thought, but said nothing.

'Would you do us the honour of performing for us a song from your repertoire, Miss Mercy?'

'My what?'

'A song. Sing him a song,' Greenwood hissed from the wings.

'Oh, I see.' Mercy Faith Désirée took several deep breaths, paused, and then deflated. Then she asked if there was someone who could accompany her on the piano. She pointed to the piano at the rear of the stage.

'Fetch Old Tom,' Barnum shouted to Greenwood.

Greenwood went, leaving Mercy Faith Désirée to repeat her full range of pouts, flutters and exposures.

Ever since Jenny Lind, it had been Barnum's dream to promote himself to the status of impresario and to work with more culturally elevating performers. He wanted to present classical actors and world-famous opera singers; he wanted to be able to announce himself to the world as the patron and employer of the greatest literary figures of the age, most of whom he had already unsuccessfully approached. But most of all, he wanted to be written about by those same men of letters, to have his name immortalized by them as well as by his own handbill printers.

Greenwood returned, leading Old Blind Tom on to the stage. There was little need for Greenwood's assistance; for a negro blind from birth, Tom 'saw' as well as any of them, and knew every twist and turn of every gallery, staircase and corridor of each of the Museum's five floors as well as he knew the notes of the keyboards he continually played. He sat at the piano, lifted the lid and ran his fingers lightly over the keys. He grinned broadly as he played, holding up his face to reveal its thick white bristles, as long on his chin and cheeks as it was on his head.

'You name it, Lady, I'll get close to it,' he said, breathing deeply as Mercy Faith Désirée approached him.

'We're in the presence of a cultivated young woman, Tom,' Barnum called out to him. 'So watch your tongue.'

'I smell her, Mr Barnum, sir, I smell her.' The notes shivered in anticipation beneath his fingers.

39

Barnum had a great affection for Tom, having 'rescued' him twenty years earlier from a bar, where he played for drinks, only afterwards discovering Tom's ability to reproduce exactly any piece of music after only a single hearing. A modest man, Tom considered this to be the Lord's gift to him, and although he accepted his lifelong board and lodgings from Barnum – he shared a room with Cherry in the attic – he refused to take more money for playing the piano than he needed to get drunk each night.

'Cultivated, Tom.'

'Why, thank you, sir,' Mercy Faith Désirée said, ready to resume.

'I still smell her, sir.'

The smile fell momentarily from the Brooklyn Nightingale's face.

Tom began to play, and the clear sharp sound filled the empty hall.

Anna and Captain Bates held each other more tightly and rested their heads on each other's shoulders.

After a minute of Tom's expert playing, Mercy Faith Désirée shouted, 'Stop, stop, stop!'

'What's wrong, my dear?' Barnum asked her.

'I don't know that tune. I ain't never heard it before in my entire life.'

'It was very popular with Miss Lind.'

'Then perhaps it's from Sweden or wherever,' Mercy Faith Désirée said. Her voice was louder and coarser, but rather than disappoint Barnum, this appeared only to excite him further.

'Just tell Tom here what it is you want,' he said.

'You know "Three Merry Milkmaids on the New Jersey Shore"?'

'I know it,' Tom said, and began immediately to play the bar-room song.

'Slow down; you're playing it too fast. I thought you said he could play,' Mercy Faith Désirée yelled at Barnum.

'Tom?'

Tom slowed down and Mercy Faith Désirée prepared yet again to begin.

Barnum sat back in his seat and folded his arms.

Henry Butler braced himself for the worst.

It came.

Mercy Faith Désirée burst forth with a singing voice as tuneless as the Museum had suffered since the King of the Carolinas had exhibited his singing racoons.

'Ah,' Barnum said quietly, sinking a little in his seat.

'Ah,' Henry Butler said, leaving the utterance open to every possible interpretation.

'Yes,' Barnum said.

'Yes,' agreed Henry Butler.

At the back of the room, Anna Swan and Captain Bates were unable to suppress their laughter.

At the piano, Tom faltered momentarily and then resumed with vigour, raising the volume. The Brooklyn Nightingale noticed this, and she too began to sing more loudly, looking angrily from Barnum and Henry Butler to where Anna and Captain Bates sat with tears in their eyes and their hands over their mouths. She stopped singing.

Tom continued for a few notes, stopped and turned to gaze milkily in her direction. 'She finished?' he asked.

'They were laughing,' Mercy Faith Désirée said, stamping her foot and pointing at Anna and Captain Bates. 'What are they doing here, anyway? Can *she* sing?'

Anna Swan stopped laughing and held up her hands in a submissive, apologetic gesture. And then, sliding Bates's arm from beneath her own, she rose slowly and majestically from her seat until she had gained her full height.

'Oh, sweet Lord have mercy,' Mercy Faith Désirée said, taking several steps backwards, her mouth open in amazement.

'Hallelujah!' shouted Tom, trilling his fingers up and down the keys.

After stretching her arms, Anna sat back down and everyone waited in silence.

Then Mercy Faith Désirée came to the front of the stage and leaned forward. 'Well?' she said, looking directly at Barnum.

'Well, my dear,' Barnum began, 'it's true that you have a . . . a –'

'A certain elusive and indefinable quality,' Henry Butler offered.

'Precisely. And in affording you the appellation you so clearly deserve –'

'The what?' Mercy Faith Désirée stood with her hands on her hips.

'Your talents, Miss Désirée, which, if I may be so bold, are not for a humble place such as this. In a private salon is where your multifarious abilities might garner their fullest appreciation.'

'A saloon!'

'Mr Greenwood,' Barnum shouted. 'Take Miss Désirée's full particulars. I do assure you Miss Des – Miss Nightingale, nothing would give me greater pleasure than for me to reacquaint myself with –'

'*He's* what's wrong up here,' Mercy Faith Désirée shouted down at him. 'You expect me to sing at my best when all I got for accompaniment is an old blind field-nigger?'

Tom stood and bowed. 'Thank you, ma'am.' He took off his hat and held it to his chest.

Greenwood led Mercy Faith Désirée into the wings. Her voice could be heard long after she had gone from view.

'Nevertheless,' Barnum said to Henry Butler, 'she did have a certain quality, don't you agree?' He mopped his brow and wiped the spittle from his lips.

Greenwood returned and announced that four more acts were waiting to perform. But by then Barnum had seen enough. Earlier in the week he'd had an offer from a zoo of a worn-out gorilla and had now decided to accept.

'Gorillas, Mr Butler. At once so human, and yet at the same time so . . . so –'

'Gorilla-ish?'

'Precisely! Gorilla-ish. Sufficient of an attraction, would you say?'

'Sufficient,' Henry Butler agreed, as he too grew tired of the proceedings.

Barnum rose and left, instructing Greenwood and Henry Butler to stay behind and witness whatever remained to be seen. He passed Anna and Captain Bates and said he was pleased to see the Captain safely returned.

After his departure, Greenwood left the stage to join Henry Butler in the stalls.

'Did you get her address?' Henry Butler asked him.

'Address? She's upstairs in his office waiting for him now.'

Before Henry Butler could respond to this, another woman walked out on to the stage leading a child.

'How old?' Greenwood shouted.

'Eight, nine,' the woman said, instructing the child to dance, which he or she – it was difficult to tell which at that distance – did immediately.

'Mercy Mercy Desirable,' Greenwood said, nudging Henry Butler.

'He also recites from Shakespeare, Charles Dickens and you-name-it,' the woman called down. 'Mostly word-perfect.'

The child clutched its chest and began to recite a speech none of them recognized.

'What's to come?' Henry Butler asked beneath his breath.

'A girl with eight fingers on one hand and a boy with a nose like the snout of a pig.'

42

'Could we take him on as Byron's handler in place of Vivalla?'

'I doubt it. Byron has better dress sense.'

'On stage, Blind Tom played a slow march to accompany the child's recitation.

'Thank you, that should be enough,' Greenwood called up.

'He can walk on his hands,' the woman said.

'Fine.'

The woman left the stage, followed by her son walking on his hands.

'It's getting worse,' Henry Butler said. 'We haven't seen anything recently worth having.'

'The demand's falling. I blame the war. Too many cripples around, too much sympathy and regret, whatever. Don't worry, he'll turn something up.'

They were distracted from their conversation by the appearance on stage of yet another child.

'Carn de ol digga shud ub?' It was the boy with the snout.

Tom stopped playing and waited for further instructions.

'Id's a grade pridledge do be here,' the boy said. His snout, rather than being solid and slightly upturned like Byron's, was flaccid and hung in a curve over his lips like a stubby trunk.

Before he could say any more, Anna Swan rose in her seat and shouted for him to stop. She explained that he wouldn't be employed and that he ought to leave right there and then and not humiliate or disgrace himself any more than was necessary. She told him she was sorry, but that was how things were.

'Bud id's a real fleshy snoud,' the boy said, gripping his nose and pointing it towards them. 'You could bill me as whadever you like.' He looked pleadingly from Anna to Greenwood and then Henry Butler.

'Tell him,' Anna said to Greenwood.

'It's like she says, son,' Greenwood said dispassionately.

'Coward,' Anna said.

Beside her, Bates nodded in agreement and support.

The snout-nosed boy left the stage.

'Now see what you've done,' Greenwood said. 'Now what's he going to do?'

'It can hardly be any worse than what he'd be forced to do in here in the unlikely event of Barnum ever taking him on.'

'Hear hear,' Bates said.

Henry Butler appealed for peace. 'I understand precisely,' he said. 'We all do. And we all sympathize, believe me, but this kind of behaviour isn't going to help anyone.'

Anna dropped back into her seat, where Bates immediately held her.

'Touching,' Greenwood said, striding up the aisle beside them, leaving the theatre and slamming the door behind him.

Henry Butler went to join Anna and Bates. 'I really do sympathize,' he said. Henry Butler's first child had been born weak and sickly and had mercifully died less than six months old. A second child had been still-born, after which a doctor had recommended that there should be no more children. He lived now with his invalid wife on Canal Street at the junction of Division, in rooms to which many of the Museum's inhabitants had once been frequent visitors.

'Barnum should take on the singer and bill her as the Brooklyn Crow. He could hold a competition to find someone worse,' Anna said.

Lowering his voice, Henry Butler asked them if they were any nearer to fixing a date for their wedding.

'Alas not,' said Bates, but with no real disappointment in his voice.

On stage, Blind Tom resumed his playing and all three stopped speaking to listen to him and to clap along with the tune.

5

MADAME JOSEPHINE CLOFULLIA Fortuna was the first bearded lady to display herself to the American public. Her booth in the Museum was decorated and furnished in the style of a French salon, with lacquer-work tables and a slender chaise-longue, upon which she sat and fanned herself as the visitors filed past. Occasionally, especially when doubts as to her sex were raised, she sang. Her voice was high and fine and perfectly pitched, and most were immediately convinced by it. Those who were not were pointed in the direction of the framed ruling of the Tombs Court, made over a decade earlier, certifying that she was indeed a woman. Similarly displayed was the birth certificate of her son, Esau, who was occasionally exhibited alongside her, his own young face already as silky as a terrier's.

Fortuna's beard was full and luxuriant. She trimmed it weekly, and where it spread across her cheeks, she experimented by shaving it into various patterns. It grew rapidly, as did the hairs on her head, arms and shins. These last she shaved daily, and because it was equally important to stress the feminine aspects of her character, she wore dresses in the latest French fashion and a finely embroidered lace veil, beneath which little was visible.

Swiss by birth, Joséphine Boisduchêne had married René Clofullia Fortuna, a mediocre and unsuccessful French artist, in 1850. As with Elizabeth and her single eye, Joséphine Fortuna's hairiness was considered by many to add to rather than detract from her feminine appeal, and René was a devoted husband with eyes for no one but her. He defended her when challenges to her femininity were made, and stood beside her in all her dealings with Barnum. She, in turn, demanded of Barnum that René and her son be afforded every comfort in their quarters while she was on view in the Museum. In addition, René continued with his painting, the results of which were sometimes hung and offered for sale to the wealthier visitors.

Barnum had taken to her immediately upon her arrival from France, and when his claim that the bearded Fortuna was indeed a woman had been first challenged, he had wasted no time in insisting that she be inspected by a doctor and a matron in a room adjoining the court in which he and Fortuna's accuser waited in the presence of a judge.

Initially, the whole affair had distressed Fortuna and René, and he had pleaded with Barnum to prevent her from having to endure such an indignity. Fortuna, however, realising that her credibility, and thus her livelihood, was at stake, had convinced him that the tribunal would settle the matter once and for all, and that afterwards both she and he could face the world without the slightest fear of their accusers.

To avoid attracting attention to herself when she was out walking with René, Fortuna frequently dressed as a man, wearing a cumbersome overcoat, even in summer, to further disguise her figure. It was rumoured among the other inhabitants of the Museum that René – so complete was his devotion to his wife – collected up her weekly beard clippings and used them to make himself new brushes.

René made sketches of everyone who worked in the Museum, including many of Barnum himself, and these hung in Fortuna's rooms alongside those of the city and the surrounding countryside. Often, while his wife was on show in her French salon, René would stand behind her backdrop of drapes and whisper endearments to her. Barnum disapproved of this, but René persisted.

It was René who had painted many of the boards which hung on the outside walls of the Museum, and who had decorated the hoardings displayed in the entrance hall. He was currently employed in stripping down and repainting the Museum's many automatons, several of which were beginning to show signs of wear. True to form, rather than engage a mechanic or engineer to dismantle and then reconstruct these, Barnum had instructed René to give them a new coat of paint.

The couple's only true regret was that their son should have inherited his mother's hirsute characteristics, developing an even broader spread of fine hair across his entire face, including his nose. This could be shaved away in part, but repeatedly grew back to cover any exposed flesh. The boy himself was not unduly saddened or concerned by this, but already he was being referred to as 'dog-boy' by some of the visitors, and this pierced the hearts of both Fortuna and René every time they heard it. Sensitive to his parents' hopes and fears, no one resident in the Museum ever called him this.

Both Fortuna and René had resisted Barnum's attempts to 'secure' the boy's future in the Museum, but equally both were slowly coming to the realization that few realistic alternatives now remained open to him. Upon their arrival in America, it had been their intention to make their fortune and then return to Versoix, near Geneva, Joséphine's birthplace, where they would live in comfort with their son far beyond the public gaze. This was still their intention, but with each passing year they saw their goal receding swiftly ahead of them – almost as swiftly as René's youthful ambition of becoming a great artist had receded ahead of him. A delicate and exquisite lily, he said, could not sustain itself in a field full of weeds, where to survive even as a weed had become a great and proud achievement.

*

Barnum was excessively fond of his automatons, several of which had formed the basis of his collection when he'd first acquired the Museum from the unhappy and unsuccessful Scudder sisters. Some had toured the palaces and stately homes of the world before coming to rest with him, and most, in addition to their celebrated and life-like mechanical functions, operated as time-pieces, chiming the quarter hours throughout both day and night in the Museum, their presence most obvious during the latter.

The chess-playing Turk was the first of Barnum's acquisitions, larger than life-size and announced as a machine with a mind of its own, challenging spectators to sit with it at a table and outmanoeuvre it on the board.

Outwardly, the Turk was constructed of wood and dressed in a flowing Oriental robe, Turkish slippers, each curled and pointed toe-piece capped with a bell, and a turban from which rose a plume of scarlet feathers. He sat on a backless chair and was shown before each performance to be connected to neither the stage upon which he sat nor the maple desk upon which the chess board and pieces were set before him.

Originally the property of the infamous Maelzel, the Turk had toured Europe and been viewed by royalty in every country he had visited. A door in his smooth walnut chest revealed the intricate machinery by which he 'operated' himself, and with which he considered and made his moves on the chessboard – cogs, levers, nuts

47

and bolts, his arterial web of wires, his cylindrical gut of gearwheels. A second door in his broad and polished back revealed an equally impressive and incomprehensible array of moving parts.

Having had his innards thus revealed, the Turk was then positioned at the table, and a member of the audience was invited to sit opposite him and begin the game. Invariably conceding the first move to his incredulous opponent, the Turk would then come swiftly to life, raising his arms and flexing all ten of his fingers, each hinged at every knuckle. Moving slowly over the board he would select a piece, lower his arms and gently take hold of it. The move he made would be swift and certain, and his still uncertain opponent would duly respond. Then the Turk would make his second move, more complicated than the first, perhaps, but equally decisive and swift, moving his forearm in an identically prescribed curve, pausing only to consider his strategy, and then bringing it back to rest on a carefully positioned cushion.

Occasionally, after every fourth or fifth move, the Turk would hesitate for a longer period than usual, then raise his hand to stroke his wooden chin, appearing to be uncertain about his next play. Barnum, like Maelzel before him, would announce that he was thinking; or he would gratify the Turk's opponent by telling him that he was a better player than those who normally approached the table. And then the Turk, having considered his move, would make it and once again take control of the game. It was claimed that the Turk won nine out of every ten games he played.

On the occasion of Barnum and Maelzel first becoming better acquainted – as competitors in adjoining rooms of the Boston Concert Hall – Maelzel had become drunk and had confessed that the machine had not been built by him, but that he had acquired it from elsewhere and improved upon it. Originally, he confessed, the Turk had won every game he sat down to, but now, under 'instructions' from him, he lost an occasional match and had become an even greater attraction as a result. Ten dollars was offered to anyone who managed to beat him, the fees from the crowd gathering to watch the game seldom failing to compensate for this occasional small loss.

The Turk had once played Napoleon in Berlin and had concluded the game by sweeping all the pieces from the board after the emperor had repeatedly made false moves. In Baltimore he had played Charles Carroll, the last surviving signatory of the Declaration of Independence, and in front of a capacity crowd at the Merchants' Hall had shown the good grace and tact to admit defeat at the hands of the ninety-one-year-old man.

Rumours spread about how the Turk was really operated. Edgar Poe believed that a midget was employed who was also an expert chess-player, a man small enough to conceal himself within an inner cavity at the centre of all the mechanical workings and to remain out of sight while those impressive but confusing internals were being revealed. Similarly, it was believed that a child prodigy operated the machine, also concealing himself in some part of the mechanism not shown to the public. Whatever the explanation, the Turk and other thinking-machines were in demand, and Barnum, in establishing his Museum, was quick to realize and capitalize upon this.

Some did little more than light and smoke cigars, whereas others undressed themselves until they sat only in their underclothes, whereupon the show was ended and decency maintained by the lowering of a curtain. Another drew a pistol and fired into a target, and yet another – an attractive female – set a complete table and poured coffee, inviting three of the spectators to join her, the three usually being men, who were then encouraged by Barnum to speculate upon the advantages of having such a woman for a wife.

During one such show in 1845, at which an automaton sharpshooter was the main attraction, a man in the crowd, who many afterwards claimed was drunk, repeatedly challenged the man he believed to be inside the hollow wooden shell to reveal himself. Initially, the sharpshooter ignored these gibes, but the man persisted, until after almost an hour of ridicule and abuse, the automaton slowly turned away from his target and aimed his pistol directly at him, fixing him where he stood as those around him moved swiftly away, several of whom, angry at the man's interruption of their own enjoyment, were now privately pleased at the prospect of what they were about to witness. The wooden arm of the sharpshooter clicked into a locked position and his fingers creaked as he tightened his grip on the trigger of his pistol. There followed a minute of silence, after which, perhaps because he believed that the machinery he had earlier scorned had wound down and betrayed the sharpshooter, the heckler regained his nerve and began to laugh. An instant later the automaton fired and the man fell to the ground. A dozen women screamed and panic ensued. Raising the pistol into the air, the sharpshooter fired three more shots and then continued to release the hammer on to empty chambers.

The heckler, it was afterwards discovered, was neither dead nor wounded, but had fainted with fright, and the bullet which had been aimed at his forehead was found embedded in the wood of a nearby pillar.

6

A FORTNIGHT AFTER the installation of the new aquarium, came another great day in the annals of the American Museum, reported in all the New York journals and heralded in the Museum itself by Hackaliah Cherry in his own inimitable style – a style he was perfecting in readiness for his triumphal announcement that the war was finally over. Blind Hope were Hackaliah Cherry's middle names.

'The General's a-comin'! General Tom Thumb! Here! Today! Soon! Now! Been an' gone an' yet to arrive! Don't miss it! General Tom Thumb! Here! Today! No extra charge! No! Extra! Charge! Due any second! Due any hour! Come an' gone away an' come right back again!'

He raced along the gallery, turned into the narrow entrance and collided with Zip, who was descending the stairs about to take up position in his booth.

Picking himself up, Cherry resumed his yelling until he was silenced by Zip's hand held firmly across his mouth. Even then he tried to continue, like a mechanical toy smothered beneath a cushion by an angry father, stopping only when he began to have difficulty breathing. This he signalled to Zip with his eyes and Zip took away his hand.

'Is it true?'

Cherry took several deep breaths. 'Sure is,' he said proudly. 'Here, today, any minute now.'

'And free of charge? Are you sure?'

'Mr Barnum told me so himself, told me personally, him and me, man to man.'

'So why all the excitement? You don't even like the little runt.'

'No sir, but Mr Barnum paid me to run up and down all the floors screamin' in a state of high excitation that he was a-comin'.'

'When?'

'Late afternoon, Mr Barnum reckoned.'

'It isn't yet mid-morning, Hack. Why start so early?'

Cherry checked himself to ensure he remembered precisely what he'd been told, practising the sentence before speaking. 'To ensure a sufficient and consummate degree of expectation.' He was proud of having remembered. 'To Mr Barnum's way of thinking, it won't hurt anybody to think the General's right here right now. He reckons it'd get them moving round a whole lot faster if they were all lookin' for him.'

'But he *isn't* here.'

'No, but the way I see it, neither are they being charged any extra for not seeing him. It all makes good sense.'

Barnum logic, Zip thought. 'Barnum tell you that, too?'

'Yes, sir. He even put a notice up outside announcing the General's eminent presence.'

'He's doing us a big favour,' Zip said coldly.

'Sure is. Mr Barnum reckons Thumb could still be earning a million dollars per annum year, if he wanted to. How much is a million?' Cherry spread his fingers and studied them.

'You could buy yourself a new broom every day until you passed on, Hack.'

'Every day! Holy Ohio! Place be cleaner than Barnum's ugly statue.'

They were joined by Franklin, who arrived with the Aztec children, one on each arm.

'They wanted to know what all the yellin' was about.'

'General Tom Thumb's a-comin',' Cherry told him. 'Tom Thumb, the one and only, the original.'

'Oh, is that all?'

Believing Franklin had misunderstood him, Cherry said, 'No. The General's comin' *here*, today, any minute now, right here, among all us common folk.'

'And when he gets here he'll pass among us scattering pithy epithets and kind and wonderful words of wisdom and self-improvement,' Zip said. He drew a piece of candy from the ears of both Bartola and Maximo and gave it to them. They searched for more.

'I see.' There was a recess in the narrow corridor and Franklin sat on the couch it contained. He mopped his face and brushed the sweat from his exposed, quivering shoulders. 'They thought it was a new tiger or some such, another woolly horse. I've just taken them to see the turtles in the fountain.'

52

Bartola and Maximo chattered unintelligibly to each other. Bartola's hair had been brushed out by Elizabeth into a globe which doubled the size of her small head, and Maximo's beard trimmed to a severe point.

'I been gettin' 'em ready,' Franklin said, watching them affectionately.

'General Tom,' Cherry said to them, crouching until his face was level with theirs. 'You must remember General Tom Thumb.' He dropped to his knees and mimicked Thumb's squeaky voice, but succeeded only in frightening them.

'Don't,' Franklin told him. 'They don't understand what you're trying to tell them.'

'They're igrant, that's why,' Cherry said dismissively. 'I know for a fact that the General could be earnin' himself a clear round million dollars per annual year if he wanted to. You know how many brooms that is?'

'And *I* know for a fact that up there in his toytown mansion, he and the delectable Lavinia, Bumpus as was, employ nigger boys to wait upon them hand and foot and don't pay them barely ten dollars per annual year,' Zip said.

This stopped Cherry, and he considered the information for a moment.

'And on his yacht,' Franklin said, 'he has a white crew for above decks, where everyone can see 'em, but down below in the coal stacks and boiler room, he only has short skinny niggers working for him.' He didn't know this for certain, but it didn't matter, rumour and fact being constantly and easily interchangeable currency in the Museum.

'You just jealous on account of how *you* ain't got no yacht,' Cherry said, unwilling to believe what he'd been told.

'It'd sink the moment I was piped on board,' Franklin said. He saluted and made the glugging sound of the yacht going down beneath his weight. The Aztec children copied him.

'You're neglecting your duties,' Zip said to Cherry.

Cherry put his head back out into the corridor and yelled, 'General Tom Thumb! Himself! Here today! In person! In the flesh! Don't miss him!'

'Free of charge,' Zip prompted him.

'At no expense whatsoever to faithful members of the public! Free of charge! Value guaranteed! The world-famous bargain of the decade!'

In the distance a rising stampede of feet could be heard as the public rushed to the source of the announcement to find out more.

'The place will be full all day,' Franklin said wearily.

'I think that was the intention,' Zip said.

Elizabeth arrived and she too asked them what the commotion was. Zip told her, with Cherry echoing most of what he said. She hadn't been at the Museum when Thumb had ruled supreme there, but had heard enough about him from the others to now share their dislike of the man.

'I look forward to meeting him,' she said.

'We'll all get our chance. Barnum won't pass up the opportunity of showing him round and introducing us all like long-lost friends.'

'Mr Barnum made a point of confiding that very thing to me personally,' Cherry said. ' "Cherry," he said, "Cherry, seeing the General will act as an encouragement and a spur, especially in these times of trouble and unrest",' – here Zip and Elizabeth exchanged a glance – ' "revealing to you all the heights to which you too might yet as-pire." That's what he said. "The heights to which you all might yet as-pire." I told him about my own heights and he guarantee me that the war be over and done with in a year.'

'Whereupon you'll snap your broom over your knee and march proudly out into the cheering throng singing loudly of your freedom, I suppose,' Zip said.

'I'm free now,' Cherry said proudly. 'Got papers to prove it. And these broom-handles cost twenty cents each.' He was interrupted by the distant voice of Barnum shouting 'Che-ree, Che-ree!' whereupon he left them and resumed his excited proclamations, softly at first and then with increasing volume and vigour, as though he were running towards Barnum from a great distance.

'At least *he's* excited,' Elizabeth said.

'And the children,' Franklin added, wiping their mouths.

'Barnum will take him first to Astor House for lunch, and then when they've all had enough to eat and drink he'll parade him up and down Broadway for an hour or so until half the city knows he's here. Then, when the queues are long enough, they'll make their grand entrance.'

Franklin told her of the time he'd posed with Thumb and Lavinia a month before their wedding, and how he'd stood with the crowds outside St Paul's Church on the day the ceremony took place.

'We were all there,' Zip said. 'Barnum closed this place for the day and told us all to turn up.'

'Was it a good ceremony?'

'We don't know. We turned up in all our best finery and then discovered that we were expected to wait outside and lead the cheering when the happy couple emerged.'

'Barnum came out immediately behind them,' Franklin said.

'And Thumb turned up dressed as the Duke of Wellington. Barnum wanted Franklin to crouch down on all fours and for Thumb to sit on his back holding up a sword.'

'I have difficulty crouching down like that,' Franklin said, a note of shame in his voice. 'The doctor back home said it was on account of all my inside pieces and parts shifting around.'

'So in the end, Barnum sat Thumb and Lavinia on each of his knees, passing kisses between them.'

'I was told to act embarrassed,' Franklin said. 'I sat with my hands up over my eyes. Like this.' He showed them, and afterwards there was a long silence, in which all they could hear was the distant Cherry, racing through the Museum like a fire-raiser through a field of dry cotton stubble.

'They thought it was a new tiger,' Franklin explained to Elizabeth, handing the children over to her. 'They like the tigers.'

'I think one of the tigers in the basement died last night,' she said.

'I'll take them down to see it, pay their last respects,' he said, rising laboriously and holding out his hands to the children.

When the three of them had gone, Elizabeth asked Zip if he knew how old the retarded twins were.

'I'd say thirty,' he said. 'But they haven't changed any while I've been here and I don't see any sign of it happening in the future. Barnum once brought in some doctor to examine them, and he reckoned they'd stopped at about age two.'

'Why "Aztec"?'

'Same reason I wear the monkey suit and jump up and down like an imbecile all day.'

'And there was me thinking all along that you did it because you enjoyed it.' She helped him on with his jacket and brushed the dirt and cobwebs from his back. 'You're an educated man,' she said. 'Tell me, where did the original Cyclops come from? I mean the very first, the giant.'

'Out of someone's imagination,' Zip told her. 'And of all the places to come from, that's the most dangerous. Look what it's doing to us.' He let his arms swing low and jabbered like a monkey.

Barnum appeared with Thumb and Lavinia at five in the afternoon. It was a bright, warm day, and upon leaving the Astor, their procession had gone as far north as Union Square, circled it several times and then returned to the Museum. Aware of what was happening, and anxious to see both Barnum and the midget couple, the crowds lined Broadway from Chamber to Canal Street, and the queues waiting to get into the Museum itself stretched as far as Allen Street and the Blessed Sacrament Asylum.

'I am putting myself forward free of charge,' Thumb said to Barnum. 'And yet, in addition to seeing me pass in the street, they are also fighting to hand over their money to you.' His voice, like that of his wife, was high-pitched and childlike, making it sound as though each word was being forced with some effort along a narrow and brittle reed.

'Also to see everything else I have on display,' Barnum said quickly, anxious lest Thumb or Lavinia now went back on their deal and demanded some kind of payment for their appearance.

'Can they see my jewels fully?' Lavinia asked, standing at the carriage door and waving regally out at all those who waved back.

'The entire city, prompted by me of course, has been talking of nothing but your arrival for days, and even when you are long gone they'll keep right on expecting you to pop up from some hidden corner or other so that they might prolong the pleasure of your company and marvel anew at your achievements.' Even Barnum, seldom embarrassed by his excessive hyperbole, felt a slight discomfort at hearing the words issue from his lips. He'd drunk two bottles of champagne, double his usual lunchtime ration, and wondered if he were not now in some way affected by the drink. Unhappy at such introspection, he shook the thought from his mind.

'No doubt some hidden corner of the Museum,' Thumb said, belching loudly and fanning the smell of the drink from his face.

Lavinia cast him an angry glance.

'You carry on waving for both of us,' Thumb instructed her, then, turning to Barnum, said, 'Where, Phineas, did you ever see such a woman as devoted as that woman is to me? Tell me, where?'

'Nowhere,' Barnum said. 'I've seen them all, and yet never have I come across another Lavinia Bumpus.'

'Thumb,' Thumb said angrily. 'Lavinia Thumb.'

'Of course.' Barnum let himself sink in the soft carriage seat. In addition to the champagne, he'd drunk some weaker wine, no more than a bottle, and several glasses of brandy.

'I brought eight costumes,' Lavinia said, still waving.

'We'll only be there for an hour at the very most, my dear.' Thumb paused, and then said to Barnum, 'Did I tell you we were dining at Irving House with Gordon Bennet tonight?' He smiled to himself, avoiding Barnum's eyes. 'I believe Mr Bennet – James – is a great friend of your own Mr Jeremiah Bergh.'

Barnum almost choked at the mention of the names. 'Bergh! Bergh! He's no friend of mine, I assure you.'

James Gordon Bennet was the proprietor of the *New York Herald*, and an old adversary of Barnum's. Along with Louis Gaylord Clark of the *Knickerbocker*, he frequently used his paper to mock Barnum and pour scorn upon his Museum and its exhibits. It was Bennet and Clark who had together exposed his Joice Heth hoax, a twisted stick of a Negress claiming to be the 161-year-old nursemaid of George Washington. A loathsome old wench, according to Bennet and Clark.

'Compose yourself, Phineas, compose yourself.' Thumb smiled again.

Jeremiah Bergh was the recent founder of the American Society for the Prevention of Cruelty to Animals. He was a man who would unashamedly stop sickly-looking horses in the street and unharness them from their carts; a man who would cut the thongs of turtles in the fish markets, freeing their flippers and allowing them to make their bids for freedom in the East River. He interfered in dog fights and wanted hunters to shoot at straw bales instead of moving, edible targets. Turning his attention to the Museum, he had attacked Barnum for the manner in which his animals were kept, threatening to outlaw their unhappy presence there before the year was out. Barnum had laughed at this, but for a second, perhaps less, the laugh had faltered in his throat in the face of Jeremiah Bergh.

It was true – a tiger had died in the basement the previous evening, and he became suddenly anxious in case Jeremiah Bergh, in advance of the taxidermist, might choose to make something of Thumb's arrival to bring his own crusade once again before the public.

He was brought sharply back to the present by Thumb's scratchy voice telling him again of his invitation to Irving House.

'Ah, yes,' Barnum said. 'Send Bennet my kindest regards. Unfortunately, I am otherwise engaged this coming evening. For several consecutive evenings ahead, in fact.'

'You weren't invited,' Lavinia told him bluntly.

'No. Bennet is most particular these days,' Thumb added.

'I was only writing as much to Mr Dickens,' Barnum said. 'He too could not see eye to eye with Mr Bennet on a number of topics.'

Lavinia turned. 'Mr Charles Dickens?'

'Is there another?'

'I sincerely hope not,' Thumb said in defence of his wife. 'We find his works unbearably heavy, a real strain upon the wrist.'

'I much prefer his illustrations,' Lavinia said. 'He ought to collect them and bind them together in a separate volume.'

'Lavinia is something of an artist herself,' Thumb said.

His tiny wife shook her arms and her bracelets rattled. At her every movement a further cheer went up from the crowd.

It had been almost a year since Barnum had seen either Thumb or Lavinia, and over two since they had married and left the Museum to set up a home of their own. They had still toured with him in the following months, but even then Thumb was tiring of the demands being made upon him, and a year ago the couple had sailed upon a cruise of the world, effectively severing all links with their old promoter and manager, and the source of their not inconsiderable personal fortune. The distant friendship had remained firm, however, until, ill-advised by Greenwood, Barnum had started the rumour of Lavinia's pregnancy. Afterwards, Barnum genuinely regretted this, but by then it was too late and the damage had been done. A few weeks later, Minnie, Lavinia's midget sister, had died in childbirth following her marriage to an English fancy skater. The child, too, had died, and the joke had soured for ever relations between Thumb and Barnum. He was only visiting the Museum now because his own craving for public adulation was as great as Barnum's. Barnum understood this, and an uneasy truce was maintained by both men.

Arriving at the entrance to the Museum, Barnum rose unsteadily to make a short speech, to which both Thumb and Lavinia listened with every suggestion of interest. Before Barnum was half-way through, Thumb rose beside him and thanked him. His words were drowned by applause and cheering twice the volume of that which had greeted Barnum. Acknowledging this, Barnum left the carriage and helped his guests down. They had both gained weight on their world cruise, and he was unprepared for this as he took Lavinia's hand and lowered her awkwardly to the sidewalk. Ahead of them, Thumb strutted in a circle, throwing open his arms and shouting his thanks to everyone who had turned out to see him. He patted his stomach and announced that he was a little changed in appearance since last they met, but that he hoped no one was disappointed by what they now saw. The crowd cheered him again, and then again as Lavinia arrived beside him and curtsied stiffly to the onlookers.

Barnum wanted to urge them indoors and so tempt the crowd to follow through the turnstiles of the ticket office.

'Rain,' he announced. 'It may rain. The General and his charming wife are now accustomed to more tropical climes. Let us hurry them inside where their safety, comfort and dryness can be unequivocally assured.' The crowd cheered. Few looked up into the blue and cloudless sky.

Hackaliah Cherry appeared in the doorway, holding his broom and bowing each time either Thumb or Lavinia glanced in his direction. Barnum signalled for him to go back indoors, but as he did so, Thumb spotted him and shouted, 'Hackaliah Cherry, you old black rascal! It is, it's you! It's been a long long time, too long, far too long. How are you, my friend, my dear dear friend?' He embraced Cherry's thigh.

The gesture surprised Cherry, who had exchanged barely half a dozen words with Thumb during his years at the Museum, but, prepared now to accept that his own memory was at fault, he put aside his broom and let himself be drawn into Thumb's arms, until the midget's face came to rest between his legs. He alone caught Barnum's scowl as it passed swiftly across his face.

'Oh, Cherry, Cherry, Cherry, dear friend. How we've missed you. How often we've thought back fondly of our times with you when upon some dark and distant ocean.'

The noise of the crowd fell to a reverential murmur as everyone stood and watched and shared in this emotional reunion.

Beside her husband, Lavinia watched with disgust as Cherry reached down and patted Thumb's head.

Thumb withdrew and pulled Lavinia forward. She held out her hand.

'Hackaliah Cherry. How could we ever forget? Ever the faithful friend.'

Cherry bowed, his eyes wide with wonder at the unexpected warmth of his reception.

'They all knew you were a-comin', General Tom,' he said.

'Rain!' Barnum shouted, holding out both palms, to which no one paid the slightest attention.

'Then shall we enter the palace of multifarious and nebulous delights and greet the remainder of our old and faithful comrades,'

Thumb said loudly, lifting his elbow for Lavinia to slide in her hand.

'There's Zip, and Anna, and them two ree-tard characters we calls "children",' Hackaliah Cherry began, before being silenced by Barnum, who, pulling a handful of coins from his pocket, scattered them before the crowd and shouted, 'Treat yourselves,' indicating the Museum entrance, and then stepping aside to avoid the rush.

Thumb and Lavinia went inside. Barnum pushed Cherry aside and followed immediately behind them. The crowd swarmed eagerly into the narrow entrance in their wake.

Inside, Thumb and Lavinia, accompanied always by Barnum, Cherry and a further crowd of visitors, greeted the other residents in the same effusive manner before moving quickly on.

Zip, catching Barnum's eye, rattled his chains and gave a weak growl. Lavinia ignored him, and Thumb referred to him as 'that poor unfortunate creature'.

Arriving at Elizabeth's booth, Thumb was struck by her looks and asked to be lifted up so that he might approach her more closely.

'Why, Mr Thumb,' Elizabeth said, pretending to be flattered by his attentions. 'You are fatter than I imagined. And taller.'

The remark appeared not to register. Thumb stood beside her and simply stared.

Greenwood arrived to join Barnum, and Barnum immediately whispered some instruction to him. Greenwood asked Lavinia if she would do him the honour of accompanying him to see the new aquarium recently installed in the basement and not yet on view to the general public. She tried to attract her husband's attention, but Thumb was still entranced by Elizabeth and didn't hear her. Greenwood led her away, feigning interest at everything she said. All along, it had been Barnum's intention to separate them once they were inside the Museum, thus creating two moving attractions and affording everyone who had paid to enter the opportunity of seeing at least one of them.

Now he watched the midget carefully. Thumb's weakness for women of normal height and build was well known to him, and in the years before the arrival of Lavinia, when Thumb was still resident in the Museum, he had frequently pandered to the amorous demands of his star attraction under cover of darkness.

'Phineas,' Thumb said unexpectedly, his gaze still fixed upon Elizabeth.

'General?'

'Perhaps Mr Thumb wishes to make some remark upon my outstanding beauty,' Elizabeth suggested. 'As advertised.'

'Beauty,' Thumb said absently. He reached out to stroke her leg, but she withdrew it and slapped the back of his hand. She indicated the sign beside her which said 'Definitely No touching Or Engaging In Excessively Lengthy Conversation'.

'But I'm General Tom Thumb,' Thumb said, unaccustomed to such treatment.

'So?' Elizabeth smiled down at the women in her audience. She had their sympathy and most smiled back at her or acknowledged their support in some other way. Further along the corridor, she saw Franklin, still with the Aztecs, both of whom waved vigorously at her.

'General,' Barnum said, as cheerfully as possible under the circumstances, 'I'm sure there are many other old friends eagerly awaiting your arrival.'

'Oh, eagerly,' Elizabeth said.

Thumb, still oblivious to her mocking tone, said, 'Yes, I suppose there are,' and he reluctantly made his way back to the edge of the booth.

'General Thumb, General Thumb,' Franklin called out to him, leading Bartola and Maximo through the crowd. 'They wanted to pass on their regards.' He pushed the children forward. Both stood stiffly for a moment, and then Maximo bowed and Bartola curtsied. 'I taught them,' Franklin said proudly. 'They thought at first you were another tiger, but then I explained all about you and they've been looking forward ever since to meeting you.'

'Is that it?' Thumb said. 'Is that all they can do — stand there looking stupid? Are you sure they fully comprehend who I am, in whose presence they are now standing?'

Franklin came forward and retrieved the children. 'They thought at first you were a tiger,' he repeated, anxious for them not to be humiliated any further in front of the crowd.

'So you said. In which case, I am sorry to have disappointed them. You'll understand that I am now far more accustomed to moving in culturally and intellectually elevated circles than in — in —' Thumb indicated to Barnum that he wished to move on.

Before he left, Elizabeth motioned for Franklin to lift the children up to her, and in full view of Thumb and the crowd, she kissed them both fully upon the lips.

7

LADY MACBETH ENTERED stage-left, a bloody dagger in her hand; Cleopatra sat at the centre of the stage and considered the length of her nose in a looking-glass; and away to the right, a doleful, ageing Hamlet clutched a skull to his chest and wept loudly, throwing out his free arm every few seconds as though he were broadcasting seed-corn into the audience. Off stage, Hackaliah Cherry beat upon a drum and blew loud, piercing notes from a conch shell.

Barnum, Anna Swan and Zip sat at the rear of the theatre, but only Barnum sat with a broad grin of satisfaction on his face; only he sat with his fists clenched in anticipation of this grand finale to the drama he had witnessed several hundred times already.

Turning to Anna, he indicated the moisture in his eyes. 'Call me a sentimental old fool,' he said, waiting until she had seen his tears before dabbing them dry. 'Happens every time. What a master! What a genius! Between us, he and I will elevate the masses to a truer and finer appreciation of all that is worth knowing. Drama, tragedy, humour, all human life is here.'

Anna looked past him to Zip, who was mouthing the words as Barnum spoke them.

'And you, Zip,' Barnum said, leaning forward to address him. 'Do you not feel a certain uplifting of the spirit, a release of the inner, truer emotions?'

'Cramp,' Zip said, massaging his legs, which were bent double in the confined space between the rows of seats.

'Ah, yes.' Barnum sat back, disappointed.

'They enjoyed it,' Anna said to him, indicating the audience around them as the curtain began to fall and they called out for more.

'That's the secret, Anna,' he said. 'Selection and emphasis, selective presentation, a heightening of effect. What is to be gained by having so many powerful and memorable characters spread so thinly throughout such a great and diverse body of work? It confuses, it confuses and dilutes. Same with the speeches. You see how our talents combine, you see how perfectly matched we are with regard to the modern age?'

'And putting on a dozen plays in under an hour?' Zip said.

'Compression, Zip. Artistic compression. Who but the English would sit for three hours and witness within that time one solitary murder, the loss of one son or daughter?' Barnum wiped his face with a handkerchief. 'Shall I reveal an even greater secret, Anna, one of my best?'

Anna shrugged, knowing that whatever she said he would reveal it anyway. The first of his treasured secrets he had divulged to her had been the fact that, although appearing level with the other booths, the one in which she exhibited herself was raised by almost a foot to make her appear even taller than she already was. Similarly, the drapes and furnishings of Franklin's booth were narrower by comparison with the others to make him appear even broader.

'The secret,' Barnum said, 'is to pack the Italians into the first few rows. They're so starved of this kind of enlightened entertainment that they'll laugh or cry at anything. Fine race of people, some of them, but they do have this propensity to divulge their every feeling, their every emotion at the slightest prompting. Put them on the front row and they become infectious. They laugh, and everybody else laughs; nobody wants to be left out – nothing worse than paying the same as everyone else and then finding yourself enjoying it less. Works every time. The only thing to avoid is to get too many Russians sitting together. You ever see such a cheerless breed, Zip?'

'Never,' Zip said, because that was the only answer Barnum would have heard.

'Their idea of fun is a man juggling with two balls, or a dog leaping through a hoop wide enough to accommodate a horse. Little wonder they flock away from that depressing country. I tell you, I fear for the sanity of my fellow-showmen in that place.'

'Perhaps they have other priorities,' Zip said.

'Such as?'

Unwilling to enter into an argument with Barnum, Zip conceded to him.

'It's an illness, Zip, a madness. You either look up or you look down, you come out of yourself or you go in. Look at the Italians, look – God forbid – at the French. What do you see? I'll tell you –

you see people ready to embrace and enjoy the fullness of life. Look at the Russians and all you see are men walking round with their eyes to the ground mumbling to themselves. It's a disease, a sickness.'

'You see them like that here,' Zip said. 'America. Perhaps they don't have a great deal to be cheerful about.'

To Barnum this was incomprehensible. Beside him, Zip saw Anna signalling for him not to pursue the matter, and he too acknowledged the futility of going on.

'Do you have any new shows lined up?' Anna asked Barnum, thus diverting his attention.

'I have a dozen, all waiting for some small decrease in the popularity of the production presently before us. As you both well know, my own tastes lean towards the more refined of the performing arts – opera, ballet and diversions of that nature – but I fully accept that in the eyes of my –' Here he was cut short by Hackaliah Cherry, who, having entered the rear of the theatre unobserved, leaned over Barnum's shoulder with the conch shell at his lips and blew loudly into his ear, causing him to leap sideways in his seat and cry out.

'You all hear that victorious Roman fleet gettin' back into port all right?' Cherry said, shaking a few drops of moisture from the shell.

'We heard it fine, Hack,' Anna told him.

'And the storm,' Zip added, rising from his seat.

'The drumming,' Barnum said. 'The drumming at the finale is still far too loud.'

'Sounded fine to me,' Zip said, winking at Cherry.

'Too loud. They're fine and noble words, Hack, written to inspire and encourage and elevate. You, on the other hand, are someone beating a skin with a stick.' Turning to Anna, he held her arm and said, 'I've been thinking about a song.'

'A song?'

'To end the show. Get them all lined up dancing and singing. Something patriotic. One or two of them waving a Union flag.'

'I could walk among the audience banging on the drum,' Cherry said. He made the motions with his arms. 'Stir 'em up.'

'Alternatively, you could stay right where you belong and make sure you get the scenery shifted in time for the next performance. So, Anna, what do you think? A song, something to send them all out of the theatre with a tear in their eye and a spring in their step.'

'Wouldn't it extend the performance?' Zip said.

'You could cut out the scene at the beginning with the mule,'

64

Cherry suggested. 'People don't expect no mule to get up on its back legs and start talkin' to 'em. Especially not a mule surrounded by all them fairies, which everyone can see are practically the same size as the mule itself. Not *my* idea of a summer night's dream to have no talkin' mule parading itself around givin' speeches to a load of fairies.'

'Your suggestion is noted,' Barnum said curtly, exasperated, once again defeated by the unpatriotic philistinism with which he was surrounded. He rose and left them.

Zip kissed Anna's hand and then he too left the theatre.

She watched him go, and for a moment her face was creased with worry at a distant memory.

Ten years ago, perhaps longer, when Barnum had been at the height of his power, almost intoxicated with that power and with the overwhelming sense of his own seemingly boundless popularity, he and Zip had been much closer, and had shared a mutual trust and understanding which, in the beginning, had been strong enough to survive the many barriers which grew between them. Anna, too, had shared in that friendship, and on many occasions she and Zip had been Barnum's guests at Iranistan, his beautiful country house, sometimes for the evening, travelling to and from the city in his carriage with him, sometimes over a whole weekend. There they had mixed with the highest of New York society. Only Charity Barnum had ever objected to their presence, and without ever being openly hostile towards them in her husband's presence, she had nevertheless made her feelings known to them. She had acceded to Barnum then because their daughters were still young girls and could have had little real idea of the true nature of their father's relationship with these people. Anna carried the girls on her shoulders, and Zip allowed them to brush his topknot and fasten it in ribbons. Charity, always believing herself to be the perfect hostess whenever her husband entertained, contributed nothing to the long and wide-ranging discussions which took place, and she resented the ease and conviction with which both Zip and Anna made their own contributions, speaking and arguing as equals with whoever else was present. She resented also their intelligence and natural good humour, their ability to move with the conversation and then to firmly anchor it with a witty or enlightened observation which was uniquely their own. Many of his visitors envied Barnum his companions.

Slowly and unavoidably, however, this relationship had changed. During his prolonged absences abroad, Barnum's daughters grew up

65

into younger replicas of his wife, and the invitations to Zip and Anna to visit his home stopped coming. He had tried in his own confused way to apologize to them, but apologies had never been his strong suit, and in the end there was no need: Zip and Anna understood perfectly what had happened and why they were now being excluded.

Those had been the happiest of their days together, and everything since had been somehow soured or tainted by comparison. From being merely awkward with his apologies, Barnum, prompted by Charity, came to look upon them as a weakness, and it had eventually become almost physically painful for the three of them to look back on those times and speculate upon the alternative paths they might now be travelling. Equally painful for Anna alone was the recent increase in the animosity she had noticed between the two men, from Zip in particular, who on occasion now seemed to be wholly motivated in his dealings with Barnum by a submerged and destructive grudge against him, perhaps as a direct result of his own hopes and ambitions during those happier times.

No one was to blame for what had happened – not even Charity, for she was simply a mother protecting her daughters from her own worst fears; it just so happened that a new order had been established and that everything had changed as a result.

Anna was jolted from her reverie by Hackaliah Cherry, who once again blew into the shell, this time for the simple pleasure of hearing it echo around the walls of the empty theatre.

'Best go out and get the next lot excited,' she told him.

Cherry left her, and she sat alone in the dim light contemplating the empty stage and hearing the voices of the actors behind it preparing for their next performance. Beyond their muted conversations she heard the even more distant drumming of the Redskins, and then their screams and war cries as they began to dance, the pounding rhythm of their feet slowly transmitting itself throughout the entire building until it reached into the empty theatre and passed right through her, causing her to tremble, and then, inexplicably, to shudder, as though at a sudden and violent premonition of the future.

8

ZIP AND YOUNG Herman walked along the wharves which skirted
the Battery Gardens. It was Sunday and a cool wind blew in off the
confluence of the rivers. Every few minutes, Herman turned himself
into this and breathed deeply. He had been suffering from a chest
cold, and only the previous day Barnum's physician had declared
him cured and fit to return to work after a week's absence from his
booth. Around them worked gangs of labourers, busy on the massive baulks of the new wharves under construction, and occasionally
they saw the small family groups of recently arrived immigrants still
familiarizing themselves with their new city. Some had been landed
from the ferries that same day, and these new arrivals stood in even
tighter groups, their possessions in trunks and bundles at their feet,
looking as lost as they were. As they passed them and heard them
speaking, Herman tried to identify their nationalities. Zip paid them
little attention, his eyes instead on the passing young women who
appeared every Sunday in their twos and threes to take the air along
the tree-lined waterfront.

'Herman's a German name,' Herman said.

Ahead of him, Zip stopped, turned and asked him what he'd said.

'Herman Ferguson.' There was still the edge of an accent in his
voice, which he now exaggerated, as though trying to prove some as
yet undisputed point. 'I was born here. In Buffalo. My mother and
father arrived here in New York twenty-five years ago.'

That, in essence, Zip knew, was the start of everyone's story
of the city. He sat on a baulk of wood which lay across the path. 'So?'

'Nothing. I just wanted you to know. It was a big achievement
for them, that's all.'

'Is that where "Ferguson" came from?' Zip said. ' "Ich vergesse,
ich vergesse"? Did he come through looking hale and hearty and
happy to take whatever they gave him?'

67

Herman nodded and Zip apologized for the unkind remark.

'It's just that every time I see them coming ashore,' Zip said, 'I see them all as a brand-new audience. If they weren't forever arriving, then those who were already here would come and stare at us once and then lose interest.' He understood perfectly the imperfect logic of the remark and stopped speaking to watch two of the strolling young women who passed close by. He wore a high collar and a tie held in place with a diamond pin, and a Brown Derby hat raised by several inches to accommodate and disguise the cone of his head. 'We're the lucky ones,' he said. 'I put my hat on and you hold your chest in and we're just like any of the rest of them. But that's as far as it goes. If I keep my hat on and you hold your chest in, we're worthless.'

Herman began to cough violently, his chest and arms shaking at the exertion, making it only too obvious that he was not yet fully recovered from his illness.

'I'm all right,' he said through gasps for breath.

'Meaning you can't afford to lose another week's money. What do you do with it all – send it back home to Buffalo?'

'They need it,' Herman said. 'You?'

'No family. I'm a free spirit. Come and go as I choose. With my hat on, of course. Look at this pair.' He indicated two more of the young women who passed in front of them. A group of labourers on the river called to them, but the women ignored them, and instead cast glances at Zip and Herman.

Herman blushed.

'Nothing to be ashamed or afraid of,' Zip said. 'This is it, the big, wide, real world. This kind of thing happens every day out here.'

'I've been to London,' Herman said, hoping Zip would do or say nothing to further attract the attention of the two women. 'With Barnum.'

'And did they smile and flutter their eyes at you there? They should. You're a handsome young man with prospects.'

Herman lowered his face even further.

'Shall I raise my hat to them?' Zip asked. 'That's what they expect. That's what would be considered polite and customary. I raise my hat and they either curtsy and continue on their way, or they giggle and stand there waiting for us to approach them and offer them our arms.'

'Don't,' Herman said, suddenly afraid of the possible encounter.

'Don't worry. If I raised my hat they'd probably run and throw themselves in the river screaming "Monster".'

'You're not . . .'

'I'm not what? I'm not a monster?'

'Of course you're not.'

'To them I am. To all these proud honest labourers who would come to their rescue and beat me to a bloody pulp I would be. I could clear the quay from here to Wall Street if I threw off my hat, tore open my shirt and roared. So could you.'

'But I never would,' Herman insisted.

'No – but don't you see – that's the true nature of the only power we possess. I've been thinking about it a lot lately. I don't know why. Guess I'm just unfortunate in having an inquisitive mind, as Cherry might put it. Listen, I'll tell you something. A year after I came to the Museum – I'd spent two years before that on the road travelling with Barnum all over the Middle West – a year after my arrival I was in my booth, monkey-man Zip, when a woman fainted in front of me. We were all curtained off in those days and she'd wandered in alone not really knowing what to expect. Anyhow, she saw me and fainted, and because there was no one else around to help her, I climbed down and tried to help her up, to revive her. She had on a tight collar and I unfastened it for her to help her breathe. Then she began to come to, saw what I'd done, took one look at me and screamed at the top of her voice. Two or three men ran in, saw me kneeling over her in the monkey suit, made up their own minds as to what had happened, and started to kick and punch me. Others came rushing in, saw what was happening and helped them along a little. I tried to defend myself, but inside the suit it was next to impossible.' He paused, the memory more painful than he had imagined.

'What happened?' Herman asked him.

'What happened was that I just had to lie there and let them get on with it. Levi Lyman was the manager then, and he arrived with Cherry and Vivalla and stopped them. The woman was still screaming, shouting to everyone that I'd messed with her clothes. She started demanding money and Lyman had no option but to pay up. I think she settled on two hundred dollars.'

'And you?'

'I just lay on the ground making my monkey noises. I was a brainless imbecile straight from the jungle, how was I supposed to know any better? How was I supposed to feel the pain and suffer as *real* people suffered? I remember Vivalla holding my head and whispering to me, keeping me down until Lyman had got the men and the woman out of the booth. I had lumps and bruises on my chest, arms and face where they'd kicked me.' He paused again. 'I never told you, but I used to be billed as the Museum's original Missing Link before Barnum got the monkey up in the Dinosaur Room.'

'You?' Herman said excitedly.

'You sound impressed.'

'Well –'

'Don't be. And don't think for one second that I'm flattered.'

'I didn't mean to –'

'I know. It's just something else you've got to learn about us all. You'll understand soon enough. Don't let it bother you.' Zip wiped a hand over his face, and took a deep breath of the cool invigorating air. He laughed. 'Look at me – from the original Missing Link to this. They changed the billing fast enough when the new model arrived. Stuffed animals tell fewer tales than men in monkey suits. A big responsibility bearing the weight of mankind on your shoulders. You read anything by Mr Darwin yet?'

'I've heard of him.'

'Soon everyone will. He makes a lot of sense. Everyone's up in arms about his theories, but they make a lot of sense as far as I'm concerned. Who knows, one day they might even begin to explain why we're like we are. I tell you, after that beating I knew exactly where I stood in relation to my so-called fellow-man. And Barnum knows it now just as well as we do. Why do you think he keeps us out of reach of them? Why do you think they're encouraged to have one good look and then move on right along?'

'I hadn't really thought about it,' Herman said, more proud than embarrassed at having been taken into Zip's confidence.

'You'd have gotten round to it. Eventually.'

'I suppose so. I never really thought they looked at us like that.'

'What did you think – that they were jealous?'

'I don't know.'

Both sat for a minute without speaking. The two young women, receiving no encouragement, had moved on. Ahead of them, another of the massive timber supports was being lowered and hammered down into the brown water. A blue and white ferry passed by, trailing behind it a wash which rose to the waists of the working men. There was construction work taking place too on the distant shores, and flotillas of small craft moored to the islands in the bay.

'About the young women . . .' Herman began.

'You don't have to tell me,' Zip said.

'I like them, I like them a lot.'

Zip cupped his hands over the stub of a cigar and concentrated on keeping it alight.

'My parents write every week from Buffalo. Perhaps not that often, but at least once a month. They're doing well. Half of what I send them they manage to save. My father's an engineer. He wants me to join him one day and we'll set up in business together. It's a growing town, Buffalo.' He looked out over the river as he spoke. Both men had revealed a secret and a moment of readjustment was called for.

When 'Young' Herman had first come to the Museum, Barnum, always on the look out for novel ways of publicizing his new attractions, had taken him to a succession of tailors in the city and ordered a suit to be made for him. Deflated, Herman's chest measurement was thirty-eight inches, expanded to its fullest it reached almost sixty. After a first measurement, Barnum would announce himself dissatisfied and ask for another, whereupon the tailor would discover Herman's chest to have grown by several inches. Apologizing for his 'mistake' he would return to the chalking out of his cloth. Again Barnum would express his doubts, and again the tailor would apply his measure, this time discovering a discrepancy of almost a foot. By the time the hoax had been played to its limit, the tailor's tape would no longer meet at its ends. Then, of course, the joke was exposed, and because no one had been offended and no money lost, it was all taken in good spirit. Newspaper reports of the 'Expanding Boy' spread quickly and widely, and the novelty-seekers arrived at the Museum to see for themselves.

In his booth, Herman stood naked from the waist up, and waiting until the floor beneath him was crowded, he began his process of expansion, growing with each intake of breath until his chest was stretched to its fullest and people began to believe he might explode. As he grew, his skin grew tighter and paler, until eventually it became translucent and the outlines of his breastbone and ribs could be clearly seen beneath the inflated surface. Encouraged by Barnum, people also convinced themselves that they could see his beating heart and other organs, but this was not so, and when the first demand was made to have these features pointed out, Herman was under strict instructions to start to deflate, and afterwards to sit down and appear weary and faint, as though this great and sustained effort had taken its toll of his strength.

Recently, that was precisely how it had started to feel to him, his head spinning and a moving red light flickering across his eyes. His chest colds, too, were recurring with an alarming regularity, and often as he inflated, he would wheeze and lose some of his shape.

Resuming their walk, they rounded Water Street into Government Lane, and entered a basement there, where more labourers sat drinking at long wooden trestles. Several recognized Zip and raised their hands to him. Zip removed his coat and hat and sat in a corner of the room, indicating to the nervous Herman to sit beside him. The barman left glasses and a bottle before them and went without asking for money.

In awe of their new surroundings, Herman looked around him, catching the eyes of several of the men, who returned his gaze.

'Best not to stare at them too long,' Zip warned him. 'They take offence very easily. Don't worry, they're none of them as menacing as they like to pretend.'

'Me stare at *them*?'

'A novel situation, eh.' Zip laughed, drawing his palm over his exposed skull, to which few in the room paid even the slightest attention.

'Do you come here often?' Herman asked, taking the drink Zip offered him, and then choking on its unexpected strength and bitterness.

'As often as I can. I usually come in here with Anna and Bates. It's unhealthy spending too much time inside Château Barnum.'

'You bring Anna in here?' Herman said incredulously.

'She brought me. Don't tell me – you don't think this is the kind of place respectable women should be seen.'

'I didn't mean to –'

'Well, Anna Swan's the most honest and decent and respectable woman I know.'

'Me, too,' Herman said, ashamed of the implications of what he'd suggested.

Zip drained his glass in a single swallow, refilled it and emptied it again. It was one of Barnum's rules – but one which he no longer strictly enforced other than to gain an advantage in some other matter – that no liquor should be allowed in the Museum outside of his own and his managers' offices.

'Tom occasionally comes in to play the piano,' Zip said.

As they spoke, the low murmur of the room was broken at intervals by the shattering of glass and the high, shrieking laughter of the few women present. These sat among the men, frequently in their laps, and Herman avoided their faces as assiduously as he avoided the men's. He tried to prevent Zip from filling his glass a second time, but was unsuccessful, the liquid running over and through his fingers.

'It'll clear your chest,' Zip told him, and Herman sipped at it.

'I heard something a few days ago,' he said.

'And?' Zip waved to several new arrivals, one of whom was Señor Vivalla, who came in with an attractive woman, both of her arms wrapped around one of his own.

'I heard Mr Butler and Mr Greenwood talking about Barnum. They were talking about an offer they were going to make him to buy the lease of the Museum.'

'And us along with it, no doubt.' The news came as no surprise to Zip.

'That's the impression they gave.' Herman was clearly worried by what he'd overheard.

'They tried it before, ten years ago, took it off his hands when he went into his so-called premature retirement in that fancy pile of his over in Bridgeport. I hate to admit it, but they don't possess between them even one tenth of his skill or his flair for the business. They lost money then and they'll lose it again. He got bored with putting his feet up and having his daughters play the piano and sing to him, and so he came back, took up where he left off and started making money all over again. Things might not be going too good for him right now, but if that pair were given the reins they'd run the whole kit and caboodle straight to hell.'

'I heard them say all that. They seemed to think that this time they could make a better go of it. They said the times were changing and that they were more capable than Barnum was to change with them.'

'Greenwood's been itching for something like this for a long while now,' Zip said more seriously. 'If they were successful, and Barnum did agree to sell them the lease, I dare say they could make the place pay its way with all they've picked up over the past ten years. But it'd be Greenwood's show, not Henry Butler's, make no mistake about that.'

'I don't much like the idea of having him as the new owner.' Herman screwed up his face and took another sip of his drink.

'Me, neither. He plays too often at being lord of the castle already. Then again, Barnum *might* be ready to retire again. He's always wanting more time to work on that autobiography of his. It's been finished ten years and he still keeps altering it, putting things in, taking them out, a lie here, a hoax there, puffing himself up. He doesn't want to leave anything out, so each time he feels he's achieved something new, in it goes.'

'Bringing everything up to date.'

'Splashing a bit of truth over all the lies. Tell me, how serious did Greenwood and Butler seem to you?'

'Very. They said they could raise the money from their newspaper friends.'

They were interrupted by the arrival of Vivalla and the woman. He introduced her to Zip and Herman. Zip she already knew, but sitting herself beside Herman, she took his hand into her own and asked him what part he played in Barnum's house of horrors.

'He doesn't,' Zip told her, glancing at Vivalla to ensure he understood him. 'He's the new trainee manager.'

The woman looked at Herman suspiciously. 'Two arms, two legs,' she said.

Herman, realizing what Zip had done, could think of nothing to say, and feeling the woman pressed close to him, he blushed.

'Offer the lady a drink,' Zip told him.

Herman took the bottle and poured, but his hand shook and she held it for him. He emptied his own glass, and after a few minutes of sitting beside her he felt a little more at ease, proud almost to be with the two men in the bar, the first he had ever entered. The woman told him about herself and he told her of his parents in Buffalo.

'You heard anything about Barnum's plans to retire again?' Zip asked Vivalla.

'All the time. He's going to buy a chicken farm in the country and raise four-legged birds. He's buying up all the camels in Araby and setting up against Wells Fargo in Texas. He's got a herd of elephants ploughing up the prairies. What's new?'

'Our young friend here seems to think that Greenwood and Butler are getting serious again about taking over from him if they can persuade him to sell.'

'I hear Barnum's wife's been a sick woman recently. The trials that poor creature has to face, I don't wonder.' Vivalla drank as easily and as quickly as Zip.

'I think there's something to it this time,' Zip said.

'Greenwood's Gallery of the Gruesome and Grotesque. I'd leave. There'd be no place for an ex-acrobat, plate-spinning, stilt-walking pig-minder like me if Greenwood had his way. I'd go back to Cuba. Let's face it, Barnum only keeps me on because I've been with him since the beginning.' The possibility of his departure from the Museum did not appear unduly to upset Vivalla.

'Greenwood would have you juggling with broken bottles.'

'I already do. What do you think we should do – confront Barnum?'

'I just think we ought to know one way or the other. We've still got a few demands of our own to put to him.'

'I'll tell the others.'

'Not all of them,' Zip warned him. Then the two men turned their attention to Herman and the woman.

'She's deserted me,' Vivalla said, pretending to be hurt as the woman ignored him in favour of the much younger Herman.

An hour later, Zip and Herman left the bar together and walked back towards Broadway. It was by then late afternoon, and the crowds of earlier had thinned. Ahead of them men sat in their drunken stupors on the sidewalk. It had rained, and the passing carriages sprayed everyone with liquid mud. Herman complained at this and wiped at the broad check of his suit. The street was littered with the materials of construction, and above them men on flimsy scaffolding towers shouted to each other as they worked. Blocks of stone and pails of water were raised and lowered on ropes.

Entering Broadway, Zip asked Herman if he looked presentable, raising his collar and positioning his hat. Herman, still slightly drunk despite the sobering effect of their walk back, inspected him and told him he was.

They came to the Museum and entered it by the side entrance, passing one of the actors on his way out with Byron and Apollo, both pig and dog straining to be the first through the door.

From the first floor came the voices of Anna and Elizabeth, singing to Tom's accompaniment. Revealing to Herman the neck of a bottle he had brought with him from the tavern, Zip led the way upstairs to join them.

Bates, Fortuna and René were also present, Bates reading a newspaper, Fortuna working on a sampler, and René sketching his wife as she sewed. He alone resented the arrival of Zip and Herman and the likely disruption of their hitherto quiet afternoon's entertainment.

75

Tom sniffed the air and asked who had the bottle. Zip handed it to him and he drank from it while continuing to play with his free hand. Anna brought out a tray of glasses and poured drinks for everyone else except Fortuna and René, who declined. René's views on drink were well known to all of them, and only a glance from his wife prevented him from making a short disapproving speech on the matter. She asked to see his sketches, and upon being handed them she admired them all.

Several months earlier, René had been commissioned by Barnum to paint a portrait of him, which now hung behind his desk in his office. In it, beside Barnum, were Charity and his three grown daughters. René had been carefully instructed beforehand on the details of the painting, on how each figure should look. Barnum, although of equal height to Charity, was made to appear several inches taller. The smile on his face was one of benevolence and understanding, and the remaining features of his face were even and perfectly proportioned. Because of his added height, he appeared less stout, and the colour in his cheeks was a pale, healthy brown, rather than his usual steamed pink. He alone was looking directly out of the painting, and Charity and his daughters were all glancing slightly towards him with looks of respect and admiration on their faces.

At Barnum's insistence, René had gone to his home to make the preliminary sketches for the canvas, warned in advance of the beauty, grace and elegance he was about to encounter there, and which he would undoubtedly find difficult to capture to the fullest degree in his painting. René had found Charity to be dutiful and tolerable, but Barnum's three daughters he had quickly grown to despise. If they did possess a beauty, then it was one that he could neither discern in the flesh nor recreate with any honesty in his work. Barnum hovered constantly at his shoulder, suggesting and then insisting on changes as the portrait took shape. Surely Charity's eyes were more blue than grey, her figure fuller? And surely the combination of eloquence, femininity and intelligence was far more evident in the girls than René had been able to capture? On several occasions Barnum had seized the brushes and threatened to improve upon the portrait himself. In every instance, René had acquiesced to his demands, afterwards despising himself for his weakness.

Once, René overheard Barnum complaining to Charity about how the portrait was turning out, and when she expressed her satisfaction with it in regard to the beauty of their daughters, Barnum had shouted, 'Beauty! What does the man know about beauty, for heaven's sake! He married a woman with a beard! He has a son growing up with the appearance and manners of a dog! Beauty? Beauty! *This* is beauty – this, here, all this, everything with which I have struggled and fought and strived to surround us. *This* is beauty. Not that, none of that, none of that. This! *This*!'

René found himself having to leave the house and walk in its grounds as he regained his composure. It was then that he had vowed to destroy the almost completed painting. He re-entered the house determined to do this, but found the canvas gone from his easel. Sending for him, Barnum informed him that he had taken it to his vault for safe-keeping, and that as far as he was concerned, the picture was finished. René had tried unsuccessfully to put the matter from his mind ever since, but the five smiling faces he had created still came back to shock him awake from his dreams.

Taking Anna to one side, Zip told her and Bates what Herman had told him of Greenwood and Butler's plan to try and take over the running of the Museum.

'Meaning Greenwood alone,' Bates said.

At first Anna was doubtful, but she too came to accept the possibility of what might be about to happen and what it would mean to them all.

At the piano, Tom shouted to say he could still hear drink splashing around inside the bottle. He castigated Zip for buying the cheapest liquor available and said he ought to be ashamed of himself for passing it off on a poor old blind man.

'He ought to be ashamed of himself whatever liquor he buys,' René added, unable to resist the rebuke.

'I am,' Zip told them, begging them all to forgive him, removing his hat with a flourish, clasping his hands in prayer and dropping to his knees.

9

THE FOLLOWING MORNING the taxidermist arrived to prepare the
skin of the dead tiger. He carried with him his leather case of
tools, and his assistant dragged into the Museum entrance the crude
wooden frame of legs, skull and spine upon which the skin was to
be eventually mounted and padded. Greenwood called for Zip and
Franklin to accompany the two men into the basement, which was
to be again cleared of the public for the day, a notice upon the door
announcing that something of particular interest was being prepared
for them. This was Greenwood's idea; since the visit of Thumb and
Lavinia, Barnum hadn't been back to the Museum; he was, however,
expected back later that same afternoon.

'The frame's too big,' the taxidermist's assistant said, having
manoeuvred it down the basement steps with a great deal of difficulty and cursing. All four men considered the corpse. 'A man-eater,'
Barnum said. Tall as a man's shoulders and eight feet long not
counting its tail.' The frame they'd brought would have ruptured
the skin everywhere it touched.

Zip and the taxidermist shared a smile.

'You've heard of a baker's dozen,' the taxidermist told his assistant.

'Yes.'

'Well now you've met the Barnum foot.'

Zip handed him a saw and he began to reduce the frame.

'Mr Barnum's animals always shrink upon being called by their
Maker,' the taxidermist said. 'He pays the least and expects the
most.' From his case he took out several rolled lengths of additional
tiger skin, which he spread around the corpse on the floor.

'It's a good match,' Franklin said.

'That's why he hires me. I acquired this skin from Mr Peale's
museum – a man far less particular about the whys and wherefores
of his trade. I believe that if we mount the animal against a rear

78

panel, I can take some skin from its blind side and give Mr Barnum an extra foot in overall length. The tail can easily be extended.' He made several quick calculations with his tape as he spoke and then instructed his assistant where to reduce and where to extend the frame.

Slipping his arms through a leather harness, Franklin pulled the animal from its cage and dragged it across the basement to one of the private rooms adjoining it. There, Zip and the assistant lifted it on to a solid wooden table. Still wearing his top hat and frock coat, but now with the addition of an apron and a pair of elbow length gauntlets, the taxidermist held up a long curved blade ready to begin.

He withdrew immediately at the first incision. The three other men also took a step backwards.

'How long did you say it had been dead?'

Zip and Franklin had been instructed to tell him that it had been discovered dead that very morning.

'Since some time last night,' Franklin said hesitantly.

The taxidermist smiled again at Zip. 'Then I think we can safely say that the cause of death was putrefaction whilst still alive. That, gentlemen, is not fresh tiger meat, not fresh any meat. Perhaps we have encountered that other great phenomenon of our age – the Barnum Day.' He drew a line with the curved blade from the tiger's chin to the root of its tail. The carcass sagged, and the assistant immediately thrust a pail to the side of the table, into which many things fell. There was little blood, and without its innards, the unfortunate tiger shrank even further.

'Can either of you gentlemen get a good price on any of this?' the taxidermist asked, indicating the meat and the pieces alongside in the pail. Both Zip and Franklin shook their heads. 'Good. Then I'll take it for my scholar friends to pinch and probe.'

Several flies had settled on the corpse and were now investigating the massive open wound, indifferent to the taxidermist's blade and the repeated swatting of his assistant.

Zip and Franklin sat on a bench and watched, in no hurry to return to their booths now that they had a legitimate reason for being absent.

'Anything worth seeing arrived recently?' the taxidermist asked them, cutting, peeling and probing as he spoke.

'There'll be something for the aquarium soon,' Zip told him.

'Ah, another mermaid, no doubt. Tell Mr Barnum that if that's what he wants then I can let him have one at a week's notice. I have a remarkable tuna-fish awaiting my attention at this very moment.'

Only the assistant laughed. He carried the pail from the table and returned to help strip the skin from the gleaming carcass. To do this the tiger was attached to a simple pulley and its head and forelegs were raised above the table until it hung in a begging position. A careful incision was made around the full circumference of its neck, and then the skin of its body and legs was peeled downwards from it. At the exposure of its meat and muscle, Franklin became squeamish and afterwards continued to watch the operation out of the side of his eye, making small noises of surprise and disgust at every new revelation.

'Tell your friend he's perfectly welcome to leave,' the taxidermist told Zip.

'We know.'

The assistant grunted as he pulled the skin and its underlying membrane over the tiger's pelvis, pausing to wipe his brow as it stretched and stuck fast, refusing to come any further until the taxidermist had made several more incisions around the animal's hind legs; after which the black and yellow fur hung like a pair of loose pants, ready to fall.

'The hindquarters always present us with the greatest –' The taxidermist also grunted '– problem.'

Together the two men managed to slide the fur down until eventually only the tail remained covered. Watching from between his fingers, it still looked to Franklin as though the whole process might yet be reversed, and everything pulled back up and smoothed into place. The tail came off as easily as a woman's woollen stocking, the skin and body being finally separated by a loud plop. The rope was released and the skinned carcass dropped back to the table, slithered across it and fell to the floor.

The assistant then turned the skin completely inside out and the taxidermist recited Longfellow's poem about Hiawatha's mittens. Then, taking a cleaver from his satchel, he chopped at the head and paws still attached to the carcase, brought all five pieces back to the table and removed the last of the skin from these too. By then, the stench from the dead animal was overpowering and all four men held cloths to their faces. Zip produced his flask, from which they all drank.

The taxidermist left the head until last, positioning it on the table so that it faced them where they sat.

'I understand that Mr Barnum, with the war so content to

continue along its own unstoppable bloody path, is embarking upon yet another lecture tour to implore and exhort a further patriotic hurrah from us all.'

'He never stops,' Zip said.

So far that month, Barnum had addressed the Ladies Aid society, the Union League, the Loyal Publication Society and the Sanitary Commission. His war-work, to which he was fervently devoted, was another of the reasons for his increasingly long absences from the Museum. In the past year he had toured as far west as California, and had spoken in Europe about the righteousness of the Union cause in fighting the war; he was taken up and fêted by sympathetic leaders wherever he went.

'It keeps him away from here for weeks on end,' Franklin said.

'And while the cat's away, the rats come out to play?'

'Quiet!' the taxidermist warned his assistant.

'I think he knows that events are bound to catch up with him,' Franklin went on. 'The way I see it, he fears that folk might forget him if he fails to make one last effort to remind them all of his downright patriotism and championship.'

'I see,' the taxidermist said. 'But is he also aware that there are rumours abroad in this city that an attempt is about to be made by certain more daring and reckless members of the Confederacy to raze it to the ground? Perhaps even by sympathizers in our midst.'

'How?' Franklin said.

'How? By fire, of course. By arson, bombs, incendiaries. By Greek fire.'

'You surely can't be serious?' Franklin said, now clearly alarmed at the prospect.

The taxidermist and his assistant shared a smug glance, as though they too might have been conspirators in the terrible plot.

'Oh, but we are,' the assistant said. 'Look what's happening in the South. Seems to me like no one was particularly reluctant to start tossing around lighted torches down there, were they?'

'And you think the Museum would be a target?' Zip said.

'Mr Barnum is a very vociferous champion of the Union cause.'

'Fire,' Franklin said, still absorbing what he'd been told. 'We'd all be burned alive in our beds.' He took the flask from Zip.

'I wouldn't worry yourselves unduly, gentlemen,' the taxidermist said with a smile. 'I'm only passing on what I've heard.' He was pleased with the effect his warning had had upon them, Franklin in particular.

81

'It might happen. It *could* happen,' Franklin said, beginning to perspire even more heavily. 'How would we all get out if it came in the middle of the night? How would *I* get out?'

'Middle of the night's when they reckon it would come, sure enough.'

'Is all that you in there,' the assistant asked Franklin.

Franklin said, 'Sure. Why?'

The taxidermist looked him up and down with a lascivious look, allowing his tongue to protrude slightly from between his lips. 'A man could make a name for himself, a reputation, with something like that to work on.' He made a measurement with his hands, assessing the width of Franklin's broad shoulders.

'What do you mean?' Franklin said, still anxious, and now uncertain what they were proposing.

'Only passing an observation, friend,' the taxidermist said, tipping back his hat and wiping his brow. 'The air down here is foul. You probably got sewers running around you at higher than floor level. Seepage. It's not surprising that nothing lives down here for very long. That aquarium out there, it's a death-trap. Barnum might just as well fill it with clams and sell them off to the hungry idiots who pay to stand and gawp at all this rubbish.'

'I take it that includes us,' Zip said, his mind still on the likelihood of an arson attack on the city. He had heard the rumour before, in the taverns, and even then had known that it was not entirely impossible, that the attempt might be made, and a great propaganda victory achieved if it were to succeed.

'Naturally. No offence meant, friend.'

'It's got yellow teeth,' the assistant said unexpectedly, lowering himself until his face was level with the tiger's mouth. 'We could clean them up and then build a bit of length on to the two long ones. How long are they reckoned to be?'

'No doubt the longest teeth of any tiger in captivity,' the taxidermist said. 'And Barnum gets what he pays for. Incidentally, he still hasn't settled up for that turtle's head I stitched on to the possum for him. Nor the dodo I mocked up out of all them turkey feathers. Is he still showing that?'

'Fell apart,' Zip said. 'Shoddy workmanship.'

'Fair enough, friend. I told him it would. He tampers with nature the way most other businessmen are happy to tamper with their creditors' accounts. A spot of that too, if I'm not mistaken.'

'He still has plenty of those,' Franklin said, relieved that the conversation had taken a turn on to more familiar ground. 'He has his own seat in the debtors' court.'

'Ah, perhaps, but they're tiring of the pursuit,' the taxidermist said. 'Every condemnation of the braggart only encourages a greater display of misplaced sympathy and concern from his devoted public.'

'True,' Franklin said.

'When do *you* think the war will end?' Zip asked the taxidermist.

'I don't think it will ever end,' he said seriously. 'The way I see it is that you could kill them all but one, and he'd sprout and flower and scatter his seed until they were all built up and back again and running to their unholy slaughter.' His voice acquired the supercilious tone of a travelling preacher.

Several weeks earlier there had been a rumour that Confederate desperadoes planned to sail over the city in hot-air balloons and bombard it from above. Sharpshooters had been positioned on the rooftops of all the prominent buildings ready to drive them off.

'The animals wouldn't stand a chance,' Franklin said, his thoughts having unhappily returned to the prospect of a conflagration.

Still taking delight in his fears, the taxidermist said, 'And I dare say Mr Phineas T. Barnum is not exactly a great favourite among the insurers of this city. I'd look to your own escape plans if I were you.'

'There isn't going to be a fire,' Zip said loudly and firmly, rising from the bench and snatching his flask from the taxidermist's assistant. 'We're all going to end up like the tiger. Hung, drawn and quartered, stripped down, painted up and put back on display. We aren't going to burn.'

'We aren't?' Franklin said, eager to be convinced.

'No.'

'I wish I had your strength of conviction, friend,' the taxidermist said. He too rose, returned to the table and resumed his skinning of the tiger's head. Franklin watched fascinated as the black and pink of its gums were split, the scalpel scraping bone, and as this flesh was peeled away from its teeth, making them appear instantly larger and more ferocious. The full globes of its eyes were uncovered, and the assistant prodded one of these out with his finger and held it against his own face. Then he threw it into Franklin's lap, where it settled in the sag of his pants and stared up at him. Franklin jerked his legs and shook it to the ground, where it lay against the dismembered carcass like a shiny round pearl amid the gouged flesh of an oyster.

When the skin of the head was fully removed, the taxidermist held it over his palms for them to see. His assistant wrenched the teeth from the skull with a pair of pliers.

'I don't imagine Mr Barnum is in any great hurry to have his Prince of the Jungle returned,' he said. He laid the skin loosely over the wooden frame and made several further calculations. 'Tell him I want payment upon results this time.' He began to return his tools to his case, peering through the dim light of the room for anything he might have forgotten.

'What about that?' Franklin asked him, indicating the pile of bloody meat.

'What about it, friend?'

'Aren't you going to take it with you?'

The taxidermist laughed. 'Chop it up and fry it for your dinner. You look as though you could use it.' He looked again over Franklin's bulk. 'Lord Jesus, what I couldn't do with –'

He was cut short by Zip, who pushed him against the wall and told him to shut up.

'Only speculating, friend. Only speculating.'

'Then save it for the war and your arsonist friends.'

'No friends of mine, I assure you.' He held up his hands in a gesture of surrender. His assistant came close, ready to help him but not prepared to tackle Zip unless it became absolutely necessary.

Zip released him and the man tugged down his coat.

'You're awful jumpy for a man with such strong convictions,' he said.

The assistant laid out the skin on a broad piece of cloth and carefully rolled it into a tube, deftly smoothing out the wrinkles with his fingers. Then he wrapped up each of the four paws, the skull and the skin from the head.

'Tell Barnum I want payment in full.'

'You already told us that.'

'This time I mean it. No cash and I might just be tempted to sell the skin to recover some of what he already owes me.'

'You wouldn't dare,' Zip said, knowing that the man would be no match for Barnum in the courts.

Beside them, Franklin rose strenuously to his feet. 'But what are we going to do with that?' he asked again, carefully stepping over the carcass and other pieces.

'You'll think of something. Feed it to that hippopotamus I hear Barnum has coming. Tell me – where did he find that? No – let me guess – the North Pole?'

Zip pushed open the door leading into the basement showroom and jerked his thumb towards it.

'We're leaving, friend. We're all finished here, and we wouldn't want to keep you or your fat friend here from whatever other pressing business you might have to attend to.' He shared a smile with his assistant.

Zip followed them out, waiting for Franklin, who manoeuvred himself sideways through the doorframe, pushing the folds of his stomach around the obstacle and then holding them as he eventually cleared it.

'Peace to the Union, freedom to all slaves,' the taxidermist shouted as they ascended the stairs to the ground floor. Stepping outside, into the fresh air, he breathed deeply. Zip waited again for Franklin, helping him to negotiate the second doorway before telling him to return to his booth and rest.

'I hope for your sake that nothing happens to this place,' he said to the taxidermist as he was about to leave.

'Me too, friend. Me, too.'

'Because, believe me, I'd come looking for you and skin you alive if it did.'

'I believe you, I believe you. Am I not as great a friend and champion of the Union and its cause as your own Mr Barnum? And until he settles his debts with me, would it not . . .' He stopped at the arrival of Greenwood, who asked him if he had what he needed and then told him to go, indicating to Zip that he too should return to his booth and prepare to exhibit himself.

*

Later that afternoon, Greenwood and Henry Butler confronted Barnum with their plans to take over the running of the Museum from him and thus afford him the opportunity to retire. The meeting took place largely at Greenwood's insistence; Henry Butler, despite his support and involvement, remained an unwilling participant in the move and would have been happy for Greenwood to have met Barnum alone. He knew that if they succeeded in their plans, then Greenwood would quickly become the dominant partner and that he, Henry Butler, was as certain to be taken advantage of and eventually ousted as Greenwood now hoped to oust Barnum.

The meeting, however, was not a successful one, Greenwood

having allowed himself over the previous few weeks to become far too confident of his powers of persuasion.

Barnum, who had known for several days in advance of the confrontation, feigned surprise and hurt, then interest and concern, and finally indignation.

'And Mr Butler is with you to the end, come what may, in this venture?' he said when Greenwood had finished his opening speech, which dealt largely with the supposed advantages of retirement to Barnum – points which, to Barnum's mind, were considerably less than the likely pleasures Greenwood considered them to be.

'He is,' Greenwood said quickly. 'Resolutely,' a glance indicating to Henry Butler that he would remain their spokesman.

'Mr Butler?' Barnum asked, probing the obvious weakness of the pair.

'Resolutely,' Henry Butler said, clearing his throat before and after the word.

'I see.'

Greenwood smiled and curled the fingers of both hands across his palms.

'You tried once before,' Barnum said. 'And not, if my memory – seldom less than perfect, despite what you clearly consider to be its progressive wear and tear as a consequence of the excessive demands made upon it daily – serves me right, with any great success.'

'We learned many valuable lessons,' Greenwood said, having disentangled Barnum's reply.

'Ah, so at least I'm a good teacher, not entirely useless.'

'The best,' Henry Butler said, feeling some contribution from him was needed.

Barnum bowed. 'My friend Horace Greeley also thinks I should abandon all this chicanery and humbuggery and spend my days in quiet, and no doubt miserable contemplation with him upon the banks of some river angling for dull-witted fish and the slippery eels with which he has – although his own imperfect memory serves him less well on the matter – frequently compared me in the past.'

'You deserve it,' Greenwood said, immediately regretting the remark.

'No one deserves Saint Horace Greeley day in day out, not even the fish. I would rather sit with a bear and take my chances with that considerably more entertaining of beasts.' Barnum's face went suddenly blank for a moment, and then a smile began to spread slowly and cautiously from its centre. 'Bears,' he said again. 'Bears,

bears, bears,' turning to each of them, as though the word were some cryptic challenge to which they were both intended to respond.

But before either of them could speak, he slid a sheet of paper from his desk, wrote upon it and quickly folded it. Having reached the distant boundaries of his face, his smile then began its retreat, withdrawing finally back to his lips, where it vanished like a bubbling spring which had suddenly ceased to flow.

Greenwood coughed, prompting him back to his line of thought.

'Bears, yes,' Barnum said, returning to them. 'Yes, indeed. I hear they catch salmon on the Pacific coast by fishing for them with their paws. Tell me, was it I, or was it someone else who said, "I despise the fish as food fit only for invalids, but treasure it for the precious jewel its stomach might disgorge"?'

Greenwood and Henry Butler shared an uncertain glance, Greenwood in particular beginning to despair of the labyrinthine trails of thought and language by which Barnum had already started to defuse their assault upon him.

'You, probably,' Greenwood said.

'No, I doubt it. Twain, perhaps. Or perhaps one of these Oriental philosophers. They grow them, you know. Take them out to caves in the wildest country as small boys and leave them there. Not much else for them to do, see, but philosophize. No other distractions. I, on the other hand, am the kind of philosopher whose very philosophy of Life itself is wholly and extensively founded upon distraction. I search for distraction in every corner of every land, and in every corner of every room I enter for the first time. It is this searching in corners which has made me what I am today.' He was now in full flow, the words dependent only upon the ability of his lungs to sustain breath. 'And when, on those few occasions I cannot peer too closely myself, I have the eyes and hearts of others ready and willing to do my peering for me. Why, only this morning I received this.' He pulled from behind his desk a large hessian sack, in which sat something heavy and formed into coils. 'A snake, gentlemen.'

Both Greenwood and Henry Butler leaned back in their seats.

'A hooded cobra, I believe, is its true title, and edging yourselves out of its reach is virtually an impossibility. The hooded cobra – my sources being as accurate, precise and reliable as ever – is one of the deadliest reptiles known to both man and beast. It could, if it so wished, strike from here –' Barnum lowered the sack on to his desk '– and there would be no corner of this room in which you or

I would be safe.' He looked at them both. Neither of them took their eyes from the sack.

'The hooded cobra,' Greenwood said. 'I've heard about it.'

'Ah, yes, but have you ever seen one? People had heard of a great many things but had never seen them until having them set before them by me. They had heard of birds of paradise, of turtles twice the length of a man; they had heard of polar bears and men half grown as women, and women men. They had heard of dinosaurs and of men tattooed from their loftiest thoughts down to their grow-ing toenails, but had they ever witnessed such beauty or such strange-ness before coming here, to me?'

'No,' Henry Butler said, almost involuntarily, his eyes wide, as though he were hearing all this for the first time.

'No! No, they hadn't.' Barnum exclaimed.

On the desk between them, the sack remained motionless.

'Fish!' Barnum said suddenly. 'Charity, may the Lord bless and keep her, consumes an inordinate amount of fish.' The statement saddened him. 'Tell me, Butler, Henry, how is your own dear wife?'

'As well as can be expected,' Henry Butler said, equally sadly.

'Ah, yes, as well as can be expected.'

The two men looked at each other, and, in the moment their eyes met, a deep yet fleeting understanding passed between them.

'Can we at least outline our proposals to you in greater detail,' Greenwood said impatiently, drawing a sheaf of papers from his coat and spreading them on the desk.

'Mind the snake,' Barnum warned him.

Greenwood decided to rise to the challenge. 'Mr Barnum, Phineas, Mr Barnum, you doubt our ability and our fortitude. I say to you here and now that –'

'Here and now,' Barnum repeated, amused by the new deter-mination in Greenwood's voice.

'– that there is no snake in that sack. Or that if there is, then it shares in common with a great deal else within the Museum the condition of Death.'

'Rigorously mortified,' Barnum said. 'You are wrong in both particulars, Mr Greenwood. John.' He rose, tugged the drawstrings to the sack, and the material fell down to reveal to them a finely worked and engraved metal serpent, its four heavy coils in precise replica of a real cobra, its curved head – fangs bared and tongue protruding – rising upright from the deep basket of its body.

'Another automaton!' Henry Butler said.

'Precisely. No less the attraction and its longevity guaranteed. You do understand the term "longevity", Mr Greenwood.'

Greenwood nodded grudgingly. He inspected the serpent, holding its body and feeling the hundreds of hollow and flexible rings of which it was constructed ripple limply through his hands, just as the body of a real snake might do.

'Impressive, is it not?'

Again Greenwood grudgingly agreed that it was.

Barnum told Henry Butler to take hold of it and feel it. 'We should all become accustomed to handling serpents of one kind or another. Who knows how many of them there are hiding in the grass just waiting for the chance to rise up and strike us in the back?'

Henry Butler did no more than rest his fingertips upon the snake.

'Horace Greeley,' Barnum went on unexpectedly, following yet another line of thought. 'I suppose you've both heard the story of how he assisted Mr Thoreau in the construction of his so-called cabin at the dreary Walden Pond, from which he produced that equally dreary little book of his – a book, I might add, which no one has yet bought, let alone read. *That*, gentlemen, is the true consequence of enforced idleness and too much philosophizing without any actively sought distraction to maintain a balance of sanity. More to the point, that is how *I* would end up in a matter of mere days were I to devote myself to idle contemplation away from this place, my pride, my joy, my temple, my altar.'

'Times are changing,' Greenwood said harshly.

'So they are, so they are. And only for the better. Soon all hostilities will cease, and when that happens, believe me, there will be a public clamour for diversion and entertainment on an unprecedented scale. Theatres will be built right here in New York. Our councillors and commissioners are old women, New England old women, and they'll be swept away in a tide of demands for more, more, more. And who is best placed and best able to provide all this, to meet those demands? Why, *we* are! So you tell me why, in all conscience and sanity, I should relinquish my hold on this place, this goldmine, and gamble its future with you.'

There was nothing either of them could say; their challenge had finally been defeated and laid to rest.

Barnum went on: 'True, Charity and my daughters make their demands on my time, but so does my country. You see my predicament, gentlemen. My country and my country*men*.'

Greenwood retrieved his sheaf of papers and slid them back into his pocket.

Barnum offered them both a cigar.

'Where will it go?' Henry Butler asked him, indicating the metal cobra.

'I don't yet know. I have half a mind to keep it in here, solely for my own entertainment. Is it not truly a thing of exquisite beauty and craftsmanship? Let me show you.' Lifting the serpent from the desk, he positioned it on the floor, carefully arranging its coils and propping its head at a slight backward angle. He took from his pocket a key and inserted this into a space between the snake's eyes, hitherto hidden by a hinged scale, turning until the mechanism was fully wound. Then he motioned for them to move away from it. 'I received it only this very morning. This is the first time even I have seen it in operation.'

The serpent's tail began to vibrate, and the motion passed slowly along its entire length, unsettling the coils until they hung more loosely, still vibrating as the motion progressed up into the cobra's cowl and head.

Both Henry Butler and Barnum cried out with surprise as the hood in which the snake's head was framed suddenly doubled in size and became rigid, revealing the design of a skull on its rear, its slender inner ribs conveying their own slight motion to the head and jaws. A light shone in the snake's eyes.

Barnum said, 'Good Lord,' and moved even further away from it as the creature slowly rose from its coils and turned its head to gaze at each of them in turn.

'The reality, the reality,' Barnum said, unable, as were both Greenwood and Henry Butler, to take his eyes from the serpent as it rose even higher, almost to their own height, further opening its jaws and taking up the slack of its coils until it stood taut and quivering, ready to strike out at them with its glistening fangs.

'Good Lord, good Lord,' Barnum repeated, a note of true fear in his voice as he watched the slender forked tongue emerge to test the air.

The cobra continued to turn its head from side to side. The rattling in its tail increased in volume, and the flatter of its coils doubled in size and grew firm. Then, without warning, it struck out at them, slowly drawing back its head until it was facing the ceiling, its fangs extending slightly, before lunging suddenly forward with a loud rush of air and a distinct hiss and clack as its jaws snapped firmly together at a distance five or six feet ahead of the bulk of its body, and only inches from where the three men stood.

Barnum held his chest and caught his breath, still mesmerized, as the snake, somehow sensing that its attack had failed, drew itself back, lashing wildly from side to side as though to cover its retreat and leave its prey still hypnotized and immobile. Then, just as unexpectedly as it had struck out, it appeared to relax, withdrawing its head into the uppermost of its coils, the loose skin of its hooded cowl folding down to its original size. Finally, with a last warning flicker of its tongue and quiver of its tail, it fell completely still and lay staring at them with its dull and lifeless eyes.

None of the three men spoke.

Eventually, Barnum said, 'Miraculous.'

'Truly,' Henry Butler said, and was the first of them to let out his breath.

'Which of us,' Barnum said, 'which of us did not, for one awful moment, feel his very heart cease to beat? It is a mechanical device, and yet for that one terrifying moment, which one of us would have sworn that it had not taken on a life all of its own? Miraculous, truly miraculous.' He circled the snake several times before finally summoning up the courage to touch it and satisfy himself that it was once again inert, whereupon he lifted it back to his desk and sat before it in rapt admiration. All thought of the reason for his managers' visit had now gone from his mind completely, and believing their business with him to be over, he asked them if they required anything else of him before leaving to attend to their duties elsewhere. It was clear to them both that there was now nothing more to be achieved by persevering with their demands.

Greenwood was the first to leave, followed a moment later by Henry Butler, and when they were gone, Barnum caressed the snake and laughed, pleased and reassured by this vindication of his complete dominion over them. The cobra, he finally decided, largely because of its role on this auspicious occasion, would remain with him in the office for his own private enjoyment, now too prized a possession to put before the common mass of visitors to the Museum.

10

HACKALIAH CHERRY SAT alone in the small attic room he shared
with Tom and gazed intently at the map upon which he had been
following the fortunes of the war, plotting its comings and goings
with a confusing assortment of tacks and thread, and from which
he also took the names of the rivers he had come to substitute for
his more commonplace profanities. Profanities and foul language of
any kind, his mother had told him as a young boy, were a sure and
undeniable sign that the devil had somehow gotten hold of a man and
was speaking through him. From his tongue the rot would spread to
his heart, and from there to his soul, and when that happened then
that man was lost to the Lord and might just as well put a pistol to
his head or set out to swim the ocean back to Africa and set up home
in the trees with all the other devil-worshippers.

No, sir, if profanity wasn't a sure sign, then nothing was. This
was the same mother who, at other times, Hackaliah Cherry said
he had never known, being a poor orphan child, unwanted and
unloved.

As a rule, Hackaliah Cherry had grown up believing everything
he was told, and afterwards accepting as the truth everything he
then passed on to others. He found thinking and reasoning for himself
difficult and time-consuming, and he had long since discovered that it
was by and large unnecessary. Other people got an idea of you and all
you had to do was let them get on with it and make of you whatever
they wanted.

He believed Barnum when Barnum told him that he should live
at the very top and the rear of the Museum because all the dirt and
dust entered from the bottom, and that in his constant war against
it he should be careful not to let it encircle him and attack him from
behind. It all made perfect sense to Cherry, who had recently learned
a great deal about stratagems and campaigns from the reports of the

war, afterwards applying this in his own daily battles against the dirt which assaulted the Museum from all directions. He was proud of the strategist he had become, rushing at some accumulations with his brush fully extended, pretending to pass others by and then round on them, deftly flicking them into his dustpan.

Looking at his map, he traced a line up through the Carolinas, over the Appalachian mountains and down through West Virginia, Kentucky, Tennessee and Alabama. Recent reports had been confused: in some parts the fighting was over and the land was beginning to recover; in others there was still bloodshed on every plantation and in every copse, and the crops in the ground were scorched to death without even a chance of growth.

'Shame, shame, shame,' he muttered to himself, moving several of his tacks at random from one town to the next, fording rivers and crossing mountains. Barnum had given him the map and tacks, along with the suggestion that he should display the engagements of the war, particularly those resulting in victory for the North, and that this might afterwards serve as a constant reminder to every visitor to the Museum of the suffering and bloodletting taking place on their behalf. He wasn't entirely convinced that Cherry was equal to the task, but Cherry assured him he was. Barnum's original idea had been to hire someone to masquerade as an escaped slave, who would stand in his broken fetters and move the tacks and pieces of thread daily, thus presenting to the public an accurate and up-to-date picture of exactly what was happening far beyond their own horizons. But Cherry had pleaded with him to be given this responsibility and Barnum had reluctantly agreed.

Cherry, however, adopted a very individual and imaginative approach to his representation of the vicissitudes of the war, and the prospect of displaying the map as a serious public service was quickly abandoned. He listened to the daily reports, to wishful thinking, rumours and speculation and then decided for himself which were truthful and which were filled with lies; in short, and contrary to his philosophy in other matters, he believed what he wanted to believe and rearranged his tacks and thread to support his own freely given predictions about the outcome of each month's campaigning. Initially, he had anticipated that the war would last for six months, his reasoning based on the belief that once the fighting had started then everyone would want to join in for at least a short while before growing tired of it, abandoning their weapons, disobeying their leaders and returning home. Cherry was convinced that this

93

was how wars progressed, and that each side took out some kind of renewable option dependent upon a factor of combined boredom and bloodlust. He saw nothing wrong with this arrangement. As a child, his mother had told him week after week of all the deceitful slayings and outright murders in the Bible. It's the Lord's will, she said: Man had to kill man. He had to know that it could be done and he had to see it being done. That's why Man was man, and not God. By this, Cherry understood that God killed only indirectly via flood, disease, famine, tempests, plagues and the like. It was difficult to find fault with some killings, no matter how hard you tried.

'Chlockonee,' Cherry intoned. 'Suwanee, Caloosahatchee, Pee Dee, Chatahoochee, Clinch, James,' and 'Fear'.

Fear. That was a good name for a river, and running through North Carolina was a good place for a river of that name to be right now.

'No doubt filled an' runnin' red with the blood of the Confederate slain,' he said to himself, nodding sagely at the realization and tracing the line of this bloody gutter to the sea.

'Ocmulgee, Oconee, Ogeechee.' Who decided on these names? Savages? Who made them up? Naked red savages who boiled and ate their own children? Probably.

West of the Mississippi was an unknown land to Hackaliah Cherry. It might have existed, but as far as he was concerned it was wiser to keep all that kind of lawless country right where it belonged – in the minds of men who had nothing better to think about. Know what you know, his mother had said. What you don't know you don't know and it can't do you no harm not to know it. It's out there, away in the distance, someplace else. Leave it in peace. Let other men lose their lives exploring it. If the good Lord had wanted you to scamper all over the land, he'd have given you four legs, like a horse, or even a thousand legs like one of them insects you hear about. And what does the good Lord do with those thousand-legged creatures? Puts them right under boulders, that's what – makes sure they don't get the itch to start wandering. All they know is the underside of that boulder and the darkness, and they're as happy with that as the devil is with sin.

'Hallelujah!' Hackaliah Cherry called out, the memory as clear to him now as the day she'd said it.

'We lived in Mississippi then,' he said, turning and holding his lapels as though addressing an audience. 'Up from Winona on the Yazoo. Times was hard but we was happy. Ma and Pa and all us little uns runnin' barefoot around 'em.' He stopped and shook his head and started again. 'Yes, times was good back in Tuscaloosa, Alabama, on the Warrior River.' He stopped again, searching for Alabama and then Tuscaloosa on his map, locating the first but not the second. 'It's here someplace,' he said, allowing himself to be distracted by the scribbled blue line of the Chickamauga, and then the Dismal, the Gasconada and the Trinity.

He began to sing:

> Oh, Marietta County is a Godless place,
> Oh, Marietta County shames the human race,
> Oh, Marietta County daren't show its face,
> When the great Almighty comes a-calling.
> Oh, Marietta County is a shameful place,
> Oh, Marietta County –

He was stopped by a voice far below him calling his name. He was accustomed to this, and made small wagers with himself whenever he had a few spare moments how long it would be before someone shouted for him. He knew immediately every time who was calling. Usually, he bet himself a cent that he couldn't enjoy a minute of unbroken silence and was seldom proved wrong. He wished now that he'd bet himself a dollar every time, because by now he would have been a wealthy man.

The voice below called for him again.

'Summons to arms,' he said, holding his broom like a rifle and saluting. 'General Hackaliah Cherry at your service, at the service of his country and the Almighty.'

When the time comes, his mother had said, you stand up, get yourself counted, and then you die. And if the dying didn't kill you when that great day came, then the shame of not dying surely would.

'Surely will,' echoed Cherry. There were times when he could have cried for all his lost memories of his parents.

The voice called again, this time from somewhere much closer.

Cherry left his room, ran silently down a flight of stairs and along a corridor, stopped and began brushing and whistling.

Greenwood appeared and said he'd been calling for him.

'For me?' Cherry said, pushing a finger into his ear and shaking it.

Greenwood told him to follow him.

Cherry complied, whistling his Marietta County song, stopping abruptly at the Fiery Gates of Hell and the overpowering stench of sulphur and the burning bodies within.

95

'Get rid of that,' Greenwood said, indicating a large dead rat, its tail snapped and folded behind it, its skull crushed. 'There are no rats in the American Museum.'

'No, sir.' Cherry scooped up the body in his dustpan and walked away with it at arm's length. We're all the Lord's creatures, his mother had told him, but like everyone else, the Lord had his good days and his bad days.

'You and him together,' Cherry said to the rat, and walked on, whistling.

There were rats all over the Museum, all over every building in the city most likely, but today nothing was to be allowed to detract from the splendour and majesty of the arrival and installation of the hippopotamus in the new aquarium. Everywhere, at every level, along every staircase and balcony, and through every gallery and booth, the splendour and majesty of the Museum was at its most splendid and majestic.

Cherry encountered Franklin, struggling along a narrow passage-way to his booth.

'What's that?' Franklin asked, pausing to catch his breath.

'I bet Mr Almighty Greenwood that I couldn't put a spell on him and turn him into a rat and he just stood right there and laughed in my face.'

'It's not a particularly big or mean-looking rat to say it's Green-wood,' Franklin said.

Cherry looked at the creature. 'I suppose not.'

'Where you taking it?'

'Feed it to one of the snakes, I expect.' Windfalls in the Museum were seldom wasted.

'They got that hippo coming today,' Franklin said, his tone soliciting Cherry's opinion of the new arrival.

'Reckon so,' Cherry said.

'The basement will be full for weeks. Who'll want to go on looking at us when there's something new to stand and gawp at?'

'I'd come along and keep you all company except I'm kept busy all day.'

'Appreciate that, Hack.'

'Always nice to be appreciated.'

'You ever try telling Greenwood that?'

Hackaliah Cherry smiled and prodded the dead rat. 'You listenin' to all this?' Turning to Franklin, he said, 'I'm gonna feed him to the smallest snake I can find, one that's gonna take a good long time to swallow him, one that looks like it ain't ever gonna succeed in gettin' him down, and the two of 'em can just sit there, half in half out, their eyes bulged like a crawdad and just –'

He was stopped by the unexpected reappearance of Greenwood at the far end of the passageway, who stared into the gloom for a moment and then shouted to Franklin that he should already be in his booth. It was almost seven and he was about to open the doors.

'Right away, Mr Greenwood, sir,' Franklin shouted.

When Greenwood had gone the two men saluted him and burst into laughter. Cherry blew an imaginary trumpet, dropped the rat from his dustpan and kicked it ahead of him towards the light.

*

On the morning of what was to have been his latest triumph, on the day his name would once again be on the lips of the entire city, the day when people would crowd the sidewalks along Broadway for a glimpse of the arrival of his hippopotamus, on that day, Phineas Taylor Barnum was not a happy man.

He had woken a happy man, the prospect of his renewed and, hopefully, ever-increasing popularity before him, but he was not happy now, and the sole reason for this unhappiness was to be found in the *New York Herald* he held across his lap – the *New York Herald*, in which, alongside news of the impending arrival of the hippopotamus, was a snippet, no more than three sentences, of table gossip – little more than a joke, a remark passed on imperfectly from mouth to mouth until it had now acquired the status of a commonplace fact in the typesetting hands of James Gordon Bennet. The *Herald* was filled with such pieces of information, and usually, whenever Barnum or the Museum were mentioned in some derogatory way, they failed in their attack and served only to satisfy Barnum's own urge for constant self-promotion. But this one – this one – the one he read now, on this of all mornings – this one he most certainly took no delight in. This one, Bennet had the nerve to suggest, had come from none other than General Tom Thumb, Barnum's one-time greatest exhibit, still his close friend and confidant, and the maker of his first fortune.

Barnum had started to read the *Herald* on his way to the Museum, largely to satisfy himself that the advertisements he had placed announcing the arrival of the hippopotamus had been

97

prominently displayed, which indeed they were, adding to his early state of near delirium on that bright warm morning.

And the nature of this joke which, though barely a column inch in length, had done so much to blacken his mood and have him arrive at the Museum entrance in a foul temper? Simple –it suggested, or, rather, Thumb had suggested to James Gordon Bennet, that upon the first publication of his autobiography, Barnum had toyed with the idea of giving away free to everyone who purchased the volume one of his own hairs, clipped painlessly from his scalp and carefully inserted between the leaves. In this there was some truth, but as swiftly and as easily as the idea had entered Barnum's head, so it had been dismissed as impractical, not to say impossible, his hair having even then, ten years ago, retreated to a thin and disintegrating wreck of a nest resting uneasily upon his ears. And now, because even this carefully tended wreath had largely disappeared, he would become a laughing stock, pointed at and ridiculed on the very day when the city should have been kneeling before him and singing his praises. He couldn't remember having mentioned the proposal to Thumb, but felt certain that he must have done, the two of them having once been so close. And now – now this. James Gordon Bennet had even possessed the gall to extend the joke and squeeze a further laugh from it by suggesting to Barnum that a wiser course of action might be to save his finger- and toe-nail clippings and award these as prizes to the first visitor to provide the *Herald* with satisfactory evidence of any or all of his countless frauds.

Even as he read this, and as he felt his cheeks redden, Barnum could see Thumb and Bennet together, sharing brandy after a good dinner at Irving House, amusing themselves at his expense. Perhaps the portly Lavinia had been present and shared their laughter. It was all too much for him to even think about, and by the time he pounded on the Museum doors shouting to be let in, he was in a rage.

He'd torn the *Herald* to shreds and had crossed the street to scatter the pieces on the boardwalk in front of Bennet's office. He'd then stood and cursed him and defied him to come down and face him man to man. Several faces had appeared at the upper windows, but Gordon Bennet's was not among them, whereupon Barnum had called up that he was an even bigger coward than he'd thought, and had stormed back across to the Museum, where, attracted by all the noise, Greenwood had let him in.

This, then, was the cause of the dark temper in which Barnum passed that day, and from which he was unable to free himself even during his inspection of the preparations being made for the arrival of the hippopotamus.

Taking both his managers with him to the basement, he asked Henry Butler for details of the creature's procession through the streets.

Unaware of the true cause of Barnum's anger, Henry Butler was careful with his answers, and read to him from a folded sheet he took from his pocket. Only Greenwood, having already seen the offending piece in the *Herald*, derived any real pleasure from Barnum's discomfort.

'We're expecting it on the steam vessel *Machias*,' Henry Butler read. 'She left Toronto eight days ago.'

'Via the distant Nile,' Greenwood whispered.

'Arriving where?' Barnum snapped.

'One of the South Street quays. Between three and four this —'

'Too close,' Barnum said.

'Too close? We'd planned to bring it ashore at Catherine Street and then parade it down East Broadway and Park Row.' They had worked the route out together several days earlier.

'I don't think it'll be able to walk that far,' Greenwood said, hiding his smile.

'Not walk! Not walk!'

'It weighs several tons,' Greenwood added. 'It probably won't even be able to turn in its tank as it is.'

'The steam pump's fitted and working,' Henry Butler said. He switched on the pump which it had been his idea to install alongside the aquarium to ensure a continuous flow of air and clean water through the tank. He alone still insisted on making every effort to ensure that the hippopotamus would be content, or at least survive longer than any of its predecessors in the basement. 'Constantly recycled clean water,' he said. 'The hippo can —'

'Not "hippo", Mr Butler — hippopotamus. It's a big, fine, round name. Use it! The bigger the name, the better the value. I want *you* — *you* personally — to supervise its unloading. I assume there will be no mention of Toronto in evidence on its cage. The creature has just been captured at great expense and with loss of life in the foaming white mouth of the Nile within view of the pyramids themselves.'

'It'll come crated,' Henry Butler said. 'Crated, not caged.'

'Crated! Crated! A vicious killer like that in a flimsy wooden crate!'

'I'm assured it's perfectly adequate. It's really a very placid, docile creature, born and bred in the Toronto zoo.'

'Adequate! Docile! Placid! Is that how you want me to advertise the beast? Docile! Placid!'

'I'll arrange for it to be lowered to the quay in a cage.' Henry Butler made a note on the sheet of paper.

'Raging with terror and anger. Take a hat-pin with you, a long one. I want to hear it roaring from here. It does have its own teeth, I assume.'

'Big ones,' Greenwood reassured him, indicating the length with his hands.

'Good. Sharp?'

This time it was left to Henry Butler to answer. 'Not particularly. It lives on a diet of cabbages and weed.'

'Cabbages and weed! Impossible! It's a monster, a man-eater!' Barnum held a hand to his brow and sat down, finally defeated by the successive and unavoidable blows of an unkind fate.

'I think it'll be happy in the tank,' Henry Butler said.

'Happy! Who wants it to be happy? Tell me, Mr Greenwood –' Barnum lowered his voice and shielded his face from Henry Butler, who he knew would be unhappy at what he was about to suggest – 'Tell me, in your opinion, if this – this weed-eater of the mighty Nile were to break free from its flimsy wooden crate – clearly inadequately packaged for its journey by the ignorant heathens at its point of departure – would it be possible for it to, say, rampage around a little on the quayside for a while, apparently in a great temper, and hell-bent upon some form of destruction?'

'That would certainly be possible in my estimation,' Greenwood said.

'Good. Then I think the day might yet be saved.'

'Unless,' Henry Butler said anxiously, having overheard. 'Unless it managed to launch itself into the river and escape.'

Barnum considered the possibility, and felt the unfairness of it all like yet another physical blow. 'Have I paid for the beast in advance?' he asked dejectedly.

'In full.'

'In that case we must content ourselves with its roaring and its *attempts* to escape en route.'

'I understand,' Greenwood said.

During one of Barnum's voyages to England one of his elephants had crushed to death a member of the ship's crew. Hoping to capitalize on this, Barnum had arranged to have the animal taken into police custody upon their arrival in Liverpool. However, unhappy at the publicity, and thus the profit about to be made by Barnum, and by the loss of his man, the ship's captain had winched the creature from its cage on the deck, swung it over the side of the ship and let it drop. He did all this under cover of darkness, and the following morning, upon the discovery of the empty cage, had professed not to know what had happened. In an attempt to retrieve something from the now profitless killing and later disappearance, Barnum, upon his arrival in England, had exhibited the elephant's grieving mate and orphaned offspring with equal success.

Vivalla and Lord Byron entered the basement and made their way past the three men.

'How's the porker?' Barnum asked him.

'He feels the warmer weather now that it's on its way.'

Byron lived in a sty to the rear of the basement, with access to a narrow sunless alley which ran alongside the Museum, and where most of his exercise was taken. All four men considered the pig. Byron, dressed again in his tight-fitting velvet suit, had found something beneath one of the seats and was probing for it.

'A big day,' Barnum said to Vivalla. 'Everyone up there excited, I suppose.'

'They certainly are. Talk of nothing else.' He avoided Barnum's gaze and pretended to occupy himself with Byron, pulling him away from whatever it was he'd found.

'Maybe I'll close the Museum an hour early one night, give them all the opportunity to come down here and see the magnificent creature for themselves. Think they'd appreciate that?' Barnum had turned from them and was gazing into the depths of the tank.

After sharing a glance with both Henry Butler and Greenwood, Vivalla said, 'I'm sure they would.'

'Would what?' Barnum said, turning back to them.

'What you said. Appreciate the opportunity to come down here and look at the hippo.'

'The hippopotamus,' Henry Butler said quickly.

'Oh.' For a moment Barnum had forgotten about the attack in the *Herald*. 'Yes, of course. To look at the hippopotamus,' he said absently. He turned back to the glass, reaching out to touch it and to feel the vibrations of the pump-driven bubbles rising through it.

Behind him, the three men and the pig left the basement as quietly as possible.

Alone, Barnum stood looking into the empty tank for several minutes longer until the steady tramp of feet above him signalled that the Museum had opened its doors for the day and that his presence was probably required elsewhere. Turning, he was surprised to find himself alone, and he paused briefly to inspect the room around him before climbing the stairs and presenting himself to his public, many of whom, he guessed, would already be repeating Gordon Bennet's libellous slurs.

'BARNUM'S BRAVES', HIS own tame dozen or so Redskin savages, were ready to leave the Museum and return to their homes in the West. They had grown increasingly restless of late, knowing that the second and final summer of their term of employment was coming, and anxious in case Barnum now tried to find some way around his promises of return railroad fares and parting gifts.

The experience of the East and the Museum had been an unhappy one for the Redskins, and as they counted the passing of each full moon over the Museum roof so their determination to return home had grown even stronger. In truth, Barnum himself would be happy to see them go, but he was equally determined not to be seen to accede too readily to their demands. He knew that the other residents at the Museum were watching carefully, all aware of the many small shifts in balance which had taken place over the previous few months, and it was this, the fact that he felt himself to be under close and unfair scrutiny, that now determined his actions.

Bad news from beyond the Mississippi always increased demand for the Braves, but recently there had been neither massacre nor any other atrocity committed to stir the blood of the civilized East, which had anyway been too engrossed over recent months with the spectacle of its own larger-scale and better-dressed savagery.

Two years ago, Barnum had believed the war to be nearing its conclusion, and despite the warnings of both Henry Butler and Greenwood, he had prided himself on being the sole possessor of the foresight necessary to maintain the Museum's pride of place in the public eye when the fighting did finally draw to an exhausted halt. That public, he insisted, would keep up its interest in the butchery with which it had become so familiar over those unhappy years and would demand to have that interest satisfied by other means. Hence the Braves, who, again in Barnum's sole opinion, were a far worthier target for civilized aggression – their reduction and eventual extinction being a justifiable and profitable aim in the eyes of everyone not directly involved in the process.

Now he wasn't so sure. White men were fighting and dying over slaves the colour of coal, and voices were already being raised in defence of the Redskin, calling him noble, proud and dignified, and even suggesting that he had a right to the unhindered occupation of the land he had possessed and lived upon for centuries – a proposition, Barnum believed, which would prove both unreasonable and unfeasible to anyone who stopped and considered it at any length. All this, of course, he kept strictly to himself.

It had been another of his agents in the West who had originally suggested the possibility of collecting together a small, harmless and willing group of Redskins and sending them East, and Barnum, having swiftly realized the profitability of such a scheme, made the idea his own, suggesting to the public that he alone had the confidence, integrity and vision required to make such a spectacle succeed, and thus, in his own mind at least, satisfying both sides of the Redskin argument and leaving himself free to present the braves in whichever way the public demanded to see them. 'Tame Savages' – Henry Butler's phrase – captured his feelings and intent precisely.

He wired the agent to proceed and then set about creating the maximum amount of publicity for the venture. He negotiated with the railroads for the Indians to travel in a special guarded carriage, and for the journey to be broken as often as possible at every jerkwater halt, giving the inhabitants of the towns along the track the opportunity to witness the spectacle for themselves and to be in no doubt as to the final destination of the braves. Having guaranteed his agent high-quality hotel accommodation along the journey – which in total lasted fourteen days – he then cancelled all reservations and made additional arrangements with the railroad companies for everyone to be bedded down somewhere open and central and, most importantly of all, somewhere which afforded the inquisitive public an unrestricted view of the proceedings. Food and kindling were provided, and although the agent objected on the Redskins' behalf, they themselves understood and accepted what was happening to them.

Upon their eventual arrival in New York, a triumphant parade had taken place, Barnum at its head, flanked by two young warriors riding bareback, preceded and surrounded by men carrying placards warning the public to keep well away from the procession, this being the unpredictable savages' first encounter with civilized living. Additionally, Barnum's bravery in riding alongside the braves – estimated by Greenwood to be between fifteen and seventeen years old – became a talking point among the thousands who had witnessed the parade for days afterwards.

Upon disembarking from their long train journey, however, the Redskins had presented a considerably less remarkable spectacle than even Barnum had anticipated. They wore vests and pants provided by the agent, displayed no war paint whatsoever, and had scarcely a feather among them. The women were old, overweight and ugly, and the old men looked ready to drop by the roadside at the slightest exertion. They were to look like this to Barnum throughout the duration of their stay in the Museum.

Anticipating their less than savage appearance after their journey, Barnum, having prepared himself for every eventuality – right down to the hiring of several armed men to walk alongside him in the procession – arranged for the Redskins to be disembarked in private, and then had delivered to them a dozen painted ponies and a carriageload of feather head-dresses, tomahawks and spears. Following a twenty-minute speech of welcome which none of them understood, he then set about preparing them for their triumphal procession to their new home.

Despite what had happened since, Barnum still remembered that day with much pride and some fondness.

It became immediately clear upon their arrival at the Museum, however, that despite being impressed by its size and magnificence, the Redskins were not happy with either their own living quarters or by the way they were then treated by the public which came to stare at them. They had been told by the agent that once in New York they would be admired and honoured, both for their previous brave deeds and for their bravery in making such a journey, but upon arrival they quickly came to realize that they were little more than the latest of Barnum's fleeting amusements. By then, however, it was too late: they had agreed to come and their own agent had signed the two-year contract on their behalf. Barnum afterwards left it to Elizabeth to explain to them how many passages of the moon two years involved. Initially, they had despaired upon realizing how long they would be absent from their homes, but they then stoically agreed to honour the agreement in the hope that conditions in the Museum might improve.

Their first public display was as disappointing to Barnum as their disembarkation from the railroad car had been. Instead of a frenzy of flailing limbs and savage cries, their war dances consisted of little more than a prolonged and intolerable murmuring and a dance which consisted of lifting one leg and then the other and shuffling around in a small circle with their eyes closed. After witnessing this sorry spectacle for a minute, Barnum stopped them and made it clear what he expected of them when they performed in front of the paying public. He agreed to a week's settling-in period, and they in turn promised to perfect a new and considerably more exciting dance for him. This they did, and as they came to understand the true nature of their appeal to the public, so they felt happier about the artificiality of what they were presenting. Barnum's only problem then had been to stop them pilfering from his visitors and to prevent them from dancing on the roof of the Museum every time a full moon presented itself in the night sky – something they appeared to him to have calculated with a remarkable degree of accuracy for primitive savages.

Because they exasperated him, and because by nature he was not a patient man, Barnum allowed Elizabeth to act as his intermediary in all his dealings with them. Awed by her solitary eye, they treated her with admiration and respect, which to Barnum's two eyes, bordered dangerously on idolatry. Elizabeth enjoyed this, and having been familiar as a child and young woman with the peaceful Indians of her native Minnesota, she understood their reaction to her appearance and was careful not to insult them by refusing to allow herself to be used in this way. She and they grew rapidly to understand each other and several strong friendships developed, particularly between herself and the two young braves who had flanked Barnum at the head of his procession, the youngest of whom, an Oglala Sioux called Crazy Horse, had the greatest difficulty in bowing to Barnum's will and making the changes demanded of him.

Elizabeth was invited to their rooftop ceremonies, where she was decorated by them with paint and feathers. She shared their food and gradually they learned more of each other's language, until eventually they were able to hold simple conversations. Crazy Horse was the quickest to learn, but at the same time he was also the least willing to become excited or even pleased by this achievement. It was also clear to Elizabeth that, of them all, he alone was determined to benefit in some more substantial way by their encounter and their enforced stay in the city. He was the proudest of the braves – none of them more than youths upon their arrival – and only he, Elizabeth guessed, had a vision of the future in which he could truly believe. Despite their friendship, however, on the few occasions she tried to draw him out he told her not to ask, simply to wait and see. The braves trusted her, and because of this she was unhappy at the way in which Barnum took advantage of her friendship in his own dealings with them. After two or three months she knew that Crazy Horse was capable of taking over as their spokesman, but she never suggested this to him and he too avoided all mention of it, preferring instead for her to retain this valuable function as their intermediary.

When she was alone with them she allowed them to paint a circle around her eye, and as a sign of their mutual respect invited them to share her 'gift' by gently touching her forehead with their thumbs.

The other inhabitants were also pleased at their arrival, and at Barnum's discomfort upon discovering that his control over them was considerably less than he would have liked.

And now, after almost two years, they were ready to leave, forcing him into the unwelcome position of wanting to agree to their demands without actually appearing to. Why, he tried to understand, did every act of kindness or generosity on his part lead to such a predicament – one in which he had nothing to gain and yet might lose so much? He was reminded of the time he had offered to employ men mutilated in the war as walking advertisements for his Museum and the outrage this had caused at the time; and then of his offer of free admission to all those who had suffered obvious or visible injuries in service of the Union cause. That too had been unaccountably unpopular. These memories, and the unhappy connection thus established, only increased his present sense of grievance and unwarranted persecution. He had recently written a short and popular history of the life of Jesus Christ and had been constantly amazed by the similarities which existed between that man's wrongful persecution and his own. He'd pointed this out, albeit indirectly, in his preface to the book, and was afterwards frequently able to reassure himself by the similarities which continued to occur.

He wanted in some way to be able to blame Elizabeth for what was happening to him now, but knew that without her the problem of the Redskins' departure would almost certainly have arisen much sooner and would have proved considerably more intractable. Even now, after they had honoured their contract, he could not accept that he himself was the only barrier to an agreeable and acceptable solution. He still believed that there would be a renewed interest in the Indians and in the land problem in the West when the war was over, and consequently he maintained his conviction that there was still therefore a profit to be made in keeping them at the Museum on a basis more agreeable to him. The only question now was how long the war was likely to last.

The previous day, news had reached the city that Grant had lost no fewer than 20,000 men – some had the figure as high as 40,000 – at the battle of Spotsylvania and that he was withdrawing, his forces in disarray.

'Forty thousand good honest Union boys,' Barnum said loudly to himself, accepting, as usual, the highest of the figures involved.

During their two years at the Museum, two of the older Indians had died, and two of the squaws had given birth. Thus had the numbers been maintained and the smallest print of their contractual obligations fulfilled. Even this Barnum now considered to be part of the overall conspiracy against him. 'No respect!' he yelled. 'No damn respect!' He stood with his arm around the shoulders of the bust and spoke to himself in René's family portrait which now hung above it, drawing some strength and reassurance from both.

He had negotiated with Elizabeth for the Indians to leave in two months' time, at the height of the summer, by which time, he hoped, his basement aquarium would have risen to prominence as a new and major attraction. In accepting this date, they in turn had demanded blankets and cooking pots from him to take home with them, and to this too he had agreed.

When he'd told Charity of the conspiracy against him she had shuddered and calmly remarked that back home in the West was where the savages belonged, out of harm's way, where they need remind no one of the debased and uncultivated side of human nature. She spoke of the West as though it were a dark and distant planet, and one which need not concern her or her daughters in any way whatsoever. To avoid argument, Barnum had agreed with her. The wedding of his eldest daughter was starting to close in upon him, and because the preparations for this existed only within the province of the four women, he felt himself excluded, an unnecessary hindrance to the proceedings.

During their first week in the Museum, the Redskins had killed, skinned, cooked and eaten three snakes and had attacked the largest of his stuffed bears, laughing like children as they dismembered it to reveal its sawdust and horsehair innards. He had pleaded with Elizabeth to prevent them from committing any other outrage. Since then an uneasy truce had existed, and as far as possible Barnum had delegated his responsibility for them to Henry Butler, who had worked with considerably more sympathy and understanding with Elizabeth.

His hand absently stroking the shoulder of the bust, he cried out again: 'Forty thousand dead! Forty thousand true and honest souls!' What hope was there for the barbaric Redskin if such a tragedy could befall even that most advanced and civilized of nations?

*

Leaving his office, Greenwood made his way to the floor above, knocked on Elizabeth's door and entered without waiting for her response.

She sat in bed, reading, and with the paraphernalia of letter-writing scattered around her. She showed no surprise that he should have entered without being invited, but nor did she show any pleasure at his arrival. Her long hair was unbrushed and hung over most of her face, held away from her eye by a pair of tortoiseshell combs.

'Feel free, why don't you,' she said, drawing her bedjacket together and indicating a chair beside the bed.

'I only wanted to see you,' Greenwood said, considerably less certain of himself than usual. 'I suppose you heard about our attempt to get Barnum to hand over the running of the place.'

She looked from him back to her book, carefully marking her page before laying it down.

'I've always thought I could talk to you,' he went on hesitantly.

'You could talk to any of us – talk, that is, and not order around – if you chose to.'

'I know. But I always felt as though you and I, as though we had some affinity.'

'Perhaps,' she said. 'In the beginning.'

'I see. Whatever. The fact is I can't talk to Barnum because he only listens to what he wants to hear. And Butler's afraid of raising his voice, let alone –'

'Before you go on, you ought to know that I think a great deal of Henry Butler. We all do.'

'I know. Whereas I – you do realize, all of you, that if it wasn't for my presence in the Museum – mine, yes, mine – then Henry Butler would have been dispensed with long ago and Barnum would have probably sold up or otherwise relinquished his control of the place.'

'We know that, too,' she said.

Greenwood moved closer to her bed.

Elizabeth withdrew her hand from his reach and warned him that if it was his intention to behave in any way dishonourably towards her, then she would shout for Zip, who was at that moment in the room directly above her, and who would respond immediately to her call.

Greenwood looked up at the ceiling. 'I only wanted to talk,' he said, pushing himself back to his original position.

'About what? About some new damask drapes for my booth, about a more comfortable seat? Or perhaps Mr Barnum wants to negotiate with me to accompany him on his next tour of the European capitals. No – don't tell me – he's spent everything he had on the hippopotamus and the rest of us will have to wait for whatever it is we want or need.'

'If I were able to get the lease for this place from him, I'd tear up your contract and you could do whatever you wanted,' Greenwood said.

'And leave me penniless and destitute?' she replied, provoking him, knowing that this was not what he meant.

'I'd buy a house,' Greenwood said.

'And I'd be your wife, the mother of your children? Is that what you came up here to suggest to me?'

'I once believed it was all I'd ever want,' he said quietly.

'No,' Elizabeth said, taking his hand. 'I know you mean it, or at least that you think you do, but when I've gotten what I need from this place I'll leave and no one will ever hear of me again.'

'Impossible,' Greenwood said, regretting the word immediately. 'Aren't you even prepared to consider my proposition?'

'Why should I? If I hadn't come to this place, you'd never have known I existed.'

'Everything comes to this place one way or another, sooner or later. Barnum's wrong – the taste for all this is going to fade and disappear. If I got my hands on the place I'd turn it into . . .' He stopped himself, angry at having allowed himself to be so easily diverted from the purpose of his visit.

Realizing this, Elizabeth drew aside her hair until her full face and high forehead were revealed. 'Look at it,' she told him. 'Look. Look at it hard. I might have had three noses, a dozen ears, other mouths.' Her single eye stared at him without blinking. 'And now look at this.' She pressed her finger into the vestigal scar of her other socket. 'See – red. It's going red, discoloured. It's old skin, loose, ready to sag, and the older I get the more readily it betrays me. The cold air makes it sore. Each morning I apply my powder, and each night I wipe it off and study what lies beneath. Someone soon is going to start complaining, shouting "Fraud!" What then? You've seen all our contracts. There's no provision for anything like that in them. Barnum tears them up because we've failed to live up to our side of the bargain, and instantly we cease to be so attractive and become what we once were before he so benevolently took us under his wing.'

'Which is why –'

'Which is why you think you want to save me from all this, to take me off to your so-called home and allow me to live the life of a million other women.'

'Yes,' Greenwood shouted.

Elizabeth shook her head and composed herself. 'It's not what I want,' she said. 'It could never work.'

'I'd *make* it work,' Greenwood said.

'And the morning after we moved into your grand new house, I'd wake up and look in the mirror and still see this looking back out at me.'

'Just give me the chance.'

There was a knock at the door and Zip entered. He looked from Greenwood to Elizabeth and asked her if everything was all right, knowing from her tone as she answered him that she was relieved to see him, but possibly for no other reason than that she no longer wished to be alone with Greenwood and his impossible dreams.

Embarrassed, Greenwood could think of nothing to say. Zip knew how he felt about Elizabeth, and how she felt about him.

'She's in no danger from me,' Greenwood said unnecessarily.

'I know that,' Zip said, offering him a cigar.

'We were discussing the failure of our – mine and Henry Butler's – attempt to take over from Barnum.'

'How did you ever hope to succeed? He's drawing in his horns. He's getting old and defensive. He sees everything as a threat.'

Greenwood, surprised by Zip's percipience, could only nod in agreement.

'Buy this place and let us all run wild through the streets,' Zip said. 'How does that sound?'

'Theatres, they're the thing. I'd buy up every empty building and empty site from here to the Bowery. Plays, comedies, tragedies, that's what people will want to see, not the fake moralizing Barnum gives them here when the fancy takes him. He can't see that, but I can. He should have agreed to our offer and let us get on with it.'

'We'd still be running wild through the streets,' Zip said.

Elizabeth retrieved her book and resumed reading.

'He's living in the past too much,' Greenwood said.

'He's an institution.' Zip paused to blow out smoke. 'This place is a trap. He's pulled the stick away and it's fallen down and caught us all inside, you and Henry Butler included. Some of us can see that, some of us don't want to, and some of us would be terrified to death at the very thought of any kind of life outside it.'

'Tell me – what would you do if you were given the choice?' Greenwood asked him.

Zip and Elizabeth shared an uneasy look, both familiar with the topic of conversation, and uncertain about revealing their feelings to someone for whom those alternatives were more than idle speculation.

'That choice doesn't exist,' Zip said flatly. 'And you can spare your efforts in trying to convince us otherwise.'

'He's right,' Elizabeth said. 'All the negroes are soon going to be free, but they're still going to be black, and in more ways than one nothing's really going to change for them. Give us our freedom and ten thousand dollars tomorrow and Zip here is still going to be a pinhead, Anna's still going to be a giant and I'm still going to be a cyclops.'

Greenwood winced at the word.

'That's right – a cyclops,' Elizabeth said. 'It doesn't hurt, but the fact that it makes you shudder to hear even *me* say it proves our point.'

'That's the catch,' Zip said. 'We don't want it, but we can't live without it. You say it's all going to come to an end, and perhaps you're right, perhaps it is, but how many of them niggers down there on their plantations are genuinely set to start dancing and cheering when it all comes true for them? Not many, I can tell you.'

'He's right,' Elizabeth said again. 'I can't speak for the negroes and the plantations, but he's right about all this, about us. And you're right too – it *is* all going to have to end some day, and probably sooner than any of us realizes. We all know that, we've known it all along. We know it every time Barnum announces something new and exciting, when all he's really got is more of what he's had before. People are going to realize that soon.'

'And when they do . . .' Zip said, holding up his palms. 'So you see our predicament.'

Greenwood nodded. 'The Spragues are coming back,' he said. 'And the Albinos. Today some time.' They were all ready to leave the subject for fear of being drawn into anything more painful.

'Where have they been?' Zip asked him.

'On tour with the Asiatic Menagerie, Wyoming, Colorado, Utah.'

'Be good to see Isaac again,' Zip said. 'What is he now?'

'Somewhere between fifty and fifty-four pounds,' Greenwood said. 'Barnum wants to weigh him before he puts him back under contract.'

'In the meat market, no doubt. Anna will be pleased, too.'

Elizabeth had arrived at the Museum after the departure of Isaac Sprague and his family, and consequently she knew nothing of them. Likewise, the Albino family.

'I advised him against taking them back on,' Greenwood said. 'The travelling shows are all losing money. That's the real reason they're coming back.'

'Running for home,' Zip said. 'And no doubt he's taking them back at a reduced rate.'

Greenwood nodded.

'How about Chang and Eng? Barnum heard anything from them recently?'

'Only a newspaper report that they'd lost most of their plantation in the fighting and that their grand house had been burned down. They're still a big attraction. Whatever they've lost they'll make it up in a year.'

'But only if they put themselves in Barnum's hands?'

'If that. I heard a rumour that they hadn't lost their plantation as a result of any military action, but that they'd been burned out by the townspeople where they lived.'

'Why would they want to do that?' Elizabeth asked. She knew about the Siamese Twins from the others in the Museum.

Both Zip and Greenwood considered their answers before telling her.

'Being able to come and look at something in here is a different proposition entirely to having it turn up as your neighbour flaunting a fortune,' Zip said.

'Then they married two local girls,' Greenwood added. 'Sisters. Built two separate houses and spent one week in one, one week in the other. The doctors said there was no way they could ever be separated without them both standing a good chance of being killed in the process. Something to do with the internal organs they shared.'

'And then they started breeding,' Zip said. 'They must have almost twenty kids between them by now.'

'Twenty-one,' Greenwood said. 'Out there in North Carolina it's a big problem, but if Barnum could get them to leave everything and come back here, perhaps with their wives and some of their offspring, then they'd be a bigger draw than ever. He'd make another fortune on their backs and they'd make another for themselves. In fact, the way I see it, we'd all –'

'Not us,' Elizabeth said, stopping his excited speculation.

'And will they come?' Zip asked him.

'Barnum seems to think so. He's been in touch. One thing's for certain – the hippopotamus isn't going to draw the crowds.'

The hippopotamus had arrived at the Museum the previous day and was being given several days to accustom itself to its new surroundings before being put on public display.

'It's a big disappointment,' Greenwood said.

'How long is it expected to survive?' Elizabeth asked him.

'Long enough to recoup its cost, hopefully.'

'In that tank? It'll be dead inside a week,' she said.

'I doubt it. Butler's seen to it that it has a constantly recycled supply of fresh water. It's very advanced.'

They sat in silence for a few moments, Zip sharing his cigar with Elizabeth.

'He's even thinking of bringing in some bears,' Greenwood said, shrugging as they turned together and asked why. 'My point precisely. It's medieval. Where's the novelty in bears?'

He left them, and as he went he heard their shared laughter through the closed door. He didn't resent this, but felt instead as though he had somehow been taken into their confidence and been made aware of something that would give him an advantage over Barnum when the time next came to challenge him.

*

Later that same night, Herman and Franklin stood in thoughtful contemplation of the hippopotamus. Neither had seen one before, and of all the Museum's inhabitants, they alone were eager to acquaint themselves with the new arrival. Both were familiar with the appearance and history of the creature from Barnum's extensive advance publicity, but nevertheless there was still something about it which held them in awe, which caused them to follow its every move and then step back a pace as it turned to face them through the glass.

With the hippopotamus installed, the aquarium looked suddenly much smaller, and Barnum's exaggerated claims for its holding capacity had already been called into dispute by a labourer who had helped to install the 'Savage Behemoth'. Having been excited by all Barnum's advance publicity, few could now fail to be disappointed by the placidity of the creature's movements and the sorrowful anguish of its gaze in the watery light of the basement.

Similarly, there had been no sign of its advertised Arabian keeper, Salaama, but Barnum knew that if the demand to see him became too great to ignore then he could easily acquire an Arab from the basement dens on Beekman or Frankfort Street to stand in for him at little extra cost.

It was past one in the morning and the Museum had been empty of its visitors for over an hour. Herman held an oil lantern, and this alone illuminated the giant tank and the creature within it, which hung almost motionless in suspension, occasionally paddling its stubby legs and sending a ripple through the water around it. The glare of Herman's lantern reflected on the water cast moving shapes of light all around them. Far above them, somewhere in the heart of the building, Tom played the Moonlight Sonata. As usual, he had grown progressively drunker throughout the day and now only the slow, melancholy progress of the notes revealed his condition.

Herman cocked his head to listen, reassured by the sound. He had been back in his booth for over a fortnight following his short illness, but the pain had not entirely gone from his chest, and each night either Anna Swan or Elizabeth bound him in bandages soaked in a solution of grease and camphor to ease his cramps as he slept. He woke frequently as he turned in his sleep, and often, as now, he put off retiring to his bed for as long as possible, occasionally accompanying Zip on his night-time journeys through the city, playing poker with him and Vivalla, or simply listening to Fortuna, Elizabeth and Anna reminiscing until he fell asleep where he sat and Anna carried him to his bed.

'He's a genius,' he said now, meaning Tom and moving his fingers with the notes.

'He's a pianner-playin' nigger,' Franklin said. 'Five a dollar in any county fair you care to visit. Barnum says he's a genius, but all he is is a pianner-playin' nigger. None the worse for any of that, but that's what he is all the same.' In his hands he held a large meat-pie,

115

a foot in length from one side of the crust to the other, and six inches deep.

'You going to eat all that?' Herman asked him.

'Have to. Might not want to, but I have to. Simple as that.' Franklin took his first bite of the pie, its crust cracking and falling in pieces into his lap, where the material of his pants was stretched tight to catch it.

In its tank, the hippopotamus drifted slowly round to face them, its broad dumb-bell of a nose touching the glass and releasing a trickle of bubbles from each nostril.

'I get the feeling it understands us,' Herman said, standing as close as he dared to the tank.

'It's a dumb animal. How can it understand us?'

'It's watching you eat that pie.'

Franklin immediately wrapped a protective arm around his pie. 'Nothin' it can do about it,' he said. Despite his previous eagerness, he too was becoming disappointed with the animal. 'That all it can do?' he asked. 'Float around lookin' miserable as sin. I don't see the attraction in that.' He continued eating.

Herman, however, sat fascinated by the animal, his own reflection cast dimly on the glass between them.

Above the tank, Barnum had erected a notice which read 'Hippo-potameus', considering the extra vowel a legitimate and worthwhile addition in the midst of so many others. 'From the Greek Hip-o-pot-ameus,' he told everyone. He himself pronounced the word to rhyme roughly with Nicodemus. In addition, the creature was described as the 'Marvel of the Animal Kingdom, the Great Behemoth of the Scriptures and a Frightful Antagonist when Threatened', its Herculean jaws and great strength crushing everything which came within reach – none of which had been in evidence since its arrival. In honour of its presentation to the public, Barnum had renamed the basement the Aquarial Hall.

There had been no rampaging around the East Street wharves, no desperate last-minute bid for freedom, and no forty-foot plunge into the river. The captain of the *Machias*, who had been previously employed by Barnum in bringing other animals from the Toronto Zoological Gardens, and who was only too aware of his need for spectacle and publicity at other people's expense, had fed the animal throughout its journey on potatoes boiled in a cauldron of cheap liquor, and had regularly topped this up at the first indi-cation of any sound or movement. Consequently, upon its arrival the hippopotamus had been lowered to the wharf in a stupefied, almost insensible state, seemingly more dead than alive, and the only moment of real excitement had come when its slumped and bulging body threatened to break the tarpaulin sling in which it was secured.

From the wharf it was transported to the Museum by a dray and a dozen horses, where it was then manoeuvred down into the basement and finally lowered with great difficulty into the waiting tank, reviving momentarily and thrashing its legs, causing a wave of overflow to flood the basement to a depth of several inches, drenching the workmen and plumbers who were there to make the final adjustments to its new home.

'Are we the first to see it?' Franklin asked disinterestedly, still concentrating on his pie, the jellied meat of which had slid from its casing in a single lump into his hands. 'I mean the first of all us regulars. At least if we was the first it'd be something to talk about.'

'It can't be much of a life,' Herman said. 'Floating around inside there all day and night.'

'Huh?'

In response to this, the hippopotamus rose effortlessly to the surface of the tank and blew the air from its lungs in a loud and lasting snort.

'It stinks,' Franklin said, wiping the fine spray from his face and shoulders.

Herman left the tank and returned to sit beside him.

'Zip was telling me all about a naturalist in England,' he said.

'And?'

Herman seemed reluctant to go on. 'Apparently, he's warning us that we're all descended from monkeys.'

'Heard about him,' Franklin said, much to Herman's relief. 'And you got it wrong. We're not all of us descended from monkeys, only some of us. I know which ones he means.'

'Who?' Herman asked him, wondering if he'd misunderstood what Zip had told him.

'The niggers. They're the ones he's talkin' about. Not us. Think about it. Makes sense. Leastways it makes perfect sense to me. Tell me – you see any monkey in me?'

'No – he meant all of us,' Herman insisted. 'And what he's saying is that if we aren't more watchful of how we behave now that we've come this far, then we might start right off on the path to being monkeys again.'

'Nobody's telling me I'm on the way to being a monkey.' Franklin licked at the jelly in his warm palms. 'Anyhow, I still say you've got it all wrong. I read all about him. What he says is that we've evoluted and that the monkeys is what some of those who've evoluted less quickly might once have been. Like I said – the niggers. He ain't talkin' about us white folk, and especially not us professional people. He might spread the net a little to include some Italians or Irish, but I can tell you for a certain, sure-fire fact that me and you ain't included, so you can stop your worrying. Anyhow, why would we set off back to bein' monkeys if that's where we come from in the first place? Not that I'm sayin' we did, you understand. It just don't make sense. I tell you, I worked in the fairs with some so-called monkey-men and they was the sharpest, cheatingest card-players I ever come across. Is that what he's sayin' – that we're all turnin' into card-sharps? No. Thought not. None of it makes sense. You listen to me, I'm tellin' you right.'

'For our sins,' Herman said seriously. 'That's why we'd all turn back into whatever we once were.'

'For what?' The piece of pie on its way to Franklin's mouth stopped several inches short.

'We've all sinned, and the more we sin, the further we get back to being monkeys. That's how I understand it.'

'Sinned? We've all sinned? I thought the good Lord made up the reckonin' on all that. We surely ain't answerable to Him *and* this Mr Darling of yourn. Ask me, that don't seem right nor fair.'

'Darwin. No.'

'Seems to me as though the more you think about it, the more there is to set you worryin'. I ask you again – do I look as though I'm evoluted from a monkey? Maybe I'm evoluted from one of the trees the monkeys swing around in, but I don't see how I could have gotten up to this from being a scrawny little monkey. No way. Even before I started eatin' for the shows. No way, no sir.'

'Perhaps you're right,' Herman conceded, unconvinced, but unwilling to force the argument with his friend.

Swallowing the last of the pie, Franklin brushed the flakes of pastry from his lap, pointed to the hippopotamus and said, 'If I'm evoluted from anythin' then it's more likely to be one of them things than a miserable little ape. Come to think of it, I wouldn't mind floatin' around in a tub of warm water for a day or two myself. How does it do that – keep its head and all under the water with its eyes open without any air? No, don't tell me – it's evoluted so it don't have to sit out here with us listenin' to all this nonsense.'

The hippopotamus continued to stare out at them with the same resigned and mournful look upon its face.

'It looks how I feel after a good souse,' Franklin said, slapping the folds of his stomach.

'The niggers are only black,' Herman said, stopping to listen to Tom as he went on playing above them.

'Only! Only! It's because they're *only* black that your Mr Darling gets his fancy ideas and puts the fear of God into good honest folk like us by wantin' us to believe –'

'It's because we've sinned against *them*,' Herman said, pressing his hands together, his head bowed.

'– to believe we've – Sinned against who?'

'The niggers. It's a judgment.'

'But not from the Almighty, it's not,' Franklin said. 'Niggers is niggers, and there's good niggers and bad niggers just like the rest of us. You might just as well say we've sinned against the rats Cherry catches and kills.'

After a full minute in which neither of them spoke, and in which the silence was broken only by the distant piano and the almost inaudible bursting of bubbles on the surface of the tank, Franklin said, 'Perhaps now, perhaps because of the war, perhaps you think they'll start turnin' white, evolutin', and we'll start gettin' darker. If that started happenin', then that'd be a judgment I'd show some respect for.'

'It's what we've been fighting for,' Herman said, exasperated, knowing that he'd lost his grip on the poorly-reasoned argument.

'*We* haven't been fightin' for anythin',' Franklin said, equally uncertain of his motives for prolonging the discussion, but at the same time sympathetic towards Herman's beliefs. There had been a rumour in the Museum that Barnum wasn't happy with Herman's illness and was thinking of taking him out of the building and attaching him to one of his travelling shows in place of the Spragues or the Albinos until he was fully recovered. Such a move, Franklin knew, would be too much for the boy to bear, and his recovery, were it to come about, would be unnecessarily prolonged. Herman himself was aware of this rumour, and despite his suffering he was making an effort not to bring himself to Barnum's attention until he was well again and able to expand himself to his full extent without fear of causing himself a permanent injury.

'I wonder how long it'll survive,' Franklin said. 'A month? Two?'

Following all the other basement mortalities, no one was able to completely ignore the fact that the new attraction was unlikely to survive for any longer than its predecessors, and Barnum had taken this into account when making his calculations of the animal's appeal. A sea-lion, Old Neptune, had been the longest survivor in the first of the tanks, living almost three years until his normally glossy black body was blotched with white and he succumbed to a disease about which not even the name was known, but which Barnum, upon exhibiting the corpse, referred to as a direct result of 'homesickness'.

Herman lowered the flame in his lantern, drawing in the walls around them until the two of them sat in a globe of feeble yellow light.

'Can I tell you something,' he said, his voice almost a whisper.

'So long as it ain't that you've already started growin' a tail and eatin' bananas or such like.'

Herman blushed and continued to lock and unlock his fingers. 'I've met a girl,' he said quickly.

'A girl? What sort of girl? A girl girl? I shake the hands of hundreds every day. Pretty girls, too. Pretty as my sisters.'

'No – a girl. Outside. Nothing to do with this place. She works in the kitchens at the Astor.'

'Oh, that kind of girl,' Franklin said, and sighed. 'So?'

'I think . . . I think –'

'You think you're in love with her.'

Herman blushed deeper and nodded once.

'Does she know about you, about all this?'

'She came to see me. She brought all her friends. I make her laugh.'

'And do all her friends laugh, too?'

'She said – she said she thought I was handsome.'

'You are, Herman. You are. How many times you seen her?'

'Six times so far.'

'Here or outside?'

'Five times here, once outside.'

'So she spends twenty-five cents a time to pay you a call.'

'No, I . . .', Herman stopped and looked up.

'You what?'

'I told her I could get her into the Museum for free. I gave the ticket girls the money beforehand and told them she was coming.'

'How about her friends – you get them in for free, too?'

120

'She said she couldn't come without them, that she'd be too embarrassed to walk around alone. I can understand that.'

'And you make her laugh,' Franklin said. 'Have you kissed her yet?'

'Once.' Herman held up his finger.

'And when you kissed her, were you alone with her or were these friends of hers hangin' around?'

'She couldn't see me alone,' Herman said defensively. 'Not like that, not under those circumstances.'

'Of course not. You told Zip about her yet? You and him gettin' pretty thick these days. He was the one started you off on all these excursions out there, in and out of taverns. It was bound to happen sooner or later.'

'But I wanted it to happen,' Herman said.

'Sure you did. That's not what I'm sayin'.' Franklin paused and smiled. 'Girl kissed me once at the Greensboro Hog Jamboree. I was voted Greensboro Hog Champion and she was the Queen of the Fair. Sat right in my lap and kissed me on the lips, come and gone before I'd had a chance to pucker up and start blowin' back, though.'

'I only kissed her cheek.'

'That's only the start of it,' Franklin said, and then, with more enthusiasm, 'Women – now I can imagine *them* being evoluted from scheming monkeys.'

'Blowing?' Herman said. 'You said –'

'Hot and cold mostly. We're men of the world, you and me, Herman. When you seein' her again? You never even told me her name.'

'Nancy,' Herman said proudly. 'Her name's Nancy.' He savoured the name as Franklin had savoured his pie.

'Fancy Nancy,' Franklin said. 'No disrespect. I'll keep an eye open for her, let you have my considered opinion. I take it you've already put the cash in the drawer for her next visit.'

Herman nodded, pleased and relieved at his shared secret.

'She bringin' her friends along?'

'Two or three of them. She's a very popular girl.'

Franklin was going to say 'I bet,' but thought better of it and stopped himself. 'I imagine you and her reckon –'

'Listen!' Herman said suddenly, lifting the lantern and staring intently at the doorway.

Above them the piano-playing had stopped and there were only the creaks and groans of the building to be heard, a distant door opening and closing.

'I can't hear nothin',' Franklin said, but sensing that he was about to.

In the tank, the hippopotamus rasped loudly underwater and a trail of bubbles shot quickly to the surface and burst.

'It's the hippo,' Franklin said, moving closer to Herman and the lantern.

Then they both heard the footsteps coming lightly down the stairs towards them.

'Shout out and ask who it is,' Franklin whispered, his cheeks and chins quivering.

'Who is it?' Herman said softly.

'Louder. We don't want to scare them when they get down here. Probably just Old Tom lookin' for one of his hidden bottles. You're right – he is a genius. Shout again, quick.' Sweat had filled the creases around Franklin's eyes, and this shone in the dim light. He was grimacing, tensed in anticipation, the inner folds of his cheeks and first chin encircling his wet lips in an almost complete circle.

'We know you're there,' Herman called out.

'Whoever you are. And what's more – we ain't scared.'

The footsteps had ceased, but both were convinced that they could now hear someone breathing in the darkness just beyond the glow of the lantern.

'Swing the light round,' Franklin whispered.

Herman moved the lantern from side to side, throwing up light and shadow all around them, making it even harder to see whoever might be there.

In the darkness at the foot of the stairs, a voice said 'Whooooo,' and was followed by a burst of suppressed laughter.

Franklin jumped and clutched at his collar.

Beneath him, Herman felt the bench shake.

'I'll believe it, I'll believe it,' Franklin called out. 'We're all evoluted from monkeys, I'll believe it. We're payin' for our sins and Old Tom's a genius.' Despite being four times as broad as Herman, he pressed close behind him and peered over his shoulder.

'There!' Herman said, holding out the light, and pointing as a small glowing skeleton walked into view.

Franklin let out a long sigh of relief. 'Isaac Sprague, you dumb ass. You almost had the boy here skeered right outta his skin. Don't you know no better than to go creepin' about at all times of the night dressed like that and puttin' decent folks in fear of their lives. Just as well for you that I didn't have my bird gun with me.'

'Sure is – you'd shoot your own foot,' Isaac Sprague said, stepping daintily into the centre of the pool of light and shielding his eyes. He was wearing the two-piece black suit upon which the bones of his skeleton had been embroidered in white, and which now glowed in the darkness. 'And besides which, I can't help but creep around. How do you expect me to do anything else?'

The newly-arrived Sprague stood five feet two inches tall, weighed fifty-two pounds, and walked stiffly, his arms swinging by his side.

'This the hippopotamus?' he said, approaching the tank.

'The hipp-o-potameus,' Franklin said. 'What's it look like?'

'Like every other hippopotamus I've ever seen in every other town in this country.'

'Marvellous. So now you're the hippopotamus expert,' Franklin said, annoyed that their solitude had been interrupted. He had known the Spragues before they left the Museum to join the travelling show, and considering the man more self-important than he had a right to be, he had not looked forward to their return. 'How's Bella-Grace and all the young uns?' he asked.

'They cry most of the day and she's chafing because Barnum won't let her go out in case somebody recognizes her and spoils his grand announcement of our return. It's all very understandable, I suppose, but still annoying.'

'Oh, I'm sure it must be,' Franklin said dismissively. He himself hadn't been outside the Museum for a month, and then only to make one of his regular journeys to Fulton Street to be weighed.

The return of the Spragues was not the momentous occasion Isaac Sprague might now have tried to make it appear. They had returned to the Museum because there had been nowhere else to go and the travelling show was losing money, and because there was still a year left to run on his contract with Barnum.

'And I wear this skeleton suit because it's the warmest I've got,' he said, holding out his arms until the bones again caught the light and became distinct.

'It's very effective,' Herman said, introducing himself and showing Sprague the bandages around his chest when Franklin insisted he did so. 'We came down to make sure the hippo was settled in all right.'

'I only got up to shut up that piano-playing fool,' Sprague said. 'Bella-Grace is a very delicate sleeper. She has her disposition to think of and woke with a terrible hunger. Barnum's provisions wouldn't scarcely keep a skinned cat in flesh.' Sprague, despite his appearance, ate four full meals a day, and like Franklin's meals, these were taken publicly as part of his show. 'Fat boy here,' Sprague said to Herman, winking to him as he spoke, 'once had an idea to run away with Bella-Grace – run, *him* – but she's the faithfullest woman alive and never had eyes for anyone but me.'

Franklin denied this loudly, but stopped when he saw that both Sprague and Herman were laughing at him.

'Herman here's in love,' he told Sprague.

'Blessed with any progeny?' Sprague asked.

'Progeny?'

'He means have you got any uncontrollable brats runnin' round your feet yellin' and screamin' all day long.'

'No,' Herman said, unable and unwilling to attempt the leap between himself and Nancy as they now were and what Franklin had described.

'They're still at the cheek-kissin' stage,' Franklin said sagely, leaning back and causing the bench upon which they all now sat to creak ominously. Flanked by their worried glances, he smiled. 'You're puttin' on some weight, Sprague. You want to step careful otherwise Barnum'll find some excuse to tear up that contract and kick you and all your prodigies out on to the street. If I was you I'd get myself down to about ten or twelve pounds soonest. Let's face it, folk only come in to feel sorry for you and say nasty things about your mama for not feedin' you up right as baby.' He nudged Herman so that he might share in the joke. 'And don't you go too near the old hippo there, otherwise he might just take you for an eel, leap out and snap you up for his supper. I expect you've read all the warnings.'

'Better than being mistook for his brother,' Sprague said.

'Impossible. According to young Herman here, we're all evoluted from monkeys.'

'I heard it said, and I believe it to be only a matter of time before such a notion is thoroughly and completely discredited.'

'My belief entirely,' Franklin said. 'He's got a lot to learn.' And suddenly the two men were friends again, bound as one in their attack upon the theory of evolution and the sum total of expert opinion. They shook hands, Sprague's chest barely the thickness of Franklin's forearm. This sudden affinity Herman took to be the result of their shared pasts working in the travelling shows and fairgrounds, something of which he as yet had no experience, and which, after the relative security and prestige of appearing in the Museum, seemed to him to represent a kind of banishment, exile even.

'Better be getting back upstairs,' Sprague said.

'Give my regards to Bella-Grace.'

'And mine,' Herman said.

'You intent on sitting down here all night long just staring at that thing?' Sprague asked.

'A few minutes longer, that's all.'

Herman walked with Sprague back to the foot of the stairs, lighting their way with the lantern until Franklin complained of being left alone in the darkness and Herman went back to him. They listened to Sprague climb out of the basement and make his way back up through the building, his slight footfall fading rapidly along the boards.

'I've been thinkin,' Franklin said, happy to concede part of his argument now that it had all turned out so amicably. 'This notion about the monkeys. Does that mean that some of us are descended more from, say, gorillas, while other folk might have more in common with the chimps and their kin?'

Unconvinced, Herman said, 'It might do.'

'It'd make more sense.'

'I think the real idea is that we might even be descended from something way back even before the monkeys, that they themselves might once have been something else.'

'Such as?' Franklin said, unprepared for this sudden twist in the argument.

'I don't know,' Herman said, unable to bring himself to suggest to Franklin that he might in fact be descended from a fish, which in time had learned to walk on the land, swing from trees, dress itself and then go on to steal kisses from pretty girls at county hog shows.

'I believe one thing,' Franklin said, motioning towards the aquarium. 'I believe you're right about that critter knowin' what we're up to. It hasn't taken its eyes off us for the past ten minutes. Think it's just waitin' to evolute itself and leap out and join us?'

The hippopotamus, still recovering from its journey, sank to the floor of its tank, where it took several paces forward, turned awkwardly and made the same progress in the opposite direction.

'It's lookin' to curl up some place and go to sleep,' Franklin said.

The animal, having exhausted the few possibilities of its new home, lifted one foot and then another and slowly rose, pausing midway to the surface to look back out at them, its shadow drawing a curtain on the room around them, its bubbles moving like small disembodied flames across the ceiling. It opened its mouth to reveal an expanse of flabby gum and rounded, yellowing teeth.

'It's weary,' Franklin said, watching it closely. 'Probably too weary to even know what evolutin's all about.'

'Probably,' Herman said, moving to the exit and waiting for his friend to join him.

A WEEK LATER a small crowd gathered in Zip's room with the intention of forming a delegation of their own to visit Barnum. Their demands were to be for more money for those of them who were the least well paid, improved working conditions for all of them – although few had any real idea of what these were to be or how they were going to demand them – and the closure of the Museum at eleven rather than midnight, giving the occupants more time in which to relax and socialize with each other. The extent of such socializing as already took place had been unforeseen by Barnum upon deciding to use the Museum as both exhibition space and living quarters for the more profitable of his performers, and it had surprised him to see how many deep and lasting friendships had been struck up – friendships which, he had been convinced from the start, would in time, like the world at large, only serve to conspire against him.

The idea to make such a representation to him had been growing over the previous months, and following Greenwood and Henry Butler's recent approach, the time was now considered ripe for making another, the assumption being that Barnum might respond magnanimously in his victory. Not everyone was fully convinced of this, but the need to present a united front, they knew, was greater than their more realistic individual concerns.

Zip read out their three major aims to everyone present, soliciting a murmur of assent. Tom applauded, and hearing this, Apollo rose to his hindlegs and walked among them barking.

Herman shouted, 'Bravo!' and Isaac Sprague, prompted by Bella-Grace, said, 'Hear hear!'

'Where?' Tom asked him.

'Here,' said Franklin.

At Sprague's voice, however, several heads turned in surprise.

'We've as much right as anybody to go along,' Bella-Grace said quickly, preparing her husband's defence before he was even aware of the attack upon him. 'We might not have been back long, but we've as much right as that blind fool or that stupid pig.'

By the door, Byron grunted and strained at the leash held by Vivalla.

'He understands every word,' Vivalla warned Bella-Grace.

Bella-Grace turned her back on him and folded her arms across her chest, the gesture indicating to them all that she was adamant and immovable, characteristics which all those who had known her previously immediately recognized.

In view of her husband's slight appearance, Bella-Grace had created within herself the strength to protect them both, and this strength, allied to her growing sense of injustice and persecution in the travelling shows, had doubled and then doubled again, until now she found something either suspect or offensive in almost everything that was said to her. In addition to which, she certainly wasn't going to put herself or Isaac second behind a fancy-dressed pig or card-playing dog.

Zip called for silence and everyone turned to face him, except Tom, who concentrated on searching his pockets.

Originally, it had been thought that a single spokesman would best suit their purpose, the men electing Zip, the women Anna. Then it was agreed that the pair of them approaching Barnum together might better serve their collective needs. Then this show of strength was improved upon by the addition of Elizabeth and Captain Bates. The selection should have stopped there, but didn't, and Bella-Grace, upon securing herself a place on the side of the women, then insisted that Isaac should be included with the men. Seeing the unfairness of this, Zip invited Fortuna and René to join them, which they both did. Tom, Franklin and Herman were happy not to become so directly involved, but then the point was raised that if so many of the others were going, then all of them should attend. Herman and Franklin acquiesced and Tom announced that he would be happy to fall in with popular opinion.

'I'll stay behind with the animals,' Vivalla volunteered, seeing how the inclusion of a dog and a pig in the bargaining party might weaken their cause.

'And I say they come along,' Bella-Grace insisted, much to the embarrassment of her husband. 'Nothing like having one of them two critters getting set to mess on his nice clean rug for getting Barnum to make up his mind in a hurry.'

Zip conferred with Anna Swan, and seeing how much time had already been lost, she agreed to the inclusion of the two animals.

'How about these two?' Elizabeth asked, drawing the Aztec children out from behind her skirts.

'We certainly don't want them along,' Bella-Grace said contemptuously. 'They don't barely work a full day between them as it is. Give them an extra dollar and they'll most likely think it's a plaything.'

'They're still entitled,' Herman said.

'Who asked you, sonny?'

Herman took a step backwards and stood beside Franklin, who moved forward ready to protect him.

'So we're decided,' Zip announced, tightening the drawstring on the meeting. 'We *all* go.' He repeated again their aims, ensuring everyone understood what they were about to attempt to do.

'Hallelujah!' Tom shouted, finally pulling a small bottle from his vest pocket.

Then they left the room and marched in a parade, two abreast, along the corridor to Barnum's sanctuary. They believed he had no idea of their plotting, but he had in fact been aware for several weeks beforehand of their growing unrest and the likelihood of such an approach being made to him.

It was not yet six-thirty in the morning and the early sunlight fell in a dusty column through the window at the end of the corridor along which the delegation marched. Within it, like a statue in a temple, stood Hackaliah Cherry, propped on his broom and holding his face to the meagre warmth. At the sound of their approach he quickly began to sweep, but then seeing who it was, equally quickly stopped.

'Sainted Matagumi,' he said. 'Y'all gettin' set to march on Atlanta?'

Zip waved for him to keep his voice down. They paused at the door leading to Greenwood and Henry Butler's outer office, beyond which lay Barnum's own. Elizabeth explained to Cherry what they were about to attempt.

Cherry laughed. 'Stand more chance of finding a fifty-dollar note,' he said. He felt certain that such a note existed, somewhere.

'Ignore him,' Bella-Grace shouted.

'Says who?' Cherry retorted, rising to his toes to see who had called out. 'That the skinny feller's trouble-makin' wife back again?'

Bella-Grace pushed through the ranks to confront him, and as she approached, Cherry's resolve deserted him and he held out his broom as though a bayonet were attached to it.

Anna and Captain Bates stopped the fight before it began, both uncomfortable in the low space.

'Well, *he* ain't included,' Bella-Grace insisted as she let herself be led back to Isaac.

'Suits me,' Cherry said, regaining his bravery as soon as she was out of reach.

Franklin and Herman began telling him in greater detail about what they hoped to achieve and he wished them luck, again declining to join them, the terms of his employment at the Museum being different to theirs.

Fortuna and René approached Zip, and René said anxiously that they ought to enter and begin. At seven Barnum was likely to lose what little patience he still possessed if the doors to the Museum were opened and none of them were in position.

Zip called for silence, and when they were all again paired up, Vivalla at the rear, clutching the reins of the straining animals like a charioteer, he knocked on the outer office door. There was no answer, but this had been anticipated. Henry Butler had been absent the previous day attending to his sick wife and was not expected to return for several days yet. And Greenwood had spent most of the night away from the Museum at the telegraph office negotiating with the British Government for the purchase of Shakespeare's cottage, which Barnum had discovered in a state of shameful dereliction during his last visit to England. It was his intention to transport and reconstruct this inside the empty arcade adjacent to the Museum.

It was for news of his success in this venture that Barnum was at that very moment waiting behind the second set of closed doors.

Zip and Elizabeth led the way into the outer office. Hackaliah Cherry saluted everyone as they passed him, his broom at his shoulder, until Apollo snapped at his shins and he withdrew into the sunlight from which he had emerged.

There were problems getting Franklin through the door, which was far too narrow for his bulk, and Herman and René were forced to knead his stomach around the frame until he was able, exhausted and perspiring, to pass through. Bella-Grace made a remark about a camel and the eye of a needle before Zip once again waved them all to silence. Casting a final unhappy glance over his ill-assorted troops, he knocked on the door of Barnum's office.

Immediately Barnum swung it open to confront them, and with dismay Zip and Elizabeth saw that he was prepared for them.

The inner office was warmer than the one in which they were gathered, and tinted by the pall of cigar smoke which coloured its lush gold and maroon furnishings.

Seeing his portrait of the Barnum family, René covered his eyes and groaned and Fortuna slipped her arm around his shoulders. In her beard she had tied a delicate bow, and this pleased him, providing him with something upon which to focus as the bargaining with Barnum began.

'We've come to seek an audience with you,' Zip began hesitantly, his confidence increasing as Barnum looked over his shoulder at the others gathered behind him.

'What – all of you?'

'All of us.'

'It's mutiny,' Barnum said softly.

Anna Swan and Captain Bates entered the room and stood like pillars on either side of Zip and Elizabeth. Unlike most of the rest of the building, the proportions of Barnum's office suited them perfectly and they were able to stand upright and even stretch their arms above their heads, the draped and tasselled ceiling still at least four feet above them. Bartola and Maximo motioned to be lifted up so that they might play with the tassels, and Barnum watched anxiously as Bates lifted them up on to his shoulders.

'Tell him,' Bella-Grace shouted to Zip from the rear of the delegation.

Alone, and feeling himself surrounded, Barnum called back, 'Always a pleasure and a delight to have you back among us, Bella-Grace. Your appeal, to *me* at least, is scarcely diminished. I only wish I could somehow convey it to my customers.'

Everyone was forced forward by the arrival of Franklin at the second doorway. This one too presented him with difficulties, and rather than exhaust himself again by attempting to negotiate it, he volunteered to remain in the outer office. Herman offered to keep him company, but Franklin told him to go in with the others, and was joined instead by Vivalla, Byron and Apollo.

Waiting for silence, Zip announced their demands to Barnum. After each, the other members of the delegation nodded in assent with varying degrees of conviction.

Stepping forward, Captain Bates said, 'We believe they're fair and reasonable and that no one will lose by them.'

'*Me*, I'll lose by them,' Barnum said. 'More money, fewer hours. It's unheard of! And as for improved working conditions, what can you mean? I pay you all a prince's ransom to sit around all day in comfortable surroundings. You're not coalminers, you're not stone-masons, you're not cotton-pickers or railroad workers.'

'We know what we're *not*, we know that all right,' Herman answered, surprised by his audacity, and afterwards proud of it.

'I certainly ain't no coalminer, no sir,' Tom shouted. 'No stone-mason, neither.'

'What we want –' Bella Grace began, losing patience with the way things were progressing.

'Ah!' said Barnum, dropping into his padded seat. 'Want, want, want. The clarion call of the century. You want, I want, we all want.'

'What you want that you ain't already got?' Tom asked him, causing the others to turn and look at him. 'No offence,' he added.

Barnum, having quickly assessed the delegation's weaknesses, began to probe. 'You name it, Tom. Whatever you want, you just name it and I'll do my best to get it for you. Don't stop to take into account any selfless charity on my part in picking you up out of the gutter, giving you a home and declaring your genius to the world, don't stop to let any of that worry you. You demand away. I'm a reasonable man, I'm listening. Don't stop to consider that I've got an erratic heart and a sickly wife whose bedside I've attended every hour of this very night, don't stop to consider any of that. Not to mention a barrelful of debts that would drown any other honest man, and a daughter getting set to bust me ten times over with the biggest mismatched wedding of the decade. No, sir – you just go right ahead and tell me what it is you want.' Barnum sagged where he sat, forcing a cough and then prolonging it by slapping his chest. 'My only hope is that you all find someone as kind-hearted and charitable to take care of you when I'm –' he glanced upwards '– dead and gone, buried and forgotten. Play me something sweet at the burial service, Tom. Promise me that much, at least. Don't *you* give me cause to have to constantly glance over my shoulder, don't you give me cause as I stagger and sink to my knees to have to look up into those kindly and understanding eyes and say, "Et tu, Tom?" Dear Tom, old friend.'

There was a silence. Barnum held his hand over his heart.

'Ate two what?' Tom said.

'Eating?' Franklin called in from outside.

Glancing angrily at the doorway, Barnum went on: 'If I've got any money that isn't already owed, then it's yours. Take it, take it. Relieve me of the burden.' He emptied his pockets of the few small coins they contained. 'Take it all. Only leave me sufficient to scrape by on. Leave me enough for Charity's medicines so that I might ease her passing as she makes way for my own sweet journey to that Promised Land. Leave me that much, at least.'

Unconvinced and unmoved by this act, Elizabeth stepped forward and asked him about the eleven o'clock closedown.

'Might as well close down for good,' Barnum told her. 'Put up the shutters and lock me inside. Let the creditors prowl around the place howling like wolves.' But upon this point he had underestimated their determination, and none of them were to be moved. Of the three demands, they all knew it was the only one in which they were likely to be even partially successful, and now, realizing that the others were unlikely to be met, a new determination grew and they refused to be talked away from the point.

'I wonder,' Barnum said. 'Does any of you truly understand the cost of running a place like this, the cost of constantly seeking out and putting before the public new attractions? Why . . .' He paused and brought a look of surprise on to his face. 'Why, only last week I was negotiating with a Maryland farmer for the trunk of the very cherry tree George Washington himself chopped down.'

'That'd be the one Joice Heth was hiding up before you snatched her down from the branches and started coaching her,' Zip said, which gave rise to a ripple of laughter.

Undeterred, Barnum continued: 'And today, now, this very hour, am I not embarked upon the most delicate and costly negotiations to bring William Shakespeare's – *the* William Shakespeare's – very own cottage to this country so that my fellow-Americans might be spared the great expense I personally have endured in paying my homage at that shrine of literary excellence?'

'William who?' Tom said from the rear.

'Shakespeare, Tom,' Barnum called to him, adamant now that the discussion should follow the tracks he was laying down for it. 'A masterpiece of Plantagenet design and construction, every brick, every timber, every mote of dust and piece of thatch imbued and alive with the genius it once sheltered. And shall I tell you how little Shakespeare's own countrymen think of him?' No one responded to this, but he went on nevertheless. 'A butcher's shop, that's what – they'd let the place be turned into a butcher's shop selling offal. That's what.'

It had already become clear to Barnum from Greenwood's pro-longed silence at the telegraph office that his bid for the building had been unsuccessful. The cherry tree too was likely to come to nothing. A tree which had been felled by the young George Washington should by now have been exhibiting at least the first signs of rot and decay, whereas the trunk he had been offered looked about to burst into bloom. Two years earlier he had equally unsuccessfully bid 2,500 dollars for the oak at Newstead, upon which the poet Byron had carved his name and to which he later dedicated a poem, and all this now weighed heavily upon his mind as he faced his small crowd of dissenting exhibitors.

'Ah, Madame Fortuna, Joséphine.' He held out his arms.

Fortuna and René made their way reluctantly to the front, where René could no longer shield his gaze from the portrait.

'Mes amis,' Barnum said, now with a note of sadness in his voice.

René could not bring himself to speak. There was not a single feature or ornament in the room which appealed to him. Every inch of straightforward design or plain colour, it seemed to him, had been embellished upon by embroidery or painted pattern. This diversity of brashness and conflicting tones made him almost dizzy and he stead-ied himself against Barnum's desk. Solicitously, Barnum offered him a seat, which he accepted. Fortuna stood beside him, ready to defend him if anyone accused him of defecting so readily to the enemy camp. The bow in her beard touched his ear.

'An hour at the end of the day would be appreciated,' she said.

That, in essence, was the crux and force of their argument, beside which all else had become merely a confusion of the issue.

'One hour,' Anna Swan echoed.

Prompted by Zip, Elizabeth moved to stand beside Barnum, and with her hand resting on his shoulder, she too said, 'One hour.'

Barnum wiped his brow, considering the request as though it were a demand made upon the last hour of a dying man, casting himself in the lead role of the tragedy.

'We ladies of the house need our beauty sleep,' Bella-Grace Sprague shouted, sensing along with the rest of them that he was preparing to refuse them in all three of their demands.

Franklin appeared in the doorway and called in to ask how the negotiations were progressing.

'I'll throw in an extra turnip for the pig and a bone for the dog,' Barnum said. Around him, several clocks chimed the quarter hour, rising to a crescendo of bells and then one by one drawing out the passage of time until all were once again quiet. In this new silence, Barnum declared that they had reached an impasse, that he was sympathetic to their aims but that he did not see how he could help them without suffering himself.

'I could economize,' he said. 'In this city of growth and plenty and opportunity I could start saving nickels and dimes. I could turn the Albinos out on to the streets and save money in that way.' The Albinos' absence had provided him with this small advantage, as had his knowledge that they were liked better by most of the others than either Sprague or his wife. 'I'm the last man in the world to attract your attention to your contracts in a friendly discussion such as this – contracts you yourselves have read and signed – but if you force my hand, then you leave me with –'

'I ain't signed no contract,' Tom announced proudly.

Barnum quickly slid open a drawer.

'Beg to differ, Tom. I got a cross here says you did. It may be a bit of a shaky cross, but a cross it certainly is.'

'I don't remember signing no cross,' Tom said.

Barnum held up the contract for Anna Swan and Captain Bates to see.

'It's your contract, Tom,' Anna told him.

Tom, seemingly more pleased than disappointed at the revelation, again pulled the bottle from his pocket and drank from it. 'Glory be,' he said. 'I wrote my own cross.'

The delegation, it was now clear, had failed, and Herman left the room to pass on to Franklin everything that had happened.

René rose unsteadily and Barnum remarked to him how proud he felt every time he looked at the painting hanging above them; proud too to have an artist of René's stature and calibre living among them. He said he was thinking of having more portraits painted, of his daughters separately; he felt that their individual virtues and qualities had been somehow dissipated and lost in the group sitting in which those qualities and virtues had vied with one another for space on the canvas. Didn't René agree? René held a hand to his brow and allowed Fortuna to lead him back into the centre of the group.

'Was there anything else you wished to raise with me?' Barnum asked. 'I'm a busy man, but I've always got time to listen to my friends. Well?'

Everyone exchanged uneasy glances, and one by one they shook their heads. Fortuna and René left the room, followed by the others until only Zip and Anna Swan remained.

135

Waiting until the outer office was empty, Barnum said to them, 'What did you expect?'

'Thumb clicked his fingers and you jumped,' Zip said.

'That was Thumb. There isn't one of you that can command even a tiny per cent of his commercial attraction.' There was now something hard and gloating in his voice. 'Is that what you wanted me to tell *them*? Do you think my creditors wouldn't be up in arms against me if they thought for one moment that I was slacking off, that they weren't going to be paid? You, Anna – am I genuinely the heartless rogue you want them all to see me as?'

Anna shook her head, angry with herself at even that slight capitulation.

Zip took her hand and led her out of the room. Closing the door, they stood together for a moment in silence before passing through the outer office to the corridor where the others were waiting.

Hackaliah Cherry reappeared and stood with them.

'Fat lot of good you two were,' Bella-Grace shouted as Zip and Anna came out.

'They did their best,' Herman said.

'Closing on seven o'clock,' Cherry announced. 'Better get on out to your booths before they open the doors. Queue's down to Murray Street already.'

They all regarded him with an air of weary resignation. Zip asked him to leave and Cherry said he'd be happy to, that he couldn't understand how so many people could be so miserable over such a little thing as an hour.

'I signed my own contract, Hack,' Tom told him proudly, holding Cherry's arm and allowing himself to be led to his piano down in the entrance hall, where he played for the first hour of every day before moving to another of his instruments elsewhere in the Museum.

Then Fortuna and René left without speaking, proposing to visit the Albinos before Fortuna prepared herself for her booth. René asked her to take out the ribbon from her beard and she gave it to him for safe-keeping, watching as he kissed it before tucking it into his pocket.

Elizabeth led the Aztec children away, neither of them aware of the attempt which had been made and lost, content solely to remain within their own small world in which one was never out of sight of the other.

'We were never going to do much more than make him aware of how we felt,' Anna said to Zip in an effort to console him.

'She's right,' Bates added.

Zip slid his feet into his monkey suit, which he had brought with him and left in the outer office. 'Then why didn't you say so before we made such fools of ourselves in front of him?' he asked them. Neither had an answer for him.

'Still, it's good news about Tom discovering he can write his name,' Franklin said, having misinterpreted Herman's telling of the discovery.

Pulling the black hairy pants to his waist, Zip began to howl and to beat violently upon his chest.

THE FOLLOWING FEW weeks were not a good time for anyone in the Museum, owner, managers and occupants alike. The full heat of an early summer arrived, and with it the fetid smells off the rivers worked their way inland and up every drain, along every thoroughfare and down every dismal alleyway. In the poorly ventilated Museum, the higher one went the higher the temperature rose, and people were inclined to seek their pleasures outdoors, along the fresher shoreline of the Battery or further north, around Madison Square and in the open spaces of the Park.

It was the same every summer, and there was little even Barnum could do to make up for the consequent loss in trade. In previous years, a younger man with a younger man's energy, he had packed his bags, chosen his exhibits and toured Europe with them, returning in the late summer or fall when the sharper winds of the coming winter had cleared the city of its disease-ridden vapours. This year, however, there was to be no tour. Tours were always a speculative gamble, which might lose a fortune just as easily as make one, and Barnum now had too many creditors insisting to the courts that such a gamble should not be allowed to take place at their expense. This grieved and annoyed him. In the past, his European ventures had proved momentous and celebratory occasions, and he had been praised and fêted wherever he went, establishing his name in the minds of millions. But that had been back in the days of Thumb, the Siamese Twins and Jenny Lind. What did he currently possess to compete with any of these?

Alone now at his desk with only his memories, he raised his fists and banged them down. Opposite him, the mechanical cobra quivered in its coils, and he waited for it to become still again before rising and pacing the room. He was still not yet entirely convinced that the mechanism which drove life into those coils would not somehow secretly activate the serpent when no one was present and that one morning he would arrive at his office to find it moving towards him across the floor; or, worse still, that he would sit at his desk only to see its eyes and tongue flicker into life and then watch helplessly as it rose to strike at him where he sat.

Dismissing these thoughts from his mind, he continued to pace the floor.

Open on his desk lay the *New York Eagle*, in which was a report of the death of General John Sedgewick, killed in May at the battle of Spotsylvania. Sedgewick's last words, the paper announced, were uttered upon his sighting of the Confederate artillery at a considerable distance from his own troops. Upon lowering his eye-glass he was heard to say, 'Why, they couldn't hit one of Barnum's elephants at this dist–' whereupon a ball from one of the distant canons exploded beneath him and his horse, scattering both in several directions at once. It was the only kind of publicity Barnum decided he could do without. He admitted that there was a touch of ironic humour in the report, but it was also the joke of a tragedy, a species of joke with which he himself had become only too familiar. There hadn't been an elephant in the Museum for the previous six months – something he hoped to remedy in the very near future. The creatures invariably proved to be an expensive investment and were costly to keep, but the public still enjoyed seeing them and returned to the Museum in their thousands whenever one was present.

'Poor John Sedgewick,' he said, picking up the *Eagle* and studying the photograph of the man's face. 'Is this how history will remember him, scorning the skill of a Confederate gunner before that sharp-shooter had the opportunity to wipe my name from his lips?'

He returned to his chair and read the report of the battle in full. Accompanying it was one of Matthew Brady's photographs of the scattered Confederate dead pictorially rearranged for his public. But he found himself unable to concentrate on the tightly packed print, reflecting instead upon the events of the past few weeks within the Museum and their consequences for its future.

The demands made by the delegation had angered him in ways few of those present could have guessed. He could have quite easily met their requests throughout the slack summer months, and by doing so might perhaps have recouped something from them in the fall when trade once again improved, but doing this at their insistence rather than at his own suggestion would have felt too much like backing down in the face of their assault. First the Redskins, now this.

During previous summers, even without his foreign tours, he would normally have stopped away from the Museum for long periods, either in his city house close to Washington Square, or further out still in his new Bridgeport home with Charity and his daughters.

It had been seven years since the loss of his beloved 'Iranistan', and although he now played down its underinsured destruction in the face of his creditors and business acquaintances, he still mourned and regretted its loss, and seldom more so than when he found himself trapped in the stifling heat of Manhattan, growing ever more crowded and uncomfortable as the immigrants continued to pour ashore and linger, sometimes for ever, before their dispersal to those parts of the country which might actually benefit by their presence.

Today, other than make his arrival known, he had done nothing, and he was considering how best to go on doing this, when he was startled by the sudden movement above him of the newly installed fan, erected by Henry Butler and operated from the same steam engine which drove the air and clean water through the aquarium. Its broad blades turned in a slow circle, barely stirring the air it seemed to him, but creating a sufficiently refreshing downdraught for him to tilt himself back in his seat and face up into it.

Henry Butler had erected several other fans above the ground-floor booths, and a larger model above the notice boldly proclaiming their efficacy and the fact that they were there solely to increase the comfort of the Museum's customers, and at no extra cost other than to Barnum himself. Henry Butler referred to the process as 'air manipulation', but Barnum felt this description unequal to the devices and came up with several phrases of his own. He had little idea of how the connection between the basement engine and his own fan had been made and he made no attempt to find out. Sitting back, he stared up at the wavering movement of the blades and let the refreshing breeze play upon his face.

In previous years he had been forced almost daily to buy ice from the Cutter Street ice men in order to preserve the more perishable of his exhibits, and each day an hour or so of his time had been taken up in arguing the price with them and then deducting the percentage of this which had turned to water and drained away while these negotiations were taking place. The recollection of these confrontations amused him and he smiled at the memory, before being brought abruptly back to the present by a sudden rattling noise as the blades above him spun slowly to a halt.

They'd known about the decrease in the trade during the summer months, they must have done. Otherwise why approach him then, rather than sooner or later? And why so soon after Greenwood and Henry Butler? The possibility of revenge upon them had afterwards come from Greenwood, who suggested that if Barnum were to reduce the price of admission for the final hour of the day then he would also increase the number of customers during that last hour, especially as there were many people wandering out of the taverns and eating houses at that time. And if the demand were seen to increase then there could be no question of the Museum closing an hour earlier than its usual time of midnight. There might be some problems relating to the likelihood of intoxication among these new customers, but Greenwood was sure this could be dealt with if and when it arose. Henry Butler was less enthusiastic about the scheme, but kept his thoughts to himself, choosing instead to warn Zip and Elizabeth of the plan now under consideration. It was his belief, Greenwood told Barnum when they were alone, that everything that passed between him and his managers was also related to the others. Henry Butler was aware of their suspicions and was in turn careful not to antagonize them and thus jeopardize even further his own position in the Museum. The fact was, he had worries of his own outside the place. His wife Delilah had recently suffered yet another relapse, her condition made worse by the rising heat and the claustrophobic circumstances under which she attempted to convalesce, and which, despite all her husband's pleading, she refused to leave in search of a healthier environment for the summer. Henry Butler calculated that she hadn't been outside in the fresh air for almost nine months, and recently, every moment his attention had not been in demand somewhere in the Museum, his thoughts had turned back to her and to the succession of poorly-qualified and inept nurses she insisted on employing to sit with her and take care of her in the belief that their meagre knowledge of her condition – upon which no two medical opinions had so far agreed – would somehow help her to improve.

By comparison with many in the city, Henry Butler was not a poor man, but equally he never seemed to have the money necessary to make any of the improvements to their lives he had long since planned. A great deal of what he earned was spent on the useless medicines and 'cures', and upon the succession of medical opinions – however hopeful or otherwise – Delilah appeared to need simply to survive in her weakened condition. 'I cling to life,' she frequently told him, 'I cling' – making it patently clear to him that the physicians and nurses, and not he, knew what was best for her. His contribution consisted solely of paying for all these dubious services – not one cent of which he had ever denied her or truly regretted. He loved Delilah, he had always loved her, he always would, and he had long since acquiesced in her belief that a single harsh word from him might have the power to kill her where she lay.

Greenwood, too, was growing increasingly restless with the rising heat, still angry, a month after the event, at his failure to wrest the lease of the Museum from Barnum and steer it along a more profitable course. He considered the place now to be rudderless, drifting with the tides of fickle public opinion, whim and fancy towards the rocks of that same public's capriciousness and, eventually, its disgust. It seemed to him as though a cycle of decline had begun, moving slowly now, but one which would surely gather speed and momentum as it continued, as destructive and relentless as a whirlpool, towards its conclusion. When he had mentioned this to Barnum, Barnum had responded by announcing that he was going to invite Thumb and Lavinia to return to the Museum for a short stay, and that if they accepted his proposition then he was prepared to share the profits with them. Greenwood knew immediately that the scheme was doomed to failure; public interest in Thumb and all Barnum's other midgets was no longer what it had been in the past, and Barnum, he knew, was still blinkered by the success Thumb had once been and the fortunes they had both once made together. He even suspected that Thumb himself, despite his own craving for attention, was also aware of this fact.

Thumb had grown fat and irascible, and Lavinia complained at everything she saw and was asked to do. Greenwood tried to explain all this, but Barnum refused to listen. Then Barnum revealed that he had also written to Chang and Eng, the Siamese Twins, offering them a similar contract. This Greenwood considered to be a more profitable proposition, but upon hearing that the twins and their families would expect to be accommodated at Barnum's expense, he began to despair at this scheme too. When he let his feelings be known, Barnum turned on him, and jabbing him in the chest told him he knew what he could do if he was no longer happy with his position in the Museum. Barnum still blamed him for not having acquired Shakespeare's cottage, and told him so to his face for the first time. The fact was, there had been an outcry in England and a public subscription had been raised to save the building. Barnum had known this was likely to happen, but this in no way defused the violence of his attack upon his manager.

In addition to all this, external pressures had also recently been brought to bear on the Museum. The Vauxhall Gardens were now seldom without a competing attraction of a 'higher cultural nature'; shows and exhibitions were being staged at the Bowery Amphitheatre, at Madison Square, the Concert Hall, the Lyceum Gallery and even the Mechanics' Institute, all of them within brisk walking distance of the Museum; and now, in the warmer weather, the fashion was growing for entire families to travel to the Coney Island bathing resort, where they sat in the sand or stood in the water. Barnum could not imagine how anyone could possibly enjoy such an experience: the water carried disease, and drowned people; ships sailed upon it in which people also suffered; it was the home of sharks, giant octopuses and other unimaginable horrors, the sole aim of which was to terrify; and the beach itself was composed almost entirely of sand, the most irritable substance known to man. Admittedly, the sea might have been invigorating, but what real consolation was that when all these other discomforts were so obviously present?

Recently, new calcium floodlights had been erected around the Museum's upper balconies in the hope that their brilliance would draw back the crowds as effectively as they drew their own swirling galaxies of moths and other insects each evening. In addition, trade improved slightly as a result of the reduction in the entrance fee at the otherwise slow times of the day. This, however, also led to the problem of congestion, which Barnum overcame by the addition of a second exit leading out on to Ann Street. The expense of this annoyed him, until he had the idea of posting signs along each of the galleries encouraging his customers to 'Visit the New Egress', to which the inquisitive crowds flocked in long, hopeful lines. The joke, although earning him little, pleased Barnum, and unexpectedly revealed to him something of the man he had once been a quarter of a century ago, when his reputation as a hoaxer was still in its infancy. In many respects, it was still no real failing or disappointment to become the victim of one of Barnum's jokes.

On another occasion he had hired a vagrant at a dollar a day to walk along Broadway and Church Street depositing bricks from a trolley he pulled at regular intervals along the sidewalk, under strict instructions to speak to no one who asked him what he was doing. Inevitably, he attracted a large crowd, which followed his trail right into the entrance of the Museum, where Barnum was waiting to greet them and hand out free additional tickets to the first fifty people willing to pay and enter.

When he'd first brought the largely unknown Jenny Lind to America, he'd had the idea of auctioning the tickets for her first show, thereby creating an inquisitiveness and then a demand to see her. The highest bidder for the very first ticket had been a neighbour of the Museum's, John Genin, a hatmaker, who had paid the unbelievable sum of two hundred and twenty-five dollars. Secretly, Barnum had encouraged him to bid way beyond his means with the promise of the increased business the publicity would bring him. Reluctantly, Genin had agreed, and in the year following his purchase he had sold ten thousand hats and retired shortly afterwards a popular and wealthy man.

All of this Barnum remembered as he stared up at the now motionless fan. By comparison, the present disappointed him, offered him no real challenge; the simple truth, he believed, was that he had done everything there was to do, seen everything there was to see. No one believed in mermaids any longer, let alone the creatures he had once professed to have seen grazing across the pastures of the moon through a powerful telescope (and for which the Ladies' Missionary Society had immediately offered him funds to lecture upon). No – the present was a great flat empty stage, upon which the actors were growing tired and jaded, their lines regurgitated with a stale and predictable dullness. Not only this, but he was still appearing monthly in the courts to account for his financial dealings, and his creditors still gathered around him with their mixed expressions of resignation and hope depending upon how long they had been waiting for their money and how soon they expected to receive it.

There was a similar air of restlessness evident elsewhere in the Museum, too. In the days since their failed delegation the other inhabitants had felt aggrieved and uncertain, aware only that nothing had been achieved by the confrontation and that they might even have lost something by it, having made what they believed to have been their strongest gambit only to have it dismissed out of hand. Some took the defeat harder than others.

Zip, in particular, refused to be placated for days afterwards, despite the constant reassurances of Anna Swan and Captain Bates that the effort had been worthwhile. Elizabeth, too, had grown quickly disillusioned at her realization of Barnum's power over them all. She began to spend more time with Fortuna and René, who, after weeks of pleading with her, was finally given permission to paint her portrait, promising her that it would be the greatest achievement of his career.

Fortuna was happy with the arrangement, and the two women spent most of their free time together as René made his preparatory sketches, working painstakingly and lovingly over every detail, constantly surprising and amusing them with the virtues he found to extol in every feature. The walls of their rooms were covered with the drawings and paintings he had done of Fortuna, some dating back to the time he had met her in France, her figure as slim as a girl's, and then becoming shapely as she grew older. Her beard too had changed – from the feathery lightness of the early portraits to the full black mass of the present. It was a relief to Fortuna – but one she kept strictly to herself – for René to have found someone else upon whom to devote his attentions, which at times became unwelcomely overpowering, despite her unwavering love for him and respect for his ambitions. The three of them spoke frequently of their pasts and of what they hoped for the future. It was common enough talk in the Museum, a waking dream almost, and one over which the shadow of reality was seldom ever knowingly cast.

Of them all, Bella-Grace Sprague was the most vocal in her condemnation of their collective failure, her anger rising in direct proportion to the number of times she sat down and thought about what had happened and the number of times her husband pleaded with her to forget it. He alone was aware of the precariousness of their present position in the Museum. Bella-Grace's fury was not helped by the installation of the new lighting, which shone glaringly into their own quarters, and which was not extinguished until the early hours of each morning.

Herman and Franklin had resigned themselves to the failure even as it happened, and now considered it their duty to lighten the load of the others by avoiding any mention of it. Depending upon their mood, those others either appreciated or resented this. Herman and Franklin became firm friends, and following negotiations with Greenwood, occupied adjoining booths, from where they could call to each other round their drapes.

Zip dwelt the longest over their failure, blaming himself for the wavering and indecision which he believed had lost them their advantage. It would be months, if not years, before another such attempt might be made, and for a week afterwards he was inconsolable and avoided all company. Later, he returned to them and they accepted his apologies for his behaviour.

'What if we were just to get up and walk out,' he said once

to Elizabeth, Anna and Bates, not entirely serious, but needing to hear their response. All three of them knew the answer, but no one spoke. Their reckoning might have differed, but the end result of it all could only ever be the same, and none of them was prepared to appear brave simply for the sake of satisfying a need in the others. 'Precisely,' Zip had said. 'Like runaway slaves.' Upon which Anna had criticized him for being so insensitive. Zip apologized again.

They had afterwards been joined by the Albinos, who had heard of the failure of the delegation and who had come to offer their sympathies as a means of introducing themselves to those who they didn't already know.

They were not a true family, but rather a collection of albino negroes who had met at country shows and who had come together into a single group. Two of them, the 'father' and eldest 'daughter' had been exhibited at the Museum before, and it was through them that Barnum had now secured the services of them all.

The war had revived interest in the Albinos and many questions were asked concerning the contradiction inherent in their negroid features and white skin. They were considered to be much weaker physically than true negroes, and dangerously susceptible to every illness and disease, and it was for this reason that they seldom exerted themselves or ventured out of the Museum into the humid city beyond. Barnum had arranged for politicians, theologians and other learned men to visit them at his expense in the hope that their informed debate on the Albinos would appear in the newspapers and other journals and thus stimulate further interest in them.

Within the Museum, Hackaliah Cherry was their severest critic, always unhappy at their approach, and convinced that they had in some way deliberately deceived and then betrayed their race. 'They jumped the gun,' he said accusingly, referring to the equality he believed all negroes were shortly to be offered. He declared himself repulsed by their pink eyes, their white hair, their watery, almost colourless lips, and by the listless way in which they moved from one part of the building to another.

Tom, however, befriended them, and they frequently gathered around him at the piano to sing with him. They were all blessed with good singing voices, and when they stood together to perform they worked in perfect harmony, providing the Museum with an additional attraction. It was the belief of some visitors that all negroes would, through each successive generation, gradually lighten and turn white, and here, for some, was the evidence that this was already happening.

The Albinos were intelligent and considerate, and because they knew as little about the reasons for their condition as anyone else, they seldom disagreed with any of the imperfect suggestions put forward, no matter how ridiculous they might appear to anyone else. They had been together long enough now as a 'family' to function as one and to protect each other from their harsher critics or accusers.

Barnum was as pleased with them as he was displeased with Isaac Sprague and his wife. The public found little to marvel at in the fifty-two-pound man, and seeing their lack of interest, Bella-Grace had taken it upon herself to accompany Isaac into his booth and harangue them for being uncaring and insensitive. Unaccustomed to being spoken back to in this manner, the crowds had walked quickly past in search of something less offensive. When this was brought to the attention of Barnum, he insisted that Bella-Grace remain with her children in their quarters while her husband was on duty. Isaac hid his relief at this, but Bella-Grace would not submit without a fight, eventually driving Barnum to the point where he held out her husband's contract and threatened to tear it in half. Only then did she turn back and stamp away from him, her loud mutterings of discontent audible long after she had gone from sight. Barnum told Isaac that he understood his predicament, but at the same time made it perfectly clear to him that he would tolerate no further disturbance from Bella-Grace. Isaac guaranteed it, and afterwards waited anxiously for the first sign of her return.

His predicament was the predicament of them all in those warm, fermenting months of early summer, but if Barnum, sitting beneath the motionless fan and contemplating the fangs of his mechanical cobra, believed he had overcome the greatest of his own problems, then he was sadly mistaken and was soon to be severely disabused of any such notion.

14

THE FIRST INDICATION that Barnum was not about to be allowed to lick his wounds and recover in peace and privacy appeared three days later in the self-righteous and sanctimonious form of Jeremiah Bergh, defender of sick and maltreated animals everywhere, Live Menagerie and Museum Exhibits a Speciality.

His arrival was announced by Cherry with his usual excited fanfare as he ran from the Museum entrance, at which Jeremiah Bergh and two of his spinsterish acolytes had just arrived, to where Barnum sat in his office, preparing himself for his fresh assault upon the difficult days ahead. At the first faint and distant mention of Jeremiah Bergh's name he covered his face, groaned, rose, checked his appearance in a looking-glass and strode purposefully out to do battle with his old adversary. Jeremiah Bergh had his sources, and was usually well informed as to the arrival of new exhibits at the Museum, and avoiding him had become a near impossibility once he'd covered all the entrances and exits to the building.

Barnum met Cherry in one of the second-floor galleries, resting against a case of iguanas and catching his breath.

'Bergh,' Cherry said hoarsely upon his arrival, pointing in the direction of the entrance.

'Compose yourself, Hack. He hasn't to my knowledge yet been elevated to Sainthood — though I dare say that is only a matter of time if martyrdom does not overtake him first. Nor is he the all-powerful, all-consuming leader of men he likes to think he is.' Hearing himself speak added to Barnum's resolve, and as he prepared himself for the confrontation ahead, he came to look upon it as yet another turning point in his present fortunes; success in the venture, therefore, acquired a new significance, and he waited for Jeremiah Bergh with his jaw firmly set.

'Two of his women with him,' Cherry said.

'Crows, Hack. Crows and scavengers. Fluttering around him to pick up the few meagre titbits of self-serving indignation he scatters in his wake.' He went to the window to look down upon Broadway and the gathering crowd. The appearance of Jeremiah Bergh at the Museum was always a guarantee of free entertainment.

'You going down to him, Mr Barnum?'

'Am I . . . ? Cherry, I have been provoked in my lair, roused in the sanctity of my domicile, goaded at the very centre of my —'

A roar went up from the crowd outside and Barnum went again to the window. Beneath him, the two women accompanying Jeremiah Bergh had taken out their trumpets and started to play.

'I thought so,' Barnum said. 'Accompanied by the holy blowers of his righteous crusade.'

Beside the trumpeters stood a further two women, each with a placard denouncing Barnum as the cruel abuser of innocent animals, one with a tambourine, the other a drum, playing together in tuneless chorus, and already starting to obstruct the natural flow of visitors into the Museum.

This was more than Barnum could stand.

'Follow me, Cherry. We are about to do battle with Mr Jeremiah Bergh and determine once and for all who is the public's favourite.' He marched off stiffly in the direction of the stairs. Cherry, waiting until the two of them were several feet apart, slipped behind the cabinet of iguanas and crouched down. Barnum, therefore, left the gallery and descended to deal the first blow of the campaign without realizing he was alone. Cherry, meanwhile, having held back from this first line of assault, rose and went to the window to watch.

In the entrance hall Barnum met Greenwood. Outside, the crowd had doubled in size, but few were willing to pay and enter the Museum when all the excitement might now be about to take place out in the street.

'Me and Cherry here —,' Barnum began.

'Cherry?' Greenwood said, causing Barnum to turn.

'Deserted,' he said. 'Abandoned in the face of the —' He was interrupted by the loud deep voice of Jeremiah Bergh challenging him to go outside and face up to his accusers like a man.

'Don't go,' Greenwood warned him.

'I have no intention of doing so,' Barnum said, intending to draw his accusers inside and then face up to them like a showman with their money in his pocket. He hurriedly reconsidered his plan of attack.

'We'd benefit more by whatever it is he wants if you could draw him inside,' Greenwood said.

'Like a Judas goat.' Barnum smiled at the prospect.

'Let him in for free and then charge everyone who follows him.'

Barnum, realizing that this was now the only profitable course of action open to him, called out his greetings to Jeremiah Bergh.

'Still hiding behind all your friends, Barnum?' Bergh shouted in, his voice rising above the small band of musicians which accompanied him, and which caused Barnum to wonder if something similar couldn't be got up on his behalf to provide him with a little additional moral and musical support the next time Bergh appeared.

'They aren't your friends,' Bergh went on. 'They despise you, they despise you as I despise you, as every God-fearing animal-lover in this nation despises you.'

'Outnumbered again,' Barnum said, manoeuvring Greenwood between himself and the door and peering over his shoulder at the crowd outside.

'Don't answer him,' Greenwood advised. 'Retreat. Let him think he's got you on the run. There must be over a hundred people out there waiting on the outcome.'

'You're right,' Barnum said, already moving away from the entrance as the people outside began to press to come in.

Greenwood accompanied him back along the line of booths in which Zip, Elizabeth, Franklin and Herman stood and watched what was happening.

'We have a plan,' Barnum said to Elizabeth as he passed quickly along the corridor.

'He has a plan,' she said to Zip when the two men had gone.

'I saw. It's called running away.'

Franklin whooped with delight at what was happening, and Herman left his booth to join him and speculate on the likely outcome of the confrontation.

'Butler thinks he's heard about the hippopotamus,' Greenwood said as he and Barnum reached the second floor.

'That profitless tub of lard! Why can't it do the decent thing and go the way of all its forebears and save me all this trouble and expense? Is it insured?'

'For five thousand dollars,' Greenwood said.

Barnum's speculations were cut short by the rising stamp of feet following him up the stairs, and then by the voice of Jeremiah Bergh again, rising above the crowd of excited onlookers.

'He's inside!' Barnum said with alarm. They were surprised by the speed with which they had been followed, and both turned to look in the direction of the pursuing mob.

Every time Jeremiah Bergh appeared at the Museum, Barnum expected to see him with his sleeves rolled up, waving a silk banner on a golden staff, his free arm pointing victoriously forward, its forefinger aimed at a spot directly between his own eyes.

The marching mob turned a corner and came closer still, and Barnum knew that the time for action had finally come. Pushing Greenwood in the direction of the noise, he ran back into his office and locked the door.

Ahead of Greenwood, the gallery door was flung open and the cries and music from the crowd, Jeremiah Bergh still at their head, swept over him like a moist warm wind, the vanguard of an approaching hurricane.

Momentarily safe, Barnum sat at his desk and made several attempts to compose himself, angry and frustrated by the sudden turn of events which had afforded Jeremiah Bergh such an obvious advantage over him. He'd had other opponents in the past, but none so persistent as Jeremiah Bergh, and none so harmful as he might yet prove to be. Others, men *and* women, had risen up against him on one pretext or another in fierce and vainglorious battle only to exhaust themselves against the shield of his impenetrable popularity and his own personal disregard for the consequences of his actions; opponents who had fallen back, spent, many to be trampled beneath the feet of his loyal public who had come to see for themselves what was happening, and who in most instances appointed themselves judge and jury of the occasion. There had been times in the past when his attackers and competitors had come at him from all sides, when one was tripping him and another pushing him, but when he had still walked the streets with impunity, ever more popular in his victory.

Recently, however, there had been a wind-change; not a particularly strong one, but one sufficiently chilled for him to feel even in the refuge of his office. He had seen it in the faces of men and women in the public galleries of the courts, and he saw it now in the eyes of the crowds gathering behind Jeremiah Bergh; and he, Phineas Taylor Barnum, perhaps more than anyone else in the city, knew that a man who was made by the people was also destroyed by the people.

Now, sitting alone and preparing himself for his inescapable confrontation with Bergh, this thought worried him. He reminded himself of past victories over the man and his cohorts, and sought desperately for the means to gain one now. Leaving his desk, he stood with his ear pressed to the door.

Bergh and Greenwood were arguing, and although he couldn't make out with any certainty what was being said, he was able to gauge the progress of the debate by the collective cheer or groan of the crowd after each man had spoken. He was grateful that Greenwood and not Henry Butler was standing at the breach. Henry Butler, he felt certain, would have given way almost immediately. In fact he wouldn't have put it beyond Henry Butler to have defected completely to the enemy camp.

And then the noise outside fell and faded completely. Silence. Barnum pressed his ear closer to the door. The outer office had been penetrated, and as he strained to hear what was happening someone approached and rapped loudly on his own door, causing him to jump back holding his ear. Then Jeremiah Bergh shouted in to him that he should come out and face the public instead of cowering inside like a beaten rat.

'Rat!' Barnum said aloud, somewhat fortified by the insult. 'Rat!' He took a cigar from the box on his desk, examined it and then exchanged it for one considerably larger. He lit this and then examined himself again in the looking-glass.

Unlocking the door, he stepped cautiously out.

'There he stands!' shouted Jeremiah Bergh. 'He appears before us with all the gall and arrogance of a Roman emperor, of a Caesar, a Herod, of a very Pilate himself!'

Barnum felt himself shudder, as though each of the names had been a jabbing finger pushing him back a step. He rallied, however, and blew a long plume of smoke directly into Bergh's face. Jeremiah Bergh neither smoke nor drank; he ate no meat, did not indulge in licentious behaviour with man or woman and had never raised a finger in violence or anger against any living thing. It was the certain knowledge of this latter upon which Barnum's returning confidence was now largely founded. Bergh was a full foot taller than himself, but in sight of all his customers he faced up to him with a steady grin, his thumbs tucked into the pockets of his silver and scarlet vest.

'A-ha, a smokescreen!' Bergh called out, waving the smoke from his face. 'He cannot – nay, *dare* not face us fairly and squarely in the clear and honest daylight as the good Lord intended.'

Someone at the back of the crowd shouted, 'Hallelujah!' and

immediately Barnum recognized the voice of Hackaliah Cherry.

'Thank you, brother,' Jeremiah Bergh called back.

'You're welcome,' Cherry said, pleased at having acquired for himself a role in the proceedings. 'Night-time, I always say, and my mother before me, God rest her soul, is the dishonest man's day.'

'How right you are, brother! How right you are! Night-time is the time for sinners and for sinning, for drink and debauchery amid the myriad mazes of degenerate waywardness.'

'Hallelujah!'

Barnum signalled to Greenwood to pass through the crowd and get rid of Cherry. There was nothing Bergh liked better than the answering call of agreement from someone unknown to him, the voice of the people, upon which to construct his own probing hyperbolic forays.

Guessing that the time had now come for him to make a more determined move, Barnum raised his hands and waited for silence. Greenwood slipped easily through the crowd to where Hackaliah Cherry was beginning to push himself forward.

'The only screams of agony and torment I hear,' Barnum shouted, 'are the noises produced by the members of Mr Bergh's own harem, his concubines, no less, who have been chosen – no, who have been *commanded* by him, their leader, their Lord, their *prince*, to publicly display their musical ineptitude. I apologize for this. A refund for anyone among my faithful and loyal patrons who finds themselves aurally discomfitted, if not physically and permanently deafened by this outrage. I have never personally skinned a cat alive, and believe that I now never shall.' This received some laughter and applause, upon which Barnum was quick to capitalize. 'Nor do I eat more than three small children per day. Nor, except when it is absolutely necessary, do I stick sharp pins into any of my performers. They are chained to the walls of their cells and beaten only when the Museum is closed. When it is open, they are free to wander round their booths and the corridors and to do whatever they please.' The laughter erupted even more loudly.

'That's right – joke, laugh, make fun, scornfully disregard *His* teachings.' Bergh shouted, holding a Bible up into the air and silencing everyone.

'Halle –' Hackaliah Cherry shouted, before Greenwood's hand was clasped across his mouth.

Seeing that they had arrived at an awkward impasse, and knowing that he dare not now say anything which might be interpreted as blasphemous, Barnum repeated the word 'concubines', at the same time raising his eyebrows and drawing deeply on his cigar. He was certain that no one in his audience would understand the true meaning of the word, but equally certain that their own inaccurate assumptions would lead them all to the same general desirable conclusion and serve his purposes just as well.

Turning to Jeremiah Bergh, he said, 'Tell me, why is it, Mr Bergh, that your following is composed almost entirely of elderly spinsters, women other men might consider past their prime? Look at them, ladies and gentlemen; do these women look impoverished to you? Indeed, do they not look like the kind of women who might not have considerable personal fortunes ready to be devoted and donated to a good and worthy cause?' No one answered him, but he believed he could almost hear their minds making the connections he hoped to suggest. 'Of course they do! And ask yourself this – what hold does Mr Jeremiah Bergh have over these women? He accuses me of facing *him* through a cloud of smoke, but I doubt if there is a man – a *real* man – among us brave enough to face *them* in any other way. Perhaps, in my wayward life as a sinner, I am mistaken – perhaps they are excited solely by the righteousness of Mr Bergh's cause, and not by his manly physique and intelligence and the use to which he puts both. See how they slavishly follow him around from one lost cause to another, braving public contempt and ridicule in their obvious desire to please him, and perhaps, who knows, even to satisfy some strange and inexplicable desire within themselves.' He paused, allowing his words to acquire their full impact.

Of them all – audience and musicians alike – only Jeremiah Bergh was prepared for the attack. He stood without speaking, barely colouring, staring Barnum squarely in the face.

' "Cursed is the sinner who understands his ways and yet repenteth not",' he said, conducting his delivery of the words with the forefingers of both hands.

'Don't tell me – the Bible,' Barnum said quickly. 'Mr Bergh knows his Bible from cover to cover, ladies and gentlemen. Oh yes, he certainly does. Tell me, which of you would dare to face him in a contest of Bible-spouting?' No one answered. Those at the front of the crowd took several paces backwards.

' "He that twisteth the words of good men shall feel their blows a thousand times over".'

'And a thousand times he's been in here *free* of charge threatening me with this quotation and that. And with that book that he holds so dear.' It had often occurred to Barnum that he ought to respond in a similar fashion with a copy of his autobiography held high above his head; it was, after all, a heavier and more impressive-looking volume. 'What he *cannot* threaten me with, however, is the law. And why can he not do that? I'll tell you why. The answer is very simple. Because I am breaking no law, that's why.' He drew the words out, pleased with this unexpected turn the confrontation had now taken. He searched for Greenwood among the faces, hoping he was witness to this small triumph of public oratory.

' "An honest man, sincere in his righteous cause, may step from side to side of his path, but not once shall he forsake it for another",' Bergh shouted.

But now the crowd was tiring of his quotations, and Barnum saw this. The argument had risen to its crescendo and fallen, and had not provided them with the spectacle many had hoped for.

Recently, Bergh and his devotees had been ridiculed and had lost some support as a result of his passionate plea on behalf of the passenger pigeon, which, he said, was being slaughtered month after month and in such numbers that soon they would be extinct, lost for ever. Remembering this, Barnum cast a glance in the direction of the window and the small wrought-iron balcony beyond, upon which sat several pigeons.

'Quick! There! Bergh, save them,' he shouted, surprising everyone. 'Time's running out!'

The crowd turned as one and looked. The pigeons shifted nervously into a tighter bunch.

'They look about to expire before our very eyes. Bergh, implore them to move away from the edge lest they fall off.'

Jeremiah Bergh looked uncertainly from Barnum to the birds.

Barnum puffed on his cigar and grinned at the crowd. 'Take pity on them,' he shouted. 'Get beneath them ready to catch them should they fall.' Turning to the others, he said, 'And I suggest that those of you who wish to leave accompany Mr Bergh back down to the street and see for yourselves what a marvellous crusade he is embarked upon.'

There was a murmur of dissent.

Greenwood reappeared and Barnum signalled to him.

'Ladies and gentlemen,' Greenwood announced, 'the creature which is the cause of so much concern to Mr Bergh, and which he considers to be so deplorably treated, is at this very moment wallowing in a warm bath and feeding itself to capacity on the finest cabbages and apples money can buy. Apples, I have no hesitation in saying, that you or I would be happy to pluck from our pockets and eat ourselves. If this is cruelty, then yes, I am guilty. Barnum, too. Take us both and throw us in jail. Disregard the many thousands of dollars that has been expended on saving the life of this gentle creature and transporting it here for you to gaze upon in wonder. Disregard also the expense of equipping it with every convenience and luxury necessary to its well-being.'

'A Nile hippopotamus belongs in the Nile, where it is free to wander among its own kind, just as the good Lord intended,' Jeremiah Bergh declared loudly in response, knowing even then that his assault upon Barnum and the Museum had failed, and beginning to plan his retreat. He did not believe Barnum's claims regarding the origins of the hippopotamus, but nor was he certain enough of its true history to invoke this in support of his argument.

'To wander among lawless and Godless savages and ferocious crocodiles,' Greenwood shouted. 'Ladies and gentlemen, I guarantee that you will never before have seen such a placid and trusting creature.'

Barnum's original idea to capitalize on the supposedly vicious and even murderous nature of the animal had been quickly abandoned in view of all the contradictory characteristics it had so far exhibited since its arrival.

Listening to all this, Barnum was beginning to lose interest in the argument now that he had deflected its first and harshest blows. Greenwood was skirmishing, but the engagement had already been won by himself, and following his earlier self-doubts he now felt justifiably pleased with his achievement. Announcing that he had urgent business to attend to, he begged forgiveness from the crowd for leaving them alone in the company of Jeremiah Bergh and his musical minions.

'Those of you who have ever kicked a dog, whipped a horse or thrown a stone at a howling tomcat in the night had better beware, for Mr Jeremiah Bergh will surely find you out, and under his directions the good Lord will equally surely punish you.'

'How true, how true,' Jeremiah Bergh said, losing the last of the crowd's dwindling sympathy.

Beside him the trumpet-players and tambourine-bangers stopped playing.

'At least I am capable of blowing my own trumpet as and when required,' Barnum said loudly, bowing to the applause of the crowd as he left them and returned to his office.

Several minutes later, there was a knock at the door, and Greenwood entered holding Hackaliah Cherry by the arm.

'I thought you might like to see him,' he said.

Barnum rose from his seat without really knowing what he wanted to say to Cherry.

'Holy Madawaska!' Cherry said, forestalling him. 'You really showed 'em, sir, Mr Barnum, sir.'

'Madawaska?'

'I thought them pigeons gonna come right in off that balcony and sit on your shoulders like that Saint Francis in the Bible. Yes, sir.' Cherry stood grinning.

'Let's try and keep the Bible out of this, shall we, Hack. Bergh may yet build an almighty burning cross out of the damn things and nail me to it. I tell you, Hack, if ever there was a man more sinned against than –'

'I believes it, Mr Barnum, sir.' Cherry tried to pull himself free of Greenwood's grasp.

'Did you want something, Greenwood?' Barnum said.

'I thought you might have wanted a word with Cherry concerning his defection and subsequent –'

'A word?' Barnum said.

Cherry asked what 'subsequent' meant and began to proclaim his innocence.

Exasperated, Greenwood said, 'Inadmissable, reprehensible, undermining, treasonable . . .' He faltered as he searched for more.

'Thank you, sir,' Cherry said, finally pulling himself free and tugging straight his sleeve. 'Ever occur to you that "reasonable" is made up of two other words. Seems to me that the more I am able to offer my assistance in these matters, the more valuable an ass-et I become. You understand "ass-et", Mr Greenwood, sir?'

Greenwood's answer evaporated in his rising anger.

'Finish with that cigar, Mr Barnum, sir?' Cherry said, leaning forward to retrieve Barnum's stub.

Barnum motioned for him to help himself after he had already done so. 'Cherry, Hackaliah, Hack,' he began.

'No need, Mr Barnum, sir. Working here and serving you is thanks enough. Poor, ignorant boy like me, I ought to be down on my knees prayin' for your salvation from trouble-makers like Jeremiah Bergh and his scrawny women. Scrawny women nothin' but trouble. They have scrawny thoughts and scrawny dreams.'

'How right you are,' Barnum said. The thought of himself as a latter-day Saint Francis appealed to him and he paused to consider it for a moment.

'Scrawny women go for whatever they can get, and all the scrawniest of 'em here can get is Mr Jeremiah Bergh.'

Undermined, outmanoeuvred and flattered, Barnum sat back in his seat and closed his eyes. When he opened them again he was alone, peaceful and content, and with only the sound of distant footsteps no louder than the beating of his heart for company.

15

A WEEK LATER, Greenwood arrived before the Museum opened to find Zip with Bartola and Maximo, the Albino and the Sprague children all gathered in the entrance hall by the ticket office. Their attention was clearly upon something, but as he entered he could not immediately discern what this was. Only Zip turned to acknowledge his arrival.

'What's wrong? Someone try to escape in the night, fall and break their neck?'

Zip said nothing, simply smiled at him.

There was a new, almost fetid smell in the air, and Greenwood paused to breathe it in. After a few seconds a look of disbelieving and unhappy recognition crossed his face and his mouth fell.

'Got it in one,' Zip said. Around him the children called out with joy and applauded. From somewhere in the shadows beyond them came a shuffling sound, followed by a grunt.

The first of the morning light had scaled the rooftops opposite and seeped into the Museum, advancing ahead of Greenwood like an unrolled carpet, along which he now made his way. In front of him stood three bears, the largest on all fours, the two smaller animals standing upright, one dressed as an old woman with spectacles, a shawl and a bonnet, the other as a Napoleonic general with a plumed cap, a sword and a walking stick. The old woman curtsied at Greenwood's arrival. The general put a long-stemmed pipe to his lips and looked him up and down. The third animal simply stood and watched, unclothed and clumsy, like an overgrown country cousin at a family wedding. Everything the animals did was greeted by a further round of applause from the children.

'I don't believe it,' Greenwood said, slapping a hand to his brow.

'Apparently, they're very intelligent creatures,' Zip said, still smiling.

'Not them – *him – Barnum*.'

'He's been in an hour.'

'With our Wild West friend, no doubt,' Greenwood said, composing himself and taking stock of the situation.

'Grizzly got into the city late yesterday.'

'And Barnum thought he'd work something out with him behind everyone else's back.'

'He still owns the place,' Zip said provocatively, joining the applause as the larger of the bears stood upright, swaying unsteadily and threatening to fall. It stood at least nine feet tall, and seeing it rise above him, Greenwood took several paces backwards.

'It's barbaric, medieval. We told him. I suppose this is another of his attempts to revive public interest in this doomed enterprise. Well, it won't work.'

'They're supposed to be very popular, bears.' Zip avoided looking at him, enjoying his discomfort, and watching as the creature shifted the balance of its bulk from one foot to the other.

'He must have arranged this weeks ago. Grizzly Adams is still billed as appearing in California.'

'Perhaps he's come back to help his old friend fight off all his attackers. They do appear to have multiplied of late. Like blowflies breeding in an open wound.'

'Help him? They're performing bears! What this city needs is great actors, opera singers, not . . .'

The bear dressed as a French general coughed to attract their attention, and then proceeded to gesticulate as though it were delivering a speech, beating and then clasping its chest, throwing out its arms, and finally bowing to its audience with an elaborate flourish. The children and the other bears applauded it loudly.

'They're vicious creatures,' Greenwood said. 'You shouldn't have brought the children down.'

'Barnum asked me to. They wanted to see.'

'Safe enough if the beasts have been fed, I suppose.'

'I think the old lady wants to shake you by the hand,' Zip said, indicating the smallest of the bears, which was now coming towards them with her paw extended, patting the heads of the children like an affectionate grandmother as she came.

'Keep it away, tell it to get back.' Greenwood rapped the floor with his cane and the bear stopped coming, a puzzled and then hurt look upon its face.

'You've offended her,' Zip said.

'I'll do more than offend her if she – it – comes one step closer.'

The general came forward to comfort the old woman, his eyes on Greenwood, his free hand on his sword. He, too, patted the heads of the children. The giant unclothed bear waited in the background and raised its lip to reveal a flash of pointed white.

'I'm going directly up to see him and let him know what I think of it all,' Greenwood said.

'He doesn't want to be disturbed. They're discussing business. As I said, they're old friends, go back a long way.'

A moment later, almost as though on cue, the empty Museum rang to the sound of footsteps and the voices of Barnum and Grizzly Adams as they descended from Barnum's office.

Arriving, Barnum guiltily acknowledged Greenwood's presence, and Adams hugged each of his bears. He told the children to come closer and sat the bravest of the young Spragues upon the back of the largest animal, which dropped back down on to all fours at a word from him. It turned in a circle for them, watched solicitously by the old woman and the general.

Adams was dressed as usual in his suit of frayed and tasselled buckskin, with a switch in his hand and a leather pouch at his waist. His shoes were also of buckskin, and upon his head he wore a fur cap which merged imperceptibly with his untidy hair and overgrown beard. He was heavily tanned and smelled as strongly as his bears, with whom he professed to spend his every waking and sleeping hour.

'You should have let us know you were coming,' Greenwood said, declining the hand Adams offered to him. 'We had Thumb in a few weeks back and Mr Barnum met and treated him like royalty; I'm sure he'd have wanted time to prepare the same for you, old friend that you are.'

'I neither need nor crave any of that,' Adams shouted. 'I'm a simple man, simple ways, always have been . . .'

'– and always will be,' Greenwood said beneath his breath.

'And always will be, right?' Barnum said, clapping his old friend on the back and then studying his palm to see if it contained anything other than the dirt with which it was now smeared.

'True enough, true enough, Phineas. Hetty, a handkerchief for Mr Barnum.' He held out his hand and the old woman pulled out a pressed white handkerchief from her sleeve and presented it to him, waiting for it to be handed back. 'Been entertaining the young 'uns, I see, General. Good, good.'

The general sucked on his pipe and then leaned closer to Adams as though he were whispering something to him.

'That's Greenwood,' Adams told him. 'Got his measure yet, General?'

The bear looked Greenwood slowly up and down again, nodded and withdrew, the sword rattling by his side.

'This here's Bruin,' Adams said, slapping the giant bear on its flank.

'Very original,' Greenwood said, again beneath his breath.

Both the general and the old woman turned immediately to look directly at him.

'Exceptional hearing, Mr Greenwood,' Adams said. 'They have it; I have it.' He paused and looked around him. 'You don't by any chance have any coconuts in the Museum, Phineas? A new delicacy. They squeeze them open and suck out the milk. The bigger the better. Size of a man's head, twice the strength and generally more hair.' He accompanied this with a loud guffaw and slapped Barnum in precisely the same way he had slapped the bear. This winded Barnum and he took several minutes to fully recover.

Zip helped the Sprague children down from Bruin and lifted up the same number of Albinos.

'And how are you, Zip, old friend?' Adams said. 'Get Barnum here to send you out West to the California Menagerie. Men can be men out there, Zip. It's wild and free. You can breathe, do anything you like.'

'Zip's a pillar of the Museum,' Barnum said anxiously. 'I couldn't do without him.'

'Let me know when you're set to go back,' Zip said to Adams, not entirely serious, but wanting Barnum to believe that the prospect appealed to him.

His words were followed by a long silence. The old woman and the general bowed their heads. Bruin, because he had not understood, went on turning circles with the children upon his back.

'Alas,' said Adams. 'Not to be, old friend. No going back. I've seen the last of that dear and precious land.'

Barnum moved to stand beside him. Greenwood groaned.

'Saddest news, Zip, saddest news,' Barnum said. He pressed a hand to his chest.

'What's wrong, are you ill? Is the Menagerie closing down?'

'When?' Greenwood asked, cheered by the prospect.

'The former, old friend, the former.'

'Saddest, saddest, saddest news.'

'Is it bad?' Zip asked.

'The physicians say six months. I ain't healing like I once used to.' He pointed to his head, and Zip, Barnum and Greenwood looked hard at it for as long as his finger was held there.

It was common knowledge that following a vicious attack by a wounded wild bear ten years ago, part of Adams's skull had been smashed, the loose fragments of bone from the top of his head having to be removed afterwards to prevent them from penetrating his brain. At the time the operation had been undertaken only as an emergency measure; he had not been expected to live. During the months of his miraculous recovery, however, a thick, semi-transparent membrane had grown over his exposed brain, and this now protected it in place of the missing bone. Apart from the obvious physical damage, Adams appeared to have suffered no other injury, and had afterwards exhibited himself to his customers at no extra charge. Now, it seemed, he was at last beginning to suffer, and his decline could not be halted. He had come to New York because he knew it was there, managed more closely by Barnum, that he might make the greatest amount of money in the short time still available to him, and that this could then be used to provide for his bears and the other animals of his menagerie after his death.

'We've rented Wallack's Theatre,' Barnum said, hoping to divert them all as swiftly and painlessly as possible from the morbid avenue along which their discussion had unavoidably taken them.

'So you're not coming back to exhibit these creatures in the Museum itself,' Greenwood said with relief.

'I doubt they would tolerate your company. Despite having been beaten to a jelly, torn almost limb from limb, and nearly chawed up and spit out by their wild brethren, these creatures are the most sensitive, caring and affectionate I've ever come across. I speak from long experience in these matters.' He paused. 'You, on the other hand, are motivated solely by greed and personal advancement.'

There was another moment of silence. The Albino children on Bruin's back cheered.

'Are you going to let him speak to me like that?' Greenwood asked Barnum.

Barnum wrung his hands. 'Six months, they said.'

'Six months during which he is at perfect liberty to go round insulting decent, honest –'

'I meet so very few of them in this city,' Adams said. He turned and winked at Zip.

'Six months,' Barnum repeated, hoping by this reminder to resolve the confrontation and release the tension which now existed between the two men like a taut wire drawing them slowly together.

'Stand up to 'em more,' Adams told him. 'Forget to stand up to a bear and they let you know soon enough of your failings. Do what you do because it's got to be done and not for any other fanciful reason.'

'Frontier philosophy?' Greenwood said, lighting a cigar and puffing the smoke in the direction of the animals. Most animals, he knew, were offended by the smoke, but the old woman and the general appeared positively to enjoy it. The general, his pipe being now extinguished, took out a cigar case of his own, selected one and lit it. It was clear from the aroma of the smoke that it was a considerably superior cigar to Greenwood's.

'Nothing but the best for my bears,' Adams said proudly. 'They do their utmost for me, I do mine for them.'

'My philosophy entirely,' Barnum said, causing them all to turn and look at him.

'So you definitely won't be exhibiting in the Museum?' Greenwood said.

'Is he also deaf, Phineas?'

'Wallack's,' Barnum said.

'And we shall be announcing our arrival by a whole host of charity events. Performing for the poor and sick and needy.'

'Big audience,' Greenwood said. 'Workhouse poor or pickpocket poor?'

'Hospitals, orphanages, at the bedsides of the sick and weary,' Barnum added. He had performed few other wholly charitable acts in his life, but it had been at Adams's suggestion during his last visit to the city that he had taken three elephants to perform outside the window of a sick child. The free shows were being undertaken at Adams's insistence, and having agreed to them, Barnum was now desperately trying to work out how to recoup the cost of his enforced generosity.

'I need to give something back,' Adams said. 'Particularly now that I got such a short time left in which to do it.'

Barnum regretted Adams's sudden concern with his own mortality, but said nothing.

Zip helped the Albino children down and sat Maximo and Bartola upon Bruin's back.

Adams watched fondly. 'That creature could carry a new-laid egg over a mountain and hand it over safe and sound.'

'Very useful,' Greenwood said. 'I hear bear steaks are very popular in the most fashionable restaurants.'

'Eaten them myself,' Adams said proudly, thus instantly deflating Greenwood's provocation.

Elizabeth arrived, and delighted at the sight of the bears she went immediately to stand between the old woman and the general.

Adams kissed her hand and she shook paws with both animals.

'It's no lie, Phineas, I declare. I don't know which is the more beautiful, your Elizabeth or my Hetty here.'

'I think that tells us a great deal,' Greenwood said to Zip behind his hand.

'Indeed, has not Emerson himself written that the secret of ugliness consists not in irregularity, but in being uninteresting. You married, Greenwood?'

Elizabeth waited for the remark to sink in before asking Adams if he thought Bruin would give her a ride around the ground floor when Bartola and Maximo had finished.

'I'd go down on all fours myself for that privilege,' Adams said.

Greenwood said, 'Disgusting,' and left them.

'He's a mite too touchy, you ask me,' Adams said loudly enough for Greenwood to hear as he made his way up the stairs.

'He has a lot on his mind,' Barnum said, this being as much as he would say in defence of his manager.

'His scheming, you mean.' Then Adams opened his jacket and pulled out a folded newspaper. 'I wondered if you'd seen this. Might be a dollar in it for you.'

The mass of tightly packed print confused Barnum; his own preference was for capitals, black borders and exclamation marks. He searched the paper in the dim light but saw nothing.

'Livingstone,' Adams told him, pointing out the small article. 'Just got himself back to London. Been lost in Africa.'

'Oh?'

'Seen more of that place than any white man alive, they reckon. I envy him that.'

'Ah, Livingstone,' Barnum said, not wishing to appear ignorant or behind the times.

'Back to get more cash and he's going to return. Leave him in there for a few years and he's bound to get lost again, perhaps for longer this time.'

'Scot!' Barnum said, having suddenly remembered. 'He's a Scot. They speak with a certain afflicted waywardness which can only be poorly and at best partially understood by most other civilized men. They claim it to be the same language, but, believe me, I've been there among them and I might just as well have been wandering in China for all I learned of them from their own mouths.'

'So you see nothing in him?' Adams said.

Barnum thought about it, rubbed his chin and fluttered his hand in assessment. 'Maybe, maybe. Old World, New World. If there was some American interest attached next time, perhaps. Someone who could come back and tell us all about Livingstone's adventures in a language we could understand. In London, you say. No rush, the world can wait. What's a year or two when a man . . .' He stopped, having realized his blunder in front of a man whose own life was about to become one continuous hurry in the face of death.

'No matter, old friend. I ain't gonna allow myself to be feather-bedded now. These hard old bones are too set in their ways to allow that to happen.'

They were interrupted by the arrival of Bella-Grace Sprague, who, upon seeing all six of her children so close to the bears, threw up her hands and screamed. Both the children and the old woman took fright at this and moved to stand beside Adams.

'Calm yourself, madam, calm yourself. You're putting a fright into them. Harmless as rabbits, harmless as rabbits.'

Bella-Grace, however, remained unconvinced and called for her children to move away from the animals, which they all reluctantly did. The old woman waved her handkerchief at them and the general saluted.

Zip assured Bella-Grace that he would not have let her offspring come to any harm.

'Let me introduce my old companion, Grizzly Adams,' Barnum said. 'Of whom, no doubt, you have already heard.'

Bella-Grace had, and she considered the buckskin-clad figure with a mixture of suspicion and distaste.

'Phineas, I declare it, you're turning this place into a palace of beauties. Goddesses every one. Permit me to kiss your hand, madam.'

No one had ever called Bella-Grace a goddess before, not even Isaac, although that was frequently how he looked upon her. She tucked a loose curl of hair behind her ear, pulled her lace collar together at her throat, and held out her hand. She even pretended not to smell Adams's fur cap as he bent forward to plant a kiss upon her wrist.

'Bella-Grace is the devoted wife of the celebrated Isaac Sprague, Human Skeleton Extraordinaire,' Barnum said.

'*The* Isaac Sprague?' Adams said immediately, Bella-Grace's hand still in his own, making it clear to everyone except her that he had never heard of Isaac Sprague. 'Madam, permit me to kiss you again. *The* Isaac Sprague. It's an honour.'

Bella-Grace beamed proudly at them all over his shoulder.

'Madam, I come from California, where the fame of Isaac Sprague, Human Skeleton Extraordinaire, outweighs even that of Creaking Duke Coffey.' This was praise indeed in Bella-Grace's ears.

'And you say they're harmless,' she said, indicating the bears.

'Harmless as doves, harmless as doves. A free show for the young uns. Sand to Arizona, I know, but a small free entertainment amid this veritable cornucopia of curiosities and delight.' He released her hand. 'And afterwards at Wallack's Theatre four times daily.'

The Sprague children, taking advantage of their mother's flattered bewilderment, ran back to the bears.

Elizabeth helped down Bartola and Maximo and climbed on to Bruin herself. She held out her hands and both the general and the old woman came forward to stand beside her as they set off on their tour of the Museum.

Adams followed them at a distance, followed in turn by the children and Zip.

Alone with Bella-Grace, Barnum said that Life was a joke and Death the punchline, leaving her confused, her hands still held out as though someone else were about to take them up and kiss them.

*

Zip alone continued to brood over the failure of the delegation to Barnum. His sense of defeat grew stronger, and because he was now unable to do anything about it, he found himself once again slowly withdrawing from the company of the others, all of whom, he felt, had accepted too easily Barnum's dismissal of their challenge, and some of whom – Franklin and Herman in particular – had seemed almost relieved that the confrontation was over and that nothing had changed. Consequently, he spent longer and longer periods away from the Museum, leaving as soon as possible after midnight, and frequently staying out in the city until only minutes before he was expected to appear in his booth dressed in his hated monkey suit.

He sat morosely, ignoring the demands for him to perform, occasionally rising and dashing to the front of his booth and roaring out at the more persistent complainants, or at those who, for no apparent reason, offended him in some other way. No one was completely fooled by the suit, and in most instances their jibes and taunts were intended as tests of their own bravery rather than Zip's patience.

Little of this escaped Barnum's attention, but, aware of the delicacy of the situation, he instructed Greenwood and Henry Butler not to take any disciplinary action against him. He was growing tired of Zip's increasing demands and his restlessness, and he knew that when the time for a second such confrontation came, he would now hold the upper hand by virtue of Zip's unreasonable behaviour and his own apparent fairness and fatherly indulgence. He also instructed Greenwood to be more rigorous in his inspections of the booths and the performances being given. He felt that recently he'd become too lax, too generous in his concessions, and that this had in some way exposed him and left him a vulnerable target for the plotting not only of his exhibitors, but of Greenwood and Henry Butler too; not to mention anything of the world at large and the millions of people within it who might also be about to rise up and challenge him.

As the summer rose relentlessly to its climax he went less and less often to the Museum. The heat and the crowds gave him a headache; everything gave him a headache. And when he did turn up, he spent his time alone in his office and invariably left at the first opportunity.

One morning, knowing Barnum was unlikely to be present, Zip was late in returning from his night out in the taverns. He'd slept in the street and returned in a dishevelled state to the Museum. He let himself in at the side entrance, ran to his room and got himself ready, calling for Elizabeth to help him into his suit and chains and lead him down.

As she took him into his curtained booth from the rear, Greenwood was waiting for them.

Elizabeth began to explain that Zip's lateness was her fault, but Zip, his eyes never leaving Greenwood's, told her not to bother. He asked her to leave them and she went.

Approaching Greenwood, Zip held out his loosely manacled hands to be secured by a long chain to the floor. Before doing this, Greenwood slowly took out his pocket watch, studied it and equally slowly replaced it.

'Tut tut tut,' he said, a hard smile on his face.

Zip held his chains higher. 'I imagine you wouldn't mind seeing these substituted for something a little more substantial, would you?'

'The time's coming,' Greenwood said.

'Not for me, Greenwood, not for me.'

Unwilling to provoke him any further, Greenwood instead found fault with his suit and took out his pocket book to make a note of this. Having secured Zip to his chain, he then pulled back the curtain to the gallery beyond and called out to the Museum visitors to come and look at him, effectively silencing him.

Later in the morning, Henry Butler arrived to see him, drawing the curtain shut before warning him that Barnum, via Greenwood, was only too aware of what was happening.

'I know,' Zip told him, pleased with the reverberations his absences and increasing unreliability were causing.

'Then why? Why antagonize him? You may have been here a long time, but –'

'But Barnum wouldn't hesitate to throw me out on to the streets?'

Henry Butler looked guiltily around them. 'Is that what you want him to do? Is that what all this is in aid of? Surely not?'

Zip stopped and considered his answer, which was as honest as he could bring himself to make it. 'I'm not sure. All I know is what I don't want. He'd do the same to you once Greenwood had finished convincing him he could run this place without you. Walk out on him before he gets the chance. Walk out and then get out of this city. Get out and take Delilah with you. Take her to some mountain someplace, someplace with trees and fields and clear air. Living here can't be doing her any good whatsoever.'

Henry Butler bowed his head in agreement. 'It's so expensive,' he said.

'So you're prepared to face up to the alternative?'

It was something Henry Butler reminded himself of every hour of every day, every time he thought of his wife and her nurses. 'What about *your* alternative?' he said, knowing he was as tied to Barnum and the Museum as any of the exhibitors, and just as unable to do anything about this and free himself.

'My alternative is turning into an old man with a pointed head wearing a monkey suit. There isn't one of us in here who doesn't need that mountain, that air, those meadows. Anna and Captain Bates are going to build themselves a giant house in the country and we're all going to live with them. Come along. Bring Delilah.

That's the idea, anyhow. You believe that? *We* all do. Well, most of us.'

'That won't amount to anything. Barnum's not stupid. His lawyers draw up your contracts to cover every –'

'I *know* it won't come to anything,' Zip shouted, then turning and snarling at a face which had pushed through his curtain to peer inside. 'It isn't *supposed* to come to anything. It's the dream, the idea, the thought of it happening, the thought that it might happen, that it *could* still happen for us that's important. That's what matters. Up here, up here.' He tapped his forehead. 'We don't want to see the plans of the place, we don't need to pace out its foundations. All we need is to be convinced up here that it's going to happen. Just like the niggers only need to know in their hearts that freedom's coming. Up here, that's the only place it matters.'

After a long silence, Henry Butler said, 'So why all the missing nights?'

'Missing? I'm only missing from here, from this place. *I* know where I am. Don't worry, I checked the contracts. Between midnight and seven we're free agents. I don't cause any public commotion and I don't give any free shows. No monkey suit and I wear my coat and my top hat. Everybody out there knows, of course, but I spend most of my time in places where people don't spend too long looking you in the face. I tell you, it's a welcome relief after being in here all day. I pay my way, I come, I go. You'd be surprised how many places there are where an idiot pinhead like me can sit and drink without being disturbed through those hours.'

'I got drunk myself, once,' Henry Butler said unexpectedly, smiling sadly at the memory. 'When the physician told Delilah she was expecting our first child. I didn't intend to, but I was out on Lafayette with Greenwood and Lyman and a few others. I don't remember what I had, just that I had a whole lot more than I'd ever had before.'

'What happened?'

'I don't know, don't remember. Someone must have taken me home. Next thing I knew, I was waking up and feeling the worst I'd ever felt in my life.'

'I know the feeling; it gets better.'

'I don't intend giving it the chance. After that I swore to Delilah that I'd only ever again drink in moderation. We still had the birth to look forward to and celebrate, see.'

Zip watched him for a moment and then put his arm around his shoulders. It was at times like that that he was convinced that the

Museum was a repository for all the sadness in the city, every kind of sadness, painful sadness and numbing sadness, sadness that held some men together because they had nothing else, and sadness which tore others apart because they'd never known how to make room for it in their hearts. Henry Butler, he realized, was one of the latter, and he squeezed his arm, dislodging the melancholia into which he was about to sink.

'You ought to come out with me for a night or two,' he said. 'I'd make sure you drank milk all night, but you could sit and watch me, see what happens when you're ready to let go. It's easier on some nights to despise yourself than on others. On some nights I take Old Tom out with me. He needs no sleep, that old nigger, it's been bred out of him by hardship. I take him out with me down Pearl and John Street and he plays the piano in exchange for free drinks for us both. So long as he keeps playing, they keep right on setting them up. He's happy to go on playing and I'm more than content to go on sitting next to him.'

'It sounds like a welcome arrangement,' Henry Butler said, wiping the sweat from his face.

'It is. Except that it's no different from what happens here: I take Tom out, put him on show to entertain people, and I benefit, I reap all the rewards.'

'I'm sure Tom doesn't look at it like that.'

'Sure he doesn't, but it doesn't alter the fact that that's what I'm doing. As I said, it's easier on some nights to close yourself off from things because if you didn't, then they'd become unbearable.'

Henry Butler paced the bare boards of the booth.

'Did Greenwood send you?' Zip asked him.

'No. I was just anxious for you. We all are.'

'And they still hunt down and hang runaway slaves,' Zip said. 'So close to not being slaves any longer and yet they still get hunted down and strung up. Makes you wonder, doesn't it.'

'Not here,' Henry Butler said. 'This is where they run *to*, don't forget. And you're right – soon they won't have to run.'

'Think so?'

'Sure. This whole country's going to blossom soon. You can already get to California in a little over a month.'

'Ah, but only once you've started moving in the right direction.'

'I know. Delilah keeps telling me to take the chance.' Henry Butler hung his head at the lie. 'It's only her physicians and nurse who think that trying to move her . . .' They both knew it was a lie, and because Henry Butler was a poor liar, he dared not persist with it.

'You'll never know unless you try,' Zip told him.

'I'm not brave enough. I've never been brave.'

'Perhaps being brave doesn't matter. Greenwood's brave, Barnum's brave.'

'It'd be good to have the opportunity to find out, though.'

'Thousands just did, and look where they are now. Brave men buried in unmarked shallow graves under every piece of land this half of the country. Do you imagine that's what they were doing – finding out how brave they were?'

Henry Butler's response to this was cut short by the return of Greenwood, who jerked back the curtain and demanded to know why it had been drawn. A small crowd stood around him. Seeing Henry Butler, he apologized. 'We've had complaints,' he said, indicating the people beside him.

Because he was once again on public view, Zip was unable to speak; instead he rattled his chains and leapt into a squatting position on his chair. 'Chains,' he whispered to Henry Butler.

'I was just making sure his chains were secure,' Henry Butler said, lifting the links and gently tugging on them.

'That's right, ladies and gentlemen,' Greenwood announced. 'We wouldn't want this prehistoric imbecile to get ideas above his station, would we? We wouldn't want him to get free and start believing he was just like one of us, like you or me, civilized, honest, hard-working people, would we?' The crowd agreed with him.

'Get out,' Zip whispered to Henry Butler.

Henry Butler climbed down at the front of the booth.

'Secure enough, Mr Butler?'

Henry Butler nodded.

'Good. Well, Mr Monkey-man, pull and rant and roar as much as you please.' He turned to the crowd. 'I doubt if he even understands the barest essentials of what I'm saying, ladies and gentlemen. The brain inside that malformed head of his has been calculated by the most eminent naturalists in this city to be little larger than a walnut, capable of possessing only the most primitive and simple of desires. We shudder to think what might happen if he, if *it*, were to get hold of any intoxicating liquor, or, worse still, if it were to get its hands on any . . .' He needed to say no more; the crowd understood him.

From his chair, Zip sat and endured all this calmly, and of the three of them, only Henry Butler was made uneasy by Greenwood's taunts.

Annoyed by Zip's refusal to respond, Greenwood shouted: 'Behold! And all the regrettable result of ill-considered breeding. What a sorry and pathetic figure he really is.'

Zip watched Henry Butler walk away, unwilling to be a party to what was happening.

Greenwood grinned up at him, and then he too left. In his absence, the small crowd dispersed and was quickly replaced by another.

Herman called to him from along the gallery, and then Franklin.

Isaac Sprague appeared with a glass and large pitcher of water and set it down beside him. For the sake of the audience, he spoke to Zip as he might have spoken to a chained and growling dog, cautiously soothing it, and then whispering to him when he was certain no one could overhear him. With his back to the crowd he slid a slender flask from his waistband on to the seat beside Zip.

'We heard what was happening,' he said. 'Bella-Grace thought you might appreciate this.'

Zip took it and nodded his thanks.

He went out again that same night. At midnight Anna Swan and Bella-Grace visited him in his room and tried unsuccessfully to persuade him to stay. Realizing their entreaties were coming to nothing, they then searched for someone willing to accompany him out into the city and the night. They were restricted in their choice – Tom was already too drunk, Vivalla had already gone out, and René refused – until eventually Herman volunteered to go, and accepting his company, Zip then waited for Elizabeth and Fortuna to finish bandaging Herman's chest.

Nancy, Herman's girl from Astor House, had been in again with several other girls, and it was for her that he had performed so late in the day, and why he was now suffering. His chest ached and he still had difficulty breathing when fully expanded, but for her and her companions he had put on a show in which he'd stretched himself to his full sixty inches, contracting slowly, and disguising each stab of pain as his flesh and muscles shrank back to their original shape. The others considered he was being used by the girl and her companions, but no one said anything to him concerning this. Nancy still refused to come alone, and Herman still believed this to be only decent and correct. He was convinced he loved her, and seeing her in his audience he felt encouraged to make this additional effort.

He was exhausted when approached by Anna to accompany Zip, but accepted willingly, already having been told by Nancy that she and her companions might call in at some of the more respectable taverns before returning to their rooms at the Astor.

Both Fortuna and Elizabeth did their best to warn him indirectly that he was being taken advantage of, but he was unwilling to listen to them, and neither of them was prepared to tell him outright what they thought of Nancy and her friends. Franklin in particular was anxious for him; so far, only he knew that Herman hadn't been sending his regular financial contribution home to Buffalo, and that he had written to his parents with the excuse that the Museum was operating on a shorter day and that as a result of this he was earning less. Franklin would have gone with Zip in Herman's place were it not for the short exhausting walks between taverns, or the narrow entrances and alleyways he was unable to negotiate.

Applying the last of the bandages to his ribs, Elizabeth asked Herman to ensure that Zip was back some time in the early hours and not to wait until the last possible moment before returning. She said she felt sure that this was a difficult time for Zip, but that it would pass. For his part, Herman was proud to have their trust. Captain Bates, Isaac and René each gave him a dollar as he was about to leave, and upon slipping his hands into his jacket pocket he found several more there. Elizabeth waited in the entrance with the Aztec children, both of whom demanded to be kissed by Zip on his way out. Their heads were smaller versions of his own, and because they seemed to understand so little of what was happening around them they had long since formed an attachment to him on this basis alone.

Bartola presented herself and then curtsied. Maximo bowed. Zip kissed them both and they giggled, clutching at Elizabeth's dress in their excitement.

'It means a lot to them,' she told him.

'Next you'll want me to turn right round, go back upstairs with them and read them a bedtime story,' Zip said, acknowledging her transparent ploy.

'I'll do that,' she told him. 'You probably can't even read.' She brushed his shoulders with her fingers.

'It won't last,' he told her, kissing her on the forehead directly above her eye.

'I know.' She waited with him until Herman arrived and then the two men let themselves out into the darkness.

She waited in the doorway for several minutes after they'd gone, breathing in the cool night air. Along the corridor from her, Cherry

174

began extinguishing the wall lamps, creating pools of shadow where there had previously been flickering colour. She took one of the lanterns down and led the two children back up into the building.

Zip and Herman went first to Thomas Street, to a tavern filled with workmen, many of whom were already drunkenly asleep at their tables. Herman searched for Nancy, but she wasn't there. He glanced at the few women who were present and then looked quickly away before he caught their eye. Several approached and sat with them, drinking from Herman's glass and ingratiating themselves until Zip dismissed them with a shout. Zip drank quickly, mixing cheap ale with cheap spirits, until after an hour he sat back in his seat with a long contented sigh.

'You can go if you like,' he told Herman. 'Go and look for Nancy. Surely you'd rather be with her than with me.'

After looking at each of the women in the bar, however, Herman was no longer quite so keen to find her among them. She and they were different breeds, and each time the door opened he crossed his fingers and hoped that neither she nor her friends now appeared.

'Go on. You've only been sent out with me to make sure that I don't try and make a break for it, and that I get back at a reasonable hour and in a reasonable condition to present a reasonable spectacle to my reasonable public in the morning. You've nothing to worry about; I'll be there.' Zip spat into his palm and drew a cross over his heart.

'No – I enjoy coming out with you,' Herman said. After previous occasions, he was now careful to do little more than sip at his own drink. 'I don't get out otherwise. Sometimes to sit on the wharves and watch the boats coming and going, but nothing else.'

'Hasn't Nancy invited you back to Astor House yet?'

Herman reddened. 'She isn't allowed to have gentlemen callers back there, and I'm not allowed to invite her to my room at the Museum.'

'Why not? No one would let on to Barnum or Greenwood. Do it; we'll see you're not disturbed.'

Herman shook his head and Zip knew not to persist.

There was a fight at the far side of the room, and Zip cheered the two combatants as they threw slack and useless punches and then fell over the tables and chairs. The bartender separated them by beating them both on the shoulders with a pick handle until they lay on the floor gasping, and groping blindly for some way to pull themselves up. Unable to do this, they gave up and remained where they lay, until only a minute later they both began to snore.

Zip and Herman left the tavern and walked towards City Hall. Herman talked about Nancy and the future. He confessed about the money he had neglected to send home, promising to make this up to his parents. He said he was certain that soon the novelty would wear off and that Nancy would come to the Museum alone.

'She never bring any of the men from the Astor?' Zip asked him cautiously.

'Men? Sometimes. Just some of the kitchen hands and porters. They're nothing to her, she told me that.'

'I wasn't suggesting that they were.'

'No, I know. They're like us, in a way, all living in, following strict rules. There's a hundred of them. They hire and fire every day in that place.' He was talking to smother the uncertainty Zip had raised in his mind.

The next tavern they entered was on Murray Street. Herman recognized it from a previous visit, and the two men were greeted by several others already there.

'Are all these men your friends?' Herman asked Zip as they found a seat.

Zip told him that they were, that they were friends to anyone who entered with enough money to buy them a drink. He left him to collect their own.

They visited four taverns in all, and neither in nor between any of them did Herman catch sight of Nancy or her friends. At Herman's request, Zip asked around to find out if anyone had seen her, if they might not perhaps just have missed her. Several men said they thought they might have seen her, but none of them recognized the girl Herman then went on to describe to them. In one bar Zip grabbed the arm of a man who was about to drunkenly confirm that he'd seen Nancy earlier in the evening. One look from Zip was enough to silence him.

They returned to the Museum at three in the morning. Zip was drunk, but not as drunk as he'd been the previous few nights. They let themselves in by the Ann Street entrance, where a lantern still burned, and passed through a room of caged birds, Indian minahs mostly, hopping chuckling from perch to perch, their orange beaks vivid in the darkness. Two small chimps came to the bars of their cage and reached out their hands. Zip held them and then caressed the animals, encouraging Herman to do the same, which he did. The chimps pressed their heads against the bars like affectionate cats and Zip spoke to them.

They passed a glass tank in which a python lay stretched to its full length, a smug grin on its face, the tail of one of Cherry's rats hanging from its mouth like a second tongue. A parrot called out in the darkness for them to identify themselves and each of the minah birds shouted back a name. Near by, the ants in their exposed nest were still busy, flowing like blood along a braided mass of slender arteries.

Zip and Herman stopped beside a poster announcing the imminent return of Chang and Eng, the original Siamese Twins, who – or so Barnum's story now went – had been away fighting for the Union as a two-man cannon crew. Herman hadn't yet met them and the prospect of their return to the Museum excited him. Zip said nothing to discourage him.

Somewhere in the building, yet another bird let out a long shrill cry, and was answered by many others, some of which sounded almost human.

They moved up the staircase to Herman's room, where he made them both coffee. Zip heard him cry out as he lifted a jug of water and went to investigate. He found him naked from the waist up, unravelling his bandages.

'It's more comfortable without my vest or jacket,' Herman said, clearly still in pain.

Zip helped him to unwind more of the bandages, shocked and surprised by the extent of the bruising thus revealed to him. Many of the weals were blue and turning yellow; others looked as though Herman was bleeding, but that the blood had not yet come through the skin, welling instead in finger-sized mounds beneath it.

Zip asked him if he'd seen a physician other than the one Barnum employed to satisfy his own conscience. Herman said he hadn't, and nor did he want to in case he was considered unfit to continue with his exhibitions. There were days when the pain was almost unbearable, he said, and others when he felt very little. He then confessed that he had cut several inches from the middle of the tape measure so that his expanded chest appeared greater than it actually was.

'But it's painful for you now, even like this,' Zip said.

'Not really.' Herman breathed carefully until the stabbing slowly passed. 'At least when I'm performing in front of Nancy I feel there's some purpose to it.'

Zip took over the preparation of the coffee. He had returned early to the Museum for Herman's sake alone and wondered now if this hadn't been what Anna and Elizabeth had anticipated all along.

Herman reapplied his bandages, not because they eased his pain any longer, but because they hid the bruising, and because otherwise he could not help but look at himself every few minutes in the full-length looking glass opposite him. All of the private rooms had their looking glass, just as all of them had the notice above the door which read: 'Look before you leave. You see it now for Free, but others are going to Pay'. In his own room Zip had long since taken this down, and he offered to do the same now for Herman.

Herman didn't answer him, and when Zip looked he saw that he was asleep where he sat, his bandages only half wound, and that with each deep breath he gave a small involuntary gasp, as though a reserve of endurance had somehow been tapped and was now slowly being released as he slept.

Leaving the coffee, Zip extinguished the lanterns and left him, feeling his way along the almost total darkness of the corridor towards his own room.

*

The following day, Zip and Elizabeth stood at the railings of the short pier leading to the Castle Gardens and looked down into the thick brown water lapping beneath them, its surface littered with crates and planking, flattening the swell of passing vessels and beating against the hollow iron legs of the pier. Gulls rode upon this flotsam and fought over the food which drifted with it. One bird held in its beak what looked to be the complete entrails of a pig or sheep and tried unsuccessfully to become airborne with its prize, smearing itself red and creating a grisly display at every attempt. Attracted by the commotion, the other gulls attacked it and tore furiously at its catch.

'Why do they do that?' Elizabeth said, fascinated by the birds. 'Don't they know how civilized we're all supposed to be nowadays?' She threw a stone down, but this had little effect on the gulls other than the one it struck, which screamed, rose above the mêlée and flew off low over the water.

Zip looked further out, towards the haze of the open bay.

'Did you know that Barnum once approached the City Commissioners with a proposal to build a massive stone statue on one of the islands?' he said.

178

Elizabeth joined him. 'Which one?'

He waved vaguely towards the wider expanse of water.

'A statue dedicated to what, to whom?'

Zip smiled. 'Guess.'

'Ah.'

'A hundred feet high on a hundred-foot plinth.'

'Ladies and gentlemen, welcome to America, step right up, step right up. And what did the esteemed City Commissioners say to that?'

'I don't know. I don't think he was much in favour at the time.'

Zip left the railings and crossed to a bench vacated by another couple. Elizabeth joined him, briefly drawing back her veil to let the sun fall upon her face. Zip watched out to ensure that no one approached them and saw her. Occasionally, he too lifted his hat and wiped the sweat from his scalp.

The walk to Battery Gardens had been Elizabeth's idea and she had insisted that he should accompany her. Others in the first-floor booths had been given time off to make way for the arrival of a new attraction – a dozen new wax figures, lifesize and fully dressed, each a famous philosopher or statesman, writer or artist, mythical figure or contemporary celebrity, each of whom would hold silent court in the vacated booths for a day before being dispersed throughout the Museum. These had been expected for months, and came now as a bonus to Barnum, arriving as they did only days in advance of what he considered to be his greatest attraction of the year so far. It was his intention to have the figures delivered along Broadway in a dozen closed coffins and then to have these carried in through the main entrance by pall-bearers.

'If this heat continues, they'll be delivering a dozen boxes of molten wax,' Elizabeth said, fanning herself.

'He's losing his touch.'

'I feel sorry for him.'

'Sorry?'

'He was ahead of his time once, knew what everyone wanted, but he stopped moving fast enough and everyone else started to run on ahead of him. It's a disease.' She unfolded her parasol and held it between them.

'So where does that leave us?' Zip lit two cigars and handed her one.

'You're too harsh on him; he doesn't treat us so badly. Things could be a lot worse.'

'Eighteen years I've been with him. Here and in his travelling shows. Don't expect me to get sentimental. He's good because most of us are in a position to compare him with the worst.'

'And before that?' Elizabeth said.

Zip sat looking down at his feet. 'Before what?' he said, trying unsuccessfully to avoid the question.

She took his hand. 'Where were you before that? How old are you?'

'Thirty-six.'

'Half a lifetime.'

He was still thrown by her inquiry, as though it had never before been asked of him, as though those first eighteen years hadn't existed; as though to try and reclaim them now might precipitate a disastrous collision with the present.

She waited patiently for him.

'Why do you ask?' he said.

'Because all I see now is *this*, what you've become. You can't just forget what's gone and pretend it has no bearing on what's happening now and what's still to come. If it hurts, then tell me I've no cause to ask. We can talk about something else if you like.'

'I was an orphan,' he said. 'I guess that gets you into the way of believing that what went before doesn't have much bearing on what might be yet to come.'

'Did you never know your parents?'

He smiled. 'I imagine they had good enough cause to start running once they saw how I turned out. I know *I* did.'

'Nothing at all?'

'I got a blanket and a crate and a note begging God for forgiveness. I never asked it of him, but they obviously felt the need.'

'So who raised you?'

'I raised myself. I don't think my crowning glory became too much of a problem until I was going on five or six.'

'And then what?'

'Oh, a long line of people looking at me pityingly, waving me goodbye and pointing me to the nearest county line. I joined a travelling show at eight. They used to paint me up red and yellow. I danced. I used to dance around in circles screaming like one of your braves until folk felt good about being what they were, threw their pennies and went home happy with their kids. At thirteen I half killed a man and after that I . . .' He stopped abruptly, surprised by how much he had already told her. 'That enough for you?' he said. 'You could have made an educated guess at that much.'

'And were you never happy?'

180

'At times. When I ran away I lived rough in Nevada for nigh on a full year. Up in the high forest. I built myself a shack, found a stream, grew crops, killed game.' He stopped again, this time to savour the memory. 'Two prospectors befriended me, gave me a drink, beat me senseless and then unconscious, gagged me, bound me hand and foot and brought me back to civilization tied to a mule. I believe they made some small profit on their efforts.'

They sat in silence for a moment. What Zip had told her had been no more nor less than Elizabeth had anticipated.

'I wanted to show you this,' she said, taking a small card folder from her purse. She handed it to him closed and he sat with it in his lap without opening it for a few seconds. 'I would have shown it to you last night, but . . .'

'What is it?'

Elizabeth didn't answer.

Inside the card was an engraving of the two Red Indians, giants of men, holding tomahawks, almost naked except for the beaded bibs, bracelets and feathers with which they were adorned. At first Zip noticed nothing unusual in the figures, and then he saw that their heads were shaped exactly like his own, perhaps even taller and with an even more pronounced point. One of the men wore a cap of leather thongs upon which hung small bones. The other wore a plaited top-knot just like this own. For a moment he could think of nothing to say.

'I had it as a girl, in a book,' Elizabeth said. 'I wrote my parents to tear it out and send it to me. I wanted you to see it. I want you to have it.'

'Who are they?'

'They're not freaks or slaves or sideshow attractions if that's what you're thinking.'

Zip had already seen that much in the proud faces and the bearing and dignity with which the two men held themselves.

'They belonged to a tribe of Indians who used to live round-abouts where my parents farm. They're giants, each seven feet tall.'

'And their heads?'

'The story has it that the squaws used to bind up the soft skulls of their newborn with wet leather strips to shape them before the bone hardened. The sharper they could get them, the more they liked it. Some of the older settlers say they used to come across the odd one or two out in the backwoods, but they had mostly died out by the time any of us got there. Some farmers opened up a grave site once and found their giant bones.'

'And the skulls?'

'Them too. Folk had a lot of respect for them. They were our Giants in the Earth, and after that first grave we did our best not to disturb them or to enter the secret places where we knew they'd lived.'

All the time she'd been speaking, Zip had never once taken his eyes from the engraving.

'They weren't savages,' she said. 'Farmers, hunters. They cared for one another and looked after their children and their sick. We had an old saying that said every time you cried, for whatever reason, then at least one warm tear had to be allowed to fall directly on to the ground – that was the Giants' tear and it went from the living to the dead and helped to sustain them in their sleep until the time came for them to rise up again and carry on living. Some folks used to say that they'd deliberately taken their own lives when they saw how much of everything else was being taken from them.' She paused for a moment. 'So next time you have cause to cry, remember to spare one tear for the Giants.'

Zip smiled at her. 'Haven't you heard – I never once cried in my entire life.'

'I heard,' she said. 'And I never took a strong drink or put a hex on anybody with my evil eye.'

Zip looked hard at the picture. 'You're not suggesting that I might be somehow descended from savage, bloodthirsty heathens, are you?'

'You're too ugly. Why, is the thought beginning to appeal?'

Zip didn't answer her.

'Keep it. Believe what you like,' she said. 'If, as you say, you've got no real history, then it seems to me like you've got the perfect opportunity to start making one up, to get yourself the history you want.'

This thought appealed to Zip.

'What everyone else calls the truth is just the story as they see it. It never worried Barnum, so why should it concern us? He dresses us up in his fancy Latin names in exactly the same way a mortician puts fancy Sunday clothes on a dirty corpse.'

Zip rose and walked back to the railing overlooking the water. He turned to face her and leaned back on it. 'I could go there one day,' he shouted. 'See where they lived.'

'I'd take you, point it all out. We could visit my parents.'

'I'd like that.' She might just as well have been arranging a visit to a distant planet for them.

'Except once you got there you might feel the need to start blubbering like a –'

'Never!'

'They could all rise up and you could be their leader.' She crossed the pier to join him. People passing by stopped and turned at the sound of their raised voices. 'You'd be living in the best of both worlds,' she told him. 'You'd be one of them, and at the same time you'd know about all this, about what's happened since they put themselves in the ground.'

'In which case, they'd be better off where they are,' he said.

'Ugly *and* miserable,' Elizabeth said, and started walking ahead of him.

Zip slid the card folder into his pocket and ran after her.

They were expected to return to the Museum at midday, and slipping her arm through his, Elizabeth told him she intended to stay away until the last possible moment.

'We'll walk to The Tombs,' she said, leading him through the trees towards the Bowery.

They spent the rest of the morning walking together, saying little other than to remark on whatever caught their eye in the shop window displays, enjoying their anonymity, and their brief, illusory freedom.

When they did eventually return to the Museum, they found a crowd gathered around two open hearses, upon each of which lay stacked six coffins. Barnum was at the centre of the gathering arguing with the undertaker, demanding to know why each coffin hadn't been delivered on a separate hearse as arranged.

True to his trade, the undertaker stood unperturbed and dour. Long black ribbons fell from his hat to his waist.

'Heat,' he said, his lips barely moving, a solitary bead of sweat zigzagging down his brow like a bearing in a bagatelle.

'Heat! Heat! Don't talk to me about heat! Talk to me about hearses, about twelve hearses.'

The undertaker withstood the tirade for a full minute before raising his finger.

Zip and Elizabeth moved through the crowd to the Museum entrance to gain a better view of the proceedings.

Barnum fell silent. The noise of the crowd fell to a murmur.

'Wax,' the undertaker said. He chose his words carefully, as might any man who spoke the word 'death' fifty times a day.

Barnum resumed his barrage of complaint and insult.

The pall-bearers waited for a signal from the undertaker to start unloading the coffins.

Barnum appealed to the crowd, but, as usual, they were enjoying the spectacle too much to want to see it speedily resolved.

'Sophocles!' Barnum shouted. 'Icarus, Charles Dickens, Sir Walter Scott, Ulysses S. Grant. Yes, Ulysses S. Grant! Thomas "Founder of the Nation" Jefferson! All for your – *your* – entertainment.' He threw open his arms. 'And all you can do is stand about and let these mighty, these noble, these proud, these – these – all you can do is watch them arrive like so much cut timber and then side with the scoundrel who so openly and blatantly and proudly confesses his cheating in bringing – in bringing . . .'

The undertaker stepped forward. He ran his forefinger under one of the black ribbons, letting it ripple over the back of his hand as the finger moved out to point directly at Barnum.

'. . . in bringing this – this – these – and in front of a hundred witnesses. Who, not content simply to deceive and defraud me is now attempting – attempting . . '

The finger stopped an inch from Barnum's chest. The ribbon fluttered free and hung still. The man's face, already little more than a skin-covered skull, assumed a further degree of lifelessness.

His lips moved. 'Cholera,' he said.

Barnum suppressed a cry and backed away from him. 'Where?' he said.

'Wherever it chooses to strike.' For the undertaker, this amounted to a speech and he checked himself. 'Readiness,' he added, indicating the hearses. 'Preparation.'

Elizabeth nudged Zip and indicated to him a viscous stalactite of red wax beginning to form beneath the coffin marked 'Icarus'. She resisted the urge to shout out and ask who in the crowd had heard of him.

'Cholera,' Barnum said again, clutching his throat.

'Heat,' the undertaker said. 'Wax.'

The pincers of this assault closed around Barnum and defeated him. He turned and ran back into the Museum.

The undertaker raised his hands to his chest and held them as though he were clutching a pair of field-glasses, about to lift them to his eyes and ready to call out 'Fire!' or 'Charge!' or 'Attack!' But instead, he simply moved one of his little fingers a fraction of an inch and around him the men began hurriedly to unload the coffins. He wiped away the molten wax, allowing himself a grim smile as he did so. Then he took out a Bible, covered his face with it and preceded the first of the boxes into the cooler air of the Museum.

16

TO BEGIN WITH at least, it was to be a day of double celebration for the Museum. Chang and Eng were due to arrive in town to negotiate with Barnum in an attempt to regain some of the fortune the fighting in North Carolina had snatched from them. Also arriving, although this was considerably less certain, was America's first White Elephant, shipped exclusively to the Museum from Siam. Everything, as usual, at Great Personal Expense to Barnum, who had only the Interests of his Public at Heart.

The acquisition of the elephant had been arranged by one of his Far Eastern agents almost six months previously and was supposedly on its way now to replace the hippopotamus, which, to everyone's delight and Barnum's dismay, had not yet succumbed as expected to the fetid air of the basement in which it was incarcerated. For six months the elephant had waited in Colombo, where it had been losing rather than making money, and it was upon considering these losses that Barnum felt he could wait no longer, and regardless of whether the hippopotamus was dead or alive upon its arrival, he sent for it.

The hippopotamus had been a considerable disappointment to Barnum in other respects, too: it ate more than he had anticipated, did very little in return, and actually discouraged the public from wanting to see it by the doleful expressions with which it communicated its unhappiness to them. That it had lived for so long was entirely due to Henry Butler's engine and the fresh supplies of oxygen and water this provided. For the most part, the animal simply bobbed up and down in its tank of green water, darkening it with its excrement and fouling it with its scum of uneaten food, rising occasionally, sometimes sinking and walking a pace or two, but seldom turning to face the crowd it was there to entertain.

On one occasion, upon receiving his tenth complaint of the day, Barnum had gone down to the 'Aquarial Hall' in a temper and asked the crowd what they honestly expected to see. Did they want to see the creature leap through burning hoops or perform underwater somersaults? Did they really want to witness the unbridled ferocity by which it might once have gained its reputation on the Nile? Their complaints, he told them, would be silenced fast enough if the glass walls shattered – which he then felt the need to convince them would never happen – and the beast were to rampage through the basement crushing and mauling as it went – which, God forbid, would also never happen.

After that, fewer and fewer of his customers descended to stare at the unhappy creature, which as a result seemed to grow more content in its relative solitude.

In finalizing the arrangements for the now superfluous white elephant, Barnum had asked his agent in Ceylon if this newest acquisition might not be tempted to become carnivorous and thus solve two of his problems at a stroke. The agent thought this unlikely, and for the fifth time tried to explain in his letter to Barnum that the term 'white' elephant did not exactly signify that the elephant – that its hide – that its actual colouration – that in daylight – that despite being much sought after – that despite being revered by the Siamese royal family – that although no one could actually call it black or even grey . . . He had got no further. 'White!' Barnum announced. It was enough. White as snow, white as the clouds, white as freshly picked cotton. White! White, agreed his agent, unhappy that only ten thousand miles now separated him from Barnum and the Museum.

The day of this double celebration started well – for Barnum himself and for the city as a whole. It was clear, and warm rather than stifling, and there had been neither drastic bloodshed nor setback during the previous few days to sour the newspaper headlines.

Barnum, following an absence of a week from the city, returned triumphant at six in the morning, stopping his carriage at Canal Street and walking from there to the Museum, shouting his greetings and doffing his hat to everyone he met, most of whom recognized him, some of whom did not, but who guessed by his manner and cordiality on that morning that they ought to know him and had nothing to lose by returning his greeting. He carried copies of the *Sun*, the *Tribune*, the *Herald* and the *Brooklyn Eagle*, searching them as he strode joyfully along for reports of the return of Chang and Eng and the arrival of the elephant. He found something in every one and made a mental note to send each of their editors a gift. Except perhaps to James Gordon Bennet, whom he had not yet forgiven for the slanders he had helped to spread. Perhaps, too, the time was now right for a further report advertising the new edition of his autobiography, a good deal of which he had only recently revised. The public, he felt sure, always thought of him as a younger man, and in his revision he had bowed to this; they demanded that he be taller, wealthier and healthier than he actually was, and to this too he had acquiesced. When they had wanted to see him as a man with nothing, a man who had gambled everything and lost, then this was what he had given them; but when they wanted riches and success, then there was no man richer or more successful than he. When they wanted fatherly joy he poured it upon the pages by the pailful, and when they wanted pain and anguish he gave them that, too. The son of a distant cousin of Charity's had recently been killed in the war – unnecessarily, as it happened, stupidly standing in the way of the recoil of his own cannon – and had not Barnum himself felt this terrible but worthwhile sacrifice as if it squeezed his very heart? Had he not loved that distant cousin's son as though he were his very own, and was there not now, so soon afterwards, a daguerreotype of the boy on the third floor of his Museum so that all might see and share in his suffering. He felt relieved that the war had finally touched him in this distant way, providing him with the perfect excuse for a tear in his eye the next time he stood up to lecture upon it.

Arriving at the Museum, he visited each of his exhibitors with all the forced joviality of a battlefield surgeon walking briskly through his wards of the sick and dying. He shook everyone's hand, he kissed all the women, he slapped everyone's back. Anything anyone wanted, they had only to ask. They'd been through a bad time recently, all of them, himself included, especially himself, but now their fortunes were about to take a turn for the better. 'Believe it. Believe it and rejoice,' he called out to everyone he encountered.

He visited Zip, who had fallen asleep fully dressed on the floor of his room. After contemplating him for several moments, he woke him and shook his hand, said keenness was its own reward and loyalty the greatest of all virtues. Before Zip could ask him what he was talking about, he had gone.

In the basement he paused to look at the hippopotamus, which gazed serenely back at him from the warmth and stillness of its tank, chewing contentedly, its eyes half closed. Annoyed at this, Barnum slapped his palms against the glass, and the animal responded by releasing a single bubble of air the size of a melon from the side of its mouth before turning away and presenting its rear to him. Barnum inspected the engine which constantly moved the water. He lifted several levers, tapped a gauge and blew at a small feather of steam as it leaked from a valve. He cursed Henry Butler and drew back his foot as though he were about to kick the gently throbbing machine, but thought better of this and stopped himself.

He visited Fortuna and René, both of whom had only recently dressed and were waiting for him to appear. René snipped at the edge of his wife's side whiskers and Barnum complimented him on the result. Beside them on the sofa lay their hairy son, the sight of whom had always repulsed Barnum. He patted the child on the head and said, 'Good Boy'. He asked if they were excited about the return of Chang and Eng and if they were looking forward to seeing the white elephant.

Fortuna spoke for them all and said they were. After the outrage of the portrait, René could still not bring himself to speak honestly to the man. Then, seeing the draped easel at the far side of the room, Barnum went to it and drew back the cloth to reveal the unfinished portrait of Elizabeth. He froze and then gasped at its beauty, at the exquisite detail and colour, at the perfection of its techniques, and most of all at its accuracy in every detail. Beside it, the portrait of Charity and his daughters looked to be the work of an amateur.

'I'll buy it for the Museum,' he said upon composing himself, surprised when René informed him it was not for sale, but that it was to be a gift to Elizabeth.

'Then I'll buy it from her,' Barnum said sharply, angry at this refusal.

Then the hairy boy leapt from the sofa and pleaded with Barnum to be allowed to ride upon the back of the elephant. He reached up to hold Barnum's hand, and Barnum felt himself tense at the touch of the fine hair which covered the child's forearm and fingers.

Fortuna told her son to return to the sofa, which he did.

It was Barnum's opinion that the boy would only frighten the creature, that it might regard him as little more than an overgrown rat and run amok at the sight of him.

'White elephants are not intended to be ridden upon,' he said authoritatively, and after glancing once more at the portrait of Elizabeth, he left them.

René immediately covered the painting and returned to his wife, holding his hand beneath her chin and shaping the dense black hairs which grew in a circle from her throat.

In the corridor, Barnum was met by Henry Butler, accompanied by Old Tom. Barnum increased his speed, intending to pass them by, but was stopped by Tom, who held out his arm an instant before he arrived and barred his way. It never failed to amaze Barnum how precisely Tom was able to judge such distances, or how accurately he timed his words at the silent arrival of others.

'Tom has something to ask you,' Henry Butler said, stepping back.

'Name it, Tom. I'm a busy man, today of all days, no time for idle speculation, but you just go right ahead and name it, I've always got time to stop and listen to you, you know that. Fire away.'

'I've written a tune to welcome back the stitched-up boys,' Tom announced proudly.

'Stitched-up? Tom, they are joined in the flesh by Mother Nature herself. *That* is their appeal, their asset, their attraction. They are *not* "stitched-up", as you put it, and I'll thank you not to even suggest as much.'

'Whatever,' Tom said, unperturbed by the rebuke.

'And?'

'Sir?'

'You've written a song. Well done. You're a genius, I've always said so, I've had handbills printed, thousands, tens of thousands declaring as much to the public. But, as I said, I'm a busy man today.' He pulled out and studied his pocket watch.

'Six-forty-five,' Tom said.

'He wants to play it in the entrance as Chang and Eng arrive,' Henry Butler said.

'Play it? I'll have a fifty-piece band out there, I'll have acrobats, I'll have people screaming the length and breadth of Broadway from the waterfront to Niblo's that they're here, and he wants to play it – a blind old ni– negro on piano against all that?'

'It was only a thought.'

'Yes, sir,' Tom said, his hopes undiminished.

It occurred to Barnum that Henry Butler had put him up to the request. He reconsidered the possibility.

'Fine, Tom, sure, you play it. I can't cancel the band this late in the proceedings, but sure, go ahead and play. It'll be the highlight of the day. Does it have a name, this song of yours?' He looked again at his watch, anxious to continue his rounds, and doing nothing now to disguise his irritation from either of the men.

'Yes, sir. Sure has got a name.'

'Well?'

'Well what, sir?'

'Tell me the name.'

'Oh, surely. See how this grab you – "Welcome Back Eng and Chang".'

'Very original. Nothing else?'

'No, sir.'

'Fine, sure, good. "Welcome Back Eng and Chang". It certainly has a ring to it. Fine, sure, go ahead.' He brushed past them and continued along the corridor.

Tom smiled and began to sing to himself: 'Welcome back Eng and Chang, hear you lost your farm in one big bang.'

Barnum paused briefly to look into Franklin's room. Franklin was sitting on the bed, his head bowed. He looked unwell. He was redder than usual, and already bathed with sweat.

'You're looking good, Franklin,' Barnum called in. Like a big greasy hog pumped up with air and ready to explode, he thought.

'I'm dandy, Mr Barnum, sir, just dandy. Got me a touch of colic or some such, that's all.' He held the uppermost fold of his stomach.

'Fit enough for the great, once-in-a-lifetime welcoming committee, I hope.'

'Sure, sure. I just need to get started, that's all. Once I'm started, then I'm fine.'

'Eating well?' Barnum asked uneasily.

'Don't much care for my food recently, to tell the truth. Don't seem able to keep it down. It'll pass, though. I'm sure of that.'

'Me too, me too.' This was bad news, and Barnum frowned. 'Thinking of having you lead the white elephant around City Hall this afternoon,' he lied. 'I know it's a great honour and a privilege, but if you don't feel up to it . . .'

'I'll be fine,' Franklin said. 'You know me – I never let you down yet. You can depend on me.'

Even the effort of trying to smile appeared to make Franklin sweat, and Barnum watched in disgust as a succession of drops fell from the tip of his nose on to his lips.

He left, calling for Greenwood to see what he had to say about Franklin's performances over the previous week.

Elizabeth, Anna Swan, Captain Bates and the Albino family sat together in Anna's room. At Barnum's appearance, the Albino family rose and presented themselves to him, saying little, merely curtsying and shaking his hand as they edged past him to prepare themselves for their booth. Barnum waited until they'd gone before wiping his hand and offering it to Elizabeth, whose fingers he kissed. Bates stood with his arm around Anna. They were very close now to finalizing their wedding plans, but as yet still believed Barnum knew nothing of these.

'Big day, ladies and gentlemen, big day,' Barnum said, hoping to infect them with some of his own enthusiasm.

In common with all the other long-term inhabitants of the Museum, neither Anna nor Captain Bates was looking forward to the return of the troublesome and demanding Chang and Eng. As with Thumb, the twins were accorded a considerably higher status by Barnum than any of his current performers.

'I have just been privileged to glimpse your exquisite portrait, Elizabeth,' Barnum said.

'René's a very talented artist,' said Anna.

'Talented? Yes, I suppose he is. In a provincial sort of way. I fear that he is somewhat let down by his grasp of technique on occasion, but nevertheless a chiaroscuro performance. How, indeed, is he ever likely to improve upon such a beauty as our Elizabeth's? You've all no doubt seen the likeness he has approximated of Charity and my own dear girls. I think he does their honesty, charm, wit and sincerity full justice. Don't you agree?'

Their plainness, meanness and dullness, thought Anna as she nodded her agreement.

'However, as for the perfect delineation of feature ... But who are we – mere mortals – when set beside such a creative spirit? A great pity, I often think, that he doesn't come out more often from behind Fortuna's skirts.' Barnum laughed.

'We think Franklin's ill,' Anna said seriously, causing him to stop abruptly.

'Nonsense. I've just paid him a call. He's in the pink. Never seen anyone look so well. And so he ought to on all the food I provide for him.'

'It isn't open to debate,' Anna said. 'He's ill and we think he should be seen by someone who might be able to help him.'

'Why don't we ask *him* what he wants?'

'Because he'll cover it up. Because he can't afford to lose any time out of his booth.'

'I think that decision's up to him, don't you? Look, I'm a busy man. Leave it for now, for today at least, and we'll talk about it later.' He left them, not exactly slamming the door behind him, but pulling it shut with a firmness intended to leave them in no doubt as to his true feelings.

Outside, Greenwood finally caught up with him.

'I'm not happy, Greenwood,' Barnum said, moving swiftly away ahead of him, causing Greenwood to lengthen his own stride to keep up. They held a moving conversation all the way to Barnum's office.

'And to cap it all, that damn creature in the basement just sits and smiles at me. It knows, Greenwood, it knows. It's laughing at me like a big fat child, wise beyond its years, too wise for its own good.' Barnum let himself drop behind his desk before taking out a handkerchief and mopping his brow.

'What do you want me to do about it?' Greenwood said. 'Just name it and it'll be done.'

There was a moment of silence as the two men stared at each other, each making his own assessment of what had just been suggested.

'What *can* be done?' Barnum said eventually.

'You're right. Nothing. We can only wait. Wait and pray.'

'Amen to that,' Barnum said. He was the first to look away, to conceal the guilty thought revealed in his eyes.

'I've had another communication from Ceylon,' Greenwood said nervously. 'Sent a month ago, received yesterday.' He laid the sheet of paper before Barnum and withdrew several paces. 'I think you ought to read it.'

Outside, banners announcing the arrival of the elephant had been hanging for a week, accompanied by paintings of the animal, the whiteness of which dazzled passers-by when they rose in the breeze and caught the sun.

Barnum read the message, and like the needle on a gauge of disappointment and disbelief, the cigar in his mouth fell until it threatened to detach itself completely.

' "Not exactly white",' he read aloud. 'What does he mean? "Very pale and pink in places". Pink! Pink!'

'I think we may have been somewhat misled by the somewhat arbitrary use of the phrase "white",' Greenwood said.

'Misled! Misled! I've paid for white and white is what I'll get. Barnum says white and that's what the public expects – white.' The message disappeared into his clenched fist. 'Where is it coming in?'

'The Old Slip. The boat's there now, awaiting our instructions.'

'Damn!'

It had originally been Barnum's intention to have Chang and Eng arrive at the Museum riding the elephant. Now that too would have to be changed. The City Hall parade led by Franklin would also have to be reconsidered; he could cancel that now on compassionate grounds. Indicating for Greenwood to close the door, he proceeded to tell him what to do. The two men leaned close, until their foreheads were almost touching. One talked, one listened, both smiled. The animal must be transported in a cage, high above the ground on a solid cart, and brought directly from the wharf to the arcade alongside the Museum. The procession, as usual, must be as loud and attractive as possible.

Greenwood left to make his preparations and Barnum sat alone for a further hour, still smiling, still congratulating himself on his solution to the problem of the elephant which might or might not be white.

The twins were due to arrive at midday.

At eleven-thirty Barnum went down to the entrance, where a crowd had long since gathered. To his dismay he spotted two of Jeremiah Bergh's trumpet-blowing disciples proudly waving a banner upon which was depicted a dead elephant. They amused the crowd, but their presence unsettled Barnum, and sending for two fire-eaters, who were then performing further along Broadway, he paid them to repeat their act alongside Bergh's women. 'Free of charge, free of charge,' he shouted, attracting attention to the two men.

Within a minute the banner of the dead elephant was ablaze and the women had fled screaming, one of them dropping her trumpet, which the fire-eaters retrieved and incorporated into their act.

At midday there was no sign of the triumphal procession which was supposed to carry the Twins back to him.

He waited until one. Then until two.

The crowd became restless and other acts were brought out to keep them entertained and happy.

At three the crowd set up a chant of displeasure, and at four they began to disperse. Seldom in his entire career had Barnum felt so cheated or humiliated.

At five he returned to his office, calling for Henry Butler and Greenwood to join him. Only Henry Butler appeared, explaining that Greenwood was still at the wharf arranging for the disembarkation of the elephant.

'Disaster,' Barnum said, his face buried in his hands. 'Absolute, total, complete, overwhelming and final disaster.'

'Not that bad, surely,' Henry Butler said, uncomfortable in Barnum's presence.

Barnum looked up at him through his fingers,.

Outside, Tom started playing the piano in the outer office.

'That's his composition,' Henry Butler said.

'It might as well be my funeral march. *Where are they*? Why aren't they *here*? I can get an elephant here all the way from Ceylon and yet they can't get themselves here from North Carolina on time. Why? Why why why why why? They promised. They said they'd be here. I had their word. They *need* me.'

There was nothing Henry Butler could say to soothe him, nothing Barnum now wanted to hear.

In the outer office, Tom continued louder than ever to extol the virtues of the Twins. Hackaliah Cherry joined him in the chorus.

'Shut up!' Barnum called through to them, but the two men didn't hear him and went on singing.

An hour later, as he was about to leave the Museum, a messenger arrived. Chang and Eng were still in North Carolina. They had been all set to leave for New York four days previously when word had reached them that the route of the coach they were about to take was in danger of being fired upon by roving bands of Confederate rebels, and because Barnum was a well-known favourite of the Union they had considered it unwise to attempt to keep their appointment with him. This news angered and surprised Barnum, having previously satisfied himself that the Twins were unlikely to be in even the slightest danger during their journey.

He walked down through the almost empty building. Angry at his failure to keep his promise, most of the visitors had left and gone home. He paused only to ask Zip if business had been bad throughout the afternoon, and Zip confirmed his worst fears with a disinterested shrug.

As he stepped out on to Broadway, the band which had been waiting all afternoon for the arrival of Chang and Eng and the elephant, suddenly struck up and deafened him, and those few optimistic members of the public who remained turned to look at him.

He tried to wave them into silence, but the musicians and their conductor persisted. He groaned with pain and embarrassment, a broad, outward grin on his face. Then he noticed the conductor jabbing his baton away from the musicians in the direction of City Hall. There, coming along Broadway, accompanied by Greenwood, high above the street in an open-topped cage on a powerful wagon was the whitest elephant he had ever seen, the whitest elephant *anyone* had ever seen, as white as the elephants on his posters, whiter even than the dozen white horses which pulled it, and considerably whiter than the darkening clouds which filled the sky above it. Seizing upon this late-minute turn in the day's fortunes, Barnum applauded loudly and stepped out into the middle of the thoroughfare to greet the animal.

The crowd, only a moment earlier so sullen and hostile, was once again with him and began to cheer and applaud all around him.

'Saved!' he called out. 'The day is saved! Saved! Saved! Oh, glory be!'

It was only as he swung his hat in acknowledgement of Greenwood's own frantic waving that he felt the first heavy drop of rain upon his head, and looking up, he saw a distant curtain of rain racing down Broadway behind the procession, catching and drenching it as it arrived within a hundred yards of the open arcade entrance. As one, the crowd stopped cheering, and amid them, instantly sodden from head to foot, Barnum closed his eyes and let out the most disbelieving 'NO' it had ever been his misfortune to utter. Looking up, he saw Greenwood, similarly drenched, on the platform beside the elephant. He saw the dozen white horses buck and prance in the warm summer downpour and their attendants dash for cover. He saw the bunting ripped from its position around the cage, and the yellow straw which lined it become flattened and turn to mush. But most of all, he saw the whitewash running in great furrowed streaks off the hide of the elephant, revealing its true colour beneath. Raising its head and extending its trunk, the creature played a succession of long, loud notes, trumpeting its arrival.

All around Barnum the bandsmen in their colourful uniforms scattered like finches at a gunshot, some clutching their instruments, others abandoning them in the mud, all running as though they might somehow now escape the downpour.

Immobile, unable to move amid all this confusion, Barnum groaned, covered his eyes, and sealed tight the gaps between his fingers.

1 7

TWO DAYS LATER the taxidermist and his assistant returned to the Museum with the stuffed and enlarged tiger. Both men had arrived in good spirits, calling into the Museum from the sidewalk for someone to help them get the animal inside. Across the street from them a crowd had once again gathered around the *Herald* doorway, clamouring for the latest news of the events of the previous night in the city. The stuffed animal provided some distraction, but few crossed Broadway to study it any more closely.

'We knew all this would happen,' the taxidermist's assistant called across to them through his cupped hands. 'Could have told you all a month ago.' He began to sing and dance an awkward jig, until the taxidermist slapped him on the head, knocking his hat to the ground.

'Save it for Mr High and Mighty Barnum,' he said with a grin. Then, looking up at the Museum, he frowned and swore.

'What?' his assistant asked.

'We might have predicted it, but what did it amount to?'

The assistant too looked up at the Museum. 'Nothing,' he said.

'No, not nothing – *some*thing.'

The assistant looked puzzled. 'But almost nothing.'

The taxidermist stopped himself from slapping him again.

Across the street the latest news was posted and the crowd pressed more tightly upon the doorway. The taxidermist watched them and then listened to them as they fell silent.

'Nothing new to hear,' he said. 'It's over, finished; they're just scrabbling around after the left-overs, wanting to be told the same good news over and over.' He drew a ball of phlegm into his mouth and spat it noisily out.

'We are cheated,' his assistant said.

'Cheated's the word.'

The previous evening, just as the taxidermist had predicted, a series of co-ordinated arson attacks had taken place in the city. Confederate raiders had arrived undetected with cases of incendiaries – glass phials filled with Greek fire which burst into flame upon contact with air. Unfortunately for them, however, word of their attack had leaked out, and earlier that same day General Benjamin Butler had marched into New York with ten thousand Union troops ready to defend the city. The rebels, it was later discovered, had been betrayed for money, but in the confusion following the arrival of the troops they had gone ahead with their plan as best they could under the now considerably more dangerous circumstances.

Fire bombs were thrown in the Holman Hotel, in the Franklin Theater, in Niblo's and the Winter Garden, among moored shipping in the docks, in the Fifth Avenue Hotel, in City Hall and Irving House. And one bomb had been thrown into the basement of Barnum's American Museum. But this, in common with many others – some of which had yet to be discovered – had failed to detonate. Throughout the entire night the city had been in an uproar. The Museum had been closed early and then thoroughly searched. The fire-bomber must have entered as a late visitor and the evidence of his failed attempt was discovered by Greenwood at two in the morning. Elsewhere, a hundred false alarms kept the troops and the fire extinguishers running all night, and in the confusion many of the bombers had managed to escape. A sufficient number, however, were caught and the true extent of their heinous and unimaginable outrage became quickly and widely known. In the heat of the moment, the facts of the matter counted for little and were not dwelt upon at any length in the sensational reports of the *Herald* or any other newspaper.

Knowing that the Museum was likely to be a prime target of such an attack, it was the smouldering ruins of this that the taxidermist and his assistant had hoped to see upon their arrival with the tiger, the absence of which now accounted for their abrupt change in temper.

Inside, Greenwood had warned everyone to say nothing of the bomb, hoping now to take advantage of the crowds being drawn by the *Herald*. It had occurred to him to exhibit the device, but Greek fire was remarkable only for its instability and his idea had been rejected by the others. He sent word to Barnum of what had happened, glorifying his own role in the proceedings, but received no immediate reply. The only word the messenger brought back from Barnum was for Cherry to brush down the 'white' elephant until its true colour was revealed, and then for a notice to be posted indicating to the public that the Museum and Barnum himself were just as much victims of the hoax as they were. Both Greenwood and Henry Butler had considered this unwise, but Barnum, who did not intend to approach within a mile of the Museum for at least a week, was adamant that this should now be done.

It took almost two hours to raise the stuffed tiger via rope and pulleys to the balcony of Isaac and Bella-Grace Sprague's room, from where it was to be manhandled into position on the third floor. The pulleys had been installed around the roof of the Museum many years earlier when it had become apparent that the narrow staircases and passages inside were restricting the movement of anything larger than a man beyond the first-floor galleries. In addition, the raising of a new attraction via the pulleys was always guaranteed to draw a crowd, a large part of which could then be induced inside to inspect the new exhibit at closer quarters.

The first Bella-Grace had seen of the tiger was its snarling face gazing blankly in at her as it drew level with the window. She screamed and the animal fell several feet before the workmen regained their grip and pulled it back up. Henry Butler arrived, explained to her what was happening and then removed the window frame, creating a space large enough for the animal to be swung inside.

'There's your tiger,' the taxidermist said proudly an hour later as the floor around the new exhibit was cleared of dirt and shavings by Cherry. He held out his hand for payment. 'In full,' he demanded.

'There's a problem,' Henry Butler said, embarrassed by the position into which he had been forced by Greenwood, who had earlier confided to him that Barnum, despite his promises, had no intention of paying the man. 'He expected to see us burn,' Greenwood had said. 'So what does he expect now?'

Zip arrived to support Henry Butler, standing between him and the taxidermist's assistant, who had already raised his fists and was now squaring off ready to throw a punch.

'We've had one of two disappointments of late,' Henry Butler said nervously.

'Disappointments!' The taxidermist laughed and then stopped himself abruptly. He glanced at his assistant; the man was waiting only for his word. 'Cash. I don't care about your "disappointments". *My* biggest disappointment right now was getting here this morning to find this place still standing. Don't talk to me about "disappointments". Barnum must take me for a complete idiot.'

'You were the one who just bolted the animal to the floor,' Zip pointed out to him.

'And I can just as easily unbolt it and send it back down to the street.'

'I doubt it.' Zip indicated the window frame, which was then being hammered back into position, and the last of the rope being drawn through the pulley. 'It's our rope.'

The taxidermist paced the room, and his assistant, his fists still raised, paced behind him.

'You'll just have to be patient and wait a little longer,' Henry Butler said.

'I can't wait. I demand payment *now*.'

Bella-Grace Sprague arrived to examine the tiger. She asked the taxidermist what it was supposed to be, thus antagonizing him even further. Isaac followed her and stood beside the animal, barely rising to its shoulders on its new stand.

'It's a tiger,' Hackaliah Cherry told her. 'What's it look like?'

'Like a badly stuffed armchair.' She punched the animal in the chest, rocking it and causing the taxidermist to run and defend it.

'You should all have been burned in your beds, and this place should have been gotten rid of once and for all. It's common knowledge that this is what they were after; they'd still string Barnum from the nearest tree if they got their hands on him, *and* he knows it. I wager if any of us could see him now, he'd be whiter than that elephant of his, not that that should present him with too much of a problem; come to think of it, we're all whiter than the elephant. With one or two exceptions, that is.' He looked dismissively at Zip and Cherry. 'Perhaps someone should call his bluff and throw a pail of water over them new albinos you're supposed to have downstairs.'

'They're the genuine article,' Henry Butler said.

'Genuine! Genuine! You're using that word in connection with this place? The only thing genuine in here is the cash piling up in the strongboxes – cash which should by rights be mine. I'm owed it and I want it.'

Fully aware of the injustice being committed upon the man, Henry Butler suggested a compromise – the immediate payment of a quarter of what he was owed, the rest later. The taxidermist refused. Henry Butler knew that if Greenwood had been dealing with the man, he'd be out on the street by now, his demands turned to empty threats and then curses. It was Barnum's philosophy that people expected to be owed money, and that there was even something approaching prestige to be owed money by him personally. In the past, the higher his own star had risen, the further he considered himself able to push his creditors. He'd been pushing the taxidermist from the beginning, from his repair work on the Feejee mermaid and the birds of paradise which had once decorated the Museum entrance.

'It's pathetic,' Bella-Grace Sprague declared, having completed a full circuit of the tiger.

'Pathetic enough for you to scream at, madam,' the taxidermist reminded her. 'It's a wonder to me, living as you do amid all this, that you don't wake nightly screaming in your sleep. The dog bone here – your husband, is he?' He turned to Isaac. 'Stay away from those jaws, sir; it might be expertly stuffed, but you still present a very tempting target, a very tempting target indeed.' Realizing that he was now unlikely to be paid in full, he was beginning to indulge himself at everyone else's expense. He still had a legal claim to the tiger, but knew that under the circumstances that was considerably less of an advantage than it might at first appear.

Bella-Grace prodded her husband and asked him if he was going to stand there and allow himself to be spoken to in that manner.

'Habit of a lifetime,' Sprague said, flexing the muscles of one arm and bringing his entire fifty-two pounds to bear on the effort.

'How's the elephant coming, Hack?' Henry Butler asked Cherry.

'Still not white.'

'Perhaps you could bill it as the cleanest elephant in the country,' the taxidermist suggested. 'They've paid good money to see everything else. If this place *had* been burned to the ground then I'm sure he'd have been here now selling tickets for pieces of that, too.'

'Burned to the ground?' Bella-Grace said. She and Isaac knew nothing of Greenwood's discovery in the basement, and because they had only risen at the appearance of the tiger, nor had they yet been told. They were aware of the panic throughout the rest of the city during the night, but not that a murderous finger of it had reached in and gently prodded them as they slept.

'In your beds. To cinders, melted down to nothing, fur, feathers, fat, all gone. Whoosh.' The taxidermist made his hands into the flames of a vicious fire. 'Victory to the Confederacy, scum that they are.' He too was unaware of the unexploded phial.

'Absolute scum,' his assistant added.

'What's he talking about?' Bella-Grace repeated, her concern growing.

'He's scaremongering,' Zip told her, moving to stand with his face only inches from the taxidermist's, his finger held less than that from his chest. 'Right, *friend*?'

'Oh, surely, friend, surely. Whatever you say.'

Zip withdrew.

'But strange, don't you think,' the taxidermist went on, addressing Bella-Grace directly, 'every other public building of note attacked, and yet this one left untouched. Perhaps Mr Barnum's been spreading his allegiances pretty far and wide, slipping a few coins into pockets on both sides of the coat.'

'Now what's he talking about?' Bella-Grace said.

Unable to restrain himself, the taxidermist said loudly, 'It's going to come, it's going to come. I see it all. It's coming! Coming to all of you. Every single one of you. And when it does none of you will escape and I'll be out front with my ticket to watch it all come crashing down to destruction and –'

Zip grabbed him by his lapels, pinning him against the wall, looking hard at Henry Butler, waiting for him to reassert his authority over what was happening. The taxidermist's assistant pushed his arm between the two men.

'Leave him,' Bella-Grace shouted. 'I want to know what he's talking about. Are they coming back? Is that what he's saying? Will they try again and this time succeed where they failed before? I want to know. We live right up here on the third floor.'

'Third *wooden* floor,' the taxidermist said, the words strangled in his throat by Zip.

'Get them out,' Henry Butler said, and stood aside for Zip to pull the two men through the door and push them ahead of him down the staircase. Cherry followed him with his broom, and Henry Butler stood alone with Bella-Grace and Isaac, who held each other and tried desperately to think of something reassuring to say to each other.

Later, after Henry Butler had sought out Zip to thank him, they inspected the shattered glass phial of nitre and sulphur which had failed in its task. After his own all-night vigil, Greenwood had gone out, and the two men sat alone in Henry Butler's shared office.

'You think it's some kind of punishment?' Zip asked him. He helped himself to a drink from the decanter on Greenwood's desk.

'Whatever. But the war's not over yet, and if they decided to try again, we'd be the obvious target.'

Inside the broken phial was a smaller sealed glass ball. It was this which had failed to break and ignite the now dispersed naphtha gas. Zip tipped this hollow marble from side to side and watched its contents shift.

'We could empty the building now, go back down and try again,' he said.

Henry Butler showed no surprise at the remark.

'Except that emptying the building is a physical impossibility. You might get the more agile of us out, but not the animals. Apart from which, I assume there needs to be some sort of sacrifice if the insurers are ever going to be made to pay up.'

Henry Butler laughed coldly.

'No insurance?' Zip said, watching him closely.

'Very little. After the fire at Iranistan and the trouble Barnum had recouping even a small part of his losses there, this place has been underinsured for years. Look around you – it's virtually uninsurable. He ought to rebuild in stone, but says he can't afford it. He might be a wealthy man, but he's still a considerable risk in the eyes of the bankers and insurers.'

Zip poured himself a second and larger drink.

'It's all falling apart,' Henry Butler said, his head bowed at the treasonous remark.

'You're not telling us anything we haven't already known for years, for ever.'

'The hippo, Thumb, the Twins, and now the elephant. At one time he couldn't do anything wrong if he tried; now it seems like exactly the opposite is true. Everybody's seen everything there is to see. There's no more to show them. It's unnatural: they'd fight to save a cent on a sack of potatoes and then pay up twenty-five here to see a man-eating savage from Rhode Island or a card-playing dog that never dealt a card in its life. What *is* it they're truly paying for? You tell me.'

Zip passed him a drink, which Henry Butler looked at for a full minute before raising it to his lips.

'Anna and Bates are getting ready to leave,' Zip said. 'But don't tell Barnum or Greenwood.'

'I know, and I don't blame them. They'll make a go of it. What about the rest of you?'

'After we've broken free of our contractual obligations, you mean?' The two words came out with a bad taste. 'I dare say we'd scatter like animals at a burning menagerie. We'd run away from the flames and then we'd stop. Some of us would starve, others would be hunted down, but most of us would just make our way back to the open cages with our tails between our legs.'

'I'd like to help, I really would.' Henry Butler felt fortified by the drink.

'You can't. We can't even help ourselves. Anna and Bates, perhaps. Elizabeth and me, but not the rest of us.'

'And that makes you responsible for those less able?'

They both stopped speaking as someone passed by in the corridor outside.

'He'd fire you if he had any idea this conversation had even taken place,' Zip said.

'Let him,' Henry Butler said, surprising them both.

Zip refilled his glass. 'I thought you and Greenwood had plans to take over.'

'Greenwood did. Not me. I just went along with him because there was nothing else I could do. He was right to try. Barnum's losing his grip on the place. He won't come back now until everything's died down and it's safe to return.'

'Do you think he'll pull out after this?' Zip asked.

'I doubt it. He craves the attention too much to ever be without it.'

'Thumb made the break,' Zip said. 'So did the miserable Twins.'

'They're still what they are. Barnum only stopped working with them because they learned how to exploit themselves. None of you can ever be free of exploitation. I don't think *any* of us can hope for that.'

'Bates and Anna perhaps. I'd like to see that.'

'Me, too. In their home in the country. They can surround themselves with giant trees and then make giant furniture from them. They can scale up the world to their own specifications. Their visiting neighbours can be the freaks.'

'Except they'd treat any visitor with all the decency and civility they could muster. Without them, this place would be no better than that menagerie before the fire.'

Henry Butler went to the window and gazed down at the crowds still arriving to mock the elephant in the adjoining arcade. 'He's wrong in letting them know that he's just as much a victim of the hoax as they are. They don't expect that from him. They expect him to stand his ground and bluster his way out of it. It's almost as though they *want* to be convinced of their stupidity, as though they believe that with his help they can somehow turn it into a virtue.'

'They can,' Zip said. 'Their twenty-five cents makes sure of that for them. For a dollar he'd get a lynch mob, but for twenty-five cents they're prepared to stand and cheer him.'

There was a single knock at the door and Hackaliah Cherry walked in. There were diluted splashes of white on his face and arms from where he'd been scrubbing down the elephant.

'Reckon it's just about as white as nature intended it to be, but they still rollin' up to laugh at it.'

'It's a sacred and revered creature in its homeland,' Henry Butler said. 'They live in the king's palace and their every whim is indulged. They have attendants who worship the very ground upon which they walk.'

'They'll laugh even harder if we tell 'em that,' Cherry said.

'I know.'

'It sure is one big unlucky beast. All that way and all that expense just to get painted up, rained on, scrubbed down and laughed at.' Cherry eyed the brandy they were both drinking, and was just about to suggest pouring himself one when Greenwood appeared behind him and told him to get back down to the elephant.

'And what's *he* doing in here?' he said, sitting opposite Zip at the desk.

'Enjoying a drink with my friend, Mr Butler,' Zip said.

'Butler?'

Henry Butler remained looking down at the street.

'We were looking at this.' Zip rolled the glass ball across the desk to him.

'Butler, I asked you what he was doing here. It's bad enough that we have to tolerate them out there, but I draw the line at inviting them in here.'

'How very considerate,' Zip said.

Henry Butler turned to face them, his face empty. 'Supposing you could leave all this behind you, just as you can wake up from a disturbing dream and leave all that where it belongs,' he said, surprising them both with the remark.

'What's he talking about?' Greenwood said, shaking the ball and watching its contents shift around inside.

'Just supposing,' Henry Butler went on, his gaze still focused beyond them. 'Just supposing we had the strength to make that decision. To make it but not to tell anyone.'

'Sure,' Zip said, knowing it was a dying dream. 'I'll drink to that.' He studied both men through the swirling brandy before draining his glass with a single swallow and leaving them.

'You ought to be more careful,' Greenwood said to Henry Butler after a minute of silence.

'Of what?' But Henry Butler understood perfectly what he meant. He understood it as well as he understood the three powerful and destructive forces Greenwood, Zip and Barnum had now become within the overheated confines of the Museum, all three cautiously circling, each waiting for any advantage, however slight, which might yet be gained at the expense of the others.

18

A WEEK PASSED, during which time Barnum stayed resolutely away from the Museum, preferring the lesser ridicule of his wife and daughters to the disgrace and humiliation he felt certain awaited him upon his reappearance in public. For days, Charity raised the subject of Chang and Eng and the elephant at every opportunity, following him from room to room until even in his own home he was eventually forced to isolate himself behind lock and key. And even then they called through the door to him, reminding him of what a fool he'd been, and insisting yet again that the time had come for him to abandon the running of the Museum and its so-called attractions to someone more capable, someone younger, someone with a feel for the work, someone more versatile, someone with an eye to the future.

Thus wounded, his back to the wall, pricked and stung by these slingshots and arrows, Barnum tried to defend himself and his errors of judgment. But they were united in their attack and retaliated ceaselessly, their arguments well practised, deaf to his pleas, and only withdrawing and leaving him in peace when there were further wedding preparations to be attended to.

On the third night of his absence from the Museum, he woke from a nightmare in which the entire building, fully laden with its human crew and cargo, had broken free of its foundations and was moving slowly along Broadway like a triple-decker paddle steamer along the Mississippi. There were certain obvious similarities – the intricate white lattice and iron-work of the door and window frames, canopies and balconies, and the overall shape of the structure in general. And in this nightmare, only he, Barnum, appeared to have noticed what was happening. He tried to warn people, but no one paid him any notice; instead they behaved as though they hadn't heard or seen him. He ran from booth to booth, floor to floor, urging people to save themselves, through every gallery and auditorium, up and down every flight of stairs, but still no one stopped to listen to him. Cabinets shook on their slender legs as the building gathered speed, moving out of the sidewaters into the full rushing flow at the centre of the street, unstoppable now as it gained momentum and began to move even more rapidly. Display cases fell from the walls and still no one noticed. In desperation he climbed out on to the roof and shouted down, warning people to clear the way ahead of them, to flee before they were crushed beneath this uncontrollable juggernaut. This time there was some response, but instead of fleeing in terror at the spectacle, the people below formed into two orderly lines on each sidewalk and cheered the Museum's steady progress. They waved flags and threw their hats in the air. They applauded and chanted Barnum's name. He was speechless, unable to do anything but stand and look helplessly down at them, his arms held in supplication. And then, nearing the edge of the roof, he leaned over and finally saw what had caused the Museum to move and what was now steadily propelling it along its course. Immediately beneath him was a heavy chain, attached by a bolt to the side of the building. He looked slowly along this, barely wanting to reach its end, and just as he was about to do so, he awoke with a start and a cry.

He was alone – he and Charity had long since slept in separate rooms – and as he sat upright in his bed he felt the sweat squeeze out of his brow and palms. Opposite him his reflection in a mirror came upright too and sat considering him.

'More capable,' he said to it.

'Someone more versatile,' it answered him.

Even then, at three in the morning, the room was warm, and he left his bed to open the window further. There was little noise from the street below, but in the distance he could hear the noise of the vessels on the Hudson, their occasional whistles and drawn-out groans of warning to others passing close by them in the dim light. There was a distant commotion in the city, but these days, or so it now seemed to him, there was always a distant commotion going on somewhere just beyond his reach.

He lit a cigar and saw that his hands were shaking. Returning to his bed, he sat upon the crumpled sheets and tried to remember everything he'd seen in his dream, recalling in particular detail the chain along which his eyes had been travelling an instant before he'd woken.

He tried not to think about it, but found this impossible, and so he sat and waited for the first signs of dawn, unwilling to submit himself to sleep for fear that the nightmare might reclaim him. On the few occasions when he did feel himself slipping back, someone crept into the locked room and whispered 'More capable, someone – more – capable,' into his ear, and the words doused him with their icy coldness.

He smoked four cigars before the first rays of sunlight touched the parapet of the buildings opposite.

Dressing, he went quickly and quietly downstairs, where he locked himself in the library and composed a letter to the Siamese Twins, castigating them for their disgraceful and contemptible act of betrayal. He wrote the letter sixteen times, read the final version through twice until he was satisfied it expressed his thoughts exactly and concisely, and then screwed it into a ball and threw it down to join all its failed predecessors.

Then he fell asleep where he sat and was woken several hours later by the noise of this daughters banging on the door and demanding to be allowed in. He was surprised to find himself dressed and sitting at his desk, and at hearing their calls and curses. Then he remembered the dream and the letter, and he retrieved all the paper balls before going to the door and letting his daughters in upon him. He returned to the desk and insisted that he was busy and needed peace and privacy to attend to his affairs. Their silence lasted five seconds, perhaps ten, but it was only the silence of disbelief and incredulity, and every second of it struck him with yet another sharp and painful blow. Behind them, he saw Charity pass the open doorway and he called out to her. She paused, raised her chin, cast a glance at him, sniffed and moved on.

'I know,' he said silently to himself. 'Someone more capable,' uncertain for a moment whether he'd arrived at the final, humiliating station of his defeat, or merely at the starting point. His thoughts were interrupted by his youngest daughter, who planted her considerable weight on his lap, twirled his hair with her finger, kissed his forehead and told him that regardless of how much of a laughable and miserable failure he might now appear in the eyes of the world, she at least would continue to love him. And could he let her have ninety dollars to buy a dress to wear at her sister's wedding? At that moment, in the vacuum between her demand and his reply, Charity reappeared, clapped once and drew her daughters to her. All of them then turned to face him, united and ready, he thought, for their first assault of the day. He considered telling them of his dream, but swiftly thought better of it.

'The wedding,' Charity said loudly and severely, indicating to him that the time had once again arrived to leave behind him the small and despicable world for which he and he alone was responsible, and return to that other world, that happy world of social niceties and carefree concerns in which they now considered themselves to be the prime movers. His world, they considered, was a world of shadows, of fleeting and frightening glimpses, of people moving shamefully and hurriedly from one blighted corner to the next; whereas theirs, by comparison, was a world filled entirely with light and bright colours, good manners and a never-ending succession of small excitements, one after the other, each leading to the next, and all of them stretching – like the heavy silver chain of his nightmare – towards the same, essentially unattainable goal.

'The wedding,' Charity repeated.

'The wedding,' Barnum said, and he rose to join them and enter unhappily and persecuted into that altogether brighter, shallower existence.

19

A FURTHER FORTNIGHT passed, and after those fourteen long and empty days alone with Charity and his daughters, Barnum was ready to return to the Museum. He had not been entirely idle during his absence, but all the same he wished to return quietly, surreptitiously almost, and to re-establish himself once again at its slowly fading heart.

Ever since the failed arson attack he had received several communications daily from either Greenwood or Henry Butler, but their tales of dwindling receipts and increasing complaints had done little to encourage him, and as the days passed, so his conviction grew that he, and he alone, could bring about a reverse in the Museum's fortunes. He was also aware that the longer he stayed away the greater the advantage he was handing to the two men in their plotting against him, of which he was in little doubt.

Now, as he contemplated his return to the Museum, he came up with what he considered to be a masterstroke: he would sponsor the first manned balloon crossing of the Atlantic – New York to Paris or London. It was partly as a result of his enthusiasm for this project that he had decided to return. That, and the fact that he felt himself being helplessly and irresistibly drawn into the quickening maelstrom that his daughter's wedding had become. Charity and the others had flung themselves in from the shore with alarming alacrity many months ago, but it was only now, during his self-imposed exile among this tribe of strangers, that he too had felt himself tugged and gently buffeted towards the spiralling point of the Great Day itself.

His nightmares had ceased, and on the morning of his intended return he woke with a clear head and an even clearer conscience, eager to begin, to reassert his authority and burst anew upon the public, to shine in its eye. He might even go up briefly in one of the balloons himself, not too high and not too far, but just high enough and far enough for people to comment on his daring and his youthful sense of adventure.

It was as he lay in his bed contemplating this happy prospect that he heard the distant notes of a marching band. He rose and went to the window.

There, beneath him, and at a distance where everything began to lose its focus and become an unformed blur of colour and movement, was an approaching procession.

'One of mine?' he said to himself, trying to remember if he had indeed had any hand in it before the disaster of the elephant. The noise grew louder, and as he once again looked out, the shapeless pattern of men and beasts marched out of the mist into full view, and ahead of them flew several banners. Retrieving his spectacles, he peered to make them out, and making them out he stepped backwards and caught his breath. And having caught his breath, he then let it out in one long unhappy sigh.

Tom Thumb, Tom Thumb, Tom Thumb, TOM THUMB, TOM THUMB, *TOM THUMB, TOM THUMB, TOM THUMB!!! TOM THUMB!!!!!*

The chanting grew louder, swollen by the crowds which had gathered even at that early hour to cheer the midget along his route.

'Today?' Barnum said incredulously. 'Why today?'

There was no doubt in his mind where the procession was headed, the route it was taking, or the reason for its appearance.

He closed the window and stood away from it.

He heard Charity calling him from below, and felt immediately like a deer might feel, stepping momentarily from the safety of the forest into an open glade, only to find itself surrounded by a group of weary hunters, resting, their rifles loaded and cocked, and only moments before abandoning their quest and leaving for home.

*

Thumb drove along Park Avenue in his miniature carriage, drawn by six white ponies, each with a plume of ostrich feathers rising between its ears. Ahead of him marched a band flanked by jugglers and clowns, by acrobats, and by two other midgets holding aloft the foremost banner proclaiming that Thumb had indeed once again returned. The onlookers ran along the sidewalks to keep up with him, and children were invited to race alongside the miniature carriage before being stopped and showered with coins, thrown among them by Thumb himself. He stood on a low raised platform and waved to the crowds, acknowledging their applause and blowing them kisses. He was dressed as Abraham Lincoln in a tall hat and false beard, and along the sides of his carriage were draped a number of Union flags and other pennants.

Immediately ahead of the ponies walked a zebra, and upon the back of that sat a chimp in harness beating tunelessly on a drum.

Every few minutes, Thumb stood down from his platform and relaxed on his cushioned seat. He wiped the sweat from his brow and caught his breath between deep draws on his cigar. When the demand from the crowd increased he rose again and waved. From his vantage point he was able to look ahead of him and calculate the distance he had yet to travel to reach Barnum's home.

Arriving there, the band marched in circles and began playing even more loudly. On his cushion, Thumb waited for Barnum to appear, ready to greet him in full view of the assembled crowd. If his luck held, Barnum might still be in bed and appear before them in his nightgown.

Nothing happened. Thumb practised his wave of hearty welcome. He instructed the band to stop marching and to concentrate their musical efforts, just as the trumpeters at the walls of Jericho had concentrated theirs. Amid this rising cacophony, the ponies grew restless, and he rose to control them with a whip which reached far beyond their heads to the zebra and the drumming chimp.

And then a second-floor window was thrown open and Barnum stood before him. Behind him he saw the figure of Charity and his daughters. He called up to him and Barnum stepped out on to the balcony. Charity appeared beside him and shouted down for silence, her voice immediately drowned by the noise of the band, the crowd, the drumming of the monkey and the braying of the zebra, all of which flooded into her home like the climax of one of her own all too frequent nightmares concerning her husband and his business.

Barnum was jolted from his own thoughts by the arrival of his eldest daughter, the one shortly to be married. She grabbed his arm and drew him back to the window.

'Tell them to go away, to get gone,' she shouted into his face, holding her fist to his mouth. She was in her nightdress, a residue of dried cream on her face, clips of paper and bone in her dishevelled hair.

'Or we'll start throwing things down,' his youngest daughter added with a malicious grin.

Barnum knew this was no idle threat. He stepped forward, back out into full view of Thumb and the crowd. Usually when he did this he felt like a member of royalty about to address his adoring subjects. Now, however, he felt like a man alone on the gallows, lost, waiting, entirely dependent upon the whims and timing of others.

Looking down he saw the ponies and followed them back to Thumb, who rose, bowed, held his hat to his heart and began to recite the Gettysburg Address, at which the crowd roared with delight. Hats and sheets of newspaper erupted into the air, separated as grain from chaff and then floated slowly back to earth.

Barnum understood everything immediately. Out of the corner of his eye he saw the scowling faces of his daughters. He had once believed them beautiful, had convinced himself of their charms and talents. He saw the eldest raise her fist to him and then jab at the crowd below. Beside her was Charity, still unwilling to assist him. Then his youngest picked up a heavy vase, ready to carry out her threat. Her teeth were bared, and in that moment Barnum knew that unless he acted swiftly all might be lost. He steadied himself against the balcony rail and raised his hand to Thumb. Behind him he heard the windows slam shut, and he shuddered, as the condemned man might shudder at the sound of the bolt being drawn beneath his feet.

'Ladies and gentlemen,' Thumb shouted. 'I give you one of the greatest showmen of our time.' He swung his arms until both were pointing up at Barnum. 'Mr Phineas Taylor Barnum!' The crowd cheered as it turned to gaze up at him.

Only *one* of the greatest showmen? Who were the others? Barnum thought, waving mechanically and smiling back down at them.

He looked directly at Thumb. He, Barnum, had been the first to suggest the Lincoln costume; *he* had bought the carriage, imported the first six Shetland ponies; *he* had been the first to surround the midget with all this paraphernalia of showmanship and *he* had groomed him and coached him in his entrances and exits. His thoughts were interrupted by the rapping of Charity and his daughters on the glass a foot from his head. His youngest still held the vase.

'General!' he shouted down, conscious then for the first time of how improperly dressed he was for this impromptu appearance before his public. 'What a marvellous surprise, a marvellous marvellous surprise.'

Thumb didn't answer, but simply considered him with his head tilted and a dry smile on his lips. 'I'm sure it is,' he said to himself.

Ahead of him, the chimp became bored with its drumming and began to pull the ears of the zebra, stretching them back until the animal reared in pain.

'Come on down,' Thumb shouted to Barnum. 'I insist. Now. Join me. Be my guest. We're on our way to the Museum, to that palace of perambulatory perfection.'

'The Museum?' Barnum said.

Continuing in a louder voice for the benefit of the crowd, Thumb said, 'I hear you were badly let down by the slit-eyed brothers of old Siam, the cowards of Carolina. Probably share the same yellow spine. I hear someone burst a bladder and they thought it was a battle and so they stayed home with all their slaves.' This last word was spoken loudest of all, and upon hearing it the noise of the crowd dropped slightly and many faces turned to look back up at Barnum. Thumb smiled to himself. 'I believe they treat them very well,' he went on, 'and that the beatings and whippings in the cotton fields are divided equally between the two stitched-up yellow-bellies.'

There was nothing Barnum could say in answer. 'I'll come down,' he shouted.

'That was the idea. It don't pay to keep all these good people standing around like this, even if they are all getting a free show at *my* expense.' He paused, his grin spreading. 'Tell me, Barnum, are they the beautiful Barnum girls I see behind you, the Barnum Belles? Bring them out; it's selfish of you to keep them all to yourself. Perhaps they could sing for us while we're waiting for you to get dressed.' The crowd called out in agreement with this.

The thought of his daughters singing on the balcony froze Barnum's heart and he shouted down that his wife was unwell in that very room and that they were with him to minister to her. He felt a single drop of icy sweat fall from his brow.

'Down directly,' he shouted, turned and went back into Charity and his daughters. He pleaded with them to be patient, and to stay away from the window until he had gone out and the procession had resumed its journey.

'You said you weren't going back there for a month,' Charity said accusingly, unaware of his plans to return that very day. 'There's the wedding.'

'I know.' Barnum struggled with his collar, pinching the skin of his chin and neck.

'And then this shrimp turns up, snaps his fingers and off you run like an obedient little dog,' his eldest daughter added. 'It's pathetic.'

'Girls, girls, girls,' Charity said weakly, this being the extent of her loyalty to her husband in his dilemma.

Barnum listened to them squabbling among themselves and wondered how much he had lost in the past few weeks, how much more he had come close to losing, how quickly that which had gone had deserted him, and how much of an effort was now required of him to retrieve it. It was too much to think about and so he concentrated on his collar instead.

There had been talk only the previous day by all three of his daughters of visiting insurance agents to ensure that their inheritance was protected. He had tried to persuade them against this, but remained uncertain of how successful he'd been.

'We have lots of shopping to do,' his youngest said with a glint in her eye. 'So you'd better make sure we're well provided for before you rush off to your stupid freak show.'

'That disgusting place.'

'Girls, girls,' was all Charity could now say.

There were times when Barnum, seeing her sleeping in her night-dress and cap, gloves and stockings, thought she looked like a corpse in its shroud, her pale, drawn face showing only the merest signs of life, the Holy Bible on the pillow beside her ready to be slid with a lily beneath her crossed hands.

'See – you're upsetting Mother.'

He was handed his topcoat and cane and pushed out of the room.

Downstairs, two servants stood by the door which led out on to the street, the looks upon their faces suggesting that they believed the mob outside was about to storm the building and carry Barnum upon its shoulders, whether for good or ill they couldn't say.

Preparing himself, Barnum fixed his grin, held his arms ready to wave, signalled for the door to be thrown open and made his second appearance before the crowd. There was a cheer, but not a particularly loud or genuinely enthusiastic one.

'Ladies and gentlemen,' he said, gesticulating, descending the steps towards Thumb's carriage. The crowd parted for him, but the corridor they cleared was narrow and he felt unaccountably threatened as he made the short journey. He heard the word 'slave' whispered again and tried to move more swiftly towards the safety of the carriage. He felt as he did every time he ran the gauntlet of his creditors in the courts, but in the place of exasperation he now experienced a very real sense of menace. He knew this could be dispelled as quickly and completely as it had been conjured up, but for the few moments that it lasted, he felt as if he had never felt anything else.

As he approached the carriage, Thumb called for the crowd to give him more room, that he was an old man, a man not as young as he had once been, a man not even as middle-aged as he might have once been. Barnum laughed with them, feeling a second drop of sweat gather and fall.

He arrived at the carriage, expecting to be magnanimously invited aboard. Instead, just as he was about to open the door, Thumb gave a single, slight flick of his whip, and the ponies, anxious to start moving again, began to trot forward. This surprised Barnum and he asked Thumb to stop.

'Wave to your daughters,' Thumb said. 'They're watching us.' He doffed his hat and blew three kisses to the faces at the window.

Barnum paused and turned to look back up, and as he did so the carriage moved ahead of him. Rather than wave, he ran to catch it up. It was not moving quickly, but in order for him to hold its side and talk to Thumb, he was forced to walk at a pace brisker than usual.

'You're – you're alone,' he said. 'No Lavinia.' So far, this had been the only positive sign of the morning.

'Ah, the beautiful Lavinia. Yes, as you rightly perceive, I am alone.' Leaning closer to him, Thumb said, 'Address me as General.'

'General?'

'Yes.' Thumb said loudly, resuming his position on the raised platform and waving beyond Barnum to the others also walking briskly alongside.

'Yes what?' Barnum said, confused by the sudden switch from the private to this public mode of address.

'You were asking after my beautiful bride,' Thumb said, still loudly. 'You'll be very happy to know that she has recovered from her recent illness and that she sends her best wishes to yourself and the fine people of New York City and hopes that she will be with them again very soon. It was the thought of their prayers for her that helped her in her recovery. That and her never-faltering faith in the good Lord above.' Thumb glanced upwards and held his hands together in prayer for a moment. The crowd cheered. 'Indeed, it was she, Lavinia Thumb, Bumpus as was, who insisted that I bring this money for the children of those same good people, in total one – hundred – dollars.'

The crowd gasped at this generosity and faltered in its pace. Thumb scattered more of the coins for the children to fight over. In reality, the sum was nearer ten dollars, but the procession had been long and few had followed it from its very beginning, passing on the baton of excitement and anticipation as they fell away on either side, called by their work or other commitments, envious of the people who could afford to travel with it all the way to its destination.

'Amen,' Barnum said as Thumb lowered his gaze and unclasped his hands.

'Amen indeed,' Thumb said quietly, and lowering his voice even further added, 'I heard you had a spot of trouble with an off-white carcass of an elephant.'

'First in the country,' Barnum said, the pride in his voice lost in his panting as the carriage speeded up at an intersection, and as Thumb rose to wave to all the new spectators thus acquired, many of whom were drawn out into the major thoroughfare to swell the procession further.

'You should have stuck to showing them what they wanted to see. Something genuinely entertaining and value for money.'

Like you, Barnum thought.

'Like me,' Thumb said.

'Perhaps,' Barnum said, releasing his grip on the carriage door and stopping to catch his breath. Some of the crowd stopped with him, and seeing this, Thumb drew up the carriage and opened its door. He then pleaded with Barnum to join him inside, as though he had asked before, and as though Barnum, perhaps in a moment of foolish pride, had chosen to walk. The crowd applauded this gesture, and then Barnum's acquiescence.

'You see how the balance of power shifts one way and then the other,' Thumb said, clutching his seat as the small carriage tilted under Barnum's weight.

They rode in silence for a minute. On either side, people came to their doorways and windows and cheered, most at what they saw, but just as many because all they heard and saw were other people cheering and they did not want to be excluded from the spectacle.

'Tell me,' Barnum said eventually, as the parade crossed Canal Street. 'How did you know about Chang and Eng?'

'I read the papers, my dear friend.'

Barnum's own report in the papers had announced that the Twins were on a train that had been derailed by Confederate troops, that they were uninjured but unable to continue their journey until the track was repaired.

Listening to Thumb, a sudden realization dawned on him: '*You sent them the message not to risk the journey,' he said. He was calm, and looked straight ahead as he spoke.

'Me?' Thumb said, slapping a hand to his chest. 'Me?'

'You,' Barnum said, convinced he was right, still calm.

Thumb laughed and rolled sideways in his seat.

'You were jealous because they were about to return and become a part of the Museum. You were jealous and so you made sure they never got here. And then lo and behold, a fortnight later, here *you* are.'

'At which point the judge and the jury and everyone in the courtroom leaps to their feet and applauds.'

'I knew it,' Barnum said. 'And now you've made certain they can't ever come back. You've ruined them.'

'They ruined themselves,' Thumb said sourly. 'They've bred twenty half-yellow brats between them. It doesn't even bear thinking about. The two of them joined up at the belly and both in bed with one or other of their filthy women. It's disgusting.'

Whereas you and Lavinia . . . Barnum thought smugly.

'I've saved your face. If they'd come back here now they'd have been lynched. Do you honestly think anybody believes all that rubbish about them working as a gun crew? They're slave-owners. You owned them once, and now they own others. It's an interesting thought, don't you think?'

'I'd have protected them.'

Thumb laughed. 'The way I hear it, you can barely keep a grip on what you've got. Whitewashing an elephant! Good lord, we're a quarter of a century on from the Feejee mermaid and that old crone Heth. And a fast-moving century at that.'

'Precisely – and one that's been moved along by men like me,' Barnum said proudly.

'But who depend upon men like me,' Thumb said.

They turned away from each other to wave at the crowds.

'So how's Charity keeping?' Thumb said eventually.

'She suffers a great deal. And Lavinia – has she truly been ill?'

'Ah, Lavinia,' Thumb said, pausing to consider his answer. 'Shall we say that Lavinia is a little less than delighted with the way our – shall we call it "business arrangement" – has been operating of late. She's always ill. Most days she just lies around eating candy and feeding it to her blessed miniature dogs.' Unhappy at these revelations, Thumb changed the subject. 'I see Jubal came within a whisker of taking Washington. Can you believe that? All the righteousness we got on our side and Washington is almost burned to the ground.'

'What "business arrangement"?' Barnum said. '*We* have no contract.'

'Ah, that,' Thumb said. 'All it needs is your signature. I have it right here in my pocket. Wave, smile. Look out at them, imagine all the money in *their* pockets. Tell me, do you still have that one-eyed beauty of a temptress in harness?'

'Elizabeth?'

Thumb straightened in his seat. 'Elizabeth,' he said, savouring the name. He tugged at his cravat.

'It can't be done,' Barnum said suddenly, banging the side of the carriage with his palm.

'What can't?'

'You, the Museum, all this.'

'Oh, I don't intend to return. Is that what you thought – that I'd come back as second fiddle to the Siamese frauds, that I'd stand around with all those other miserable specimens of humanity and have people gawp at me all day? My dear Phineas, you forget, I'm a man of considerable personal wealth and charm and appeal.'

But one who is married to a woman who thinks more of her dogs than she does of him, thought Barnum.

'What I'm suggesting is a partnership. The future, as I see it, is in theatres. Right here, along Broadway. It's what people are going to want, and they're going to want it soon. Believe me, it's the future of entertainment.'

'And the Museum?'

'Clear it out, sell off everything that can still be sold and turn it into a theatre. Thumb and Barnum.'

'And everyone who lives there?'

'What about them?'

'You want me to just turn them out in the street?'

'I survived and prospered. It'll do them no harm. Let them discover their true worth in this land of free enterprise and limitless opportunity. Let them find out once and for all what people truly think of them.' Thumb pulled Abraham Lincoln's beard from his face.

'It can't be done,' Barnum said.

'And I say it can. I'm not alone in this venture. Greenwood also believes –'

'Greenwood!'

'He's a clever man. Ambitious, forward-looking, ready to take his chances, make changes.'

The taunts of Charity and his daughters came back to haunt Barnum. He wanted to leave the carriage and the parade and walk back alone to his home, praying as he went that he would find it empty. The pieces *they* wanted of him were relatively small pieces; what Thumb and Greenwood were now proposing to take from him was everything he possessed. They might just as well tear out his heart, his soul and his eyes. He lit a cigar and sat back in his seat. The publicity, at least, was free and profitable, and following the recent turn of events in Virginia and Maryland, the disgraced elephant was no longer the talk of the city.

'What about Elizabeth?' he said as they passed the almost completed City Hall.

'She can stay. I'll even double the price of her contract. Half for you, half for her.'

'But what will she stay *as*?' Barnum asked, unable to disguise the flat note of resignation in his voice.

'Let's just say that I'll find something to keep her occupied,' Thumb said with a leer. 'Think it over.'

'Why should I? I'm very fond of her. We all are.'

'Fondness! What does fondness have to do with anything? What I'm offering you is nothing less than your own absolute and certain salvation.'

'What you're offering me is ruin,' Barnum said, determined now that he would never accept the offer, and somewhat cheered by the expense to which Thumb had already gone in making it.

There was a further long silence between them, and the nearer they approached to the Museum, the more confident Barnum found himself becoming, the more able he felt himself to deal with what was waiting for him beyond its doors.

Following the events of the previous weeks he had grown inevitably more cautious, but now, unexpectedly, he felt like a man about to overcome all his troubles, one who had toiled to the crest of a long steep hill and was looking down at the bright, clear open country that lay ahead of him. The war would soon be over, of that he was convinced, and if Thumb was right and people did want theatres, then what was there to prevent him from building one of his own? If he could get rid of the elephant in the arcade and the hippopotamus in the basement, he could begin in the near future to change the character of the Museum to meet these new demands. He was still a leader, not a follower. His spirits were dampened momentarily by the thought of his three daughters loose in the city with his money, but what they spent in a day might yet easily be recouped a hundred times over by the balloon flight across the Atlantic.

Arriving at the Museum, the carriage pulled up at the entrance and a space was cleared. Greenwood came out to greet them, followed by Hackaliah Cherry, who saluted and held his hand to his head until Thumb returned the gesture. Greenwood arranged for the ponies to be led on, and for someone to stand with the monkeys and zebra. The band stopped playing and waited to be paid, which, Barnum noted with satisfaction, Greenwood did out of his own pocket. The two of them shared a glance and Greenwood was the first to look guiltily away, crowning Barnum's growing sense of achievement, his delight at the morning's unexpected turn of events. Here he was, back at his beloved Museum, his kingdom, his universe, and still the master of all he surveyed.

Thumb was about to go into the Museum ahead of him, but pulling him back by the shoulders, Barnum made sure that he, and not the midget, was the first to enter. He saluted Hackaliah Cherry and then began to whistle as he marched briskly in.

20

'I BOUGHT YOU this,' Captain Bates said to Anna, handing her the carefully wrapped parcel. 'Something to mark the occasion. I bought it long ago, but when you first refused me I lost the heart to give it to you.'

'I never refused you,' Anna told him. 'Not really. Not seriously. You must have known that.'

'I think so.' There was something in his manner that was unalterably honest and decent, and a formality about him that appealed to her and reassured her.

'Careful, it's delicate.' He reached out. 'I thought you might shake it.'

'What is it?' The parcel was cube-shaped, each of its sides the width of her broad palm.

'I wrapped it so you could open it and find out for yourself.' He was more anxious than Anna for the paper to be torn away.

Recently, Barnum had let it be know to them that he knew of their wedding plans, but that he would respect their wishes and make no attempt to turn the occasion into a public spectacle.

Anna had been with him at the Museum, toured America and Europe with him, for the past fifteen years. Her contract expired in a month's time, at the end of August, and she had declined to renew it. 'You can go right now,' he'd told her affectionately. 'Leave me Bates until later in the fall, but you go on ahead of him and get things ready for when it's his turn to leave.' Bates had been at the Museum only three years – giants were springing up all over the continent – and he was preparing to leave two months after Anna was free to do so. Barnum had taken out her contract and offered to tear it up, knowing that even without it she would have honoured her commitment to him, that they both would, because they were both honourable people. 'I'll miss you,' he'd told her. 'I'll miss you both.'

He frequently said this, but it was only as he'd said it then to Anna Swan that he realized how infrequently he actually meant it. 'We'll miss you, too,' she'd told him. 'And all this, everyone here.' 'You're their mother,' he said. 'I'm their father and you're their mother.' She had been unable to answer him for fear of bursting into tears.

'What are you waiting for?' Bates said, cupping his hands around her own, in which his gift was still enclosed.

And so she unwrapped it, carefully peeling away the paper and laying it to one side, until eventually an inlaid wooden case with a hinged lid and ornamental clasp was revealed.

'It's beautiful,' she said.

Bates remained impatient, still eager for her to discover what lay inside.

She slid the clasp free with her fingernail and gently lifted the lid.

Inside, on a cushion of crimson velvet, lay a metallic globe of brass and silver and gold, the size of an orange and divided into segments, each one of which was as delicately and intricately patterned as the box in which it sat.

She lifted it out, unable to speak, cradling it in the bowl of her palm. Looking at it more closely, she saw that in addition to the pattern inscribed upon the surface of each segment, there was also a letter, and turning the ball she was able to spell out the names 'Anna Swan' and 'N V Bates'.

She almost choked at its beauty.

'You don't know what it is yet,' Bates said. He sat close to her and held her. 'Here, let me show you.' He took the orb from her and set it gently on the table. Then, taking a key from the casket, he inserted it at the point where each of the segments met and turned it three times. 'Ready?' He sat back from the ball, and a moment later a simple tune rose from it. 'Chopin,' he said, as mesmerized as she was by what then began to happen.

As the tune played, one of the segments moved slowly outwards from the globe, followed by another, and then another, until a dozen or so of the pieces were all moving outwards together, pausing and falling and rising in time with the music. Anna couldn't believe what she was seeing, and she found herself holding her breath for fear that even the slightest imperfection might now be revealed to her.

'It works perfectly,' Bates said proudly.

'It *is* perfect. It's the most perfect thing I've ever seen. It's beautiful. Perfect and beautiful.'

Both sat hypnotized as the segments continued to move smoothly in and out of the globe.

'Now watch this,' Bates said.

As the music neared its climax each of the pieces moved out together, until the outer rim of their curved edge was resting on the table, pushing up the stem of the orb, which rose and then divided in a fountain of gold, each of its twenty fibres little thicker than a cotton thread. Then, before either of them had had the time to take everything in, the music slowed, the stem stiffened and sank, and each of the outer segments rose simultaneously back together until the ball was once again whole. The music finished with a slight click as each curved surface was drawn tightly back together.

Neither of them was able to speak for a moment.

'I daren't touch it,' Anna said eventually, her fingers hovering above it.

'No. I feel the same.' Bates lifted the ball and laid it back in its cushioned case.

Anna felt as though she had just witnessed a miracle.

Bates was called away a few minutes later and she sat alone with her gift, unable to take it from its case, pleased now that this object of desire was not to become the secret she had earlier wanted it to be.

Despite the termination of her own contract ahead of Captain Bates's, she would wait for him and the two of them would leave together, after which they proposed to spend a short holiday on the Hudson and then the Saint Lawrence on their way back to Nova Scotia, her birthplace, where they now intended to set up home. An agent had secured them a plot of land outside Kentville overlooking the sheltered Bay of Fundy, and several stonemasons and carpenters had been instructed regarding the dimensions of the house they wanted building there, the foundations of which had already been excavated upon receipt of the banker's draft Anna had forwarded to Annapolis Royal.

Over the past few weeks she had received an almost daily report from the agent on the progress being made. He wrote to her of the surrounding trees which had been felled and treated prior to building the walls and floors, and of the frame with its solid uncut trunk at each corner. She and Bates had specified that there should be no other nearby buildings with which comparison of size or scale might be made, and that the house should be sufficiently far back from any public road so as not to advertise itself and thus attract attention as a novelty.

To please her, Captain Bates made sketches of what the finished building would look like, and because he himself knew a great deal about carpentry and joinery, he drew for her the various stages of the construction as he imagined it to be taking place. In her eagerness for the project to be completed, Anna had – unwisely, in Bates's opinion, although he kept this to himself – already sent almost half of the agreed price of the house to the agent who was overseeing the work on their behalf. This, he assured her, had been to enable work to begin without delay, and he regularly sent her the documents and bills of sale to show her how the money had been spent, and from which Bates was able to make his drawings.

Anna had more than sufficient funds to cover the building work and then the complete furnishing of the house; she also had a separate sum set aside to provide for both their extended journey 'home' and to meet any unforeseen eventuality concerning the construction.

Now that her dream was so close to being realized, she agitated over its smallest details, and she knew that the demands upon her savings were only the smallest part of its worth. She had withdrawn her cash and bonds from the various banks in which they had been accumulating and had them all now with her in her room, securely locked inside a mahogany trunk which had belonged to her sea-faring father. This in turn was hidden inside the false bottom of a chest of drawers which stood solidly beside her bed. Because of her size, Anna was naturally stronger than most women, but even she exerted herself when sliding the doubly padlocked trunk from its hiding place, noting with satisfaction, that although she was able to lift it she was unable to walk with it more than a few paces. Captain Bates had hoped to persuade her to transfer her savings to a bank in Annapolis or perhaps Digby, but because she now felt herself so close to what she had long awaited, Anna was adamant that she and her money were not to be parted. Banks still failed; speculations ended disastrously; wealthy men were made poor overnight and lost the will to become wealthy again. Bates persisted no further; instead he transferred his own savings, these too being sufficient to cover the cost of the finished house.

One consequence of this open secret of departure and wedlock was the steady accumulation of small and treasured gifts from the other inhabitants of the Museum.

Zip had given them a tantalus, a silvered metal base upon which stood three crystal decanters. He'd seen the one Barnum kept on his desk and had gone to great lengths to seek out this even finer example for them. Around the neck of each decanter was a silver chain and disc, under which he'd had engraved the initials B and S.

It was past midnight when he brought it to her, and he was dressed for another of his journeys out into the city. He told Anna to unwrap it when he'd gone, but she insisted that he remain with her while she did so, carefully folding back the tissue and ribbon in which it was wrapped. There were tears in her eyes before she saw what it was. She hugged him and pressed his face into her side. She tried to persuade him not to leave the Museum, to wait for Bates and several of the others to join them, and then to sit with them and talk about the future. The bond between the two of them was still as strong as it had always been, but Zip declined the offer and left before any of the others arrived. It had been several weeks since he had been accompanied by either Herman or Vivalla on one of his nightly forays, and now the others no longer attempted to follow or chaperone him. He knew the dark streets and alleyways better than any of them, and on several earlier occasions he had given his companions the slip, thus absolving them of their responsibility. He felt easier being alone, unhappy when too much of this other, private life he led became known to them.

When he'd gone, Anna placed the tantalus on her chest of drawers, waiting for Bates and the others to arrive and admire it.

Elizabeth presented the couple with a carriage clock, at the centre of which was painted a single golden eye set in pale blue enamel, from which extended its slender hands. She had seen it in a jeweller's window, and because it had been displayed at head height she had been able to look into the glass between her and the clock and superimpose her own face upon it, drawing forward her hood so that no one else might recognize her. In her own way, Elizabeth too believed in omens, and this she considered to be a powerful one, causing her to buy the clock without the slightest hesitation.

Upon being presented with this gift, Anna wept again.

Through Elizabeth, she had also received a case containing six wineglasses from the Aztec children, who had taken each from its wrapping, presenting all six individually, handling them as though the giving rather than the receiving of them were a considerable honour. Anna displayed both gifts alongside Zip's tantalus before rewrapping them and storing them in her chest of drawers.

Herman presented the couple with an ornamental fireside set, Franklin with a pair of pot dogs for the mantel above, the two gifts having been bought in collaboration, and Isaac and Bella-Grace Sprague with a counterpane which Bella-Grace had quilted and embroidered herself. It was twice the width and length of a normal counterpane, and when unwrapped it covered the floor of Anna's room like a bed of wild flowers.

René and Fortuna presented them with one of René's paintings. It depicted the Museum as Anna had known it when she'd first arrived in the city. Anna herself stood in the doorway, and because of the way in which René had expertly increased the scale of other features of the building around her, there was nothing to suggest her height or size. She looked healthy and happy, young and strong. Even the Museum itself, in the absence of its jostling and noisy crowds, exuded an unfamiliar air of calm and dignity. René explained that he had been working on the painting since he'd learned of their intention to leave. He regretted that it was unfinished, needing the second figure of Bates to be included, which he would undertake in the next few days. But Bates declined this, saying that he would prefer the painting just to contain Anna. A murmur of concurrence confirmed his decision. René also promised to have the portrait of Elizabeth completed in time to show them before they left, but upon being asked what remained to be done to it, Elizabeth stopped him from telling them, insisting that they should wait until it was finally completed. In fact, all that the portrait now needed was the addition of her eye at the smooth blank centre of her forehead. René could have completed the portrait several days ago, but having arrived at this point, Elizabeth had held back, refusing to pose for this final, vital feature until she'd had time to consider the portrait as it now was.

Señor Vivalla presented Anna and Bates with a tureen from himself, Apollo and Byron. The simple verse on one of its sides had been composed by the other Byron, and upon the lid was a pig and a calf, the latter of which might be quite easily mistaken for a dog.

Tom gave them a brass candelabra, and Hackaliah Cherry two new brooms and a mop with a maple handle. They were the finest brooms he had ever seen and he had been unable to resist buying them. He hoped to own brooms like them himself one day.

When Captain Bates wound up Elizabeth's clock they all sat in silence as it chimed the full hour, and then, in a moment of resonant silence, sounded the single stroke of one o'clock, the signal for them all to disperse.

In her mind, Anna began to fill their unfinished home with everything she'd been given. She asked Bates to include them in his drawings as he added daily to each, thus creating even stronger ties between the present and the future, throwing out unbreakable ropes along which they might pull themselves if anything unthinkable were now to go wrong with their plans. She was worrying unnecessarily, but there was nothing Bates could do or say to convince her otherwise. She was too close to realizing a once impossible dream, and she could not now bring herself to consider even the smallest loss or imperfection. Once, fifteen years had seemed a lifetime to her; now she marked the passage of every day.

Bates wrote to the house agent about churches and preachers in the region. He paid for their riverboat passage and showed her pictures of the vessels upon which they would be sailing.

In its case inside the trunk inside the chest, Anna could hear Elizabeth's clock chiming throughout the night – a small and reassuring indication of its buried presence and all it now stood for.

ZIP AND HERMAN sat together in Herman's room preparing themselves for their booths. Herman was pale and had dark rings of sleeplessness around his eyes. There were beads of sweat on his forehead, but otherwise he did his best to disguise his pain as Zip, half dressed in his monkey suit, unwound his bandages.

'It should have stopped hurting by now. I'm telling you again – go and see some physician other than Barnum's.'

'They cost money. I lost enough of that already.' Herman indicated the letter he had recently received from his parents. With it had been enclosed a card print of his sister holding a baby. 'She wants to call it after me,' he said. 'They need everything they can get.'

'And you've been a little backward in forwarding your contributions, eh?'

Herman bowed his head, caught between the two pains.

As the last of the bandages came away, Zip hid his surprise at the extent of the bruising which still showed on Herman's chest. He'd seen similar injuries at the Madison Garden knuckle fights, but never before had he seen anything to match the herringbone pattern of welts where Herman's ribs now pressed against his skin.

'It's all a matter of circulation,' Herman said without any real conviction, but as though even that simple and imperfect understanding of the problem might now in some way lead eventually to its solution.

'Circulation,' Zip said. 'I'll believe you.'

Throughout Barnum's absence during the previous weeks, Herman's shows had been reduced from twelve to six a day. Greenwood had protested, but Zip and Henry Butler had convinced him of the necessity of this reduction. Demanding that Herman expose his chest to him, Greenwood had been unable to speak, had given Zip and Henry Butler a curt nod and then left. Later, upon hearing that the two men had interceded on his behalf, Herman was angry, accusing them of having lost him money he could ill afford to lose.

Zip returned each morning to help him with his bandages, and eventually their unspoken apologies were made.

Elsewhere in the Museum, other regimes had also been relaxed during Barnum's absence. Bella-Grace refused to leave her husband's booth and kept him company throughout his performances, always quick to respond to any remark or criticism, however slight, from anyone in the audience. Isaac tried to stop her, but she was determined, and he had neither the physical strength nor the strength of will to insist that he be left alone as instructed by Barnum.

Like the ill-fated hippopotamus, the Albino family proved less popular with the public than they had done with the eminent members of New York's scientific community, and consequently they were moved from their booth on the ground floor to a smaller stage up on the third, where they were instructed by Greenwood to announce their presence by constantly singing or reciting well-known speeches. Only Hackaliah Cherry was happy at their relegation, and he visited them frequently on his sweeping rounds to point out to them the error of their ways in having allowed themselves to turn white whilst still retaining the features that would forever mark them out as negroes. It was only when Tom told Cherry that he knew for certain they were black, that Cherry stopped his crowing and stayed away. Throughout this brief debate, the Albinos made no attempt whatsoever to defend themselves, as though they had long since accepted that they were neither one thing nor the other. They were a shape and they were a colour, and beyond that nothing mattered because they had no other contribution to make to the endless debates forever going on in the world around them.

Earlier when it had become clear that Barnum did not intend to return to the Museum until the news about the elephant and the Siamese Twins was old news, Greenwood had abandoned a large part of his own duties to Henry Butler, and had stayed away until late afternoon, when he would frequently arrive intoxicated, sit with his feet on his desk, shout out a dozen orders and then fall asleep until it was time for him to leave.

It surprised everyone – or at least those who were alert enough to notice – how easily and smoothly the Museum had run itself during Barnum's absence.

Henry Butler had asked Zip to act as his deputy, to which Zip had agreed, and it was in return for this favour that Henry

Butler had agreed to persuade Greenwood to reduce the number of Herman's performances.

Then a second week had passed and Barnum had at last returned in a noisy procession with Thumb.

Greenwood reappeared first thing every morning, Zip lost his position as unofficial deputy, and the Albinos stayed where they were.

Outside, a heatwave broke upon the already suffering city, and in the Museum the wooden walls grew warm to the touch. Henry Butler's slow-moving fans worked erratically throughout the day, but their effectiveness was restricted, and along the upper staircases and galleries the mid-afternoon heat became unbearable, and on several occasions women had fainted. People began to seek their pleasures outdoors, and then out along the coast and on the rivers, where the summer mosquitoes seldom congregated, and where there was always something of a breeze, however slight, to face into.

When Herman was unbandaged and dressed ready for his booth, Zip began to prepare himself, smearing powdered chalk beneath his arms and brushing loose the matted hair of his suit.

They were about to leave when there was a knock at the door and the sound of several unfamiliar women's voices outside. Motioning for Herman not to open it, Zip quickly pulled on the top half of his suit. Waiting until he was ready, Herman then unlocked the door and three girls pushed in. They presented themselves in a line, edging away from where Zip sat and watched them without speaking.

'Nancy,' Herman said, at once pleased to see her and anxious at her forbidden presence in his room.

Nancy curtsied and all three girls burst into laughter.

'Zip, this is Nancy,' Herman said nervously, checking the corridor outside to see if anyone had witnessed the girls' arrival. 'I told you about her. Nancy – Zip.'

Zip was unable to speak, and realizing his mistake, Herman explained that although he was unable to answer them, he understood everything that was happening. His anxiety deepened as he fully understood the dangerous position in which Zip was now placed. In turn, Zip did not want to go and leave Herman alone with the girls. Nothing in the Museum ever went unnoticed, and sooner or later either Barnum or Greenwood would appear.

'I ain't talkin' to that pea-brain,' Nancy said. 'We just passed a cage of monkeys further down. He ought to be in there with 'em.' She was referring to the chimps on the second floor.

The other two girls giggled, encouraging her. Then, ignoring Zip, she walked around the room inspecting its few contents.

'This here is Patsy and –'

'Emmeline,' the third girl said quickly. 'Emmeline Victoria.'

'Emmeline Victoria?' Nancy said.

Emmeline Victoria shrugged. 'So?'

Herman held out his hand to them, but the girls only giggled again.

'We come to see you,' Nancy said. 'You told us where it was and so we come up.' She continued her inspection of the room, picking up Herman's letter, turning it in her hand and throwing it back down.

'We even paid for ourselves to come in,' Patsy said pointedly. 'Nancy here said you could arrange us a refund. We come on that condition.'

'That's what I told them.' Nancy kissed Herman on the cheek and let herself fall on to the bed, pulling him down beside her. She drew up her knees until her dirty petticoats were revealed.

Only Zip saw Herman clench his teeth at the pain of being pulled on to the bed. Moving to the door, he grunted, hoping to suggest to Herman that if the two of them were to leave, then the girls would be forced to follow.

'We've got to go down,' Herman said. 'Come with us. By rights the public isn't allowed into the private quarters.'

'Never stopped them trying to get into mine,' Patsy said, causing all three girls to burst into laughter, after which Nancy said, 'Public! You sayin' I'm just a member of the public? Well, I like that. I thought you and me was sweethearts. That's what you're always tellin' me to say – sweethearts. If you don't want me to be your sweetheart no more, then you only got to say so.' She behaved offended, refusing to look at him.

It occurred to Zip to roar and to beat his chest and scare them all from the room. He watched carefully the way the three girls worked, each using the others to manipulate the situation. He grunted again and beckoned Herman to him.

'Pea-brain wants to whisper something to you,' Nancy said.

'Mind he don't bite your ear off,' Emmeline Victoria said.

Zip told Herman to get them out. He opened the door. Herman did his best to pull Nancy up off the bed, but she grabbed his wrist and he fell back down on top of her. Nancy pretended to be shocked and told him to wait until they were alone. She drew her dress further above her knees.

233

Embarrassed and in pain, Herman pushed himself upright, and because he could think of nothing else to say, he asked Patsy and Emmeline Victoria if they too worked at Astor House.

Seeing that their first attempt had failed, Zip closed the door and remained crouching behind it.

'Where?' Patsy said.

'Astor House,' Nancy shouted at her, pushing herself up beside Herman. 'Where I work – Astor House.'

'Oh, sure, Astor House.'

Patsy nudged Emmeline Victoria. 'Astor House. That's where we all work. Good old Astor House?'

'You work in the kitchens, too?' Herman asked.

'The kitchens, sure.'

'Me, too.'

'You keep any drink up here, Herman darling?' Nancy said, opening the bedside cabinet and frowning at its emptiness.

'I got some,' Patsy said. 'We having a party?'

'I ain't touching no drink with monkey-man looking on,' Emmeline Victoria said. 'Ain't he got no cage you can put him in. It ain't right havin' somethin' like that just squattin' there in the presence of real ladies. He's naked but for all that long hair.' All three girls looked at Zip, and again he fought back the urge to leap into the centre of the room and roar at them.

'We really ought to go down,' Herman said.

'Oh, ought we to? Really. Tell you what – you go, and we'll just make ourselves nice and comfortable up here until you get back.'

'I can't; it's not allowed.' By now Herman was becoming desperate.

'What ain't allowed?' Nancy stood with her hands on her hips. 'You sayin' we're goin' to steal all that money you got saved up?'

'He sayin' we're thieves?' Emmeline Victoria said.

'Anyhow, it's all in the bank,' Nancy told them. 'Fifty dollars a month, Herman, ain't that right?'

'Right,' Herman said, softly, as though Zip would not hear.

In a further effort to help him clear the room, Zip grunted again and ran in a hunch to the bed. Nancy gave a small scream as he brushed past her and then went to join the others by the door. Zip held Herman's hand.

'I have to take him down,' Herman said. 'He trusts me.'

'It shouldn't be among civilized folk like us. Someone ought to kill it and stuff it.'

'You goin' to blow up?' Patsy asked Herman. 'I ain't never seen it. Nancy told me all about it. I come to see you blow up. She says you can blow up any part you want. That right?'

Emmeline Victoria almost choked with laughter.

'That's not what I said,' Nancy said indignantly. 'That's not what I told 'em, Herman. I said you could – well – I said you was an artiste.'

'Go on, strip off and give us a private show,' Patsy said.

Zip reached out and touched her arm.

'Get it off! Get it away!'

The three girls banded more tightly together.

It was then that they heard Greenwood, still a floor beneath them, calling for Zip.

'Go, you better go,' Herman told him.

Zip left, straightening up as he ran along the corridor. Following him, Herman pulled Nancy outside and the others followed her. He locked the door and pushed them ahead of him along the corridor in the opposite direction.

The girls protested at this rough treatment, but had no alternative but to follow Herman as he raced to get to his booth.

At the end of the corridor they met Vivalla with Apollo and Byron. This cheered Nancy up.

'I seen that pig play checkers,' she told the others. 'Seen it with my own eyes.'

Byron, with his scrubbed trotters, was having difficulty negotiating the steep stairs.

'Checkers,' Patsy said dismissively. 'It can't even get down a few steps.'

Vivalla looked to Herman for an explanation of the three girls, but he realized there was no time and he stood aside to let them pass. He recognized both Patsy and Emmeline Victoria, but said nothing.

Isaac and Bella-Grace met Herman and the girls on the second landing. Bella-Grace was carrying her husband, who was drinking a glass of milk and eating a crudely constructed sandwich as they went along. They collided with Emmeline Victoria, who swore at them and pointed out that she was a paying customer. Bella-Grace ignored her.

It was as they were about to descend to the first floor that Nancy grabbed Herman by the arm and pulled him to a standstill. She told the other two to leave them alone. Realizing that there was no longer any real danger of being discovered alone with the girls, Herman waited for her to go on.

235

She held a finger to his chest. 'You've humiliated me,' she said. 'I've got a good mind to walk out of here and never come back.'

Herman forgot his pain at the thought of losing her.

Nancy leaned back against the wall and dipped her chin, looking up at him through her eyelashes. She pouted and twirled a finger into her loose ringlets. In their flight from his room, several of her blouse buttons had come unfastened, and beneath the material her white breasts rose and fell at each breath. Taking her finger from her hair, she ran it across the top of them, exaggerating their contours.

'It's just that visitors aren't allowed,' Herman said. People still moved along the corridor behind them, but no one stopped to watch or to interrupt them.

'Not even if I'd come up all alone?' Nancy said, her bottom lip now quivering as though she were about to cry.

Having Nancy in the company of Zip and the two others was the closest Herman had yet come to being alone with her.

'Would you – come alone, I mean?'

Nancy lowered her head even further and smiled to herself. 'I might. If there was something to see.'

'Such as?'

'Well, I don't know. I ain't ever seen more than ten dollars in any one place before. Be nice to gaze on a whole spread of money. I suppose you are allowed to take it out of this bank of yours when you need it?'

'Of course I can. Any time I like.'

'I think I might be tempted to look at that all on my lonesome. With you, that is – all on my lonesome with you.' She paused, pretending to think. 'Only thing is, I don't want to get you into no trouble by comin' back here again. Perhaps you could . . .' She stopped speaking at the arrival of Fortuna and René with their son between them. She pressed herself against the wall as they passed, grimacing at the sight of Fortuna's beard and the face and hands of the small boy.

'This is Nancy,' Herman said, causing them to pause.

Fortuna was about to extend her hand when she and her son were urged on by René.

'He's an artist,' Herman told Nancy when they had gone, hoping to excuse René's lack of courtesy towards her.

'I don't care what he is. You said you wanted to come and see me, just the two of us together, to show me your money. It's you I care about, just you.' She ran a finger down Herman's cheek. 'I don't care for any of these other freaks.'

'They're not –'

'Truth is,' she moved closer. 'Truth is, I never really think of you as being one of them. I only think of you as Herman, *my* Herman. So will you come?'

'To the Astor?'

'No, not there. Patsy has rooms on Cedar Street. Perhaps we could have our – our assignation there.'

The word helped Herman to dismiss his doubts. Assignations were what lovers had. Lovers who had assignations met alone, in secrecy, in private.

'Cedar Street,' he said.

'At the junction with Pearl. It's over the Pearl laundry.'

Before he could answer, she slid her arm into his and started walking along the corridor.

They separated at the private passage leading to the rear of his booth and Nancy went in search of Patsy and Emmeline Victoria, shouting for Herman to look out for them in his first audience of the day.

A minute after Herman drew open the curtains, both Greenwood and Zip arrived.

'How long have you been here?' Greenwood asked him.

Behind him, Zip held up the fingers of both hands.

'Ten minutes,' Herman said quietly. He saw that they were being watched by Nancy, Patsy and Emmeline Victoria amid the small group of people gathered in front of Franklin's booth.

Greenwood left, and Herman stood for a minute looking down at Zip, who was watching the girls. Then he was distracted by the loud voice of Patsy, who commented publicly on everything she was now seeing for the first time. She indicated Franklin and yelled, 'He's eatin' outta a pail. Some kinda mash! With his fingers! A whole pail fulla mash!'

Franklin sat and scooped out the food and rolled it into balls, swallowing it without chewing. He ate, however, with little enthusiasm, forcing the food down only to keep up his weight, which had gradually decreased over the past fortnight.

Henry Butler joined the crowd gathering in front of Herman's booth and looked on as anxiously as he had done over the previous few days.

'He's slobbering like a hog,' Emmeline Victoria shouted, still at Franklin's booth. 'I bet this one can't even reach over his belly to play at checkers!'

Nancy, Patsy and others in the crowd laughed.

Franklin looked down at them, and when Patsy called up for him to see how far forward he could reach, he obliged her. Herman felt ashamed to see this happening to his friend, especially when it was clear to him that Franklin had made the connection between Patsy, Nancy and himself. Franklin cast him a glance which said that none of it mattered, but Herman's shame remained intact, and in an attempt to draw the crowd away from him, he indicated to Nancy that he himself was about to perform, guessing rightly that she would call the others over to watch.

Nancy, Patsy and Emmeline Victoria stood pressed to the front of the booth as he removed his jacket and began his speech prior to inflating. He handed out the tape measure for them to inspect, knowing that no one was likely to spot the missing inches in the middle of its length, ready to retrieve it if anyone looked too closely. Everything Herman said, Nancy repeated to the other two girls, and it made him proud to be performing in front of them.

Along the gallery, the silence from Franklin's booth was broken only by the scrape of his spoon around the tin pail. In the background there was only the noise of the diminished crowd, and above its silent lulls the chanting of the Redskins in the almost empty theatre. This was the closest the Museum had ever come to silence in the daytime for the past five years, and the noise of the Indian dance sounded like the rhythmic humming of a railroad engine passing slowly by in the distance.

Herman began to expand, releasing the tape around his lower chest and gaining several inches with each intake of breath. The crowd fell silent, at first suspecting a trick, and then calling for more as the tape unwound and the increase in his chest became more readily apparent to them.

Looking down, Herman saw Elizabeth stop beside Zip, who, to Herman's dismay, pointed out the three girls and whispered something to her.

Catching Herman's eye, Elizabeth shook her head as a warning to him not to exceed the bounds of what he felt to be a safe expansion.

Immediately beneath him, Nancy drew her hands slowly apart above her exposed breasts, his vantage point giving Herman an even better view of them, until he almost believed that he could see them in their entirety beneath her blouse. It was then, at fifty-two inches, that the first sharp stab of pain returned, as though something had unwound and then struck out inside him. Still looking down at Nancy,

238

he felt encouraged to continue. He believed an important step forward had been made in their relationship, forgetting for the moment that he had neither a fortune in dollars nor an account in any bank.

At fifty-six inches the stabbing caused him to cry out, but he had become adept at disguising these cries, and only Elizabeth and Zip felt the pain for him.

He stopped an inch further on, drew everyone's attention to the tape and then stood with his arms out and his mouth open as his chest slowly contracted, turning the upper half of his body from side to side to alleviate this additional pain as his flesh and bones returned to their original shape. At forty-eight inches the pain subsided, and he felt comfortable enough to continue his speech to the crowd, most of whom were already starting to wander away in search of something else, attracted by the distant chanting or the prospect of the second full pail of mash already waiting beside Franklin.

Zip and Elizabeth left too, until finally only Nancy, Patsy and Emmeline Victoria remained. Herman could see that Nancy was pleased with his performance in front of her friends. He approached them, but as he did so they moved away from the front of the booth, as though they too were about to leave. He called Nancy back to him. She stopped, but did not return.

'We've got to go,' she told him.

Beside her, Patsy had taken a bottle from her sleeve and she and Emmeline Victoria were drinking from it.

'I could take a short break,' Herman suggested, disappointed by the prospect of her early departure.

Nancy turned to the others for support.

'We've got to get back to work,' Patsy said eventually.

'That's right. At the Astor.'

'The Astor. I forgot.'

'Oh,' Herman said.

'You won't forget Cedar Street,' Nancy said.

'Above the Pearl laundry.'

'That's right.' Nancy had fastened up the buttons on her blouse, and away from the glare of the lamp her lips had lost their rich deep glow.

Herman watched them go with mixed feelings of achievement and loss, as though he had been presented with both a priceless crystal bowl and the hammer with which to destroy it. It was only then, when the gallery was empty and he and Franklin were alone in their booths, that he began to consider the lie he had told about his fortune, and remembering this, he also remembered that he hadn't offered to reimburse their entrance fees.

Unable to speak to Franklin, he drew the curtains and sat in the half-light thinking about what had happened, what might yet happen, and recovering his strength ready to begin again when another small crowd had formed.

22

'SELL UP BARNUM, you old mule. Realize some capital. Build another big house. Get up into the sixties and seventies, that's where they're putting up the best these days. You can build a palace for the price of a pigsty –' and here Thumb paused to look slowly around the room '– down this end of the island. Think of the clean air. Think of the Park. Think of yourself – you're not the man you once were, and that's a fact.' He paused again. 'None of us are – not even me.'

Especially you, Barnum thought.

'Buy a big comfortable chair and sit in it with your grandchildren on your knees. Enjoy life. All this is just one big worry to you. Face it – it's wearing you out. Believe me, this is your big chance, the biggest opportunity you'll ever regret having let pass by.' Thumb stopped and slid from his chair, his chin level with Barnum's desk. He regretted the move immediately and struggled back into his seat, which, like most of the furniture in the office, was generously constructed.

Five 'bigs', thought Barnum, making no offer to help him.

Thumb had returned to the Museum with his entreaties for Barnum to sell up every day for the past week. Barnum's armour, however, was being burnished and strengthened by the ever-increasing fury of his onslaught. Today, somewhat to his surprise, that onslaught appeared to have declined a little in its intensity, and Thumb seemed slightly less persistent in his repeated musterings and charges.

Greenwood and Henry Butler were in the office with them, Greenwood supporting Thumb, Henry Butler an almost useless counterbalance on the side of Barnum.

The thought of entertaining grandchildren where he now unwillingly indulged only his daughters at once cheered and depressed Barnum. It was true that he felt worn out by the ambitious crusade his life had become. It was also true that he longed for an heir, preferably a grandson and preferably one who inherited more of his characteristics than his daughters had, one who might now snatch the baton of showmanship from his weakening grasp and run with it willingly into the future. Hand over the keys to his daughters and they'd most likely turn the place into a milliner's shop.

'You saw how they flocked to the place once they knew I was here,' Thumb said in his high, squeezed-out voice, interrupting Barnum's train of thought, which was once again leading him to the happy conclusion that the Museum would become a shrine to his own hard work and enterprise. He felt sufficiently cheered by this prospect to grin in the face of his opponents.

They flocked to the place to watch a trail of white paint dripping off an elephant; they flocked to the place to laugh at Jeremiah Bergh's hungry trumpeting spinsters; they flocked to the place because everyone in the city was either lost or uncertain of the future and their flocking instinct was still too strong to be broken.

'They flocked . . .' Barnum began. He looked hard at Thumb's face, as heavily lined and bunched as a fist, and his smile fell. Ten years ago he would have told the world that he could ask for no greater friend than Thumb.

'I've brung them in for you,' Thumb insisted. 'Me, me, *me*. But do you hear me asking for a share of your takings? Do you hear me asking that? I even brought my own band, my own entertainers, but do you hear me mention money? No sir, you do not.' He looked at Greenwood for support, but Greenwood, more aware than Thumb of Barnum's stubbornness, declined to be drawn too early into this renewed, undermanned and wavering assault. Sensing that he was about to lose his only ally, Thumb swore, dropped again from his seat and strutted around the desk. He tried to climb on to Barnum's knee, but was unable to achieve the manoeuvre without Barnum's assistance, which was not offered.

Turning to Henry Butler, Barnum said, 'How's Mrs Butler these days, Henry?' He couldn't remember her Christian name.

The question surprised them all, and made Henry Butler uncomfortable.

'As fine as can be expected,' he said, unwilling to barter his wife's illness against that of either Charity Barnum or Lavinia Thumb.

'Ah, women. They're a pleasure and a pain,' Barnum said wistfully.

'Mostly a pain,' Thumb said. He paced from the desk to the door and then back again. 'You can't sidestep this for ever, Barnum. It's coming as sure as winter. Sell up. Listen to reason. Get out. Pack up. Go.'

What happened to 'Phineas', Barnum thought. 'And winter's a cold and killing time in this city,' he said, surprising even himself by the solemnity of his tone.

For a minute no one spoke.

And then, Henry Butler, uncertain whether or not it was still permissible to discuss their respective spouses, said to Thumb, 'And Lavinia?'

'What about her?' Thumb said angrily, turning from Barnum.

'I was just wondering . . .'

'Lavinia, for your information, Mr Butler, has taken to buying clothes for all the nigger servants' children and having them with her in the drawing-room all day.'

'Very enlightened,' Barnum said.

'She buys them gifts and stuffs them with candy until they shine. She's bought a fleet of carriages and they ride around the grounds with her.' He paused and smiled. 'And then, when they get too old, when they grow too *tall*, she puts them out to work on the land with all the others. Rags to riches, riches to rags, you see, the driving force of our great nation. And all depending on how the fancy takes her. Does that answer your question? That's how Lavinia is, Mr Butler. Give her everything she could possibly want and the next thing you know she's ordering you to double it. Lavinia has her own steam yacht. She read in one of her journals about this Marie Antoinette, Queen of France before they all got the chop, and all of a sudden she wants a farmyard stuffed with miniatures to play with. There again, anything gets too big and one of the field hands leads it quietly out of sight and –' Thumb drew a finger across his throat. 'Any more questions about Lavinia?'

'I see,' Henry Butler said nervously.

'I doubt it. I doubt if any of us has the sense he was born and raised a bachelor with. With the possible exception of Greenwood here, that is.'

Unhappy at having so suddenly been made the centre of attention, Greenwood said, 'Can't we forget the women and get back to this place, it's future.'

'My sentiments entirely.' Thumb joined him by the door and the two sides once again faced each other across the battlefield of the room.

'That sound like a dying trade to you?' Barnum asked Henry

243

Butler, turning his ear to the wall, through which the noise of the passing crowd could be heard. Knowing in advance the time of Thumb's arrival each day, Barnum had rearranged many of the more popular exhibits, bringing them closer to his office and the surrounding corridors.

Thumb usually stayed no longer than twenty or thirty minutes, but today he had been there almost two hours, further suggesting to Barnum that this was to be his final assault.

'Perhaps they're pushing around looking for something worthwhile to gawp at.'

'It's still only twenty-five cents a time, whatever they find to amaze and entertain them.'

'And that's the only reason they still keep on coming.'

Having fixed his prices for over a decade had always been a source of great pride to Barnum.

'I've seen the elephant,' Thumb said. 'And I've been down into the basement to take a squint at that tub of lard you call a hippopotamus. Where's the profit in showing that? I've been to every zoo in this country and in Europe and seen a hundred exactly like it. The people down there are just waiting to see it die. And what's all this fancy rigmarole?' He indicated the blades of the fan above them.

'It's an air-circulator,' Henry Butler said, still proud of his achievement, having already noticed several others in the larger stores along Broadway and Fifth Avenue.

'And the air didn't circulate *before* you rigged it all up at Barnum's expense?' Thumb and Greenwood shared a smile. 'What circulating air? I don't feel no circulation.'

'It's designed to operate to maximum efficiency at a height approximating to chest and shoulders of a person of moderate stature,' Barnum said. 'Right, Mr Butler?'

'Right,' Henry Butler said. 'Maximum efficiency.'

'Down there where you are is where all the expelled and used-up stale air sinks to. Perhaps you might feel the benefit if you climbed up on to a chair.'

Thumb stamped his foot and began once again to pace the room.

Before anyone could speak to draw them back from this dangerous stalemate, there was a knock at the door of the outer office and Greenwood left them to answer it. The other three men waited, grateful for this brief respite. Despite the fan, the room was warm, the air stale and marbled with the smoke of their cigars. Looking up at the blades, Barnum saw the small figure of Thumb suspended from one of them, screaming and gesticulating wildly to be let down. It was true that others had already adopted Henry Butler's idea, and wherever Barnum now encountered one of the fans he himself claimed the credit for having pioneered their use.

It was seeing the fans elsewhere that had made him more receptive to a new idea with which Henry Butler had approached him. This involved the installation at the very centre of the Museum of a rising cabin, which would work on a system of pulleys and counterweights and which would raise and lower people up and down through each floor, thus saving their legs on the stairs. Henry Butler had already made his calculations and drawn up plans for the device. A basement and attic room would have to be prepared for the simple machinery to be installed, but the only other requirement would be to cut a drop through each floor to enable the contraption to rise and fall unhindered. At first, Barnum had baulked at the word 'drop' on the plans and had substituted the word 'descent'. The movement of the cabin as it went up and down inside a protective grille would even constitute an attraction in itself. Secretly, Barnum had consulted a carpenter and an engineer, and though both had expressed their surprise at the venture, neither had said outright that it couldn't be done. Henry Butler's plans were at that very moment under lock and key in his desk.

There was a commotion in the outer office, to which they all turned their attention. Elizabeth entered, and behind her followed a group of Redskins. Thumb ran his hands down his waistcoat at the sight of Elizabeth, but at the appearance of the painted faces behind her he ran to join Barnum behind his desk.

'They want to see you,' Greenwood shouted in. 'I've told them that you're busy, but they don't seem to understand.'

'That's because they're Godless bloodthirsty savages,' Thumb called back out.

'It's because they insist,' Elizabeth said, presenting herself in the doorway and waving a hand through the thick smoke as though preparing a way for her words.

'Never too busy to see my employees,' Barnum said, more grateful than any of them for this diversion. 'What's their grievance?'

Elizabeth stepped forward. 'They want details of their journey home. They need to plan their timing in order to help with the harvest and other preparations for the winter.'

'Home being the Black Hills of Dakota,' Barnum explained to

Thumb, who still hid beside him. 'And no doubt they still expect me to facilitate this ungenerous exodus out of my own pocket.' He had every intention of paying for the Indians to return home, but now wanted to repeat this magnanimous gesture in front of Thumb.

Elizabeth spoke a few simple sentences, signing with her fingers and palms to Crazy Horse, the foremost of the braves.

'They've been very patient,' she said. She came even further forward and was immediately approached by Thumb, who reached up, took her hand and kissed it. She tried to pull it away from him, but he held on to it and began to tell her yet again how beautiful he found her.

Seeing that this was not what Elizabeth wanted, Crazy Horse and two of the other young braves stepped forward and cradled the heads of their blunt stone axes, making their intentions clear.

'I'd let go of her if I were you,' Barnum said, pleased at Thumb's obvious discomfort. 'They worship her. You're right – they're heathens. Knock you on the head and drop you in the pot at the wink of an eye.' He looked Thumb up and down. Some pots were smaller than others.

'So do I worship her, Barnum. So do I.' Thumb began his retreat.

'Yes, of course. But they mean it. She's the only reason they stayed this long. They paint round her eye and set themselves off in the dark of night bellowing and howling like wolves.'

'And she lets them?' Thumb released Elizabeth, drew back his hand and wiped it on his chest.

'I let them because they're my friends,' Elizabeth told him.

'Friends! They're –'

Elizabeth beckoned the three young braves forward. 'This is Crazy Horse, this is Yellow Pony, and this is Screaming Woman Sidewalk.'

The three braves bowed.

'Screaming Woman Sidewalk?' Thumb said.

'Named after his first public appearance,' Barnum said proudly. 'If ever you feel the need for some space on a crowded sidewalk, call in here first and I'll lend you one. Works every time.'

'This whole thing's crazy,' Thumb shouted, his voice rising even higher until he squealed. 'Having them here is sheer lunacy. Out there –' he pointed to a wall. 'Out there, they're butchering innocent women and children. Out there they're tearing the scalps from young girls and torturing our young men, our proud, strong, pioneering, white young men, in ways I wouldn't even dare to mention in front of a lady.'

'Out there,' Barnum said, following the line of Thumb's pointing finger, 'is the East River and Brooklyn. This is the furthest east they got.'

Crazy Horse spoke to Elizabeth.

'He says that if you don't stand by your word then they'll go anyhow.'

Barnum ran a hand over his scalp.

'You're going to let them talk to you like that!' Thumb said. 'Crazy Horse – what kind of a name's that for a man?'

'He understands every word you say,' Elizabeth told him.

This stopped Thumb and he returned to stand beside Barnum.

'How old is he anyway? He's only a boy.'

'He's in his early twenties. He's the son of a chief.'

'Of course he is. They all are. Lord almighty, Barnum, they don't even know how to dress themselves proper and you're considering letting them get back home scot-free?' Turning to Elizabeth, he said, 'I bet he hasn't even got a single tailored suit to his name. I've got two hundred. I've got a wife can wear completely different outfits every single day of the year if she chooses. Which she usually does. I've got signed photographs of most of the crowned heads of Europe and letters of appreciation addressed from them to me personally. Me, Tom Thumb, General. What's he got to say to that?'

Elizabeth spoke to Crazy Horse, but could solicit nothing from him except a smile as he looked dispassionately down at the midget.

'I'm telling you, Barnum, that boy's trouble.'

'Tell them they're free from the end of the month,' Barnum told Elizabeth. 'With free railroad travel back to wherever it is they want.'

Elizabeth translated this and then listened as Crazy Horse replied at length.

'He says you promised them blankets and supplies, and that whatever you don't give them, they'll take.'

'Steal,' Thumb said. 'She means steal, Barnum. You going to stand your ground against these savages?'

'That isn't how they see it. They had an agreement with Mr Barnum. They trusted him.'

'Well, Barnum, is this what it's come to – having a load of heathens come all this way to tell you what you can and cannot do and then demanding to be paid for the privilege of humiliating you?'

Barnum and Elizabeth shared an understanding glance. 'Tell

them I'm a man of my word,' he said. He was wondering if they would accept the gift of an elephant and a hippopotamus to take back with them to their homeland instead of the blankets they demanded, which cost a dollar a time, and which all had to be a particular colour of red because only that colour turned back the wind.

'They sleep on the roof,' he told Thumb. 'So the stars can keep an eye on them.' He left his desk to stand beside Elizabeth and the braves. 'Last summer I drove in a carriage around Central Park with Yellow Bear, chief of the Kiowas, held by most to be the bloodthirstiest savage in the country. Came to no harm. Still in one piece.'

'And where is he *now*?' Thumb said with a sneer. 'Back among his fellow-butchers hunting down white women and snatching their babies.'

'I suppose so,' Barnum said absently, savouring his fond memory of the day, of the way Yellow Bear had at one point climbed down from the carriage to eat the bark off a tree, bringing a piece back for Barnum to try and then standing over him as he did so. Even a year ago, one New York summer and winter, now seemed like a time beyond his reach.

He asked Elizabeth if the braves wanted anything else of him.

Crazy Horse bowed slightly, spread his feather-lined arms and spoke loudly for a moment before turning his back on them and walking out.

'You stay,' Thumb said as Elizabeth prepared to leave with them.

Elizabeth glanced at Barnum, and Barnum nodded.

Greenwood showed the Indians out and returned to join them. 'They stink,' he said.

'They anoint themselves,' Elizabeth told him.

Thumb circled her. 'Why, Barnum, I do believe she'd leave with them and be their queen.' He lifted the ample material of her dress and let it fall. 'Mr Barnum tell you anything about my generous offer to buy this place and turn it into a *real* theatre, into a place folks'll be happy to pay *three* dollars to get into?' he asked her.

'I wouldn't have thought that was any of my concern.' She moved to stand beside Henry Butler and slid a hand through his arm. Both Greenwood and Thumb watched her, each suppressing their own silent envy.

'You could be very big, very big indeed under the right circumstances.'

'I know. I could be another Jenny Lind,' Elizabeth said, and began to sing.

'God forbid,' Barnum said, smiling at her.

'That wasn't what I had in mind,' Thumb said.

'I know what you had in mind . . . General.'

'I'm a very wealthy man, a man not without considerable –'

'You're General Tom Thumb the midget and I'm Elizabeth the Minnesota Cyclops. Except you aren't a General and I've never been to Minnesota in my life.'

It gave Barnum a thrill to hear her talking like this, and to see Thumb wince as she turned to look down at him, stripping him of all his pretensions and beating him down with the stare of her single eye.

'All this makes sense to me,' she said. 'You don't.'

'It does?' Barnum said to her.

By the wall, Henry Butler almost applauded her.

Beside the door, Greenwood folded his hands into fists. He alone, he knew, now had the power to retrieve the discussion of the sale of the Museum and move it forward, pulling it free of all these worthless meanderings. 'The public thinks that Thumb is still out there someplace,' he said. 'They saw him come in and they're wandering around looking for him, demanding to see him.'

'Let them look,' Thumb said unexpectedly. 'It sometimes feels as though everybody on this damn continent's paid his or her dollar to look at me.'

'I know the feeling,' Barnum said, and the two men shared an understanding smile, their first since Thumb's reappearance in the city many weeks earlier.

Finally losing his patience with them both, Greenwood said, 'I've had enough,' and left, leaving the four others staring at the slammed door behind him.

'No patience,' Barnum said. 'He won't go far.'

Thumb sighed. He too had finally realized that the time had come to abandon his assault and unfurl the flag of surrender. 'Not like you and me, eh, Phineas. No imagination. No spirit. I don't suppose you could arrange for a posse of your savages to chase me down Broadway when I leave.'

'I could, but I couldn't vouch for the consequences.'

'They'd stick me like a pig.' Picking up his hat and cane, Thumb prepared to leave. 'I heard they captured all the fire-bombers. The shame of it is, they hang so goddam quick. If I'd listened to Lavinia all those years ago we'd have been sitting down South someplace on our own burned-out plantation. She hates them, all of them, black, brown, yellow, red. She wants us to build another house. She wants to set her sister up in California. She's a seamstress and sews like a horse. Farewell, Phineas. Don't forget what I said about the Twins. Get them back under contract by all means, but don't bring them back to this place when it's all over, keep them moving around. On their four feet they're walking profits; sitting still they're only targets. Rumour has it, Chang flogged two of his darkies to death. Only a rumour, but rumours like that are life and death in this city. So long.'

He left them, and they heard the cheer from the crowd as he emerged from the outer office.

'I try to despise him,' Barnum said to Elizabeth and Henry Butler.

A few moments later they also left him, Henry Butler walking with Elizabeth back to her booth. He explained to her how his rising cabin would work, pointing out the part of each floor which would have to be cut away to enable it to be installed. They were joined by Bella-Grace Sprague who told them it was the most ridiculous idea she had ever heard and that it was bound to lead only to disaster. She complained that Thumb was drawing the crowds away from her husband, and that it stood to reason that if Thumb was about to leave, then the crowds would leave with him. Some days, she said, it barely seemed worth the effort of getting Isaac out of his bed.

Elizabeth left them, retrieved the Aztec children from Anna, and took them into the almost empty theatre to watch the Indians perform the first of their farewell dances. Neither Bartola nor Maximo showed any sign of fear at the loud cries or the violent actions of the dancers.

Seeing her, Crazy Horse left the stage to join them.

'Will he stand by his word?' he asked her.

'I think so.'

'Me, too. We don't have to get back for any harvest – all that's been taken care of – the truth is, we've grown sick of all this. The place has filled with bad spirits since we arrived.'

'Will it be safe for you to go home?' Elizabeth asked him. 'The war might have diverted everyone's attention for the past few years, but when it's over there will still be men coming to hunt you down because they think no more of you than Thumb does.'

'And because they're as ignorant of us as he is. I read in the newspapers that after the war they're going to reorganize the cavalry and give it more clearly defined responsibilities.'

'You'll survive.'

'I think so too, but I also think everything is about to change. You ought to leave too. You see it coming as well as any of us.'

'And what about these two?' She held forward Bartola and Maximo, who fondled the horsehair braids hanging from Crazy Horse's belt.

'They could come back with us. We'd treat them with more dignity and respect than they'll ever get here.'

'I know, but wherever they were, they'd always be lost.'

Yellow Pony called from the stage and Crazy Horse returned to join the others. There was a short silence, and then the room erupted to the beat of a dozen synchronized drums, rising to a much louder than normal crescendo until Elizabeth and the Aztecs covered their ears and laughed.

On the stage the drummers sat in a line and stared out directly ahead of them, as though they were in no way connected with the noise they were creating, and as though, by some miracle of vision, they could already see the place to which they were shortly to return, and what, in the not so distant future, was to happen there.

*

Later that same night, Barnum sat alone in the basement and looked hard into the eyes of the hippopotamus. In return, the hippopotamus turned to face him, propelling itself – impossibly, it seemed to Barnum – by the slightest flick of its stubby tail, just as a great iron-built steamship was improbably driven by its single, seemingly insignificant and inadequate copper screw.

'You're a jinx. You've put a curse on this place.' There was neither malice nor despair in his voice.

The hippopotamus blinked, afterwards raising the lid of only one of its protruberant eyes.

'A Pharaoh's curse. At least in the Nile all you had to eat were skinny Egyptians. Here, you're eating me up. Alive. What am I talking about – you haven't ever seen the Nile nor eaten a man in your entire and worthless life.' He looked up at the scum of floating cabbage leaves and other flotsam which still coated the surface of the aquarium.

A trickle of bubbles rose against the glass, fed by the hose from Henry Butler's engine. The contraption sat in its case beside the tank and hummed gently, occasionally releasing a puff of blue smoke into the already warm room.

'You should be long gone by now. The dogs should have had you and I should have had a tank filled with giant squid or an octopus. Even just sitting here looking at you I can feel myself losing money. I've felt it before. I can hear the noise in my head; it's like the noise of a pebble being thrown down into a bottomless, empty well. You listening to me? Plink plink plink. Empty as all those bubbles you're forever spitting out. Hear it?'

In response, the hippopotamus opened its other eye. A solitary bubble rose from its pink lip and was trapped in the hairs of its cheek.

'You're listening. You hear everything. You know everything that's been going on here. You're enjoying all this.'

On either side of Barnum were two glass cases, each of which contained a snake – Samson and Delilah, thus named to continue the biblical theme of the hippopotamus's advertising. They had arrived earlier in the day from one of his agents in South America, and who now promised in his every communication with the Museum to send a pair of spiders which trapped and ate birds. Barnum envisaged them in a cage by the entrance, weaving their webs for unsuspecting pigeons.

The snakes did not impress Barnum. They had arrived with neither fuss nor ceremony in sealed cases and had been immediately transferred to the basement by Henry Butler, where he believed they might now 'acclimatize' themselves to their new surroundings. Barnum could not fully understand the logic behind this reasoning of 'acclimatization', but because Henry Butler had insisted, and because he had sided with him earlier in the day, he had agreed. He suspected that the warmth produced by the engine beside the tank had something to do with it. The two creatures lay coiled and inert, their eyes like opals in the reflected light of his lantern.

He swung the light from side to side, creating the illusion of movement all around him, of creatures moving towards him through the dark and impenetrable edges of a forest.

Above him, the five floors of the empty building felt like a dead-weight upon his shoulders.

A carriage waited for him at the Museum entrance, ready to take him back to Charity and his daughters, where he would once again be called upon to inspect the more recent purchases of their uncontrollable spree, which had so far lasted five months and as yet showed no signs of ever abating. For everything he was shown, he knew there was another, equally costly item which he would never see. He felt as though all the loose ends of his life were now beyond his grasp and were already being woven by others into chains with which to bind him.

'And that includes you,' he told the hippopotamus.

A second bubble, then a third, fourth and fifth dribbled from the animal's mouth, moving slowly upwards like small indignities to burst and be lost in the greenish glow above the water.

'I've done everything a man could humanly do for a hippopotamus and what have I had back in return? Tell me, what have I had back that might yet turn a profit? There are far too many of you, for a start. You're all over the place, everywhere I look, although I don't know why, if this is all we're going to get for our money. Look at me, I got a pig that can write poetry and a dog that can sing any popular song you care to mention, including his own version of the Battle Hymn of the Republic, but what, so far, have I had from you? Besides which, a jinx is a jinx.'

He took his lantern to the case which enclosed the engine and lifted the wooden cover to reveal its workings. Amid the block of oil and grime, a pair of slender silver rods pushed in and out of their sleeves, and the balls of a small regulator spun on top of the machine like a weather-vane.

Gingerly, he touched a lever with his finger. It was warm, but not hot. He slid it from left to right, and immediately the two silver rods slowed in their action and the balls of the regulator dropped. Pulling the lever back into its original position he saw with satisfaction that the rods and balls both speeded and rose.

'Nothing to it,' he told the hippopotamus, which had by then shifted its position to watch what he was doing more closely. 'See – left right, fast slow.' He repeated the simple manoeuvre and watched as the bubbles from the submerged hose slowed down and then stopped completely. He set them flowing again and then turned his attention to other parts of the machinery.

The next piece he touched burned his fingers and he jumped back with them between his lips, taking them out only to wave them frantically and then to press them against the cool wall of the aquarium. The hippopotamus nibbled at them through the glass.

When the pain had ceased, Barnum returned to the engine and inspected another lever, this time with a piece of wood. At the slightest nudge this dropped loosely into a horizontal position and the engine stopped immediately. This alarmed him and he quickly lifted it back into an upright position. To his relief there was a chug and a plume of smoke and the machinery rattled back into life.

He left it, replaced the cover and returned to the bench facing the aquarium, where he wiped his brow and fingers. Somewhere above him, a door opened and closed, and he listened as someone made their way along one of the corridors and down a flight of stairs. The footsteps receded and he found he'd been holding his breath, as though his discovery in the basement constituted some kind of threat.

'I suppose, floating around in there all day and night and looking out at all this, that you could bring yourself to believe that you were the last creature on God's earth, and that nobody, except perhaps Henry Butler, had a thought in the world for you. You'd be wrong. Saint Jeremiah Bergh wants you released into the Hudson. He wants to find you a mate, and then that's where you'd live, upriver somewhere. It grieves me to have to admit it, but I wish that it could happen, I truly do. Then you'd have his scrawny old women hosing you down and tossing you cabbages at every hour of the day. But I can't agree to it, because if I did he'd never be away from the place, wanting more and more until there was nothing left. What we need is for you to escape under your own steam. Either that, or –' Barnum lowered his head, '– or just a plain simple straightforward expiration. Nothing we ever had down here in the past found that too much of a problem. Trouble with you is, you're as charmed as I once was.'

The hippopotamus let out a great bellow of air, which rose in a mass and broke the surface in a hiss of froth.

'I understand all that,' Barnum said, waiting until the water had stopped lapping. 'But something still has to be done.'

In the cases beside him, Samson and Delilah rose from their coils and held their heads loosely aloft.

'They understand.'

Barnum had still not yet shown to the public the mechanical cobra in his office. He had toyed with the idea of giving it to his future son-in-law as a wedding present, but knew that the veto of his daughters was likely to amount to nothing less than a physical attack upon him. Looking now at the cases beside him, he saw how dull and worthless their occupants were by comparison with the mechanical marvel which still thrilled him and caused his heart to skip a beat every time he set it in motion. He made a mental note to ask Greenwood to write to the South American agent informing him that his services were no longer required, and asking him if he knew of anyone else better suited to the position, at an increased salary if necessary.

A second noise distracted him. This time the footsteps were directly above him, crossing in the direction of the Ann Street exit. He heard the door being unlocked and then someone slipping in. The whistle of a ship at the distant quays penetrated the silence.

'That's the river. Where you belong. Trouble is, getting you there from here. So, as I said . . .'

He went again to the exposed engine, touching the levers and valves he'd already explored, becoming more confident as he began to understand the control he could now exercise over the machine. He repeated to himself the few words he'd heard Henry Butler use as the engine was installed, guessing now at their location and uses. He prodded new levers and stood back to consider their effect.

The hippopotamus turned away from him, its backside pressing against the glass and becoming paler.

'They can come and go all night for all I care,' Barnum said. 'They think I don't know, but I've known for years. They wander the streets in disguise, ready to come scurrying back here at the first sign of trouble or when the sun starts to come up or if –'

Unexpectedly, the engine stopped, letting out a last puff of smoke as the sleeves to the silver rods fell over them with a dull click. The basement was silent. A last bubble of air emerged reluctantly from the submerged hose and rose quickly to the surface.

Barnum and the hippopotamus faced each other.

'They call it giving away your daughters,' Barnum said absently, his voice low. 'You wouldn't understand – I mean – this, all this.' He stopped and turned away from the hippopotamus's dull, accusing gaze, and, retrieving his lantern, he left the basement and hurried up to the entrance and his waiting carriage.

23

A MONTH LATER, on the day that Crazy Horse and his braves left the city for their homes in Dakota, a tragedy struck the Museum that no one could have foreseen. That morning, Franklin fell from his seat in his booth and lay gasping on the floor, unable to cry out, and convinced that every short tortured breath he now took would be his last.

At the station the Indians were led by Henry Butler and Elizabeth, unexpectedly accompanied by a band and a dozen vagrants parading up and down the platform wearing boards announcing that at least one treaty with the Redskins was being honoured.

Crowds gathered to cheer, and children fired wooden pistols at the Indians.

'We should have guessed,' Elizabeth said above the noise of the band to Henry Butler, who shrugged helplessly and returned to his position between the Indians and their spectators.

A drunkard called out that the wisest thing to do would be to kill them all now, there and then, before they were free to commit any atrocity they liked. He pushed forward and volunteered himself for the job. From the steps of his railroad car Crazy Horse looked down and waited calmly for the confrontation to develop further. The drunkard snatched a child's toy pistol and staggered from side to side firing it, surprised and mystified when it didn't work. He was cheered, but only by the other drunken vagrants who had long since made the station their home. The rest of the crowd moved further back, uncertain of where this provocation was leading.

Henry Butler approached the man, but was restrained by Elizabeth. She wore her hood and veil and was recognized by no one. Approaching the drunkard, she held out her hand for him to give her the pistol. Instead, he jabbed it at her, still uncertain of why it hadn't worked for him. The other braves and their squaws sat in their seats by the windows and looked out.

'I'll take it now,' Elizabeth said, holding out her hand.

'Massacre!' the man shouted.

'Massacre!' someone answered him back.

On the carriage steps, Crazy Horse and several others began to chant, raising and lowering their heads and gently stamping their feet, the noise amplified by the broad curve of the station roof.

'It's a war song!' someone called out, causing the crowd to shuffle even further back. Several of the squaws left the train and danced on the platform in a tight circle, flailing their arms and wailing.

'Hand it over and they'll be on their way back West,' Elizabeth said to the drunkard. She moved closer until she was only a few inches from his face, and after asking him a third time to hand over the pistol, she lifted her veil and stared directly at him. To add to the effect, she hummed, and behind her Crazy Horse and his braves increased the volume of their chanting.

'Oh my Lord,' the man said, looking directly into her eye, rubbing a dirty hand over his even dirtier face and dropping the pistol. He staggered backwards, cried out again and then turned and fled into the crowd. Elizabeth knelt and picked up the toy gun. The sound of the man's yelling echoed as he ran out of the station and along the tracks.

Elizabeth drew up her hood and pulled down the veil to once again cover her face.

Crazy Horse stopped chanting and around him the dancers became still. The crowd, too, fell silent.

Elizabeth approached and embraced them. He asked her to reconsider his offer to accompany them. She shook her head. He told her that it was foreseen by his elders that another ten years would pass and then the whole country would come to know his name. She told him that she hoped it would be for the right reasons.

'I doubt that,' he said, avoiding her eye. 'Not for *your* right reasons.'

She kissed him and released her hold on him. 'Their reasons,' she said, 'not mine.'

Henry Butler began the short speech Barnum had prepared for him, much of which concerned what remained in the Museum now that the Indians were leaving. He announced that Barnum himself would have been present to see the braves off, but he feared that by simply being there he might overshadow their own great day.

Waiting patiently until the speech was finished, Crazy Horse thanked Henry Butler for all he'd done for them during their two-year stay in the city. He gave him a pendant to present to his sick wife, assuring him that in her own heaven she would be well protected by it. Henry Butler thanked him and then walked away from the small party, leaving Elizabeth alone with them.

A guard was already walking along the line of carriages closing their doors, a flag in his hand.

Crazy Horse told the others to get back on the train until only he and Elizabeth stood together. He told her he would pray for her safety for as long as she lived. She, too, was given a pendant which would protect her, and a gold nugget almost as big as her palm, which Crazy Horse asked her to present to Anna Swan and Captain Bates.

'Is this why you're going home?' she asked him, turning it in her hand.

'We're going home because in the city we have no hands and no feet, and because if we stay any longer our spirits will grow fat and lazy and greedy, like those of the people here.'

In the distance the engine let out a long whistle, followed by a plume of pure white steam.

'Get gone, Redskins!' someone shouted out.

Crazy Horse leapt on to the running-board at the back of the carriage, swaying with it as it jerked forward.

Elizabeth stood and watched the train pull away from her, closing her fingers around the nugget so that no one else would see it. Henry Butler joined her and they waved together. The faces of the braves were all turned towards them as the train pulled out of the station.

'It's a long journey,' Henry Butler said, certainly a longer one than any he had ever undertaken, even in his dreams.

'And the women expect to be pulled from the train and mistreated at every halt.'

'They never said –'

'They wouldn't. The braves expect to die protecting them.'

Henry Butler turned and watched as the last carriage rounded a curve in the track, and as the steam and smoke from the engine, flattened by the station roof, was suddenly released and blew upright in high contrasting plumes.

A small child approached Elizabeth to reclaim his pistol.

'They'll be safe enough,' Henry Butler said unconvincingly. 'Barnum's packed all their belongings in wicker trunks advertising the Museum. People will think they're part of a travelling show. They'll probably line the tracks to cheer.'

'And did he give them all the blankets he promised them?'

One of the trunks was packed with leaflets and posters to be distributed at each stop along the long journey.

Waiting until the track had stopped humming, Elizabeth turned into the crowd and Henry Butler followed in her wake.

In the carriage taking them back to the Museum she was reminded of the day she had arrived in the city and had made this same journey with Greenwood. That had been nine months ago now, but already it felt like a lifetime to her.

'He gave me this for Delilah,' Henry Butler said, showing her the pendant. 'She won't take it. All she wants now are new medicines.' He was silent for a moment, lost in his own hopelessness. 'I've stopped believing,' he said. 'I know what's going to happen to her, to me, to us all, but I've no faith in it any longer. We rot, don't we; that's what happens to us all, we rot. The only difference I can see is that some of us start before we get to the grave. We can do what we like to the Redskins, but their heaven remains intact. Nothing worries them on that score. I'll give it to her and tell her who it's from and she'll throw it across the room and start her raving and coughing. She believes all the stories, you see, reads them all in her papers and journals. She has illiterate girls for nurses because that's who she feels most comfortable with.' He stopped speaking and stared without really looking at the streets outside. 'I wonder why they ever came here in the first place,' he said.

'Just to see it all, and to know,' Elizabeth told him.

'To know what?'

'What you know.'

'We're going to wipe them all out, aren't we?' he said.

'Eventually.'

'Either that or we'll rig them up in suits and make them walk around with Bibles in their hands praying out aloud that they've been saved. That's what he's packed into another of the trunks – Bibles, and small printed cards of Jesus and the Apostles.'

Their own short journey ended, and after a moment composing themselves they climbed down from the carriage and entered the Museum, where the first thing they saw was a knot of people blocking the ground-floor corridor, and ahead of them they heard the voice of Greenwood shouting to be given more room.

Henry Butler called to him, and a moment later Herman squeezed himself through the mass of bodies towards them.

'Franklin's sick,' he said breathlessly, clutching his chest. He began to pull Elizabeth back through the crowd. 'What can we do? Barnum isn't in and Greenwood hasn't done a thing yet. You'll know what to do. You've got to come and help him.'

Slowly all three of them forced their way back through to where Franklin lay.

'Someone's gone for the doctor,' Bella-Grace Sprague said, helping them into the space Greenwood had cleared in front of Franklin's booth.

Henry Butler and Herman made their way to the private passage which led to the rear of the gallery.

'What happened?' Elizabeth asked Bella-Grace.

'Keeled over. Stood up, let out a long low sorta groan and then sunk down to his knees just like he was praying, and then – bam – flat out.' She clapped her palms together. 'Good job he's on this floor and not higher up. I was upstairs with Isaac and I felt it run through every timber and right up into my bones. We all did.'

'What are they doing for him?'

'Standing round him shouting for room and waving their arms in the air. What do men ever do in an emergency? My guess is that his legs just had enough of carting all that blubber around after all these years and gave way on him. I seen horses go down in the street in the exact same way. More than they could bear.'

They climbed up on to the low stage and searched for the opening in the drawn curtain. People were calling for it to be pulled back so that they might all see.

'Anna and Bates are in there trying to lift him back into his chair, but every time they try to raise him he just lets out another of his powerful moans and begs to be let back down again. Herman's been going frantic all the time you were gone. I feel sorry for that boy. The two of 'em seem to have struck up a good friendship. Ask me, we ought to send to the hospital for a surgeon to come and take a look-see, but Greenwood insisted on getting Barnum's creaky old physician in to give us his opinion before too much money gets unnecessarily spent.' Bella-Grace ended the sentence with a snort. 'In my opinion, best thing to do would be to get a pillow under his head and make him up a bed where he is now. Let him sleep it all off and he'll probably wake up in the morning fit as a fiddle. I'm blessed with perfect health myself, I know, but I do have some knowledge of how to alleviate suffering in others. Isaac suffers something awful with his joints. Knitting together, one physician told him, but I told him not to pay any account to that.'

Elizabeth had stopped listening and was moving ahead of Bella-Grace. A double thickness of curtain had been drawn, and penetrating the outer screen she groped in the darkness for a way into Franklin's booth. Already she could hear his painful breathing and the voices of the others as they argued over what to do for him. She called in for help and Zip drew aside the second curtain for her. Everyone turned to face her as she entered.

Herman stood at the front of the booth with Henry Butler, both of them holding the curtains closed against the crowd outside, some of whom were starting to tug at them to see what was happening.

At the centre of the booth, his fallen chair beside him, lay Franklin, his arms held out, pale, sweating heavily, and with his chest shaking violently at every breath he took. Greenwood stood over him, desperate and angry, calling out every few seconds to ask if the physician had arrived yet. By Franklin's shoulders knelt Anna Swan and Captain Bates. Elizabeth joined them and they explained to her how they had tried to lift him between them, but how difficult and painful this had proved to be.

At her appearance, Franklin called Elizabeth's name. She held her face close to his and he told her he was relieved to see her. His every word made him wince with pain, but her presence seemed to relax him and he closed his eyes. He couldn't raise himself sufficiently to see who else was present and he asked if Herman was still there. Anna assured him he was and motioned for Herman to call out and let Franklin know that he was still near by.

'He brung me this,' Franklin said, the pain of each word now greater than the last. He indicated to Elizabeth the small framed picture of his family propped beside him where he lay, and at which he could look without moving. He coughed and the spasm of pain brought tears to his eyes and a trickle of saliva from his mouth. Elizabeth told him not to speak and mopped his face with a cloth.

Everyone in the booth was as helpless as he was, and without the physician to absolve their collective responsibility there was nothing they could now do for him except stand and watch and wait, and believe that simply by witnessing his pain they were in some way able to share in it and alleviate it.

Eventually, the physician arrived, but he too was uncertain of what to do. He listened to Franklin's chest and his stomach and then prodded him in a dozen different places, each producing its own gasp of pain. He administered a large dose of laudanum, and when the pain became bearable, he slid a pillow beneath Franklin's head while Anna and Bates lifted his shoulders.

'We can drag him back here,' Greenwood said when Franklin was finally asleep. He moved aside the backcloth to the booth to reveal the small ante-chamber in which Franklin's meals were prepared. 'We'll take out the cupboards and stove and fix him up a bed on the floor. It'll be cramped, but there's no way we're going to be able to lift him right out of here or that he's going to make it back upstairs under his own steam.' He was unable to hide his relief now that the imminent crisis had passed and he could reassert his authority.

Everyone concurred with the suggestion because nothing else was possible.

'I'll fix up a new board screen behind the curtain,' Henry Butler said. 'We'll shut the booth down until he's well again.'

'No. We'll bring some of the Albinos down from the third floor. Split them up and let some of them come and stand in here, perhaps the children. It's a ground-floor booth. The last thing Barnum will want is to have it standing empty.'

'You mean open it to the public again with Franklin lying sick behind the backcloth?' Zip said incredulously.

'That's what I said.' The two men faced each other.

'It's indecent,' Zip said. 'He might –'

'And he equally likely might not. Either way, pinhead, it's none of your business. Mr Butler, clear the booth. I want everybody back where they belong. Now.' His eyes remained firmly fixed on Zip as he spoke. 'You hear me?'

'Oh, we all hear you,' Zip said. 'We all hear you.'

'Come on, Zip,' Elizabeth said, pulling him towards her. 'It's Franklin we ought to be worried about now, not –'

'Not what?' Greenwood shouted at her.

'Not ourselves,' Elizabeth said calmly, tightening her hold on Zip.

'She's right,' Greenwood said. 'You're all still employees here, no matter what kind of notions you might have been getting into your heads lately. And I'm still the manager. I said move. Go! Now!'

The others began to disperse. Elizabeth pulled Zip with her into the rear of the booth where Franklin now lay.

'We'll make him comfortable and get someone to sit with him until he comes round,' Anna Swan said. She held Zip's other arm and felt it tensed and quivering with suppressed rage.

'I'll do it,' Herman said quickly. 'I'll stay with him today.' He knelt beside Franklin.

'You'll do what I tell you to do,' Greenwood said. 'You still have your obligations to the Museum to fulfil.' He turned to look at each of the others in the circle around him. 'All of you,' he said.

In an effort to defuse the situation, Henry Butler said he thought they ought to fix up the screen as quickly as possible and that someone ought to go out and disperse the crowd.

The few pieces of furniture were moved and Bella-Grace left to fetch some bedding.

Greenwood went out to the front of the booth to make up a story for those still demanding to know what had happened.

'He didn't mean it,' Henry Butler said to Zip. 'That name.'

Zip looked straight through him, pulled himself free of Anna and Elizabeth and went to help with Franklin.

An hour later, Franklin lay on a makeshift bed. His breathing had become more regular and there was a little more of his usual high colour in his cheeks. A partition had been erected between the chamber in which he lay and the booth in front, in which three of the Albino children now stood reciting poetry and singing hymns.

'He complained of being too warm,' Herman told Elizabeth as the two of them sat beside the bed. 'Before all this started, I mean. He said he felt too warm and that his chest was tight.' He held Franklin's hand in both his own. 'Feel him, he's burning up.'

'That's the laudanum,' Elizabeth said.

'You think it's burning the fever out of him?'

'Could be.' She didn't want to have to answer any more of his questions.

Painted on the screen around them were lifesize angels, some with harps, others with long slender horns. They'd been commissioned by Barnum for Joice Heth, who, at one hundred and sixty-one years old, liked to joke that she felt more at ease in the company of angels than she did in the company of men, and later, when she was unable to speak, the painted boards had served as a constant reminder of her supposed antiquity and the company she might soon be joining.

'Too warm, and then he said he couldn't breathe. I told him not to come down here, but he insisted.'

Zip arrived in his monkey suit, pulled off the jacket and asked Elizabeth how Franklin was doing.

'I think the physician doubled up on the laudanum to make sure,' she said, careful to keep her true thoughts hidden from Herman.

'Greenwood been back?'

'No.'

'Still licking his wounds, no doubt.'

'Don't, Zip.'

'Don't what?'

'You know exactly what I mean. He's dangerous, especially now with Barnum away so much of the time. Don't do anything stupid. If Barnum sees sense he'll get rid of him once and for all soon enough. Just wait, let things calm down again.'

'Like he waited to let *this* calm down, you mean?'

Elizabeth looked at Franklin and then at Herman, who was still bowed over him holding his hand.

'Not here, Zip,' she said. 'Not now, please.'

Zip apologized. 'Anything I can do?'

'If only he could have had one of Henry Butler's fans fitted up in his booth,' Herman said absently. 'That would have kept him cool. I told him to ask for one, but he didn't want to be no bother.' He moved the family portrait closer to Franklin's face so that it might be the first thing he would see when he opened his eyes.

'The fans are worse than useless,' Zip said. 'Stopping, starting up and then stopping again a few minutes later. Butler thinks there's something wrong with the engine, a loose lever. The water in the aquarium stopped running again a few nights back, been running erratically ever since. I could have told him – nothing lasts in this place, and now it's all coming apart, everything, all of it.' He paced the small room, pausing only to listen to the Albino children singing beyond the angels. 'I saw the same thing happen to a Fat Lady in a fair in Guthrie, Kentucky,' he said. 'Fell right off the scales and crashed through the platform to the ground underneath.'

'And?' Herman said anxiously.

'Owner said she was dead before she touched the ground, and that if she hadn't been, then the fall would have killed her. Considered it a good joke.'

'But Franklin's not going to die. That was outside, at a fair, in Kentucky. He's got everything here he needs to help him recover. Tell him, Elizabeth. Franklin's not going to die.'

'Perhaps he is, perhaps he isn't,' Zip said. 'How old is he, forty, forty-five?'

'Twenty-three,' Herman said.

Zip looked down at the outline beneath the blankets and then at Elizabeth. 'Savages get off back to their happy hunting grounds okay?'

Elizabeth nodded. She asked Herman if he wanted to leave and get some sleep, but he insisted on staying. His presence placed an extra burden on them all.

'Listen to that,' Zip said, nodding in the direction of the Albinos, who had stopped singing and were now reciting poetry. 'When he does come round, that's what he'll wake up to. Greenwood ought to have closed the booth completely.'

Beyond the poetry they could still hear the crowd moving through the gallery.

Unexpectedly, Franklin groaned, and Herman spoke to him, rubbing his hand.

'He can't hear you,' Elizabeth said.

'He might.'

'The physician gave him enough laudanum to dope a team of oxen. He won't be coming round for another day at least.'

'He might, he might. You don't know. How can you know? He might. Franklin, it's me, Herman. Can you hear me?'

'She said he . . .' Zip shouted, stopping as he realized that his voice would be heard outside.

Herman looked up, lost, and frightened for his friend. There were tears in his eyes.

'You're right,' Elizabeth told him. 'He might come round.'

Zip left them, returning via the warren of concealed passages to his own booth.

'I didn't mean to dispute what you said,' Herman said to Elizabeth.

'No, I know. You're just worried for him. We all are.' She held a hand to his head.

Shortly afterwards, Bella-Grace arrived to volunteer her services. She brought with her a tureen of broth and was disappointed to find Franklin still unconscious.

Together, the two women persuaded Herman to leave and get some sleep, promising to send for him when Franklin came round.

After sitting with Elizabeth in silence for a few minutes, Bella-Grace said, 'This is it, ain't it?'

Elizabeth didn't answer. She was trying to calculate how far from the city Crazy Horse and the others would be by now.

Bella-Grace ate the broth herself and continued to speculate on Franklin's chances of recovery.

At midnight they were joined by Fortuna. She apologized for

René's absence, saying that he had fallen asleep and she hadn't had the heart to wake him.

Hackaliah Cherry arrived shortly afterwards, leading Tom.

'We come to pay our respects,' he said.

'Hallelujah!' Tom slapped his battered hat to his chest.

'He isn't dead, Cherry,' Fortuna said.

'Yet,' added Bella-Grace, preparing to leave.

'Hallelujah! I hear the wheels of a mighty chariot, a mighty chariot swinging low,' Tom said.

'Where?' Cherry asked him.

Tom began to hum softly, adding to the funereal air of the small room. Then he and Cherry held hands and sang a spiritual over Franklin.

Bella-Grace and Fortuna left. Elizabeth stayed, and when Cherry and Tom stopped singing she asked them to continue, closing her eyes and wondering where she would be and how she would feel in ten years' time when she next heard of Crazy Horse and his braves.

24

OVER THE FOLLOWING few days there was an increase in the number of visitors to the Museum, all hopeful of witnessing the fallen Franklin.

The *New York Sun* and *Brooklyn Eagle* declared him to be already dead. The *Eagle* even went so far as to print a front-page account from their reporter at the scene of the tragedy, who described Franklin's last moments in every detail, lyrically suggesting that his final uncomfortable gasp of life might be likened to the one last exhausted blow of air from a stranded whale.

All this appealed to Barnum, who felt only the slightest regret at it being, momentarily at least, untrue. He consulted with Henry Butler whether or not to sue the *Eagle* and thus heighten the sense of occasion, and perhaps even create another small and short-lasting controversy. Henry Butler warned him against this, reminding him as tactfully as he knew how of both his own recent setbacks, and of the possibility that Franklin might indeed yet die.

'You're right,' Barnum finally conceded. 'It's all a question of dignity and respect.' As he spoke he toyed with the black armband he frequently wore when presenting one of his patriotic speeches in support of the Union cause.

News had just reached the city of yet another unsuccessful and bloody attack by Sherman upon Atlanta. It was now late August and the city had been besieged since May, every assault having cost the lives of at least another thousand men on both sides, and each now undertaken with a little less vigour than the last. And all this took place as the inhabitants of that city went perversely about their duties and their socializing, affecting to ignore what was happening to them as their homes were looted and burned around them.

'We're never going to get the smell of burning out of our noses after this,' Barnum said sadly, flinging down the armband.

'No,' Henry Butler said. In both their minds, Franklin was already dead.

When he was next alone, Barnum tried to contact one of his travelling shows touring in Wyoming and Colorado to recall to the Museum Fat Mary Lou Mountain, whom he would present as Franklin's sister, come all that way to care for her sick 'brother'. Unlike Franklin, who had always appeared to Barnum to enjoy his fatness, Fat Mary Lou Mountain wept copiously every time she ate, and as one mound of her flesh built up and folded down upon another. At her last weighing she had tipped the scales at six hundred and fifty-five pounds and now needed a harness to help her stand upright. Each of her grieving tears, Barnum calculated, would be worth a dollar to him at the very least.

In Franklin's booth, the Albino children had been replaced, first by a juggler and then by a young legless and armless cripple, a survivor of Antietam, playing a penny whistle supported on a wire from around his neck. He in turn was replaced by Samson and Delilah, the two pythons. The snakes were certainly no new attraction at the Museum and under normal circumstances they would not have qualified for the prime ground-floor space. They were put there now by Barnum at Henry Butler's suggestion, to keep the more inquisitive members of the public out of the booth and away from the screen, behind which Franklin lay.

An Illinois snake-charmer at the Lyceum Gallery sold Barnum the secret of making Samson and Delilah appear more fearsome in their cages. This involved stuffing a stem of peeled raw ginger root into the corpse of a mouse and allowing them each to swallow one whole. Afterwards, as their digestive juices went to work, the snakes would writhe and thrash around with their jaws fully extended, throwing themselves against the glass and causing the few visitors who did pause beside them to move on more rapidly than they might otherwise have done.

The vigil at Franklin's bedside was kept up night and day, and the first signs of a recovery came three days later, when he opened his eyes and saw the painted angels all around him. He called out, but a pain blocked his voice. He saw that he had been undressed, and that above and beneath him the sheets were stained with sweat. Beside him he saw Fortuna, her head bowed forward in sleep, her beard jutting stiffly out at an angle from her chin. From her, he looked back to the angels, and then considered the rest of the confined space in which he lay. His hand touched the floor, moving slowly back to his chest, cautiously probing, as though frightened of triggering off more pain.

'I'm not dead,' he said weakly.

Beside him, Fortuna lifted her head and watched him. She took his hand and felt the life in his fingers.

Franklin tried to smile at her through the damp mounds of his cheeks.

Fortuna left him for a moment, returning with Herman and Anna Swan. The two women discussed what to do next and Herman fell to his knees, his hands clasped in prayer, tears in his eyes.

'What happened?' Franklin asked him.

'You collapsed. Just keeled over and collapsed. But now you're just fine. The physician put you to sleep to help you rest, but now you're just fine, just dandy.'

'Probably hunger,' Franklin said, weakened by even that small effort of speech.

Anna explained to him where he was and what had happened while he'd been unconscious. As she did so, Barnum arrived and offered Franklin a cigar, crouching to slap him on the shoulder and ask him how long he thought it would be before he was back on his feet. He explained to him how much he thought this 'mishap' would add to his appeal.

Only an hour earlier he'd heard from Fat Mary Lou Mountain in Steamboat Springs, Colorado, who was now on her way to New York to grasp this golden opportunity being offered to her.

Franklin, determined to show willing, tried to push himself upright, but collapsed again with a sudden cry of pain. More sweat appeared on his brow and collected in the sunken pools of his eyes.

'He's come round, that's all,' Anna told Barnum. 'He's conscious, but still a long way off being fit to return to work.'

Franklin, feeling the heat of the pain spread outwards from his chest, was unable to say anything for or against the argument.

Barnum relaxed; everything now depended on how long it took Franklin to recover as against how long Fat Mary Lou Mountain took to get there travelling by overland stage.

'You're surely not calculating on how to turn this to a profit,' Fortuna said to him.

'My dear Madam Fortuna, nothing could be further from my mind.' Smoke rose from his mouth to mask his eyes. 'I am merely concerned. The young man is in his prime. You do me an injustice to suggest –'

'He's gone again,' Herman said loudly, indicating Franklin, who was once again unconscious. 'It doesn't look too good, does it?'

Silently, Anna and Fortuna agreed with him.

'Is he going to die?' Barnum said.

'Read the papers,' Anna told him.

'Treason and treachery,' he said with a smile. 'All around me, everywhere I look. First Greenwood and Thumb, now this. Somebody give me a fishing pole and a pool deep enough to fall into and drown.' Ash from his cigar fell on to Franklin's sheets, and was immediately brushed away by Herman.

Then, unexpectedly, from beyond the booth came the sound of smashing glass, and fearing that one of the snakes might have escaped, Barnum pushed his head through the divide in the curtain, relieved when he saw that both cases were still intact. He left to investigate the noise, and to see what, if any, damage had been done. Few noises rang up dollar signs in his mind's eye faster than the sound of breaking glass.

Anna left shortly afterwards, and an hour later Fortuna was joined by René, who brought with him his pencils and a sketch pad to make studies of the sleeping Franklin.

*

The breaking glass, Barnum quickly discovered, had been the result of a display cabinet being toppled from its stand by the crush of people still insistent upon seeing Franklin. It had contained a number of stuffed birds, most of which were already missing, and three shrunken skulls, which lay on the floor untouched, mocking the crowd with their tight grins, stitched eyes and exposed brown teeth. The few birds which remained had fallen into the triangle made by the skulls.

Arriving at the scene, Barnum retrieved these valuable exhibits and stuffed them into his pockets. He shouted for Hackaliah Cherry and then for Henry Butler. Cherry was the first to arrive, and upon being loudly and pointedly told by Barnum that several of the birds – that several of the extremely rare and expensively acquired exotic birds – appeared to already have flown the coop, looked up at the ceiling and along the line of windows. It took a great effort on Barnum's part to restrain himself from grabbing Cherry by the lapels and shaking him.

Henry Butler pushed through the crowd and stood beside him.

Seeing immediately what had happened, he took control of the situation and asked people to stand back so that the splinters of broken glass might be safely retrieved. They moved away, but slowly and reluctantly.

'Back! Get back!' Barnum shouted at them, and they stopped moving. He held out two of the small colourful birds as though they had been the innocent victims of a recent accident.

'Please,' said Henry Butler, noting the hostile response to Barnum's demand. He waited for silence before going on: 'As I'm sure you are all aware, a tragic accident –'

'Very tragic indeed,' interrupted Barnum.

'Amen to that,' said Cherry, shaking his head.

'– tragic accident has occurred within these walls –' Henry Butler indicated Franklin's booth '– and for the past two nights Mr Barnum has maintained a lonesome and anxious vigil at that unhappy man's bedside.'

Barnum bowed slightly to hide his modesty.

'And I'm sure he would beg your forgiveness if –'

'Beg on my bended knees.'

'– if he appears before you today somewhat distraught.'

'Beg on my bended knees, knees that have been bended in silent prayer for the full and complete recovery of one of my closest and dearest friends.'

'Who that?' asked Cherry, uncertain if he'd misheard something, and if the discussion had moved off at a tangent, leaving him behind. When this happened he usually abandoned his interruptions and raced silently ahead of the conversation, ready and waiting like an ambusher upon a rock to leap back into it when he again understood what was happening.

'Friends, my noble and loyal public, I apologize. It shames me to have to look at you with these eyes that have not known sleep for . . .' Barnum made a quick calculation '. . . for . . . for –'

'For forty-eight hours,' offered Henry Butler.

'For approaching sixty long and weary hours of anxious vigil.'

'Sixty!' Hackaliah Cherry's own eyes grew rounder and whiter. 'You must be one tired man, Mr Barnum, sir.'

'Thank you for your concern, dear Hack.' Barnum indicated for Henry Butler to disengage Cherry from the conversation before he said anything to contradict him. He noted with satisfaction that several of the women in the crowd had already drawn their hand-kerchiefs and were dabbing at their eyes. Barnum copied them. A man came forward with one of the missing stuffed birds, saying he'd found it by his feet.

'Friends, I would gladly forfeit every exhibit in every case in every room of this treasure trove if only the good Lord above –' he joined his hands in prayer '– would just see his way fit to letting that one solitary upstanding human being recover his health and return to the happy life he once led among us.'

'Amen,' several answered him.

A second stuffed bird was handed back and Barnum calculated that four were still missing. He did not consider the return of only two of the birds to be a fair return on his speech; otherwise he was pleased and reassured by the way in which he had been able to respond to the situation. Encouraged, he went on.

'No price, no price on earth would be too great for that one act of divine kindness in return. I'm an old man, old and exhausted in the service of his fellow-man, and if I could lay down my own life in exchange for the recovery of that one dear and trusted friend, then believe me, I would do so happily.' He glanced at Henry Butler to assess the effect of his appeal, happy when Henry Butler signalled back to him that the crowd was once again with him.

'Except you can't,' Hackaliah Cherry said, puzzled. 'In fact, the way I figure it –'

Someone in the crowd called out, 'Shut up, nigger, let him finish. Here.' A third bird flew over the heads of those in front and was caught by Henry Butler.

'I have to leave you,' Barnum said. 'I have to return once more to that unhappy bedside. Believe me, the instant there is anything to report, you will all hear of it – free of charge on one of the outside boards.'

Someone cheered and started to applaud. Acknowledging this, Barnum made his way through the crowd to the steps leading down to the basement. Ahead of him, the onlookers parted, just as the Red Sea had parted for Moses, and the comparison cheered him even further.

Since the engine driving the pump had repeatedly 'failed', the basement had once again been closed to the public. Henry Butler had volunteered to attempt to repair the machinery himself, but Barnum had prevented him. Similarly, there had been no further discussion of his rising cabin scheme. Barnum had even suggested to him that the failure of the engine, and consequently the fans, had in some way contributed to Franklin's collapse. This worried Henry

Butler and he could not bring himself to argue against it. No one else in the Museum believed it.

In its now stagnant water, the hippopotamus seemed even more inactive than usual. It stood on the floor of its tank, took a step forward and then a step back. The water was murky, filled with particles in suspension, and the glass was already coated with a film of green along its inner surfaces.

Ensuring that the door was locked behind him, Barnum turned his attention to the engine. Having disconnected the driveshaft which turned the fans, he brought the motor to life for a few seconds, sending a rush of bubbles into the tank. The hippopotamus responded immediately by rising to the surface and swallowing them. Barnum stopped the engine.

'It isn't cruelty,' he said. 'I'm a businessman. I look at profit and loss, I weigh the two up. I look at value for money and then I work out how to increase that value while paying even less for it.'

The hippopotamus remained suspended with its mouth held open over the source of the bubbles.

'You want some more?'

He pulled the lever a second time, surprised to find that it had grown warm since he'd last touched it. He tampered with other parts of the engine in an attempt to rectify this. He pushed the lever back, stopping the rush of bubbles, and then touched it every few seconds until it had cooled down. A feather of blue smoke rose from the pump and was quickly lost in the dimly lit basement.

He took one of the birds from his pocket and held it out for the hippopotamus to see.

'See that – they're stealing from me now. From me! One of the greatest benefactors this city has ever known.' He paced in front of the tank. 'They think I can't see it coming, but I see it better than any of them. They've had me on my knees before, they've had me with my face down in the dirt before, but I've pushed myself back up, and I've done it all under my own steam.' As if to emphasize his words, a small plume of steam sprouted briefly from the pump. Barnum watched it and felt encouraged to continue. 'The worms are all eating away at the apple which supports them, and soon it'll be so riddled with their chewed and rotten galleries that it'll collapse and scatter them. Then where will they all be? Out in the cold, that's where, discarded and abandoned to their own feeble resources.'

He was beginning to warm to the speech, and so he went on with it, waving his arms, opening and clenching his fists, drawing into it his wife and daughters, the City Commissioners and the crooks who controlled its newspapers. He found something to say about the new laws and regulations governing the running of places open to the public and about those men who had changed their courses with the changing fortunes of the war.

'I'm tired, they're tired, everybody's tired,' he concluded. 'Even you're tired of just bobbing up and down and plotting against me. Trouble is, all *they* have to do is to sit back and wait for something new to come along and entertain them. They make their unreasonable demands and then just sit back and wait.' He found he was shouting, and upon hearing footsteps above him he lowered his voice.

He left the basement a few minutes later and returned to his office, speaking to no one and allowing nothing to distract him. He locked the doors to the outer office, and then that leading to his own inner sanctum.

He sat at his desk, drawing himself close to it. Feeling in his pockets, he pulled out the three shrunken heads and lined them up before him. He addressed them as his three daughters, asking them what they'd bought that day, how much more of his hard-earned money they'd spent. He heard Henry Butler arrive in the outer office and shouted to ask him how many more of the birds had been returned. Henry Butler tried to open the door and come in to him, but Barnum told him to shout his answer through it.

'All but two,' Henry Butler answered.

'Not enough. I want them all back.'

'Whoever's taken them will probably have left the building by now.'

'And gone straight to hell, I hope.'

This strong and unexpected language silenced Henry Butler.

'Well?' Barnum shouted.

'Yes, sir,' Henry Butler said.

Greenwood arrived silently beside him and asked in a whisper why he was shouting through the door.

'That you, Greenwood?' Barnum called to him. 'Been off plotting behind my back again? Tell me – who are you in league with this time?'

'I've just come from Franklin,' Greenwood said.

'And?' Barnum prepared himself for the news.

'No change. He keeps drifting in and out of consciousness.'

'And your own diagnosis, Greenwood. A straight answer.'

'He's going to die,' Greenwood said without feeling.

'Soon?'

'Soon enough. They all end up like this.'

Beside him, Henry Butler shook his head, as though to rid it of the thought just planted.

'And how about Mr Butler?' Barnum shouted. 'He no doubt has something to add on the matter. Hope eternal in life ditto. He has more cause than most of us to believe it. Well, Butler?'

On the other side of the door Henry Butler stood silent with disbelief at the callousness of Barnum's remark.

At his desk, Barnum too wondered if he hadn't said too much and was relieved to receive no answer. 'Never retract' had been from the very beginning another of the guiding principles of his business success. That beginning now seemed a long way back and receding more rapidly with every day that passed. Thirty years ago the nation would have been on its knees at his feet for a hippopotamus in a tank. Now it was smashing his cases and stealing from him. Thirty years ago it hung on his every word and new revelation; now it waited only to mock and deride what he put before them.

He picked up the shrunken skulls, and strands of hair came away from the brittle flesh. He wondered for a moment about the men they might once have been, but for no longer than a moment. Morbid curiosity had always been the most profitable kind, but to consider it at anything but a superficial level was always dangerous. There were still dark continents on the earth, but the darkest places of all still lay in the minds and hearts of civilized men. He tried to decide if this was another of his own sayings, or one he'd read someplace.

'Phineas,' Greenwood called in to him, interrupting his unhappy train of thought.

'What is it?'

'A cable from Fat Mary Lou Mountain. She'll be here in a week, ten days at the most.'

Barnum sighed and let his head fall gently to his desk.

In the outer office, only Greenwood still stood with his ear to the door. Henry Butler sat at his desk, a photograph of himself and his wife on their wedding day in his hand.

25

ZIP'S NEXT CONFRONTATION with Greenwood took place the following morning.

Zip was on his way to relieve Elizabeth at Franklin's bedside when Greenwood appeared unexpectedly in front of him. They were in one of the Museum's narrow connecting corridors, where if two people met they were obliged to press themselves to the walls in order that they might pass one another. Greenwood held out his arm and inspected his pocket watch.

'Going somewhere?' he said.

At first, Zip had been unable to identify the figure in the poor light, but upon hearing Greenwood's voice, his superior, sneering tone, he stopped and considered his response. He was wearing his hairy pants and carrying his jacket.

'Rushing off for a last look at our fallen friend before he breathes his last? Very touching.'

Unwilling to be provoked, Zip approached him with a smile on his face. 'I'd come and look at you if you were ready to die. I'd hold myself this close to you.'

'And then what?'

'And then I'd hold my breath and wait.'

'A long wait, pinhead.'

'Perhaps, perhaps not. Perhaps soon the recruiting sergeants are going to find out where you've been hiding all these years.'

Greenwood laughed. 'I'd go tomorrow if they called for me. Who's hiding?'

'Of course you would. Get out of my way.'

Greenwood made no attempt to move. 'I've always said these corridors were too narrow. Perhaps when Butler gets his blessed magic cabin installed things will get a little easier. Imagine that – going up and down in a box!' He laughed. 'I reckon Franklin can see it already.'

Zip used his jacket to wipe the sweat from his chest and stomach. Outside, the temperature had reached a hundred degrees for the fourth day in a row. Two days earlier, the *Perseverance* had docked with its cargo of corpses, all dead from cholera. People walked the city streets with cloths held over their mouths.

'You didn't answer my question,' Greenwood said.

'Sorry, Mr Greenwood, sir. It's just that we've all gotten so used to you hiding behind the mighty Thumb. That must be quite something – hiding behind a midget. Tell me, how did you manage it? Or, better still, tell me how long you think you're likely to last now that he's backed off and you're out in the open again?'

'As long as I need to put you back in your place.'

'I doubt it. This place is beginning to tear apart at the seams. Anna and Bates will be gone soon. Listen to it beginning to fall.'

Both men listened for a moment to the distant tramp of footsteps all around them.

'Who needs them? Who needs any of you?' Greenwood said.

'You do.'

'Don't flatter yourself. Just look at yourself. It's pathetic the way you've all allowed yourselves to be used.'

Zip tensed and Greenwood saw this.

'Bother you, does it, having a few facts of life pointed out to you?'

Zip refused to answer.

'Oh, come on, you can tell me. I'll be running this place one day soon and I'll need to know all these things.'

Again Zip tried to pass him, and again Greenwood stopped him.

'Elizabeth's expecting me. She's been up all night.'

'Let her wait. Keeping her eye on the fatboy, is she?' Greenwood said, realizing the joke only after he'd made it.

'Go on, laugh,' Zip said. 'Laugh as loud as you like.'

Greenwood stopped immediately. 'Oh, my mistake. I thought all you walking jokes were supposed to be able to take a joke. Apparently not.'

'Look, Greenwood –'

'*Mr* Greenwood. It's still *Mr* Greenwood to you.'

Zip tried again to push past him, but Greenwood propped himself across the corridor. 'Come on, keep trying,' he said.

Zip drew back his fist and Greenwood raised his arms to protect his face. Then Zip stopped himself and wiped his mouth.

'Wise move,' Greenwood said, and then, in a different tone: 'Tell me – you and Elizabeth – you . . .?'

277

'We what?'

'You know what I'm getting at. Are you and her at all – friendly?'

'Very,' Zip said, savouring the slight shift in balance which had now taken place between them.

'*How* friendly?'

'Like I said – very. Us walking jokes got to stick together. What else have we got but each other? She's still waiting.'

Greenwood appeared to hesitate and Zip pressed by him until the two men were wedged together, their faces only inches apart.

'Don't let me stop you,' Greenwood said. 'Might be the last you see of fatboy. And if you try to convince me otherwise, then you're a bigger fool than I already take you for.'

Zip eased himself through and took several paces in the direction of Franklin's booth.

'I'd like to continue this discussion,' Greenwood called after him. 'Perhaps after the funeral.' He laughed again, and in the confined space the sound rushed ahead of Zip and came back to hit him in the face.

He turned. 'Oh, there will be other times, *Mr* Greenwood, sir.'

'Count on it,' Greenwood said. He began to whistle and then walked quickly away.

Zip waited until the whistling had faded and then punched his fist three times into the wooden wall.

There was blood on his knuckles by the time he got to Elizabeth and, when she asked him about it, he told her he'd fallen and grazed the skin.

'It's a trying time,' she told him. 'For all of us. Just try and wait until events take a turn for the better.'

To Zip, it felt as though she had witnessed everything that had just happened.

'How is he?' he asked, diverting her attention to Franklin.

'What do you want to hear? A little better, a little worse, much the same, that I think he's going to recover, that I think he's going to die?'

'Whatever,' Zip said. He lifted her hand and kissed it.

'Why, kind sir,' Elizabeth said, pretending to be flattered and then looking at the blood on her own fingers.

'I still don't know why you didn't jump on that train with the Redskins. They'd have looked after you like the one-eyed Queen of England.'

'In my experience, people running away generally have someone or something running after them. It might not be much, but it keeps on coming at them until it's so far inside of them that there's nothing they can do about it. The past can sometimes come at you like a pack of slave-hounds, and you'd do well to remember that.' She smiled at him and kissed him back.

Again it seemed to Zip as though she were talking about his own situation rather than herself.

'Whatever's said,' she said, 'and whoever's doing the talking, they're only words, and you can use the exact same words to tell a lie just as easily as you can to tell the truth.'

They were distracted by Franklin groaning in his sleep and both turned to look down at him as his eyes opened, saw nothing, and then closed again.

'Worse, much worse, I'd say,' Elizabeth said.

*

Hackaliah Cherry stood with Tom in the room of reconstructed dinosaur skeletons, surrounded by stuffed gnu, bison and rhinoceroses, solid as stone, their heads bowed and casting malevolent glances whenever the sunlight caught the glass of their eyes. It was one of Cherry's duties to dust and polish the animals and bones, and this he normally undertook during the middle of the day when the room was at its fullest. There were a few visitors moving among the exhibits now, but considerably fewer than usual, most of the Museum's customers preferring to remain on the ground floor, where the drama of Franklin had now entered its fifth day.

Cherry had given Tom a cloth and set him in motion along the leathery contours of one of the rhinoceroses while he himself polished its horns and toes. Everywhere he went in the room, he felt the eyes of the Missing Link following him around.

He paused for a moment to watch Tom working.

'What is it?' Tom asked without stopping.

'How you do that?' Cherry said.

'You ask me that fifty times a week. What is it you want?' Tom stopped dusting and shook out his cloth.

'I was going to ask if you could feel anything watching you.'

Tom, aware of the way Cherry felt about the Missing Link, said, 'Old monkey-man, you mean?'

'It's no joke, Tom, no joke.'

'Hack, I was born blind, raised blind, educated blind and cast out blind; I live, eat, drink and breathe blind. Hack, I even *dream* blind. You got eyes – use them. That monkey-man got sawdust where you supposed to got brains. I ain't saying that that necessarily gives you the advantage, but it ought to at least tell you something about yourself in relation to *it*.'

'Such as?' Cherry asked seriously, believing an important point was about to be made.

'Oh, Lord save me from ignorant niggers,' Tom said. He took a bottle from his pocket and drank from it. He offered it to Cherry, but Cherry, conscious that he was on duty, refused.

'So?'

'So, Hack, it's a fake, one of Barnum's get-ups. If it's here and present and on display for everybody with twenty-five cents to come in and look at it, how can it still be Missing?'

Cherry only half understood this. 'You can't see it,' he said indignantly.

'Don't need to see it to know what it is. We close to a piano in here? Understand one's been brought down out of the Albinos' new room.' Tom turned in a full circle, his head tilted to one side, as though he were searching intently for the source of some faint and distant sound.

'Don't talk to me about them,' Cherry said.

'I wasn't.'

'In the corner,' Cherry said. 'Next to them million-year-old dog dinners.'

Tom went to the piano, lifted the lid and began to play. The few visitors paused to listen, applauding each piece as he finished. The notes rang clear and long in the large near-empty room.

Cherry continued his cleaning, moving from the rhinoceros to one of the bison. This was as close as he would approach to the Missing Link.

Beside the bison was the concealed door of a passageway leading to the room in which Barnum's collection of upright bears stood with their snarling mouths and outstretched paws, alternating along each wall with complete suits of armour, some still with the dents or holes by which their occupants had supposedly been killed or wounded in battle.

As Cherry passed the door he smelled smoke, and cautiously opening it, he saw Zip, still only half dressed, squatting on the ground with a cigar in his mouth.

'What you doin' here? You shouldn't be here.'

'Calm down, Hack. I just came up from Franklin.'

'How's he doin'?'

'Much the same.'

'Oh.' Looking behind him to ensure that no one was watching, Cherry stepped quickly into the passage and closed the door behind him. The sound of Tom's piano-playing followed him inside.

'All we have to do now is wait for Greenwood to starting yelling for me,' Zip said.

'You and him had words?'

'He thinks Franklin's going to die.'

Cherry shook his head and sighed. 'Might happen, Zip. Me and Tom been prayin' for him every night since since his fall, but it still might happen. We prayed for a lot of things these past few years, but we still wake up in that same old attic room, him with his empty bottles, me with my brooms, and with the war still bangin' and clatterin' away down there.'

'I know it might happen. I just don't want it to happen because someone like Greenwood says it's going to happen, that's all.'

Cherry didn't understand the logic of this, but he could see how agitated Zip was and tried to divert him.

'Me and Tom just havin' a discussion about the old Missing Link out there.' He tried to sound unconcerned; it was still an effort for him even to mention the creature's name.

'Still terrify you half to death, does it?'

'My own argument is that if it's here, how come it's still called Missing?'

Zip, guessing that this realization had been reached by Tom and not Cherry said, 'Missing the point more like.'

'What point?'

'You're right – what point?'

Cherry was by now almost totally confused. He'd thrown himself into the discussion with all the confidence of a strong swimmer diving into what he believed to be ten feet of water, only to find himself in a bed of deep soft mud a foot below the surface.

'Smoke?' Zip asked him, handing him his cigar. 'It's this place that's the missing link, Hack, all this.'

Reluctant to allow himself to flounder and sink any deeper, Cherry said, 'You're right.'

'This place, us, all of us, we're all the broken links of some chain or other that's lost its strength and don't have the know-how to get itself back into one strong length.'

Cherry tried to memorize this to repeat to Tom later.

Zip smiled. 'You believe all that?'

'Why, ain't it true?'

'I don't know.' Zip retrieved his cigar as Cherry made a last hopeless attempt to understand what might or might not have just been revealed to him.

In the distance, beyond Tom's piano-playing, they heard Greenwood calling for Cherry. Cherry remained unconcerned.

'I generally make it to him one time in every three. Usually he's forgotten what he wanted me for by the time I get there. He just keeps right on shoutin' out to make himself appear busy, generally when there's one or two young ladies round him.' In the glow of the cigar he saw the dried blood on Zip's knuckles. 'You and him have more than words?' he said.

Zip flexed his hand until a fresh drop of blood appeared at each joint. 'No. Just words.'

'I guess some words is more likely to bleed you than others. My guess is they were just putting-off words. Am I right?'

'Don't worry, Elizabeth already posted a warning.'

Greenwood called again, but this time his voice was more distant.

Tom stopped playing, and Cherry looked through a slit in the door to see him walking towards them. He hissed to him and then whispered to tell him where they were. Tom climbed into the narrow passage and sat beside them.

'Nice playing,' Zip said.

'Awful playing. I can play that well with my feet, but *they* ain't likely to know no better.' He took out his bottle, drank from it and handed it to Zip, accepting the cigar in return.

Cherry, who was now enjoying the seclusion and secrecy of their illicit conference, said, 'We ought to get together like this more often.'

'You listening to him?' Tom asked Zip.

'Zip and Greenwood come to blows,' Cherry said.

The news did not surprise Tom, who said, 'So what now, Zip? You ready for it?'

'Ready for what?' Cherry said.

'For whatever it is he's planning to do next. Can't go on like this for much longer, that much I know for sure.'

'Shut up,' Zip told him.

'Sure, I'll shut up. But just because I ain't saying it, don't mean it ain't happening.'

'Ain't what happenin'?' Cherry said, now wishing that he'd had the sense to abandon the conversation completely.

Neither Tom nor Zip answered him. Having drained his bottle, Tom took out a second, uncorked it and handed it round.

'We were discussing the Missing Link,' Zip said eventually to Tom.

'I thought we already discussed that one right up to the exclamation mark full stop.'

'We did,' Cherry said, now embarrassed that he couldn't remember how either of the discussions had ended.

'So you saw Greenwood,' Tom said, lightly touching Zip's fingers as he took the bottle from him. 'Seems to me you saw him real close. Step careful, Zip. When Anna and Bates are gone we're going to need you here.'

'Holy Wappapello! All I hear is talk talk talk,' Cherry said petulantly.

'Wappapello's a lake, Hack,' Tom said.

'A what?'

'A lake. Lake Wappapello. In Missouri.'

'How do you know that? How does he know that? I'm the one supposed to know about all that kind of thing. All *you* supposed to know about is piano-playin'.'

'Sorry, Hack. Just thought –'

'Thought! Thought! Seems to me that all thought ever did round here recently was push folk into trouble they couldn't get theirselves out of.'

'Sorry, Hack.'

Cherry tutted and folded his arms across his chest.

Half an hour and two bottles later, all three had reached some stage of intoxication, Cherry being the furthest along the road, despite having drunk the least.

'You'd better get him out of Greenwood's way,' Zip told Tom.

Cherry was half asleep and sat singing to himself and then mumbling the names of his rivers.

'I'll see to him,' Tom said. 'You want to go out and pull the head off his Missing Link, stop all his nightmares? Be better all round than trying to get your hands round Greenwood's neck.'

'Holy Musquenomenee!' Cherry shouted.

'You're too clever by half to be an ignorant nigger, Tom.'

'And you got too much going for you to lose it all by trying to get even with Greenwood.'

'He insulted Elizabeth.'

'He insults everybody. All he needs now is for Barnum to get him back down in his place, just like he thinks he keeps us in ours.'

Tom's milky eyes were staring directly into Zip's, following them as Zip looked from side to side. 'You understand my meaning?'

'I understand. Greenwood can wait. I got something more pressing to attend to first.'

'Such as?'

'Tell you later. Don't worry.'

Beside them, Cherry started to sing again, conducting an orchestra with his hands. He opened his eyes and asked them where he was.

'Celebrating,' Tom said, adding 'war's over,' but not loud enough for Cherry to hear.

Zip rose to leave them.

'It's a fact, Zip. So step easy, eh?'

Zip smiled. 'What do you know – you're only a –'

'Blind ignorant nigger. I know. Raise the flag, bang a drum.'

Zip left them, and a cape of thick cigar smoke followed him out into the room of long-dead and resurrected animals, like a curl of the mist from the primeval swamp in which they might all have once roared and hunted.

*

That same night Herman left the Museum to keep his rendezvous with Nancy above the Pearly Street Laundry.

Earlier in the evening he'd spent several hours sitting with Franklin, who, following his brief revival two days earlier, had remained unconscious ever since. His breathing, which had been regular and shallow, had become uncertain and sounded painful. Long silences, during which those keeping watch held their own breath, were followed by short gasps and then a few seconds of almost contented sighing, as though a persistent blockage were constantly being cleared, only to slip back into place, requiring the effort to remove it to be made all over again. With the possible exception of Herman, it was clear to everyone who kept vigil that Franklin was deteriorating rapidly. Laudanum was now being regularly administered by the physician, and Barnum had instructed both Greenwood and Henry Butler to stay away from the booth lest they find themselves present at the vital moment, and thus in some way be held responsible for what had happened. His reasoning on the matter was unclear; he had too much else with which to occupy himself.

When Zip and Elizabeth had been alone with Franklin, he'd asked her if she thought Herman realized what was happening.

'They're good friends,' she said. 'He's not looking that hard or that clearly.'

There and then, Zip acknowledged that when the time came, the responsibility of breaking the news of Franklin's death to Herman would be his and his alone.

By then everyone knew of Herman's assignation with Nancy, and many, including René and Isaac Sprague, had tried to talk him out of it. But Herman had insisted, and when he stepped out of the Museum at shortly after midnight, Zip, at the concurrence of all the others, was waiting to follow him to ensure he came to no harm. Vivalla had already gone on ahead, and he too was ready and waiting in the Pacific bar on Cedar Street.

Herman walked quickly to the junction of Cedar and Pearl and began to search for the laundry. Zip moved ahead of him along the opposite side of the dimly lit street and went immediately to it, where he waited in the impenetrable shadow of a doorway looking directly on to the building. He had a flask in his pocket and swigged from it as he waited for Herman to arrive.

Above the laundry were three brightly lit windows of opaque glass, and he could see the silhouettes of several people moving across them. He heard women's laughter, recognizing immediately the voices of Nancy and her two friends. He estimated that there were at least five people in the room, and he knew then that the meeting was likely to be considerably more than Herman, in his eager anticipation, was expecting.

He pressed himself even further into the shadow as Herman appeared and stopped at the laundry entrance. Billows of steam rose from vents in the wall, and through the open door a crowd of shining Chinese laundrywomen could be seen working at the tubs and presses. Herman looked up, uncertain if he would have to pass through them to reach Nancy. Someone called out to him and he backed away, out of the block of yellow light cast on to the street.

'That's it, turn round and run,' Zip whispered to himself, his eyes constantly moving between the door and the windows above. He heard a shout and the light in all the windows was immediately dimmed.

A moment later, Nancy opened one of the windows and called down to Herman below.

He held up the bunch of flowers he'd brought her. Nancy withdrew, reappearing several minutes later at a second door a short distance from the laundry entrance. She looked along the street in both directions, embraced Herman and drew him in.

Zip crossed the street as the door closed behind them. He turned the handle, but found it had been locked. Leaving it, he made his way to the narrow alleyway which separated the laundry from the building beside it, where he found himself knee-deep in refuse as he searched for another way in.

Inside, Nancy removed Herman's coat and took the flowers from him without comment. She held his arm and led him upstairs. When he hesitated she stopped and asked him what was wrong.

'Your clothes,' he said.

'You don't like them? I thought we were sweethearts.' Nancy ran her hands over her breasts and then clasped them to her waist. She wore a corset fastened with a zigzag of pink ribbons, the top of which was already unfastened. When she spoke to him, Herman looked away and could only bring himself to glance sideways at her.

Nancy pretended to be offended. 'I only did it for you,' she said. 'It's not often that a poor uneducated girl like me gets to be alone with a man of means like yourself.'

'Man of means,' Herman said, touching the pocket in which were the few dollars he had been able to gather before leaving the Museum. This amounted to little more than a month's wages, and was considerably less than the fortune he had suggested to Nancy, and which she now expected to see.

Nancy saw the gesture, understood it immediately and smiled. She kissed him on the forehead and continued leading him up the stairs. They were stopped briefly by the sound of wood on wood somewhere beneath them, and then by the sound of splintering timber.

'Someone in the laundry,' Nancy said quickly, hurrying him up the final flight of stairs.

Above them, Herman heard footsteps and hesitated.

'Boarders,' Nancy said. 'Chinese. The place is crawling with them. Yell and they all scatter. What did you expect – Hoffman House?' She drew the two halves of her corset together and indicated a door ahead of them. Pushing it open, she led him through into the darkness beyond.

Inside, he tried to turn and kiss her, fumbling to hold her shoulders and nothing else. But instead of responding to him, Nancy threw down the flowers and backed away from him. Someone grabbed him from behind, a man, two men, one of whom held his face to Herman's and shouted directly into his ear. Herman tried to cry out, but the second man punched him sharply in the stomach and then held a hand over his mouth as he tried to regain his breath.

Nancy lit a lamp, and beside her on the bed, Herman saw Patsy and the girl calling herself Emmeline Victoria. They too were wearing only their underclothes, and neither had shoes on their feet. Patsy was inspecting the skin of her inner thigh, watched by Emmeline Victoria. The room stank of liquor and there were wet patches on both the unmade bed and the floor.

'Don't hurt him *too* much,' Nancy said as the man punched Herman again.

'Has he got it with him?' the voice in Herman's ear asked.

'Breast pocket.' Nancy sat between the two girls, and all three linked arms and looked at Herman with a mixture of fear and excitement on their faces.

Herman was still unable to fully grasp what was happening to him and he implored Nancy with his eyes to save him, for her to tell the two men that the joke was over.

'He's trying to tell you something,' Patsy said, giggling drunkenly.

Nancy let herself fall back on to the bed, and she too began to laugh.

Emmeline Victoria rose and went to Herman. She removed the hand which covered his mouth, squeezed together his cheeks and kissed him, her tongue moving against his. Pulling back, she said, 'What's wrong? Not good enough for you?' She nodded to the men, and before Herman could respond, he was punched again.

Then Nancy returned to him, and without taking her eyes from his she pulled the money from his pocket and unfolded the notes, a look of disbelief and then growing anger on her face as she saw how little he had brought with him.

'Is that it?' one of the men said to her. 'You said he was worth a small fortune. All of Barnum's freaks must have pots of it stashed away, you said. You said this was going to be worth all our whiles.' He twisted Herman's arm until Herman felt sure it would break.

Nancy searched roughly through his other pockets, tearing the cloth in her rage. When she realized there was no more to be had, she pushed what she'd already taken into Herman's face and demanded to know where he'd hidden the rest.

Struggling for the breath to answer her, Herman was punched again, this time in the ribs.

Patsy came up to him. She too kissed him on the mouth, holding up his head by his hair.

'*The money!*' Nancy screamed at him, pounding on his chest.

She exhausted herself, stopped, looked into his eyes, and knew at last that there was no more to be had.

'I thought –' Herman began, and she slapped him across the face.

'He's tricked us,' Emmeline Victoria said. 'Or perhaps he ain't so much of a dumb freak as he makes out. Perhaps he only brought along a taster; perhaps he's got a load more of it stashed away back in that castle of horrors.'

Nancy considered this for a moment, but knew from Herman's eyes that this too was untrue. 'Sweethearts,' she said to him. 'You thought we was sweethearts. Grow up, freak. What do you think I am?'

Both Patsy and Emmeline Victoria laughed at this.

Then one of the men released his grip and the other pushed Herman to the ground. Both stood over him, each with a foot on his chest.

'Go on, hurt him,' Patsy said.

'No, leave him,' Nancy told the men. 'Let me think. There might still be a way to get something out of all this.'

'We aren't going to make Barnum pay up,' one of the men said, pushing his foot harder into Herman's chest.

'All his freak friends?' Emmeline Victoria suggested.

'What about it, Herman?' Nancy asked him. 'They never thought too much of me to begin with, did they? Reckon they'll gather together enough to get you back in one piece. It's only one o'clock now. Nobody's likely to miss you until when, seven?' She motioned to the men to release him. 'Stand up. Tell us what you think.'

'Sweetheart,' added Patsy.

Herman pushed himself upright. His jacket and vest were torn, revealing the bandages beneath.

'What we got here?' one of the men said, ripping away more of the material to reveal the full extent of the dressing.

'I vote we push him in the river,' the other man said. 'All this is your fault.' He jabbed a finger at Nancy. 'You promised us a nice cut of whatever he had. From where I'm standing, that don't amount to a great deal. Get rid of him, I say.'

The other men nodded in agreement.

'No!' Emmeline Victoria shouted. 'If we aren't going to get any cash out of him, I want him to do us a free show while we decide what to do. Here, now. Just for us. What about it, freak?'

Still in pain from where he'd been punched and held down,

Herman looked again to Nancy, and for the first time he saw a flicker of regret and doubt cross her face.

'Please yourself,' she said, turning away from him.

'We could take him round the taverns and exhibit him in each one. At least we'd make some money that way,' one of the men suggested.

'And be arrested in the first one we came to,' Nancy said. 'Are you too stupid to work even that much out.'

'Don't call me stupid,' the man yelled at her.

'Why not, stupid?' Nancy came closer to him, presenting her cheek to him and daring him to strike her. 'You already had your reward before he even got here. Or had you forgotten?'

Patsy and Emmeline Victoria moved to stand beside her, both unsteady on their feet, Patsy still holding a bottle.

'I still want a show,' Emmeline Victoria said. 'Now get started.'

Both men prodded Herman. 'You heard the lady. Get going. Start puffing and panting.'

'Nancy . . .' Herman said.

'Never mind her; *we're* telling you what to do now. Five seconds or you get more of what you've had already. Perhaps you'd like that? Perhaps that's why you're being so obstinate. Four seconds.'

Patsy and Emmeline Victoria finished the countdown together.

'Get his wraps off,' Patsy shouted. They unwound Herman's bandages as the men held his arms. Nancy now refused to have any part in the proceedings.

'I don't understand,' Herman said to her, still not fully able to accept what was happening to him, what she had planned and caused to happen.

'He doesn't understand, he doesn't understand.' Patsy and Emmeline Victoria danced around him as the bandages came away.

'What about your job at Astor House?' Herman said.

'The only work any of them ever gets at the Astor is in between the sheets or bent over a dresser,' one of the men said. 'Been here ten minutes earlier, you might have seen what I mean.' He prodded Herman in the ribs.

'I don't work at the Astor,' Nancy said. 'I never have done.'

'Never mind the explanations. Get these things off; we want a show,' Emmeline Victoria said.

'And then what?' Nancy asked her.

'Never you mind.' The man caught her with the back of his hand across her face. Unprepared for the blow, Nancy caught her breath, but gave no other indication of having felt any pain.

When the bandages were finally removed, Patsy and Emmeline Victoria stopped dancing and looked at the bruising on Herman's exposed chest. Both pulled faces of disgust.

'Holy Christ!' one of the men said; 'Jesus God!' the other.

'You were the ones wanted a show,' Nancy said. 'What's stopping you?'

Blood appeared to seep through Herman's skin where the punching had raised new welts. He touched them and winced.

'I said, show us!' Emmeline Victoria shouted, conscious, despite her increasing drunkenness, of being the one who had called for the show, and unwilling now to back down in front of the others.

Looking around him, Herman knew that without her they might have released him. He wanted Nancy to turn and face him again, for her to absolve herself and speak on his behalf. But she didn't; instead she looked at her dim reflection in the opaque glass, and at the even dimmer forms of the people behind her.

'I said, show us!' Emmeline Victoria smashed a bottle against the wall.

Herman took a deep breath and signalled to them that he was about to begin. He shook at the effort. The impression of a fist appeared on his stomach and his tears flowed uncontrollably down his face.

Emmeline Victoria began a slow handclap, which was taken up by Patsy.

'Sixty inches,' she said. 'That's what we want to see. And if you don't get yourself –' She was cut short as the door to the room burst violently open, and as Zip appeared, his fists clenched, shouting for them all to stop.

'It's another of the freaks!' Patsy screamed. 'They might *all* have followed him!'

Zip told Herman to deflate and relax. Herman stood as though hypnotized and Zip told him again.

'There ain't no one else,' one of the men said. 'Just this one here who got lucky.' Both men studied Zip's skull and the tuft of black hair which rose from it. Both were wary of him.

Herman began to deflate, holding himself and crying out with pain as his chest shrank. He retrieved his vest and jacket, both of which were now torn beyond repair. Humiliated and disgusted with himself, it didn't even occur to him to ask Zip how he'd known what was happening, or how he had burst upon the scene so miraculously when he did.

'Give him back his money,' Zip said, motioning Herman towards him.

One of the two men took the money from Nancy, and as he was about to hand it over he swung at Zip's face. Zip sidestepped the blow and jabbed the man between his eyes in a short solid punch. The man fell backwards holding his face. His accomplice pushed Herman aside and swung an empty bottle, which caught Zip on the side of his jaw. Patsy threw another from across the room, and this shattered beside Zip, leaving a cut on his cheek. He grabbed Herman and pushed him behind him as the second man swung again. This time he caught Zip's chin and blood flew in a fine spray from his mouth. Before the man could take advantage of this, however, Zip lowered his head and ran at him, catching him in the chest and forcing him back against the wall, where he then delivered a dozen rapid blows to his face and stomach. He went on hitting him long after the man had shouted out for him to stop, and then as he slumped forward, only prevented from falling by Zip's vicious onslaught. Emmeline Victoria tried to pull him off and he turned and struck her too. Then he turned to face Nancy, his fist drawn.

From the doorway, Herman shouted, 'No,' stopping him from hitting her.

Nancy waited, fully expecting the blow and making no attempt to avoid it.

Patsy covered her face and screamed.

The man on the floor called out that he'd been blinded. Lines of blood had already appeared in the spaces between his fingers and he was weeping, more in fear than pain. The other lay face down on the unmade bed, choking, a viscous pool of red saliva collecting around his face.

'You got everything?' Zip asked Herman, pulling him through the door. Herman nodded. Seeing the money still scattered on the floor, Zip retrieved it and handed it to him. 'You ought to be pleased with yourself,' he said to Nancy.

She couldn't answer him.

'You haven't heard the last of this,' Emmeline Victoria threatened uselessly. 'We'll get back to you one day, freak, and when we do we'll wring your neck. You should all have been strangled at birth, as it is. What if we told all the papers he tried to have his way with her? Your word against ours.'

'One sure way of finding out,' Zip said, wiping the blood from his mouth and chin and flicking it at her.

Emmeline Victoria tore at her own blouse and screamed for help. The man on the floor pushed himself up, still holding his bloody face. He looked from her to Zip, unaware of what was happening, but unwilling to tackle him again on her behalf.

Without waiting for the scream to finish, Zip pushed Herman ahead of him down the stairs. He paused at the bottom, but no one followed them. He showed Herman the narrow side entrance he'd broken open and helped him out into the alleyway beyond.

As they emerged into the street they were met by Vivalla, who took off his own jacket and gave it to Herman.

'Can you manage without the bandages?' he said, producing a roll.

Herman said he could.

'You two go,' Vivalla said. 'Get away from here. I'll wait and make sure you're in the clear and that no one comes after you. How about you, Zip?' He held Zip's face and turned it from side to side.

'I only had to blow hard enough and they all keeled over,' Zip said. 'I'd better get him back.'

There was a noise along the alley as one of the men pushed his way through the broken door.

'That's right, step right up, step right up,' Vivalla shouted to him. 'Plenty more where that came from.'

'Just watch for the women,' Zip warned him, briefly clasping his arm before taking hold of Herman and helping him along Pearl Street in the direction of Broadway.

'Your hat,' Herman said as they ran, indicating Zip's exposed head.

'I lost it. We'll take a chance. Can you go any faster?'

Herman said he could, but it soon became clear that the effort was too painful for him, and Zip told him to stop. He led him along the darker side of the street, pulling him into doorways whenever anyone approached them.

It was a warm and airless night, and they were seldom alone for more than a minute at a time, and consequently their progress back to the Museum was slow. Voices could be heard calling to each other from every direction and for a great distance around them. Babies cried and drunks sang. To Herman it now felt as though everyone in the city knew what had happened, and as though they were all making their way towards him along those dark streets and alleys, ready to encircle him and prolong his humiliation.

On several occasions they were recognized, largely as a result of Zip's head, and people called after them. Leaving Walnut Street, they were chased by a gang of youths, one of whom threw a stone which caught Herman in the back and knocked him to the ground. Zip picked him up and held him as they continued running.

They finally arrived at Broadway beside City Hall, where there was little opportunity for them to hide amid the brighter illuminations. They ran instead along the centre of the thoroughfare, and on either side of them people stopped to watch and to point. A few laughed or called out, but no one pursued them.

Arriving at the Museum, they let themselves in at the side entrance and stood breathless in the corridor after locking the door behind them. The blood from Zip's mouth had spread on to his vest and looked in the poor light like a loose cravat.

'You're hurt,' Herman said, when he could once again speak.

Zip shook his head, pushing away his hand.

'Do you think they'll come here?'

'I don't know. Perhaps.' Zip doubted this.

'I shouldn't have gone.'

'Nothing would have stopped you. Two worlds, Herman, two worlds. Ours and theirs. You just forgot for an hour or so, that's all.'

Then Zip led him to his room, where they both washed, and where Zip was able to rebandage his chest.

They were joined by Anna Swan and Captain Bates, who had been waiting for them to return.

'What happened?' Anna asked Zip.

'Nothing I couldn't take care of.'

Bates poured them all a drink. Herman swallowed his and almost choked. There were still tears on his cheeks.

'He hurts from all the running as much as anything else,' Zip told them.

'Was it as bad as you thought?' Anna said.

Zip indicated for her not to persist with Herman still present.

'It's happened to all of us, one way or another,' she told Herman. 'It's over now; you're back among friends,' she said, and he buried his face in her chest, her massive arms enveloping him completely.

Zip held his face for Bates to dab at his jaw with a cloth dipped in the alcohol.

'How many?' Bates mouthed to him.

Zip held up five fingers, and then reduced these to four. 'Vivalla should be back soon,' he said. Both men watched as Herman went on crying, and as Anna stroked his head to soothe him.

'It shouldn't happen like this to any of us,' Zip said, refilling his glass. 'So why does it go on happening?' In his hand, the glass cracked and the drink spilled into his palm. He wiped it into his cut cheek and drew in his breath at the pain.

Anna began to rock Herman in her lap, and to hum to him as though he were a young child unable to sleep.

'That house of yours built yet?' Zip asked Bates.

'Up to the first floor. We were up studying the plans when we heard you get back.'

'How's Franklin?' Herman asked, turning from Anna, but unwilling for her to release him.

'Still peaceful,' she told him, signalling with her eyes for neither Bates nor Zip to add anything to this.

'It doesn't look very good for him, does it?' Herman said.

'Not particularly,' Anna told him. 'Cherry and Tom are with him now. Henry Butler called in, but Barnum must have warned him and Greenwood to stay away.'

When Herman felt better, he insisted on leaving them and going down to sit with Franklin.

None of them made any attempt to stop him, and when he'd gone Anna asked Zip for a full account of the night's events.

Vivalla arrived as he was about to start, and when Zip asked him what had happened, Vivalla shrugged, said, 'Nothing,' and took off his cap to reveal the small circle of a bruise at the centre of his forehead.

Anna and Bates left, followed by Vivalla, who had clearly enjoyed the night's adventure, and who shook Zip's hand before going.

Alone, Zip paced his room and spoke to himself beneath his breath. He drained the last of the drink from the bottle and let himself fall on to his bed, where he lay staring at the ceiling. He clenched both his fists, and as though in response to this final small exertion, his eyes filled with tears.

26

FRANKLIN DIED LATE the following evening. Fortuna was with him, but she had fallen asleep, her head on her chest. At eleven she was woken by Elizabeth, who held a lantern over Franklin and waited for the realization to dawn. There was a peaceful, buried smile on his glistening face, and his hands lay above the sheets, as though he had drawn them out to prepare himself for his final moments. He might even, Elizabeth suggested to Fortuna, who now reproached herself for having fallen asleep, have regained consciousness for a few moments, seen her beside him and died content knowing that he wasn't alone.

Elizabeth left the booth to tell Anna, and later, in the heart of the night, when the rest of the visitors had gone, everyone arrived to pay their last respects. René tried to join Franklin's hands across his chest, but his bulk made this impossible. The Aztec children listened as Elizabeth explained about heaven to them and then knelt and prayed at Franklin's shoulders. Fortuna combed his hair and wiped away the sweat which had dried on his cheeks.

Only Herman broke down and wept openly, clasping Franklin's arm and shaking him before allowing himself to be lifted from the body of his friend by Zip and Captain Bates. In his mind the death and the events of the previous evening were now irrevocably connected and there was nothing any of them could say to him to convince him otherwise. Zip helped him to a chair and explained in a voice loud enough for them all to hear that there was nothing any of them could have done to prevent what had happened to Franklin.

The canvas screens at the front of the booth were drawn aside, opening out the cramped chamber and providing space for Franklin's body to be drawn to the centre and then for everyone to stand around it. Tom and Cherry were joined in a low hymn by the Albino family, and the Spragues and Vivalla stood with their heads down and prayed.

In his room in the basement, Apollo sniffed the air and howled, and the sound found its way like a persistent draught into every passage and chamber of the Museum.

At two in the morning, Cherry was sent to fetch Henry Butler, both of them returning an hour later.

Looking down at the body, Henry Butler saw only the pale, drained face of his wife, with whom he had so far spent yet another sleepless night. She had woken earlier in the evening complaining of pain in her chest and arms, demanding that her nurse be woken and a physician sent for. The girl she currently had attending her could have been little older than fifteen or sixteen, and upon entering to wake her, Henry Butler had come across her naked, asleep, her bed-clothes thrown aside and the window wide open to allow a cooling flow of air into the room. She was plump and ruddy, with broad thighs and full breasts, and her long dark hair lay fanned across her pillow. She smiled as she slept, her breathing deep and steady, and for a full minute Henry Butler stood in the doorway watching her, unable to take his eyes from her solid, healthy limbs, from her face; unable also to disregard the comparison between this female form with its every indication of vigour and vitality, and that of his wife, shrunken to its bones and drained of its colour and strength.

From along the corridor, his wife called to him. The girl stirred in her sleep, drew a hand across her breasts and set them quivering. Henry Butler stepped quickly outside and knocked loudly.

Upon going back into the room he averted his gaze, but the girl had retrieved her bedclothes and sat with them draped around her shoulders, rubbing her eyes. He apologized for having woken her and explained what his wife wanted. She began to dress, unselfconsciously turning towards him and slipping the bedclothes to her waist as she pulled on her blouse. He apologized again and went back to his wife, who had resumed calling for him.

It was only a few minutes after he'd returned with the physician that Cherry had arrived with the news of Franklin's death. When he explained to his wife that he had to return to the Museum she accused him of deserting her. Cherry began to explain to her the considerable difference between her own condition and Franklin's, but she ignored him, shouting at her husband to get the dirty nigger out of her house. The physician prescribed a potion but confessed to Henry Butler that he could neither locate the source of the pain nor suggest any reason for its occurrence. He said he felt sure it would have subsided by the morning and Henry Butler concurred in the prognosis. The girl sat beside his wife's bed only half awake and he promised her that he would return as soon as possible.

On their walk to the Museum through the almost deserted streets, he apologized to Cherry for his wife's behaviour. Cherry told him there was no need; he said it was a common enough mistake to make, to confuse being black with being dirty.

By the time they arrived at Franklin's bedside, only Elizabeth and the Aztecs were no longer present. Tom sat along the corridor and played a long slow funeral march.

'Barnum should be told,' Zip said to Henry Butler, having thanked him for coming.

'But not yet,' Bates added quickly. 'This way we get to keep him to ourselves for a few hours longer.' Everyone silently agreed with him.

'I'll send for him at dawn, three hours,' Henry Butler said. 'Did he –' He indicated Franklin.

'Nothing,' Anna told him. 'Peacefully and calmly.'

'What will Barnum do?' Zip asked, holding his face in his hands, suddenly exhausted by the night's events.

'I don't know. I think that's for us to decide now. What do you want him to do?' Neither Henry Butler nor Greenwood had heard from Barnum since his departure from the Museum two days earlier.

'He'll want to make something of it,' Vivalla said, leaving them to stand beside Tom's piano and share his drink.

Henry Butler told them all that Fat Mary Lou Mountain was on her way as a replacement, regretting the words before the full implications of Barnum's forward planning became clear to them.

'It's a prime site,' Zip said sourly, taking the bottle offered to him by Cherry, drinking from it and handing it on to Bates, who in turn passed it to Isaac Sprague, who had it snatched from his hand by Bella-Grace before he could drink from it.

'So long, Franklin,' Zip said, putting his arm around Herman's shoulders as Herman returned to sit beside him.

For a full silent minute they all looked down at the body.

Elizabeth returned alone, sat beside Henry Butler and asked him how his wife was. In the presence of Franklin's corpse, he was unable to answer her. She'd been crying and he comforted her, wiping at the tears which ran in a single stream along the line of her nose.

Along the corridor Tom stopped playing, and all around them

they heard the myriad creaks and groans, like the rustling of grass, as the Museum regained its empty equilibrium. A distant clock chimed three, and was answered a moment later by a second, as though the call were being answered by another lonely creature seeking comfort in the night.

The first dim light of the rising sun arrived just after five, and as though this were the signal for which they had all been waiting, everyone rose from their seats around the body and became active.

Cherry was sent back out to try and contact either Greenwood or Barnum.

Elizabeth and Anna washed Franklin's face and arms and straightened his clothes.

The bed upon which he lay was dragged back and the curtains to the outer booth were once again drawn.

Henry Butler suggested closing off the entire gallery to the public, but Zip warned him of Barnum's likely reaction to this. 'We've had our time with him,' he said. 'Barnum can do what he wants now, but we've had our time.' He pressed his hand against Franklin's chest and then left.

He went up to his own room, and from there he climbed to the top of the building and let himself out on to the roof, where he lay at its edge and looked down on the street below. There were already a number of people out and about, moving purposefully in every direction towards their day's work. Hogs rooted in the gutters opposite, and storekeepers threw pails of water over their windows and shopfronts, congregating to discuss business and the affairs of the day, the war, new construction work, bar-room brawls, recently arrived vessels. He positioned himself so that his head and shoulders hung over the parapet, closing his eyes for a moment and then opening them and looking directly down. Then he turned and lay on his back until he was gazing up into the lightening sky, blinking and watching the gulls, moon and stars all move across his closed eyelids.

Rising, he went to the side of the building and peered down into the impenetrably dark alleyway below. It was difficult to believe that the two adjoining parts of the same world could be so separate, so different, so kept apart. There was a movement in the alley, the sound of someone stumbling through the refuse and filth collected there, but nothing he could identify any more clearly.

The sound of a carriage arriving distracted him and he returned to look down over the front of the Museum. Beneath him, he saw Barnum climbing out, Cherry holding the carriage door for him, almost curtsying as Barnum stumbled to the street. A flock of pigeons flew noisily between Zip and the ground, making the distance appear even greater and cutting him off completely from what was happening below.

Inside, Barnum arrived at Franklin's booth and stood over the body with his hat clutched to his chest. He felt relieved when, after less than a minute, two tears left his eyes and ran down his cheeks, and he turned his head so that everyone might see. More followed and he smeared them along the creases of his eyes and mouth.

'This isn't good enough,' he said. 'He deserves better. He was a dear and good and trusted friend and employee. He deserves better. He shouldn't be stuck away like this, hidden like something shameful. I want him to lie in state. Nothing but the best.'

The others had prepared themselves for this, or something similar, and waited without speaking for Barnum to explain in greater detail what he now wanted to do with the body.

He quizzed Fortuna and Anna for almost an hour to ensure that he was in full possession of every detail of the death, and so that he might speak of it afterwards as though he had been present at the very moment it had taken place. To him these details were remarkably dull and unrewarding, and would require considerable embellishment before being reiterated to the public, who would demand – and get – a full account of every shuddering, final detail. On his way to the Museum in his carriage, he had already likened the slipping of Franklin's hold on life to the slipping of a great vessel from the dockyard into the sea. It was a far from perfect comparison, but the suggestion of bulk was there, of beginning and end, of achievement and of something gone for ever.

He left Henry Butler in charge of the proceedings and hurried away to capture these thoughts on paper, passing Zip on his way back down through the building.

'A sad day, Zip. A sad day.'

Zip said nothing, merely glancing at the hand Barnum held briefly upon his shoulder before leaving him.

In his office, Barnum discussed with Greenwood, who arrived a few minutes later, the ways in which Franklin's body might be moved from the restricted space in which it now lay into the larger booth, where it might briefly be shown to the pubic. He then selected a series of lavishly embroidered backcloths to be draped around three sides of the booth, and several pieces of equally extravagant furniture to be positioned around the bed, suggesting, perhaps, a recreation of Franklin's own private quarters.

'Find a band,' he said, speaking as the ideas occurred to him. 'A small one. Set them up in the back chamber and get them to play something appropriate to the occasion.'

'You don't intend to let the body be displayed,' Henry Butler said disbelievingly, having arrived and learned of these arrangements.

'Displayed? Displayed? Showmanship, Mr Butler. Showmanship.'

Henry Butler knew it would be pointless to argue. He left to break the news to the others. He knew it was what they were expecting, but still felt the exercise, and Barnum's unashamed enthusiasm for it, to be in poor taste.

Boards and rollers were brought and Franklin's body was manoeuvred on to them and slid slowly forward to its new resting place on a low platform already prepared to look like a bed. The backcloths were hung and the furniture arranged around the enclosed space.

Even before this was completed, Barnum had sent Cherry with his notice of the death to the *Sun, Herald* and *Tribune*. The city, this announced, was in mourning for one of its finest characters and attractions. Franklin, the Seven Hundred and Fifty-Pound Wonder, had died peacefully in his sleep, amid every comfort, his every need catered for, surrounded and prayed for by his dearest friends. All following a short illness, which, according to the finest medical minds in the city, was brought on by overwork, by an insistence on Franklin's part not to disappoint his devoted public. Barnum himself had been keeping his usual all-night vigil at the bedside when Franklin had woken, reached out his hands, looked into his eyes and thanked him for everything he'd done.

Key words were picked out in bold type, others in italics, and the whole message arranged in a pattern pleasing to the eye. In smaller print Barnum speculated on how the body would now be removed from its place of rest, suggesting that it might somehow be transported as the Ancient Egyptians had transported the great blocks of stone during the construction of the pyramids, or as the Greeks had raised the columns of the Parthenon at so great a distance from the quarries from which they were hewn. He was less than certain of his facts in these matters, however, and of the specific nature of the connection between these marvels of the ancient world and the dead Franklin, but the association by suggestion pleased him and looked good in the notice. There would be little else of any real importance happening in the city that day and he felt certain of securing at least two or three front pages. James Gordon Bennet would no doubt find something to crow about in the *Herald*, but the others would be glad of his copy and perhaps add eulogies of their own.

He was feeling pleased with himself, smoking and sipping a self-congratulatory brandy when Zip and Captain Bates entered and stood silently before him. Seeing them, his face fell, as though its features had been released by an invisible cord.

'Just thinking over old times,' he said in an attempt to explain his smile. 'Drink, gentlemen?' He knew immediately from Zip's response why they were there. Zip prepared to approach him, but was stopped by Bates, who had to stoop to avoid the chandelier hanging over Barnum's desk.

'Purely medicinal purposes,' Barnum said, holding out the decanter to them.

'We came to establish your plans for the day,' Bates said. 'Your arrangements.'

'Arrangements? Gentlemen, you find me only moments after having personally penned a true and moving farewell to a dear and treasured friend.' Barnum creased his brow. 'You find me exhausted, spent, worn out, physically, mentally, emotionally.'

'But you still intend to open the Museum and show his . . .' Bates faltered.

'Corpse,' Zip said.

'Gentlemen, gentlemen, come come. Don't cast me so readily in the role of ghoul. There are thousands in this city, in this continent, who would wish to pay their last respects to such a great and popular man and who might indeed –'

'Pay for the privilege,' Zip said.

'– might indeed – should indeed – should not be denied that privilege.'

'I assume that's why you've made the booth look ten times more respectable and comfortable that it was when Franklin was in it alive.' Zip moved ahead of Bates to stand at the desk. He looked around at the untidy state of the room, and then at the immobile mechanical serpent between Barnum and himself.

'You hurt me, you wound me. You accuse me – *me* – of not caring, of thinking only of profit. You wound me. Jab away; I see your mind is already set on its hurtful course. I always thought better of you, Zip. That you – *you* – of all my friends, should now turn and point such an accusing finger.' Barnum covered his face. 'You may as well approach me with a dagger and plunge it deep

301

into my grieving heart, my broken heart, a heart empty and bereft of a great and valued friendship.'

Watching this accomplished act, Bates saw how quickly and easily a shield had been thrown up and saw also how readily Barnum would be believed by others only too willing to listen to him.

Barnum let the fumes from his glass sting his eyes until two more tears were induced to appear.

'You're showing the body,' Zip said, and without waiting for Barnum's response, he turned and walked out of the office.

'Is there nothing we can say that might persuade you otherwise?' Bates asked Barnum.

Knowing that Bates would be gone from the Museum in a little over a month's time, Barnum refused even to answer him.

'Ingrates,' Barnum said to himself, when both had left him, and as he poured himself another drink.

Greenwood returned and said he'd just been told the true version of events by Elizabeth and Fortuna.

'It's *my* version that counts, *mine*,' Barnum shouted immediately, rising and pinning him to the wall. 'What did *they* tell you? That they were there, that they grieve harder than me, that they have more right to grieve, that they cared, that – that –' He released Greenwood and apologized for his overwrought behaviour. 'The truth is,' he continued, 'they were all running around like headless chickens, flapping and squawking and panicking until I arrived and took control, reminding them of our paramount obligation to the public. You at least should understand that.'

Greenwood nodded and helped himself to a drink. It was still not yet six in the morning.

'As you can see, I'm upset, distraught. Is that how I appear to you?'

'Extremely,' Greenwood said.

'Good. But I still appear to be in control, in charge of all my faculties?'

'Naturally.'

Barnum relaxed. 'Tell me, what would you do if the Museum were yours and this unrepeatable opportunity had so fortuitously presented itself? Shut it down, lose a good day's trade, dismiss the biggest attraction we've had in a month?'

Greenwood shook his head, touched Barnum's glass with his own and shared his smile. 'The Frenchman had some sketches he'd made of Franklin before he –'

302

'Passed on to a Glorious Land of Never-Ending Plenty?'

'Precisely.'

'What sort of sketches? Any good? Why didn't he show them to me? I might have been able to use them to illustrate my report. I'd have paid him, of course. It could have been his first sale in years.'

They both laughed.

'I only saw them under his arm when Fortuna told me about Franklin. He wouldn't let me look at them any more closely.'

'That's the French for you – secretive amd suspicious. Good thing we kicked them out of Louisiana. All we need now is a new and more fitting name for the place.'

Barnum State, Greenwood thought to himself as he rose to leave.

Back down in Franklin's booth, Zip told the others of Barnum's intentions.

'It's no more than any of us expected,' Elizabeth said. She and Anna had cut the front from one of Franklin's clean shirts and were arranging this over his chest and shoulders, drawing the sheets in a tight line beneath his armpits.

Only Herman protested at the news, insisting that they should join forces and stop Barnum. No one took the remark seriously.

'We've joined forces before,' Zip said. 'Remember?'

Bella-Grace Sprague fitted slippers to Franklin's feet where they extended beyond the edge of the raised platform. Isaac looked on approvingly.

At the appearance of both Barnum and Greenwood they all fell silent.

'You are all no doubt aware,' Barnum began, 'that under any other circumstances –'

'Save your words,' Elizabeth told him. 'We know what you want and none of us here is going to oppose you.'

'Oppose me? My dear Elizabeth –' He stopped himself at Greenwood's tug on his sleeve. 'Yes, well, I'm happy that the arrangements meet with your approval.'

'Have you contacted the undertaker yet?' Anna asked him, rising and standing above them all.

Barnum looked at Greenwood, who assured them that one was on his way at that very moment.

'Would you like to see him?' Fortuna asked Barnum.

'Who?'

She moved aside to reveal Franklin in his new bed.

Barnum did not relish looking any more closely at the corpse, especially now that it could be seen in the natural and revealing light of day.

'He looks happy,' he said. 'Peaceful, content, at rest, with his Maker.'

'He's dead,' Zip said.

For the first time, Barnum noticed the scar on Zip's cheek and looked at it closely. He saw too the bruise on Vivalla's forehead but said nothing about either, making a note to discover more when the opportunity next arose.

Seeing Henry Butler sitting on a chair at the rear of the booth, he asked him if he had nothing better to do, adding that it was likely to be a busy day for all of them. He made a brief inspection of the rest of the booth and then left. Greenwood told them all to prepare themselves for their own day's work.

'We're going,' Zip told him. 'But not until we've had another minute alone with Franklin.'

Knowing that he would be defeated if he tried to refuse them this, Greenwood contented himself with a hard cold stare at Zip before leaving.

Henry Butler was asked to stay and then invited to say a few words over the body in lieu of their attendance at the actual funeral. The ensuing silence was broken only by the sound of Barnum hammering up the boards in the Museum entrance announcing the death to the gathering crowd.

An hour later, the first of the visitors began to file past the body. At the head of the bed stood the Albino family, dressed in white, each reading aloud from a Bible bound in white leather. The children wore swans' wings raised above their shoulders, and over each of their heads floated a halo of feathery light.

Barnum's only regret now was that he hadn't sent for Fat Mary Lou Mountain a few days sooner. She could have been there at the bedside, praying with them and weeping copiously over her dead 'brother'. Crowds liked tears, especially women's tears, and there was nothing so contagious, nothing so designed to produce an identical response in others than a crying woman.

For the remainder of the day, Barnum stalked the galleries and corridors of the Museum with half an onion in his pocket, frequently smearing his handkerchief and pressing it to his face whenever he encountered a crowd anxious for its last look at Franklin. There could be no doubt now, no doubt whatsoever, as to whose loss was the greatest, whose grieving the most likely to endure.

To everyone else, however, it now seemed more and more as though a train of unstoppable events had been set in motion; and more than ever the noise of distant footsteps throughout the Museum sounded like the rumble of approaching thunder-clouds, of a savage storm about to crest the peaks of a mountain range and race deafeningly down upon the exposed and unprotected cities of the plain beneath.

27

THE FOLLOWING DAY, Barnum opened the Museum half an hour early in anticipation of a second rush of customers anxious to view Franklin on their way to work. This, however, and much to his surprise, did not materialize, and short of sending Cherry and Vivalla out on to the street to announce that the body was shortly to be claimed by the undertaker, he knew of no other way to stir up interest in the spectacle at such short notice. Even later in the day the crowds did not arrive in the numbers he'd anticipated, and throughout the morning and afternoon he constantly toured the Museum to see for himself how many were present, trying in whatever ways he could to lure those who were there towards Franklin's booth. In this too he was largely unsuccessful and he withdrew late in the afternoon to his office, both to await the arrival of the undertaker and to ponder his miscalculation, the latest of so many.

Hearing Greenwood arrive, he went out to him. 'What do they want, what is there I can give them, what is there I haven't *already* given them?' he demanded.

Greenwood, fully aware of the cause of this outbreak and of his own precarious role both as scapegoat and conspirator, refused to be drawn, preferring instead to enjoy Barnum's frustration and discomfort, and to calculate how this might best serve his own plans for the future of the Museum. He knew perfectly well why there had been no rush to view the corpse, but saw no need to share his secret with Barnum.

A corpse, both men knew, was merely that, but only Greenwood also knew that many of those who did now come to gaze upon it did so only to reassure themselves that they were not about to become the victims of another of Barnum's hoaxes, to prepare themselves for the miraculous resurrection if and when it occurred.

306

'Why, why, why?' Barnum said, each weakened demand an unsuccessful assault upon this unassailable truth. He sat opposite Greenwood in Henry Butler's chair. 'And don't imagine for one moment that I am not fully aware of your part in all this,' he said unexpectedly, pointing a finger at Greenwood.

'Mine?' Greenwood said, framing the words with a smile, a note of unconcerned mock-incredulity in his voice. 'Surely not. Not me, not mine.' He spun from side to side in his seat, his every movement followed by Barnum. 'It's a corpse. You're showing them a corpse, and the simple fact is, none of them is likely to thank you for it.'

There had been four hundred deaths already in the city during that long summer from typhus, and the immigrant hospital beds at Tompkinville and Ward's Island had had their occupants changed more frequently than their sheets.

'Thanks! I don't want their thanks. Just their –'

'Respect?' Greenwood said coldly. 'Money?'

Barnum wanted both these things. 'No. No!'

'What then?' Greenwood said, happy at this small victory following so many considerably larger failures. He had already made arrangements for Franklin's funeral, and this would take place at the Lafayette graveyard the following Sunday afternoon – a time calculated to attract the greatest number of mourners.

Barnum's original idea had been to have Franklin's hearse drawn by the Siamese elephant, but this had been rejected by the church officials on the grounds that the animal came from a heathen country, that its weight was likely to damage the well kept lawns between the plots, and that it would, more likely than not, help itself to the wreaths laid by grieving relatives upon the nearby graves. Barnum had conceded on all three points and had grudgingly accepted Greenwood's alternative arrangements. These consisted of a cortège of ten black horses, led by Barnum in his own carriage, and followed on foot by the other members of the Museum, walking in pairs behind the hearse. To the simple details of the marble headstone Greenwood had chosen, Barnum had added both his own name and that of the Museum, and because he knew Charity would refuse to attend the funeral with him, he had also invited Elizabeth to share his carriage. Elizabeth, however, had declined, preferring, she said, to walk beside Zip and with the others. Upon hearing this, Bella-Grace Sprague had promptly proposed herself as Barnum's companion, an offer he had declined on the grounds that he doubted if the springs of his carriage, already much weakened by age and constant use, would bear their combined weight. Unable to respond to this slur before Barnum had slammed his door in her face, Bella-Grace ran to her husband in his booth and repeated several times over what had happened. Torn between his wife and his public, all of whom were just as interested in Bella-Grace's story as they were in him, Isaac could do little more than sympathize and encourage her to tell it again, elaborating upon its finer points until the insult, if not lost exactly, at least became easier to forgive.

'What do they expect?' Barnum said, his face in his hands. 'It's a great loss – to me, to the Museum, to them all. I thought they'd be interested. I thought they'd want to share in the occasion, to participate.'

'You're showing them a corpse,' Greenwood repeated, tiring both of the complaints and of his own answers. 'That's all – a corpse.' He looked slowly around him and repeated the word for a third time.

Barnum followed his gaze, and its significance was not lost upon him.

Then, suddenly, he became excited. 'Wait until the balloon-crossing gets under way,' he said. He checked his watch. 'In fact it's already started.' He banged the desk, rose, paced a full circuit of the room and sat back down. 'They've been in the air for over an hour. You just wait, you just watch. There's adventure for you. There's life at it's most thrilling. I'll soon be the name on everyone's lips again. Just wait, just wait.'

The balloon-crossing had indeed been arranged for that very day, but had been overtaken by the recent events in the Museum itself. Three hours ago, the balloon of Tulle silk with its suspended whaleboat in which the two-man crew were to attempt the crossing of the Atlantic, had risen from a field in Brooklyn watched by a crowd of several hundred spectators, all of whom had cheered as it had risen slowly and with great difficulty from the ground, having then descended several times and bounced around before finally lifting itself clear.

Greenwood was unwilling to share in Barnum's enthusiasm for the venture: too much now depended upon its success and too little thought had gone into its preparation. Ironically, the greatest loss to Barnum would come if the crossing *were* to be successful, both he and the *New York Graphic* having guaranteed half of the 30,000 dollars prize money, payable upon a successful landing, in Paris or thereabouts. Secretly Barnum hoped for a crash-landing somewhere in Spain, possibly in the Pyrenees, whereupon both he and the *Graphic* would be obliged to pay out only a fraction of the prize money. The owners of the *Graphic* undoubtedly sat with their fingers crossed too.

'I should have been there,' Barnum said. 'They need me.'

'A lot of hot air is what they need,' Greenwood said maliciously. 'Hot air, a strong following wind and a prayer to keep them up.'

Unwilling to endure these remarks any longer, Barnum called for Cherry to run to the *Graphic*'s offices and find out how the flight was progressing. Cherry went, but grudgingly; like Greenwood and everyone else in the Museum, he too could see little real chance of the attempt succeeding. In Cherry's mind there was even some suggestion that because the attempt was being made in a whaleboat the two balloonists had some hope of assisting any following wind by actually rowing themselves across the surface of the clouds, which he knew for a fact to be composed of water. As he went, Greenwood warned him to return only with good news. He asked him if he knew what the Ancient Greeks had done to the bearers of bad news. Cherry said he didn't, but that he could hazard a guess. Barnum, equally ignorant of the custom, told him just to go and to return with the good news as quickly as possible, already calculating the wording with which the great beginning of this unparalleled adventure was about to be presented to the waiting public.

A few minutes later, Greenwood rose and left the office.

'You can tell them all we're closing early,' Barnum shouted after him. 'Out of respect for the dead. You tell them that – respect for the dead. That's something they'll understand all right, respect for the dead. Ingrates, philistines, ignoramuses.'

Greenwood put his head back round the door. 'Respect for the dead and contempt for the living. They both pay dividends in their own sweet way.'

In his rage, Barnum looked for something to throw, but the only object within his reach was the photograph of Henry Butler's sick wife. He picked this up, but instead of hurling it after Greenwood, he looked hard into the woman's face – her enervated eyes and lips, her blank, hopeless stare – and then without warning he dropped it, as though it had become suddenly too hot to hold. The portrait fell to the desk and to the floor, where the glass in the frame shattered. He stared down at this, unable to respond, unable even to bend and retrieve the larger pieces.

Leaving the desk, he ran into his own office, where he slammed and locked the door, pausing to catch his breath before sitting at his desk to await the return of Cherry with news of the upward turn in his fortunes.

A short while later, as he began to gather his thoughts on the balloon-crossing on paper, a slight movement caught his eye and he glanced quickly up just in time to see the shining metal snake quiver in its coils, settling slightly, and then, almost imperceptibly, tilt its slender head and return his gaze.

*

Throughout the day, the Museum was filled with an air of melancholy and brooding resentment.

After two sleepless nights, Henry Butler stayed away, returning with little enthusiasm to pass his days uncomfortably with his wife and her young nurse.

Barnum too would have preferred to stay away, but he was still unwilling to abandon the building in its hour of need, and even less willing to deliver himself into the thrashing and grinding machine his wife and daughters had become as the Great Day of the wedding approached. For himself, Barnum anticipated the arrival of this momentous occasion as he felt the primitive savages of Africa must have looked upon the sudden night of a total eclipse of the sun.

Only Greenwood was now fully aware of what was truly happening in the Museum, of the slow and irreversible process of decay and collapse taking place all around him, and he made sure he kept himself in a position to take full advantage of it when it finally came. He made a circuit of every corridor and gallery, every booth and staircase. He made sure everyone was where they were supposed to be and doing what they were still being paid to do. Upon overhearing Vivalla remark to Apollo that Greenwood was behaving as though he already owned the place, Greenwood turned to Vivalla and told him to believe what he wanted, but that his own days there were now numbered; Apollo's too. News of this spread rapidly and everyone became cautious in his presence – not because they felt cowed by his threatening behaviour, but because they understood even better than he did the confused and menacing state of limbo into which the Museum and everyone within it had now been cast. He moved among them like a shark among a school of fish, looking well fed and satisfied with itself, and without the slightest indication that it might at any second flick its tail, explode into action and consume one of them before they had even seen its open mouth. Some were

310

more careful than others in this respect, but overall they rallied to protect each other and always kept the weakest at their centre.

Franklin's body was finally withdrawn from public view, and Elizabeth, Anna and Fortuna took short turns of sitting with him until the undertaker arrived. Afterwards, and despite Barnum's orders to the contrary, few chose to spend the entire day in their booths; preferring instead to display themselves for a short while and then to leave and return to their rooms.

Barnum, by now convinced that a dozen conspiracies were being plotted against him, avoided them all, spending the day either in his office awaiting the return of Cherry with news of the balloon, or down in the closed-off basement, pouring out his troubles to the unhappy hippopotamus, now hanging suspended in its discoloured tank as fixed and as trapped as a fly entombed in amber.

The surface of the water was still thick with a scum of cabbage leaves and other uneaten food, and the floor of the tank was a foot deep in sludge which was stirred into clouds every time the animal descended into it, and from which large yellow bubbles regularly rose. The nature of this accumulated deposit and the foul gases it produced could only be guessed at. In his more agitated moments, Barnum banged his fists against the glass and demanded that the animal should pay him some attention.

By midday word had spread even to the visitors that there was something amiss in the Museum, and despite the uncertainty of the rumour, the flow of customers slowed and then stopped completely. Those already in the Museum were followed along the empty galleries by the sound of their own footsteps and spoke to each other in hushed voices. Many, arriving to find Franklin's booth empty, the body gone, turned back and left immediately, pausing only to pass the word to those they met outside.

An hour later it was as though a plague flag had been run up one of the flagpoles on the roof of the building.

By three in the afternoon the Museum was empty, and Greenwood, himself unperturbed by this unprecedented turn of events, locked all the doors. Out of respect for Franklin, the notice he posted said. Then he too left for an hour, walking first north, and then south along Broadway, his eyes peeled for Cherry, before returning and letting himself back into the silent building.

He met Captain Bates on his way to join Anna at Franklin's beside, but neither man spoke, and after exchanging a long steady look at each other, they went their separate ways.

Reaching Anna, Bates found her in the company of Elizabeth and the Aztecs, Fortuna and René. They asked him if he knew what was happening and he told them of his encounter with Greenwood. René said he could feel something in the air, something about to happen which they were all powerless to prevent.

Bates held Anna and kissed her cheek. Their travelling arrangements had by then been finalized and confirmed, and in a little under a fortnight they would be leaving the Museum for good, getting married and setting up home together, their impossible dream made real. Despite recent events, the others still demanded to be told every detail of these plans, and in this small way continue to share in that dream and their future.

The Aztec children, understanding nothing of what was being said, but sensing the change as well as any of them, moved closer to Elizabeth so that she might hold them both.

An hour later, the undertaker arrived, and they all helped him and his assistants to manhandle Franklin from his booth, along the corridor and out into the waiting wagon, over which the undertaker had draped a black cloth supported on wire hoops in place of his usual hearse.

At this final point of departure, Herman fell to his knees in the street and wept. Zip and Elizabeth comforted him, helped him up and then led him back inside, away from the crowd which, ever since the Museum doors had been locked, had gathered in anticipation of there being something to see, even if it was only the removal of the body. Zip alone went back out to them, asked them what they had all expected, and then cursed violently at them, causing them to back away from him in fear. Hearing him speak for the first time, a few women screamed, and several men stepped forward with their fists held up ready to protect them. Amused by this, Zip teased them, and swung punches which he knew would not reach them. He was wearing only the pants of his monkey suit, and pranced before them like a satyr, his face, arms and chest running with sweat in the warm air after his exertions with the massive coffin. Only one of the men who now faced him appeared to pose any serious threat, but before the two of them could come to blows, Bates stepped between them, and both René and Vivalla grabbed hold of Zip's arms and pulled him back towards the Museum entrance. Of them all, only Herman called out for Zip to attack the man. Bates apologized to everyone for what had happened, explaining that they were all overwrought at the recent events in the Museum. He waited for the man to back down and return to the others, at the same time making it clear to him by his own clenched fist that if he were forced to fight him then he would do so. The man, having considered the two-foot height and ten-stone weight difference between them, lowered his arms, turned and walked away, humiliated and vowing to return. Seizing the advantage, Bates then thanked them all for their concern and their support over the previous years. No one answered him, and a moment later someone threw an egg which caught him on the forehead and splashed over his face. This was followed by another, and then by pieces of fruit, thrown from several directions, and finally by a hail of stones, one of which caught Bates on the cheek, another in the chest. Anna rushed forward to hold him and lead him back into the Musuem, protecting his face with her arm. She, too, was hit on her broad back by fruit and stones. When Bates was safely inside, she turned to face the crowd and asked them why they were behaving like that. People stopped throwing; there were a few calls and jeers, but the majority of the people fell silent and watched her, sullenly waiting for her to go on, mixed expressions of shame and resentment on their faces.

For a full minute Anna said nothing, and then raising her arms, she told them all to go home, that the show was finally over.

Bates returned to stand beside her, his arm around her shoulder, blood on his cheek from the stone. The two of them stood as tall and as solid as statues, against which no harm could be done.

Slowly, the crowd began to disperse. A final stone was thrown, and this broke one of the ground-floor windows, but neither Anna nor Bates responded to it other than by tightening their grip on each other. The crowd turned, hesitated and then dispersed, like the trunks in a disturbed log-jam, moving with increasing speed back into the flow of the main thoroughfare.

Elizabeth and Fortuna came out and walked back with Anna and Bates to the Museum. Anna wiped the egg from Bates's face and then dressed the cut on his cheek.

Inside, everyone stood together in the entrance hall for a few minutes before dispersing to their own rooms. Zip apologized for having forced the confrontation and then led the distraught Herman away. For hours afterwards his convulsive sobbing could be heard throughout the deserted building.

Late in the afternoon, Greenwood came to Zip's room and entered without knocking. Zip lay stretched on his bed, a cigar in his mouth, a bottle by his side, listening to the distant strains of Tom's piano.

'I saw your little contretemps earlier,' Greenwood said, taking one of Zip's cigars, lighting it, and then helping himself to the bottle, which Zip allowed him to take. 'You versus all the decent and honourable citizens of New York City. It seemed an even match. To tell you the truth, I wanted it to happen. You'd have killed the man; just imagine what they would have been throwing then instead of rotten fruit.' He made the shape of a noose with his finger.

Zip smiled. 'I saw you watching,' he said. 'Up behind one of the third-floor shutters; you'll make a good general when the time comes.'

For a full minute neither man said anything more, and then Greenwood said, 'That's that, then: Franklin's gone, Barnum's waiting and praying for the impossible, and this place is getting ready to tumble back into the mud.' He'd expected Zip to respond to this, but Zip said nothing, having anticipated the provocation from the moment he'd entered.

'So what now?' Zip said, turning to face him.

Greenwood shrugged. 'You know that as well as I do.'

'You make him another offer, send for Thumb, turn this place into a theatre?'

'Something like that.'

'And we all pack our bags, wave farewell and go.'

Greenwood shrugged again. 'As I said, you know what's happening here as well as any of us. Better than some, I'd say.' He nodded in the direction of Barnum's office. 'You saw what happened out there. Do you honestly think they're going to stay away just because the doors are locked? You might as well tell them to stop walking the streets as to stay away from this place. They look upon coming in here as a God-given right. Take that away from them and who knows what might happen. You lot have to live here, remember; I don't.'

The two men faced each other, and for the second that their eyes met, there passed between them a precise and powerful understanding.

'I know. And I could be your doorman,' Zip said. 'A top hat, nice uniform.'

'What's the alternative?' Greenwood said. 'You think we should all just sit here like *he* does, waiting for good news to arrive out of the blue, and to pass by close enough for him to stake his claim on it. It doesn't happen like that, it hasn't happened like that for years in this place. Shall I tell you what he's doing now, right now, this very instant as his so-called empire teeters on the verge of total collapse – he's down in the basement trying to blame it all on the hippopotamus. He gave orders a week ago to stop feeding it; it stinks down there. That's what he's doing – pouring out his heart to a sick, stupid animal instead of getting his affairs in order up here. He didn't even come up to complain when I shut the place down. Earlier, he was trying to grab an extra half-hour of opening, and now he doesn't care enough to even come up and find out what's happening.'

'Good for us that you're still with us, then,' Zip said, following the words with a plume of smoke.

'You don't know just how true that is, my friend.'

'Oh, I think I do . . . friend.'

'Tomorrow,' Greenwood said. 'You get them all together first thing in the morning and we'll sort out what has to be done. Forget today – we've lost it.'

'Out of respect for Franklin your notice said.'

'Out of respect for whatever you like. Let's call it an empty day, shall we, a day to stop looking back and start looking forward.' Greenwood was pleased with this glib remark and repeated it.

'If you like,' Zip said, still unconcerned. 'But tell me – tomorrow, whose side are we all expected to be on? Us, that is, the trusted employees, as opposed to you.'

'You tell me,' Greenwood said. 'Why don't you take tonight to think it over; I'm sure you can come up with the right answer if you all put your heads together.'

'Even mine?' Zip said, fondling his scalp and top-knot.

Greenwood stared at this for a moment, at the smooth black hair passing through the dark fingers in the same repeated motion. 'Even yours,' he said, and left.

It had been inevitable that he would come, Zip knew, and for an hour after his departure he lay and considered every consequence of what was now happening to the Museum. For a while he considered leaving and making a tour of the taverns, but this, in his present mood, would end only in violence, and rather than attract any more unnecessary attention to the building and its inhabitants – all of whom were now virtual prisoners within its walls – he chose to stay. He heard Herman's sobbing and covered his ears with a pillow. When the sound penetrated even that he called out for him to stop, and when this had no effect he took his cigars and bottle and left his room, climbing up to the attic floor, and then up again until he was back out on the roof.

He walked to the edge and looked down, distant from the city beneath him, yet still a part of it, as removed and apart from it

as a ship might be from the ocean upon which it sails. He watched
the passage of the vessels on the river and then let his eyes wander
to the flapping of a woman shaking a cloth from a distant window.
He climbed to the parapet, raised the bottle to his lips and took a
long swig from it, swayed unsteadily for a moment and then stepped
back from the edge. He laughed at himself and made his way to the
centre of the roof, where he lay on his back and turned his face into the
sun. He began to sing to himself, and after an hour the cigar slipped
from his lips and he feel asleep, relaxed by the warmth, and by this
brief, unexpected freedom into which all of them had wandered like
pilgrims into an unknown and horizonless desert.

*

'He's shut the place down,' Barnum said to the hippopotamus.
'He knows I'm still here and yet he goes ahead and shuts it down
without even the common courtesy of discussing the matter with me
first. And now they're throwing stones.'

The window had been broken a few minutes earlier, prior to
which Barnum had sat staring into the tank as he listened to
the distant commotion above. Despite his objection to Greenwood's
action, he had made no attempt to reprimand him or to re-open the
Museum.

As he spoke, he tampered again with the engine beside the
aquarium. There was a brief flow of fresh water, but instead of
refreshing the fetid liquid of the tank, all this now achieved was
to disturb the thick sludge of sediment, sending it bubbling to the
surface, where it burst and fell again under its own weight; and with
it rose the putrid bubbles of gas, which quickly filled the basement
with their own rank stench. Wisps of blue smoke continued to rise
from the spluttering engine, and each part of it Barnum now touched
revealed to him its shining silver innards; other parts were still hot to
the touch, and oil and kerosene had dripped from the grime-encrusted
body of the machine to collect in a spreading pool beneath it.

'You could have saved me,' he said, 'but instead you and your
flap-eared Siamese cousin broke me; you wore me down and then
you broke me. Simple as that.' He paused, smiled to himself and
resumed. 'But what you forget, what you all forget, and what Mr
Greenwood in particular forgets, is that I've been down before,
deeper down than this, much deeper, and I've always risen to
the challenge and sprung back to confound both my critics and

creditors alike. Sprung back with new ideas, new schemes, new attractions, and every time my public has rallied behind me, has supported me, has raised me up on its shoulders and carried me to yet another triumphant victory. I've been as close as this, as close as I am now to you, to every crowned prince, king and queen in Europe; I've spoken in every city in the Union to rapturous applause night after night; I've peered into the maw of a blazing volcano and been to the theatre with Lincoln himself. Does that sound to you like the kind of man who's going to allow himself to be beaten by something like this? Well, does it?'

The hippopotamus turned slowly in its murk.

The words, intended by Barnum to reassure and encourage, were having difficulty in doing their work. He felt like a man running up a loose sandy slope, unable to pause, let alone stop and look around himself to see what he had achieved.

'No,' he said. 'No, it does not sound like the kind of man who would allow himself to be – ouch!' He was cut short as the palm of his hand touched the hot engine and he was burned. He pulled it sharply away, studying the small red weal at its centre, which threatened to blister even as he looked at it. He stood away from the warmth and the fumes and pressed his palm against the relative coolness of the glass in an attempt to relieve the pain. The hippopotamus drifted forward to investigate.

Earlier, after sending Cherry out for news of the balloon-crossing, he had also sent a dozen cables in a desperate last attempt to prevent the arrival of Fat Mary Lou Mountain. All along the line of the rail-road, it seemed, she had contrived to be one step ahead of him, her momentum now unstoppable as she approached the city, driven on by the prospect of taking over Franklin's empty booth, already practising her story and its no doubt tearful accompaniment, unaware that he was already dead.

Looking up a moment later, Barnum saw that the hippopotamus had vanished into the gloom, leaving only his own unhappy reflection peering back at him.

He glanced at the engine, at the fumes which still rose from it and the liquid that still dripped. He was about to take a cloth and shut off all the valves completely, when he was distracted by the sound of running footsteps above him, and by the excited voice of Hackaliah Cherry yelling, 'Victory! Victory! Victory!' as he raced into the empty Museum and began his journey to its centre.

'I'm here, Hack,' Barnum called up to him, already climbing

the basement stairs; but Cherry hadn't heard him and he went on shouting as he ran.

The two men finally met outside Barnum's office, where Cherry had encountered Greenwood and was standing with his hands on his knees, leaning forward in an effort to regain his breath.

'Victory, Mr Barnum,' he said between pants.

'Hear that, Greenwood? Victory, *victory*!' He shook Cherry in an effort to solicit more.

'I heard,' Greenwood said, knowing that not even Barnum, despite his present state of desperate excitation, could believe that the balloon-crossing to Paris had been made in a matter of only a few hours.

Finally regaining his composure, Cherry straightened, wiped his face and said, 'Atlanta! Sherman's taken Atlanta! Now all he's got to do is burn it to the ground, chase the rebs all the way to the sea and the war'll be over. Don't you see it, Mr Barnum – it's on its way to being finished!'

'Atlanta?' Barnum said, feeling himself sag. 'Not Atlan*tic*? I thought – I thought you . . .' He felt dazed; his mind reeled. He turned to Greenwood. 'I thought he meant the Atlantic, the balloon-crossing. That's what I sent him to find out, that's what I thought . . .' He turned back to Cherry. 'I thought . . .'

Greenwood, all the while looking over Barnum's shoulder to Cherry, saw his jaw drop at the mention of the balloon.

'The balloon . . . I . . .' Barnum repeated, finally losing himself in the unnatural maze of his stunned speechlessness.

'Oh,' Cherry said.

Greenwood guessed immediately that this did not bode well for what he was about to tell them.

'Oh?' Barnum looked to him for support.

'Just tell us what happened, Cherry,' Greenwood said.

Cherry stood unable to speak for a moment and then rubbed his chin in an attempt to suggest thoughtful contemplation.

'Cherry!' Greenwood said.

'The balloon took off the most perfect I ever heard of any balloon anywhere ever taking off. *The* most perfect. Up like a bird, up and up, higher and higher, light as a feather and perfect as a rocket.' Cherry cupped his hand and let it rise between them.

Barnum followed it up with a grin on his face, eager to be told more.

'And then it came down,' Cherry said, lowering both his voice and his hand.

'Down?'

'Down. Nice and slow and peaceful. Didn't see it myself. Someplace in Connecticut, they reckon. Thirty or forty miles away.'

'Thirty or forty miles?'

'Forty at the very minimum. Perhaps even fifty. Yes, I'd say fifty at the very least.'

'Thirty or forty,' Greenwood said. 'It went up, it came down. A flight of fancy. Whatever it did, it didn't float across the Atlantic. Ships designed for that very purpose sometimes don't get right across the Atlantic.'

'Thirty ... or ... forty.' Barnum stood and swayed, still stunned by the news of his failure, by the rapidity and ferocity with which the blows continued to come.

'Sixty?' Cherry said, wondering, now that they were moving in the right direction, whether or not it might be wiser to make the leap straight to a hundred. He was still concerned about his own imperfect understanding of what happened to the messengers of Ancient Greece.

'And no one saw it come down?' Greenwood asked him. 'We could retrieve it, and even if anyone did see it come down, they won't necessarily know what it was trying to do, and certainly nobody who saw it take off also saw it crash.'

Slowly, Barnum began to understand what he was being told.

'Hundred miles still a record flight,' Cherry said.

'Then all may not be lost, Barnum said dramatically, clasping his lapel and holding up his hand.

'Hallelujah!' Cherry shouted.

'Hallelujah,' Greenwood said.

'*Hallelujah!*' Barnum shouted louder than Cherry. 'Don't you see?' he said to Greenwood. 'Don't you see?'

'I see,' Greenwood told him.

'I see it! I see it!' Cherry shouted, looking wildly around them, and then wondering for the first time why the Museum was empty in the middle of a summer afternoon.

'Turn of events,' Barnum said, still excitedly. 'That solitary, single turn of events, and everything changes.' He told them he had work to do, preparations to make, and left them.

An hour later he slipped unnoticed from the Museum and returned to his wife and daughters.

Greenwood dismissed Cherry and then he too left the Museum.

In a sense, Barnum had been right, but neither he nor Greenwood, nor even Cherry, could have foreseen what was shortly about to take place, and which would push all thoughts of the balloon, and a great deal else, from their minds.

28

UP ABOVE THE city, as he slept in the sun on the roof, this was Zip's dream: he dreamed he'd been sleeping in a broad lush meadow on a gently sloping hillside, and that above him in the distance was a large and imposing white house. He lay possibly half a mile from this, but even at that distance he was able to make out every detail of its construction and ornamentation. The house was backed by woodland, which rose to the crown of the slope upon which he lay, and was surrounded by rows of shrubs and colourful flower-beds, and at a little distance by an abundant vegetable garden, in which three or four figures now worked. Around the house were scattered several outbuildings, all as pleasing to the eye with their white wooden walls and red tile roofs as the house itself.

At the bottom of the slope upon which he lay was a shallow river, boulder-strewn and overhung with willows and alders so as to almost entirely enclose it and hide it from view. The distance between the river and the house was a mile, but there was not a single room at the front of the building from which the flow and splash of the water could not be heard by anyone listening intently enough.

They all lived there together – Anna and Bates, Zip and Elizabeth, René, Fortuna and their son, Isaac, Bella-Grace and their children, Herman, Franklin, Vivalla and the Aztecs, Tom and Cherry, and even Byron and Apollo. They had lived there for many years and were content and secure.

There was a clock in every room of the house, and those that rang the hour were set purposely not to coincide, so that their bells and chimes might last a full five minutes from beginning to end, within which the hour itself would slip by unnoticed. Midnight was still acknowledged as being the true end of the day in the house, but by then most of its inhabitants had usually been asleep many hours, worn out by their work, and by the sharp, exhilarating air which tanned their skin and made their blood run quicker.

Sometimes during the warmer nights, small groups of the adults would gather on the porch, to smoke and drink and to discuss the events of the day. They spoke of the future and of the past, but more often than not they were content to sit silently with their memories and examine the distant constellations of stars high above them. They saw comets with burning tails, and other sudden, unidentifiable flashes of light in the great expanse of black.

It was a peaceful time, a time of calm and repose. The country was at peace, and beyond its shores the world at large was at peace. Men were exhausted after their bloodletting and were now content to divert their energies, their dreams and their hopes towards more useful and profitable pursuits.

Still in his dream, asleep in the meadow, Zip heard a voice calling to him from a distance; not from the house or from the yard and buildings surrounding it, but, impossible though it might seem, from somewhere beneath him, from deep within the earth upon which he lay: the giants in the earth were speaking to him, their voices carrying through the rock and soil as though it were the air itself. He turned on to his side and pressed his ear to the ground, but he was too late and the voices had finished speaking. He shifted position, turning his other ear to the ground, but still there was nothing, and this loss, this precious but missed opportunity brought him almost to tears: he felt as though he had been offered something, something vital to the further realization of the dream for himself and all the others, and having been offered it, had then had it taken away from him because he'd been too slow to respond and grasp it. If he'd been quicker, more alert, he would have heard the voices and understood what they were saying to him. But he hadn't, and the moment had passed.

This, then, was Zip's dream as he lay in the sun on the Museum roof, and when, in his disappointment at missing the voices, he could no longer hold on to it, he awoke from it and allowed himself to be drawn back into the present.

It was by no means a new dream for Zip, nor, he suspected, for any of the others to have, but in the full warmth of the sun high on the roof, he had dreamed it with a new intensity, and with a clarity and forcefulness he had never before experienced; he had dreamed it almost with the power of control over it, with the ability to make happen upon that broad hillside and within that tall, imposing house what he wanted to happen there. He knew also that he was living in a real world as outwardly unattractive and tightly enclosed as that of an oyster, and that within that world his dream was the small but growing pearl, something for which everything else might yet be destroyed and cast aside if the need arose.

Bella-Grace Sprague had once told him that if at least a dozen people, asleep in separate rooms, could be guaranteed to have exactly the same dream at precisely the same time, then that dream, and their own dreamed roles within it, were somehow bound to come true. At the time, this had sounded ridiculous to Zip, but it was something he had never forgotten; nor could he entirely dismiss it from his mind now that his own dream had become so perfect and so intense. The problem, Bella-Grace had then gone on to point out, was that the shared dream would only become a reality if each of the dreamers kept it to themselves, and thus did not prompt it in any way. Every ounce of gold, it seemed, was locked deep inside a hundred tons of rock.

He rose unsteadily, taking his bearings against the city skyline, and picking up the empty bottle which lay beside him, he made his way back to the parapet.

It was early evening, and the sun which had earlier remained so high for so long had begun its descent into the West, exchanging its brilliance for a deeper hue and sharper outline, the sky around it turning pink as it fell towards the earth.

In the street below a new crowd had formed, and seeing them and hearing their complaints, he knew just how far he had come from the house on the hill. He stepped back before anyone saw him, then stumbled and fell and lay where he landed, laughing at his unexpected drunkenness.

Below him someone was banging on the Museum door and insisting that Barnum should open up and let them all in. They started throwing stones again. As yet there was no real malicious intent in their actions, simply a restlessness and the contagious belief that they were still being denied something they had a right to see. This, Zip guessed, would not last, and soon, as the evening passed into night and the Museum remained closed to them, they would exhaust themselves and drift away.

He crept back to the edge and looked down. Immediately beneath him, Tom appeared on the balcony of the attic room he shared with Cherry. He called down to the crowd that Franklin's body had long since been removed and that, God willing, the Museum would be open for business as usual the following day. He told them that Barnum too had gone, and that inside everything was covered over and shut down for the night. Then, without warning, someone threw a bottle, which smashed on the wall beside him, causing him to duck and cover his face against the shattered glass. Other missiles followed, and a moment later Cherry ran out and pulled him back into the safety of their room.

Angered by what he had seen, Zip retrieved his own empty bottle, and picking out the man who had aimed his throw at Tom, he hurled it down at him and struck him on his head, knocking him to the ground and drawing blood. The man screamed as he fell, and once on the ground he lay without moving. Others gathered around him and turned to look up in the direction from which the bottle had come.

Above them, Zip had moved once again out on to the parapet, his toes testing the edge, his entire body curved to define its new centre of gravity.

'My dream!' he shouted down to them, opening his arms and briefly silencing them with this unexpected remark.

Someone laughed at him, and then several of them came forward and resumed their throwing. From their centre someone shouted out that the time had come, and this cryptic remark became the rallying call for them all; they took it up and chanted it just as they might raise a banner and wave it above their heads.

'The time has come,' Zip said to himself, acknowledging the appeal of the words, and finally accepting that his dream of the warm hillside and the beautiful house upon it now lay around him as shattered and irretrievable as the splinters of broken glass. But the time, he knew, had already come and gone, had come and gone a long time ago without any of them realizing it: it had come and gone twenty years ago with the crumbling mermaid; had come and gone three months ago with the arrival of the disappointing hippopotamus; had come and gone the previous month with the whitewash running from the flanks of the elephant; and it had finally come and gone only a minute ago with the tongue of almost invisible flame that rose from the overheated engine to lick at the fume-filled air of the Museum basement.

'My dream,' he said again, and lowering his arms he stepped back from the edge, where he had become an all too easy target for the crowd below. He looked up for a final time, and on the horizon the sun touched the distant earth and burned slowly into it, drawing with it the last of the lurid colour from the rapidly darkening sky.

29

THE NOISE WOKE Henry Butler. A dull and distant murmur punctuated by the clamour of bells, of high, unintelligible calls, perhaps screams, like the cry of gulls above the pounding of waves. He woke in the chair beside his sleeping wife, woke from a dream in which he had been about to commit an unforgivable sin. His brow and palms were beaded with sweat. He rose instantly, as though the suddenness of the action, the swift and violent passage into full wakefulness, would leave the dream even further behind him, where it now belonged.

He went to the window and looked out, watching the people in the street below, all of them running in the same direction, some of them carrying lanterns and burning torches and adding to the sense of urgency and unreality in the midst of the warm night. Extending his gaze, he was able to see to the river, metallic in the vivid moonlight.

Returning to stand beside his wife, he felt none of the urgency generated below, only the same dull sense of despondency he felt every morning upon waking. He looked down at her, preparing himself for his day at the Museum. He sat beside her and watched the flickering lights pass across the ceiling, setting ablaze the small extravagant chandelier which hung at its centre.

Momentarily, the shouts of the running figures increased in volume, and his wife opened her eyes. Henry Butler turned away from her to conceal the guilt he felt certain must still be present in his own eyes. He heard the young nurse moving around in the adjoining room; she too had been woken by the voices below.

Delilah Butler never woke slowly from her sleep, but always with the alarm of someone waiting to grasp something before it was taken away, and her first prayer of the day was invariably to give thanks for her safe deliverance through yet another uncertain night.

She too lay and watched the procession of dim yellow lights across the ceiling.

'What is it?' she asked him.

He answered her still without turning. 'Inebriates,' he said.

'At this hour? It's five in the morning.'

To Henry Butler, everything she now said implied some criticism of him. She made sins of his slightest imperfections, and had long since plucked from him any feelings of hope or pride he might once have had, like a child might pluck the wings from a butterfly. She had become the sun and the planets of her own self-regarding universe.

'Inebriates? Filthy drunkards.'

When they had first come to the house there hadn't been a tavern for a block in either direction; now there were a dozen, all of them within shouting distance.

'Just inebriates.' Henry Butler rubbed his face and rose, ready to leave her.

'Then why are they carrying torches? They are carrying torches, Henry, or are you expecting me to believe that that's just a figment of my . . . of my . . .' She lay back, exasperated, feigning exhaustion.

'Shall I call the girl?' he said.

'The nurse. Too early. Besides which, I want you to get rid of her. She takes liberties. She talks about me – about *us* – behind our backs. I'm sure of it.' She'd said the same of every girl she'd employed.

'I'll have to leave soon. You know how unsettled things have been recently. They need me to –'

'Something's happening,' she said, her head cocked. 'You can't leave me. Not with all this happening. Wait.' She closed her hands in prayer. At her instructions, Henry Butler knelt beside the bed and prayed with her.

'Sounds like they're running to Broadway,' she said, stopping suddenly and opening her eyes.

Above the clamour, the sound of a distant bell could now be clearly heard.

'A fire,' she said.

'Then God help them.' Henry Butler split his praying hands and let his face slide forward into them. He knew as well as anyone that the New York City Fire Department was capable of doing little more than add to the overall sense of occasion at most of the fires it attended, its main function being to control the spectators and keep them back from the falling debris of collapsing buildings. Even as the flames rose, there were usually speculators and builders bidding with the owners for the sale of the land upon which to build anew.

326

The ringing grew louder and then faded. There was a knock at the door and the young nurse came in. She was not fully dressed and her hair hung over her face.

'I didn't know you were in here,' she said to Henry Butler, looking from him to the bed.

'The commotion . . .' he said, hardly daring to look her in the eye from where he knelt.

His wife coughed and held a hand to her brow. She said she felt faint and complained that now she had been so rudely awoken she would be unable to return to sleep. The girl waited to be told what to do.

'What do you think it is, sir?' she asked Henry Butler.

'It's a fire, you stupid girl. Don't bother Mr Butler with your ridiculous questions, he's a busy man, very busy.' She prodded her husband in his side, as though expecting him to confirm what she'd said.

'Probably a fire,' he said. He picked up his jacket from a chair and brushed its lapels.

Back at the window, the strip of light from the river was growing broader, and Henry Butler looked down upon the vast and impenetrable darkness of the continent beyond, at the land upon which the sun had yet to rise. He tried to imagine it stretching away before him, helped by its meagre scattering of lights, some of them defining paths into that vastness which the daylight had yet to reveal.

'Better hurry,' his wife said, propping herself against her pillows and arranging the sheets across her lap as she prepared to endure yet another day.

Henry Butler kissed her lightly and felt the coldness of her lips.

He left and the girl followed him out of the room, but he neither turned nor spoke to her as he went down the stairs and out of the house. He heard her singing to herself as she prepared the medicine for his wife.

As he walked out on to the street he caught his reflection in a flame of light in one of the opposite windows. There were still people running in the direction of the fire, but considerably fewer of them than earlier, and many now ran with no real idea of their goal, pausing frequently to ask others what it was they were all so desperate to reach and see.

*

In the basement the hippopotamus floated with only its bulbous eyes and nostrils above the surface of the warm water. Having flared and died against the glass of the aquarium, the flame from the engine had caught its own wooden casing, and from there it had skimmed the panelling of the wall and established itself along the more substantial timbers of the supports to the floor above. Here it splintered and spread, fed by the drier timber and fresher air into which it then began to rise.

The basement itself remained surprisingly flame-free as the blaze struggled upwards into its richer pastures of destruction. Small pieces of dislodged timber fell to the floor and burned in isolation, but apart from this there appeared to be no other real or immediate danger to the hippopotamus other than the rise in temperature of the already tepid water in the tank.

The animal, it seemed, knew no fear, perhaps believing it had only to submerge to protect itself completely. In this, however, it was as mistaken as Barnum had been when first assessing its public appeal.

By then, the basement roof was already well alight, and the ground floor filled with eager, struggling flames, and when the supports above the aquarium finally gave way there would be nothing to protect the tank or the creature within it from what might then plummet down upon them both from above. When this happened, a bellows-rush of air would be drawn in and sent upwards through the flames, and if anything still remained of the Museum it would then surely be seized and devoured.

Sensing a rise in the temperature, the hippopotamus sucked in its breath and sank a foot lower, barely disturbing the surface of the water as it went.

A flame still spurted from the overheated engine, but now it touched nothing but the warm air.

Then, without warning, but with the noise of a whip, a crack appeared, running diagonally across the front of the tank. Water began to seep out, but only at the slowest of trickles, most of which turned to steam before hitting the ground.

Rising and taking a second, loud, full gulp of air from the surface, the hippopotamus let itself sink even further into its murky refuge, oblivious to the fact that yet another crack had appeared, silently this time, running from the front support to the back, and that the basement roof was by then almost fully alight.

And still the animal showed no real fear, or even concern. Or perhaps, having realized the consequences of the roof collapsing, it now believed it would be set free of the glass cage in which it had endured for so long, against all odds, and to Barnum's constant despair, and that once free of this it would then ascend safely to ground level and run out on to Broadway, steaming perhaps, blackened by the smoke, but otherwise uninjured, and that once there it would parade vigorously up and down among the crowds and witness with them the last spectacular minutes of the American Museum before marching off to the East River and plunging to its freedom, the hero of the hour, never again to be seen.

*

Bartola and Maximo tugged at the sleeve of Elizabeth's nightgown. They themselves were both fully dressed, Bartola in her hooped satin dress and Maximo in his tightly fitting suit with stiff collar and bowler hat. Elizabeth woke with a start as they persisted in trying to make themselves understood to her, and she saw immediately that something had frightened them. At first she imagined this to be in some way connected with the disturbance of earlier in the night when Tom had been cut by the bottle. The door to their adjoining quarters was open and she looked in to the room beyond for some indication of their distress, but saw nothing. The last time they had woken her in the night she had gone into their room to find a goat with a spectacularly spiralled single horn eating their bedclothes. On that occasion too they had dressed themselves fully before running in to her.

Unable to understand them, she tried to calm them, holding them and stroking their heads, her usual way of reassuring them. This time, however, the gesture served only to make them more agitated. She became aware that something was seriously wrong, and swung her legs from the bed ready to investigate.

Maximo made shapes with his hands and Bartola continued to tug at her sleeves.

'Was it a dream?' she asked them. 'A dream?' She made the dream shape they both understood above her head.

Both shook their heads. There was a note of terror in Bartola's efforts to communicate their distress to her, and when she tried to stop Maximo's wildly gesticulating hands, he pulled them free and continued waving.

She put on her bedjacket and started for the adjoining room, but they pulled her back, signalling instead towards her own locked door. Then Bartola began gathering up her clothes, urging her to dress herself. To appease them, she did so. She sat at her dressing table, drew her hair back from her eye and fastened it with a ribbon.

Maximo began to rattle the door, but made no real effort to open it.

'There's something you want me to see outside?' Elizabeth said.

She unlocked the door and froze. As yet there was little smoke in the third-floor corridor, but the sudden smell of it was unmistakable.

Bartola screamed, and Maximo stood beside her, desperate in his helplessness. Elizabeth immediately pulled them back into her room and closed the door. She ran to the window overlooking the alley and pushed it open. Only then did she become aware of the commotion in the street at the front of the Museum.

Stepping out on to her narrow balcony, she screamed, 'Fire!' and after repeating it until she was hoarse, she stopped and waited. She searched the windows on either side of her for signs of flame or smoke, but saw nothing. No one in the distant crowd appeared to have heard her.

Returning to Bartola and Maximo, she gave them each a sheet screwed into a knot, which she soaked in water from her washbowl. She then led them back out into the corridor, uncertain of the direction they should take, but careful not to let this uncertainty show.

Holding hands, the three of them made their way towards the central stairway. At Herman's door she banged and shouted for him until he responded. The smell of smoke was stronger now, and ahead of her she could see the first curling shapes as it rose along the banister and wrapped itself around the iron supports like vines around the branches of a dying tree.

Herman appeared in his doorway dressed in his crumpled trousers and open shirt, beneath which his stained and bloody bandages still showed. He'd been alone in his room since the removal of Franklin's body, responding to none of their entreaties to join them. A smell of liquor framed him in the doorway.

'I think there's a fire,' Elizabeth said, attempting to pull him out into the corridor, the manoeuvre made difficult by the Aztecs' tight grip. Herman studied her for a moment and then pulled himself free. He told her to leave him alone, pushing at Maximo as he too tried to pull him out.

'He's dead,' Herman said. 'And we killed him. He's dead and I don't give a damn about anything that happens to this place from now on.'

It occurred to Elizabeth that he might have thought she was playing a trick upon him, and after holding him briefly by the shoulders, she slapped him hard several times across his face. Herman began to weep and she pulled him forward and held him. Looking over his shoulder, she saw that the smoke had already climbed the last step and was now seeping along the corridor towards them. She knew that there was little time to waste, and she pushed Bartola and Maximo ahead of her in the opposite direction, towards the staircase at the far end of the corridor. Herman followed her, dazed and silent after her blows.

'You'll have to do something,' she told him. 'I've got these two to care for, and we have to warn the others.'

Herman responded to the words as though he were being brought out of a trance. He grabbed Bartola by the arm and ran along the corridor in the direction of the smoke. Elizabeth called him back, but by the time he realized his mistake, both he and Bartola had seen the danger ahead of them. Bartola screamed, and hearing her, Maximo screamed too.

From the floor beneath them, there came a loud crack, and then an explosion as a glass cabinet shattered in the heat.

The four of them ran in the other direction. Pausing at the narrow staircase leading to the upper floors, Herman released Bartola and ran up, shouting to Elizabeth that he was going to warn the others. She threw him one of her own wet sheets and told him to hurry, and to turn back immediately if he encountered any flames.

Making her way into the adjoining gallery, she almost laughed with relief when she saw that it was smoke-free, and that the smoke in the corridor behind them had barely moved since reaching the top of the stairs. Her relief, however, was short-lived, and as she began to descend the stairs at the far end of the gallery, she heard the splintering of wood and the breathless rasp of the flames beneath her.

At the bottom of the staircase they met the Albino family, all of whom ran to join her, as frantic as the Aztecs to be told what to do next.

She led them to the fountain in which the turtles sat, and instructed everyone to climb in and to soak themselves as completely as possible, and to use some part of their clothing to cover their heads. As she cupped the water and poured it over her own head, she was dismayed to see smoke as fine as dust rise from between the floorboards and then trickle out from beneath the edges of the heavy rugs.

When she was satisfied that they were all as well protected as they could be, she led them down a further narrow flight of stairs. Their only chance of escape now, she knew, would be to get to the ground floor at a part of the building into which the flames had not yet reached. With a dozen staircases and the same number of galleries and corridors by which to make the journey, the combination of routes available to them now seemed as confusing as it was endless.

Ahead of them a door was blown violently open, and they all froze at the sight of the raging furnace in the room beyond.

At first Elizabeth thought that there were already others trapped inside, but then she saw that it was the room containing the upright bears and that many of these were already ablaze. As they watched, one of the animals fell, supported momentarily on its outstretched paws before collapsing to its knees as the flames tore it apart and it disintegrated. She tried unsuccessfully to stop them from watching, but by now the Albino children were screaming as loudly and uncontrollably as Bartola and Maximo, their 'parents' mesmerized by the burning animals, all of them believing they were bearing witness to their own inevitable agonies.

'Run! Just Run!' Elizabeth shouted, pushing them all ahead of her along a divergent corridor and into another surprisingly smoke-free gallery, knowing that the wisest thing to do now would be to keep running in an attempt to dodge the flames, which might follow the maze of staircases upwards before totally consuming each floor as they went.

She closed the door behind them and told them all to catch their breath while she searched along each of the passages ahead for the safest way down.

She opened another window to let them all breathe the clean air.

They were one floor lower now, and again overlooking the alley with its distant view on to Broadway. She considered the possibility of leaping out and returning with the braver members of the crowd to come to their rescue. Before she could even call out, however, she saw a sheet of burning timber fall from the front of the building, taking with it a stream of banners, all of which forced the crowd back. The drop into the dark alley was much greater than she had imagined, and her cries for help were lost in the noise of the flames. She withdrew from the window, anxious not to create any new draught into which the flames might be drawn. She couldn't be certain how completely surrounded they were by the fire, nor if any of the passageways ahead of them were still passable.

The first staircase she tried was blocked by thick smoke, through which the flames beneath could be clearly heard.

The second appeared to offer them a way down, but as she called for the others to join her, the door at the bottom gave way to a sheet of orange, which lunged half-way up the narrow space, searing every surface before withdrawing to the doorframe, where it took a firmer hold. Elizabeth fell back at this sudden rush of hot air, and then covered her face as a burning parrot flew up the staircase towards her, the flames of its scattered feathers an extension of its once brilliant plumage. It flew clumsily upwards, shrieking with pain and colliding into the wall before eventually dropping beside her, where it flapped furiously in its agony. From the shattered case beside her, Elizabeth took out a large bone and killed the bird with a single blow.

Still clutching the bone, she made her way back to retrieve the others, and then hurried them on in the direction of the third and final staircase still available to them.

*

After a long, deep sleep, in which he was disturbed neither by dreams of his daughters and the wedding, nor of the Museum and its recent litany of unfortunate failings and miscalculations, Barnum was woken by the intermittent but insistent bell of the passing fire-extinguisher. If nothing else, the Fire Department was exceptionally adept at drawing attention to its passing, hoping, by the means of the bell and the yelling of the men who rode upon the steam-driven extinguisher and ran alongside it, to suggest to the public at large – their wages being paid solely by public subscription – the seriousness with which they undertook their work, and the air of desperate urgency with which they were able to invest each new blaze in the city. Nothing might be saved from any fire, but it was unlikely that anyone within a radius of a mile would not be instantly aware of it, and subsequently ready with their sympathy for the burned-out owners or survivors of the tragedy.

Still only half awake, it seemed to Barnum as though the clamorous machine had come to a halt in the street below. There was a brief lull in the attendant pandemonium and then it drew away, resuming its journey along Broadway. Relaxing, he let his head fall back to his pillow. In the past, he had frequently been given advance warning of the more spectacular blazes in the city so that he might attend them himself or send someone to write a report upon them before any of the morning newspapers were able to do the same. His own eyewitness accounts were always well received and had provided him with a profitable sideline in the days before the Museum had gained its full popularity. On many occasions he had even made it worth the while of the Fire Department to re-route the extinguisher so that it might pass beneath his window on its way to the fire. This, he assumed, was what had happened now.

Tomorrow was the day of his daughter's wedding, and his room, along with every other in the house, was strewn with gifts and other packages – the detritus, as he saw it, of his recent downfall, and the ashes from which he would once again rise – phoenix-like, what else? – and make it known to the waiting world that he was still the showman he had always been.

In the street below, the noise of the extinguishers was followed by the running feet and excited voices of the crowd, and it pleased Barnum to hear them. From where he lay, it was easy for him to imagine that they were racing to the Museum, all eager for news of the balloon, which must by now surely be out over the open ocean, high above the clouds and unseen by anyone until it began its miraculous descent in three or four weeks' time.

A few moments later the noise had all but faded. There were still a few running feet and shouting voices, but for Barnum the overriding feeling in that dimly lit hour was a sense of peace and calm, a feeling that the disaster, whatever it might have been, had come and gone and moved away to haunt someone else's nightmares.

Leaving his bed, he went to the window and stepped out on to the balcony, where he sat with his feet upon the balustrade and waited for the full dawn, and with it the inevitable arrival of Charity and his daughters, all of whom, now that the wedding was so close, would wake as early as possible to fill the day with their inane chatter and preparations, every detail of the occasion – of the dress, of the celebratory meals, of the trousseau – requiring a dozen opinions and fifty alterations at the very least before they were perfect. In this matter, Barnum's only consolation was that it would soon be over. With regard to the balance between being sinned against and sinning, he felt the two halves of the scale were at last drawing even.

He called down to someone in the street to ask about the fire.

'The meat markets are burning down,' the man called back up.

Someone near by said that he'd got it wrong, and that the Bowery between Christie and Forsyth Streets was ablaze.

Someone else said he thought the Governor Smith Mansion was burning.

This confusion did not worry Barnum; lies and truths were bound together in the mortar of confusion and uncertainty, and tomorrow or the day after his pamphlet would neatly reorganize and set out all the necessary details.

Charity came into his room to find out what was happening.

'I heard bells,' she said, sniffing suspiciously as she went out on to the balcony.

'Wedding bells, dearest? Perhaps you were dreaming.'

She snorted and leaned over the balcony to look along the street below.

Barnum began to hum the Wedding March.

'I think it's a fire,' she said, clutching the throat of her bedjacket. Her hair was twisted into scraps of white cloth and bone, giving her head the appearance of an overcooked meringue.

'They're burning out the Irish at Five Points. Probably set it alight themselves.'

'Good riddance. Think it'll spread to the Italians up Peck Slip?' The prospect of this cheered her up and she grinned, revealing her as yet largely toothless gums.

'It's times like this when I could happily turn back to strong spirits,' Barnum said to her, half hoping she might agree with him.

'It looks to me to be too far uptown to be Five Points. Shame.'

'Ah well, never mind. Their day will come.'

Charity sniffed again and Barnum resumed his humming.

'Perhaps they're burning out a few of the Russians in the markets,' she said.

'Perhaps, dear, perhaps. Whatever you like.'

She left him, and once again alone, Barnum took a deep breath of the freshening morning air, and for the first time in many months he felt relaxed, content, at peace with himself, almost happy. He waved and shouted encouragement to the few stragglers still passing beneath on their way to the blaze, all of them growing increasingly anxious about what they might already have missed.

*

Henry Butler, meanwhile, had reached Broadway, but despite the

335

ever-increasing commotion ahead of him, his mind had so far been on other things.

In a few weeks Anna Swan and Bates would leave for their new home in Nova Scotia. They would leave the city, never to return, and life at the Museum would be irrevocably, and perhaps unbearably, changed for the worse. Henry Butler knew that given the chance, all the other occupants would leave with them, get clear of the city and Barnum and then disappear rejoicing into their longed-for anonymity. Left behind at the helm, too stubborn to accede to the demands of Thumb or Greenwood, too proud to listen to his own plans and suggestions, Barnum would continue to let the control of the place slip through his fingers, and both he and it would dash themselves heedlessly upon the rocks of progress. And when that happened, Henry Butler knew, everything would change again and an age would have passed, never to be retrieved. More importantly, when that happened, there would be no longer any place for him in the Museum, and he would be as readily and as thoughtlessly discarded as all those others who had been unable to escape. For just as there could be no orderly abandonment of a sinking ship, so there could be no slipping away unnoticed at the last moment from the failing Museum. Life, it seemed, the world at large, always demanded its sacrifices, and some men stood out more conspicuously than others as the natural victims of this all-powerful and unstoppable tide.

All this was uppermost in Henry Butler's confused mind as he reached the junction with Broadway and turned towards the Museum.

The crowd was larger here, the people running faster and with a clearer idea of their objective; their sense of urgency was also considerably greater.

A woman ran into him and knocked him over. Shielding himself from the feet of others, he held out his arm, expecting to be helped back up, but the woman had run on. He was then almost crushed as people ran from the street on to the sidewalk to make way for a passing fire-extinguisher. Someone trod on his hand and the sleeve of his jacket was torn. He shouted out for them to stop so that he might stand, but no one paid him any attention. Eventually there was a clearing around him and he was able to pull himself up. He dusted himself down, tugged at the torn material of his sleeve and flexed the fingers of his bruised hand.

Then he looked up, and there, ahead of him, vividly illuminated against the holy light of the brightening morning sky, he saw that the

Museum was ablaze, with great tongues of flame already spitting from every ground-floor window, and with a pall of smoke and sparks rising high into the air above it, burning embers floating in this fountain of light before cooling and falling in a wide circle on to the heads of the crowd below. The sight of all this took Henry Butler's breath away. For a full minute he was unable to move, only to stand and stare, and then to gasp and cry out at the full and unbelievable horror of what he was seeing.

Still crying out, he began to run, pushing people aside and pulling others back in his urgency to reach the building. He heard the explosions as panes of glass shattered in the intense heat, and as he ran through the tightening spectators he called out for Zip and Elizabeth, for Anna and Bates, straining to hear if any of them answered him above the noise of the crowd. None did.

He reached the front of the Museum and pushed through into the small clearing there in the wake of the extinguisher. Someone pulled him back and he tried to explain who he was and get forward again. The men with the extinguisher were feeding its boiler and searching for a supply of water with which to begin their hopeless attack on the flames; others were calling into the burning building to find out if there was still anyone trapped inside.

Pulling himself free, Henry Butler moved through the crowd and made a second attempt to get forward, and again he was held back by others also struggling for a better view of the conflagration. Steam rose from the extinguisher with horse-like snorts as the firefighters built up the pressure ready to start pumping.

Finally defeated, he ran to the opposite sidewalk, to the *Herald* offices, hoping to find out from someone there how the fire had started and if anyone had yet been rescued. There was smoke in his eyes and in his lungs, and he choked as he tried to catch his breath to shout and ask if anyone knew what had happened. Other spectators drew back from the crowd with embers in their hair and with their clothing smouldering.

'They must be out, they must be,' he said to himself, unwilling for even a second to consider the alternative.

A newspaperman appeared in the doorway beside him and Henry Butler asked him how many had so far come out. The man, who recognized him immediately, looked from the blaze to his feet and said nothing.

'No,' Henry Butler said, grabbing him and shaking him.

'Fire Department's here,' the man said, pulling himself free and

337

running back indoors to embellish upon his own account of the blaze.

The heavy shutters of a ground-floor window were blown out in an explosion of flame and smoke, and the crowd moved back momentarily before rushing forward again, held in position by the constant flow of new arrivals to the rear.

By then a supply of water had been found, but the extinguisher could do little more than pump a weak, curving jet at the smouldering entrance, and it was upon this that most focused their attention in the hope of seeing someone emerge.

From his vantage point, Henry Butler examined the upper floors of the Museum instead, the windows of which as yet showed no sign of flame, only weaker emissions of smoke, which rose like ghosts and then merged. He searched each window for any indication of anyone who might still be inside, and as he looked he saw a head appear at the third-floor window above the alleyway. This, however, withdrew before he could either identify who it might be or call out to them.

He tried again to push through the crowd and to redirect the efforts of the men on the extinguisher, but again he was unsuccessful. He was punched in the face and stomach, and a falling ember branded his cheek. Then, just as he was about to give up and begin his retreat, someone at the front of the crowd yelled out and pointed to the roof of the Museum. A thousand faces turned upwards in a single motion and there was a moment almost of silence as the crowd drew in its breath. Following their gaze, he looked up and saw Zip, half naked, crouching on the parapet and watching the street below through a veil of smoke. He cried out with joy, but his voice was lost in the resurgent roar of the people around him. Believing Zip had been driven up there by the smoke and flames, he began demanding to know what could now be done to help him.

Few answered him, but hearing his pleas, one man called out, 'Let him burn! Let him burn!' and inexplicably, and to Henry Butler's further horror, the chant was taken up by others close by.

He called out and waved frantically to attract Zip's attention, but Zip was preoccupied with his own more immediate predicament, and by banging on the roof with a spar of timber in an attempt to attract the attention of anyone still in the building beneath him. It was then, watching him, that Henry Butler knew for certain that none of those inside had yet come out. The smoke brought tears to his eyes, and for the few seconds he felt could now be spared, he prayed for them all, never once taking his eyes from Zip. Around him, the crowd continued

338

its chanting, and unable to silence them, he grabbed the man who had started it and threw him to the ground. Others watched, but no one was prepared to intervene. The man rose, cursed him and then ran off laughing.

Encouraged by this first positive act, and by the fact that the flames lower down the Museum had still not yet appeared at the upper windows, Henry Butler called out again to Zip. This time Zip paused and looked down over the crowd. Their eyes met, and Zip raised both his arms, a gesture Henry Butler immediately copied, relieved that even this slight contact had finally been made. Before he could signal anything else, Zip returned to his task of trying to contact those still beneath him.

Then, in a brief clearing in the smoke, Henry Butler caught sight of the block and tackle suspended from the parapet directly above the Spragues' attic window, and immediately he remembered the small store on the roof in which the ropes were kept for use with the pulleys by which the heavier exhibits were raised or lowered, taken in or out of the Museum. The last occasion these had been used had been with the lifting of the stuffed tiger, and he personally had supervised the return of the ropes to the store.

Encouraged by this prospect of escape, he called out again to Zip, attracting his attention and then making himself clear by a series of gestures, repeatedly pointing to the block and tackle, which lay hidden from Zip by the overhang of the parapet.

Zip signalled back that he understood, leaned over as far as was possible to ascertain the exact position of the pulley and then moved back from the edge, reappearing a moment later with two thick coils of rope over his shoulders. By then, the smoke and flames had started to appear at the second-floor windows, some in a direct line with the drop of the pulley. Securing himself to the parapet, Zip lowered himself to the block and tackle and began to thread one of the ropes through it. His actions attracted the attention of the crowd and their chanting gradually faded. Someone cheered him, then someone else. Soon everyone was cheering, and some began to shout up to Zip how they thought he might best achieve the difficult task upon which he was now embarked.

This sudden change of heart in the crowd was as inexplicable to Henry Butler as their original hostility had been, and now when he tried to move forward no one stopped him. Recognizing him, some even cleared a path for him and then applauded as he emerged into the clearing and approached the extinguisher, its feeble spout of water

339

still aimed at the Museum entrance, which was now steaming, the walls on either side of it beginning to show signs of the fierce blaze within.

He exchanged words with the men working the pump, and they told him that they would remain only for as long as they considered it safe, withdrawing when anything more substantial than the cascade of embers and burning bunting began to fall around them.

Much closer now to the Museum, Henry Butler turned his gaze back up to Zip. He already had one of the ropes through the pulley and was feeding it to the ground through the smoke. Henry Butler went as close as he dared to grab its trailing end and then pull it wide of the flames through which it passed. Both he and Zip then attempted to drag the block and tackle along its rail to a part of the building as yet less badly affected by the fire and smoke. The pulley refused to budge, however; it had not been shifted from its position above the Spragues for several years and its runners had now probably rusted solid to the rail.

Above him, Henry Butler saw that Zip was still trying to attract the attention of anyone still inside. He thought he saw a figure cross one of the third-floor windows, and possibly another in the attic room directly above. He signalled to Zip to let him know, and unharnessing himself, Zip ran along the parapet to where he pointed.

He had just moved clear of the ropes when a further explosion attracted everyone's attention and the crowd turned to see a jet of flame spout from the attic window directly beneath the pulley, and two floors higher than any other indication of the blaze inside. The flame died almost immediately, but was replaced by smoke, and for the first time Henry Butler saw how unevenly the fire was rising through the building, following its convoluted passages and galleries, suppressed in some areas, drawn more rapidly upwards in others. Then, as he considered the window at which the flame had appeared and tried to understand what had caused it, the whole of the frame and sill fell forward, dragging with it the overhanging section of parapet and the pulley attached to it. He called up to Zip, and as the balustrade and pulley fell clear of the building, the rope already threaded rose in a high loop from the roof and fell with it, the whole of the smouldering wreckage crashing to the ground only a few feet from where Henry Butler stood beside the extinguisher. He released his own end of the rope and covered his face. No one was seriously hurt by the falling debris but, smashed upon the ground, the pulley no longer existed as a means of escape for anyone still trapped inside. Henry Butler could not believe how disastrous that one maverick flame had proved to be.

Zip clung to the parapet and looked down to where the wreckage had fallen and shattered, and waited for the tremor it sent through the rest of the building to subside. He indicated to Henry Butler that he was uninjured and that he still had the second coil of rope. Rising to his feet, he bowed to the enthusiastic cheering of the crowd below before disappearing from view in the direction of the side of the Museum overlooking the alley, from which little flame or smoke yet rose.

Guessing what he was about to attempt, Henry Butler ran in the same direction, arriving at the Ann Street entrance which, although not yet alight, also showed alarming signs of the blaze within.

He kicked at the door and it flew open, letting out a sudden plume of choking smoke, behind which the corridor appeared unexpectedly clear.

He ran inside and shouted. No one answered him. Half-way along the passage he saw that the entrance hall and both galleries leading from it were alight and he was unable to go any further in that direction. Tapestries dropped burning from their mountings, and from throughout the building came the sound of shattering glass and crackling woodwork.

Someone called out to him, but turning he saw only one of the firefighters in the entrance behind him. Ignoring the man's entreaties to return outside, he covered his mouth with a cloth and ran through the empty booths to the passageway in which a number of private staircases converged, calling out as he went and searching for pockets of clear air from which to gulp and sustain himself. Then, above him, just as he was about to turn back and search in another direction, he heard someone scream and cry out for help. He shouted back to them that he was coming and told them to continue calling to let him know exactly where they were. Beneath his feet the staircase was hot, and in places feathers of smoke rose and dispersed around him as he ran through them. Behind him, something fell, and looking back he saw that an entire partition wall had given way beneath the weight of the stuffed rhinocerous which had been standing above, and which was now fiercely ablaze, its head framed by wooden panelling, its skin bursting and peeling as it burned. More importantly, the creature now blocked his way back, and having stopped for no more than a few seconds, he ran forward again. There were still voices ahead of him, and pushing open the door leading into the main second-floor gallery, he saw the Albinos and the Aztecs huddled together beneath wet sheets, their clothes dripping with water. He heard Elizabeth and turned to see her at the far end of the corridor. He called to her and she ran to him, indicating that the last door down she had just tried appeared to be smoke-free. She urged the others towards it. Above the noise of the crying children and the splintering woodwork, he asked her if she knew of the whereabouts of anyone else in the Museum. She told him about Herman's dash to the upper floors in search of the Spragues, René and Fortuna, Tom and Cherry, but apart from that she knew nothing.

'What about Anna and Bates?'

'I thought they might already be out,' she said, before being pulled away by Bartola and Maximo. Henry Butler followed her to the head of the stairs and warned her about the blocked corridor below, suggesting an alternative route through one of the first-floor galleries and down to the Ann Street entrance, which he hoped would still be clear.

She tried to persuade him to go back down with them, and when he refused she took the final wet sheet from her shoulders and wrapped it around his head. Then she ran to join the others, leaving him alone.

With all the doors closed, that side of the second floor was also surprisingly free of smoke. He was at the rear of the Museum and calculated that the flames were working fastest towards the front, where the corridors were wider, and where the smashed windows were letting in more air to feed the blaze.

He ran up the next staircase, calling for Herman. Something brushed past him, and looking down he saw a pair of iguanas scuttling back and forth in panic. He picked them up by their tails and ran with them to one of the windows at the side of the Museum. Opening it, he pitched them out into the half-light, hoping they would survive the fall.

Returning to the staircase, he heard the frantic screaming of the two chimps trapped in their cage. He slid the bolt on their feeding hatch, reached in and pulled them both out. Rushing back to the window, he pushed them through and watched for a moment as they scrambled down the wall into the darkness below.

Arriving at the third floor, he called again for Herman and was answered by the sound of someone choking. A pall of thick smoke lay along the ceiling, its lower edge shifting like the swell of a gentle sea. Crouching, he saw Vivalla coming along the corridor on his hands and knees, and called out to him.

'Byron and Apollo,' Vivalla said upon reaching him. 'I've got to get them out, got to get down to them.'

'It's not so bad down there,' Henry Butler told him, guessing that by then there was little chance of the flames having reached the very rear of the building, their movement being predominantly upwards.

'She's alight from top to bottom in parts,' Vivalla told him, both men still pressed to the floor to avoid the smoke.

'Have you seen Herman? He's still up there.'

'They all are. Probably too terrified even to attempt to get down. Anna and Bates out yet?'

'I don't think anyone is.' Henry Butler realized that he had passed both Anna's and Captain Bates's rooms in the corridor above the blocked staircase. 'Why didn't I look in?' he said.

'Don't worry – I'll get them on my way down,' Vivalla said, and resumed his crawling along the corridor.

Henry Butler tore the damp sheet in half and threw a piece after him. Vivalla caught it and signalled his thanks.

Alone again, Henry Butler considered his way forward.

Having gone only a few paces further, he was stopped by the sound of other voices calling for help, and he peered through the smoke of the passage ahead of him. The voices sounded unfamiliar, distant and high-pitched, terrified children perhaps, or the last desperate pleas of someone calling out and choking at the same time. He shouted back and waited. No one answered him. He could see nothing ahead of him in the clouded light. Then, just as he was about to call out again, he was struck in the chest by the leading bird of a small flock of mynahs, which flew into him and then fell to the floor, furiously pedalling in the smoke-filled air and still calling out for help. Others followed it and flew in circles around him, disturbing the smoke, and then one by one dropping to the floor as they were overcome and asphyxiated by it. There was nothing he could do for them; instead he ran with his head down to the next staircase which would, if clear, lead him up to where he hoped to find Herman. Here he encountered another of the suffocating birds; it lay on its back shrieking and calling out for water, and he crushed it with his foot, killing it instantly before rushing off, shouting for Herman as he went.

*

Upon waking, Bella-Grace Sprague's first instinct was to scream, and this she did, instantly waking both Isaac and her children.

'What's wrong?' Isaac asked her. He wore a mask to shield his eyes, had plugs in his ears, and a fine net drawn tightly over his head to keep his carefully oiled hair in place. Upon his nightgown Bella-Grace had embroidered the same skeletal outline she had sewn upon the suit he wore in his booth. This too had a slightly luminous quality in the darkness, and it was a constant joy to Bella-Grace to wake in the night and see her small husband stretched out flat beside her, his bones glowing beneath the sheets, and looking to her like the sculpted body of a medieval knight resting upon his tomb. On this occasion, however, there was little time for such wifely adoration. A sniff of the air in her sleep had woken her, and now she sniffed it again, more deeply this time, and let out a second, considerably louder scream just as Isaac and her children were recovering from the first.

Isaac sat up beside her, the mask still covering his eyes, and turned from side to side. Bella-Grace pulled out his ear plugs and tore off both the mask and his hairnet, bringing him literally and speedily to his senses and turning his face with her hand so that the first thing he saw upon clearing his eyes was the look upon her face.

'Sniff,' she instructed him.

Isaac sniffed, detected nothing and sniffed again.

'Harder,' she implored.

Around them, their six children sat up in their makeshift beds and began sniffing the night air, craning their necks like young birds in a nest expecting food.

Isaac sniffed harder, but was still unable to detect the cause of his wife's anxiety.

One by one, the children screamed, held each other and began to sob in unison.

Then a look of understanding crossed Isaac Sprague's face, and he pulled from each nostril the small wad of soft wool by which he prevented himself from snoring and rattling in his sleep.

Taking a deep breath, he sniffed again, and this time he immediately felt the small sharp sting of smoke and began to search for its source.

'Oh, good Lord!' Bella-Grace said beside him.

For the first time, Isaac too felt like screaming.

'We'll be roasted alive,' Bella-Grace said.

Isaac began to tremble.

344

'We're on the top floor,' she added.

Isaac screamed, and in the midst of his yell, which was once again taken up by the children in a chain reaction of terror, Bella-Grace began to formulate their plan of escape. She was always at her best in a tight situation, and it had often occurred to her that her resourcefulness in those situations increased in direct proportion to the extent of the panic and confusion around her. In contrast, Isaac was by nature always quick to panic, and it was hearing his scream that caused Bella-Grace to stop and take charge, and to respond to their present dilemma as she now saw fit. Her own screaming had served its purpose; there must be no more to follow it. She told herself that she hadn't come all that way and raised all those children only to have them roasted alive in their beds before her very eyes.

'What do we do?' Isaac said, grabbing her arm and clinging to her as she swung herself from the bed and began to deliver her orders.

She ran to the small window and looked down over the crowd gathered below.

'The entire city looks to have turned out to help us,' she called out. 'These brave folks have come to our rescue.'

Her youngest daughter applauded, followed by the others.

Only Isaac refused to be convinced of their salvation. He rose, sat back down, rose again, wrapped himself in the sheets, threw them from him, and then climbed back beneath them. Bella-Grace told him not to worry. She was a mother and a wife and was not about to let them all go up in flames and be reduced to cinders. Hearing this, Isaac screamed again and stuffed the sheets into his mouth as a gag. Then Bella-Grace told him she needed him to be brave. It was a ploy for the sake of the children, and realizing this, Isaac sprang up from the bed and flexed his skeletal arms.

Bella-Grace told them all to get dressed, and when they were ready she led them out of their room, along the corridor and down the first staircase they came to, up which the first exploratory fingers of smoke were even then beginning to rise.

At the foot of the stairs they encountered their first flames, and quickly turning them all back, Bella-Grace considered each alternative means of escape still likely to be open to them. Isaac stayed at the top of the stairs and calmed the children. He shouted down to her that she was the finest, bravest wife and mother any man could hope for. Bella-Grace thanked him and then went on with her calculations.

From that staircase they could gain access into the Missing Link gallery, from which there were two possible staircases down.

Bella-Grace ran into the gallery, which was still untouched by the fire, and flung open the upper door to each flight of stairs. By then, however, both were well alight, and she was greeted by a rush of warm air and smoke at each. Securing the doors, she ran back to where Isaac and her children were waiting for her. The only other way open to them, she decided, was to return to the floor above and make their way around the Museum until they came upon a clear route of descent, possibly to the rear or south side. As she ran, she calculated their chances of finding one free of smoke and flame, keeping her unhappy conclusions to herself.

They went up, along, and then down again. At short intervals she called out to ask if there was anyone within hearing distance of them. No one answered her.

From a suit of armour she took a helmet, a shield and a hefty mace and used these to protect herself as she led her family forward.

Watching her, Isaac felt the urge to cheer her. She reminded him now of Boudicea, and simply by watching her as she cleared the way ahead of them, yelling and swinging the mace from side to side, he knew she was going to get them out.

They made their way down to the third floor, and Bella-Grace was about to open the door to the central stairwell when it blew open without warning only a few feet ahead of them, sending a roaring ball of flame directly towards them at head height. Isaac and the children froze, but Bella-Grace, emitting a loud and fearsome cry, raised her shield and mace and charged straight at the fireball, stopping it dead and then beating it down to nothing until it was finally extinguished and lay in patches of charred carpet and wallpaper all around her. Seeing her momentarily engulfed by the flames, the children screamed, but again Isaac could only gaze in admiration at his wife's quick thinking and bravery.

Checking to ensure that neither her hair nor her clothing had caught alight, Bella-Grace told them to turn back and retrace their steps.

Ahead of them, the flames already had a good hold on the gallery beyond. A creature, something unidentifiable, stood trapped in the room and screeched with pain until a burning spar fell from above and silenced it.

Leading them back along the corridor, Bella-Grace indicated a second gallery, knowing it to be their last hope if they were to get down to ground level and the safety of the waiting crowd. The fire, she realized, in addition to being beneath and behind them, was now somehow also above them, and they must keep moving if they were not to be completely encircled by it.

To her relief, the second gallery appeared clear, but as she started to cross it ahead of Isaac and the children, the entire floor sagged and then caved in beneath her. Bella-Grace threw herself back and was saved, but the planking collapsed completely, releasing the flames beneath high up into the air. Cabinets and cases plunged into the abyss. A polar bear fell in a blazing somersault, followed by a camel. Chandeliers exploded in their sockets before they too fell and shattered in the flames below. A second bear, already charred black, appeared to salute them with its broken paw as it tipped upright and then tumbled forward in a clumsy dive into the flames.

Bella-Grace stared disbelievingly and with mounting fear at the total disaster they had so narrowly avoided. She turned her family around, picked up Isaac, instructed her children to clutch her skirts, and then ran with them back in the direction from which they had just come, discarding the helmet, shield and mace as she went. She was running blindly now, all her plans having come to nothing, and as she ran, Isaac kissed her cheek and she drew some small strength from this.

The way down was now blocked completely to them, and soon other staircases and floors would begin to succumb and collapse, and the tremors of every fall would set off another until the entire building had been weakened and shaken apart. The only way now still open to them was upwards.

With Isaac still in her arms, she kicked open each of the doors they passed, but although most of them were still free of flames and smoke, none of them offered any further means of escape.

They climbed to the floor above, and it was there, as they edged cautiously along a smoking passage, that they encountered Herman, hearing first his voice as he called out for help, and then watching as he materialized like a miracle out of the gloom ahead of them. He waved to them, and the children cheered him. He called them to him, embraced them, and then led them to a side window where they were able to take it in turns to lean out and gulp the clean air, the smoke rushing out over their shoulders as they did so.

Putting down her husband, Bella-Grace took Herman to one side and told him of everything they had so far encountered, making it immediately clear to him that the route via which he had come up

347

through the Museum was no longer available to them as a way down. He asked her if they had come across Elizabeth, the Aztecs or the Albinos, and when Bella-Grace shook her head he feared the worst.

Further along the corridor the smoke thickened, and was already starting to foul the air outside.

Unable to suggest a way ahead, Herman began to tremble, and Bella-Grace held him. She kissed him and tucked his charred and bloody bandages back into his jacket. She called Isaac and her children to her and they gathered around the window, where they resumed taking it in turns to lean out and breathe what little clear air was still available to them. Bella-Grace was exhausted and defeated. Everything she had grasped had been savagely snatched away from her until there was nothing left within her reach. She began singing, but only to mask her fear from Isaac and Herman. The younger children joined her, but when she stopped, they too fell immediately silent. All around them, the air grew warmer and the sound of the flames grew louder and louder.

Still unable to admit defeat, Bella-Grace ran back along the corridor and closed all the doors leading from it. She then stuffed the carpet along the bottom of each doorway, and by these means was able to cut off a good deal of the smoke still entering the restricted space. Her face was blackened and she was choking by the time she returned to the others. Now, with the window held open the air in the corridor became more bearable, but other than this they had gained nothing. They were trapped on the fourth floor, and the only way out of the building now open to them involved a sheer drop of seventy feet on to the hard earth of the alley below.

Bella-Grace knelt and began to pray for their salvation, and Isaac and her children joined her.

Herman, by then close to tears, and unable to accept that he had achieved so little, that the end was so close, and that when it came it would come so suddenly and yet so agonizingly, left them and went back to the window. He leaned out, cupped his hands and shouted for help. No one heard him above the noise of the blaze, but he went on calling until his voice failed and he could barely hear himself.

Then, just as was about to withdraw and hold one of the children to the window, something fell from above and caught his shoulder on its way down. Thinking this to be a piece of falling timber, he threw himself aside and looked up, half expecting more to fall, and possibly to wedge itself between the small window and the blank wall of the building opposite, and thus deprive them of even this last small comfort and bring their end suddenly so much nearer. Looking up, however, he could scarcely believe what he saw: for there, not ten feet above him on the roof, was Zip, and what had hit him was not a piece of falling timber, but a length of thick rope, the end of which was coiled firmly around Zip's shoulders and chest. He reached out and grabbed this, still hardly daring to believe what was happening. Zip waved down to him and pulled in the slack until the rope hung in a straight drop to the ground. Herman waved back, but Zip simply shook the rope, rapping it against the window to suggest to him that he should act quickly and begin his descent.

Herman pulled Bella-Grace to the window, showed her the rope and then pointed to Zip above them. Bella-Grace called out to him, her hands still clasped in prayer. Again Zip rapped the rope against the window. Bella-Grace knew immediately what was required of her and signalled up to him that she understood. Zip then released more of the rope and Bella-Grace pulled a wide loop of it in through the window. Wrapping it around the chests of the two smallest children, she knotted it securely and lifted them out on to the narrow sill, gently holding them clear of the building so that they spun slightly as Zip, slowly paying out the rope, began to lower them to the ground.

As they disappeared from sight, two things happened in the narrow corridor in which the others waited to be rescued. Firstly, the door at the far end burst open and flames began to tear at the walls and ceiling. And secondly, a distinct rapping sound came down to them from the attic rooms above.

Bella-Grace and Herman looked hard at each other. The only windows up in the attic rooms faced the front of the Museum, the lower half of which must have been by then almost totally consumed.

The rapping continued until a distinct sequence of knocks could be discerned.

'Tom and Cherry!' Herman said.

'Oh, sweet Lord!' Bella-Grace turned from the window and the rope upon which her children hung to the flames already moving towards them along the corridor.

'I can still get up to them,' Herman said. 'They don't know we're here. I can get up to them and bring them directly back down.'

The door leading up to the attic lay half-way along the corridor, the flames still twenty or thirty feet from it. He and Bella-Grace silently assessed his chances: he would have to get up, find Tom and

Cherry and then lead them back down before the flames reached the door and were diverted upwards. If this happened, the three of them would be trapped with no possible means of escape.

'Try!' Bella-Grace called out to him. She tore off her skirt, ran to the flames and started beating them back with it.

Herman leaned out of the window and took several deep breaths of clean air in preparation for the attempt. Beside him, the rope went slack and he pulled it back in for Isaac to attach another two of the children.

Seeing this, knowing that at least two of them had been lowered safely to the ground, Bella-Grace shouted, 'Hallelujah!' and then resumed her single-handed attack on the flames.

Pausing only to touch her arm and look into her eyes for a second, Herman kicked open the attic door and then ran up the narrow flight of stairs in search of Cherry and Tom.

*

Fortuna had so far spent an almost sleepless night; she was restless, unsettled by the events of the previous day. Beside her, asleep, lay René, and all around them hung his paintings: they covered the walls from floor to ceiling; others were propped against the furniture, and some stood as yet unfinished upon their easels.

She had spent much of the day trying to console Herman following the removal of Franklin's body, and then when he turned everyone from his room and refused to see anyone she had gone in search of Zip, afraid that following his confrontation with the crowd he might already have left the Museum, and that now, in his anger and disillusionment, he might be about to do something stupid, something they would all regret in the days to come as they sought to regain a common equilibrium. The remainder of the day and evening she had spent with Anna and Elizabeth, secluded at the heart of the Museum, away from every sight and sound of the world beyond the locked entrance. All three were agreed that Barnum's fortunes had taken a considerable turn for the worse; equally, all three were now powerless to do anything about this.

She had slept briefly, exhausted by the day's events, and had woken suddenly and unaccountably alert, and resigned to the fact that she would stay awake until dawn.

There was a noise far below her, the sound of something falling or being dropped, followed by the scream of a parrot and the cries of some of the smaller birds. After that there was only silence.

She wished René would wake, and that the two of them could discuss the possibility of leaving the Museum. But René, despite his temperament, was a sound sleeper, and he would not thank her for being woken unnecessarily. Soon, the summer morning light would be gone, and while it lasted he rose early to take advantage of it, incorporating it into the several lifeless landscapes upon which he was currently working. Painting all morning undisturbed by anyone, he would insist upon a two-hour sleep in the afternoon, after which he would rise, dress for the evening, and make his way down to sit with Fortuna in her booth.

There was a second loud noise, this time from somewhere much closer, and above her Fortuna heard footsteps and the slamming of a door. They were all by then accustomed to the late hours Zip kept, and she imagined the sound to be that of him returning from the taverns; he would have disturbed the birds lower down upon letting himself back into the Museum.

As she turned to face the door leading to their son's small room, there was a gentle tap upon it and he came in to her. There were tears on his face and he told her he was afraid. Believing him to have had a nightmare following the events of the day just passed, she motioned for him to be silent and carefully lifted the sheets beside her so that he might join her. René did not approve of this, but feeling her son pressed close to her in her bed was still a great joy to Fortuna, and she dabbed his eyes and smoothed the silky hair over his cheeks. Recently, this seemed to be growing more thickly, and tracing along his jaw and neck, she kissed him and held him more tightly.

Then the boy suddenly pulled free of her and sat up. He breathed deeply and tugged at her sleeve and then her beard, insisting that he could smell something. To pacify and reassure him, Fortuna rose and she too breathed deeply in the night air.

'You're right,' she told him, speaking softly in French. She swung herself from the bed and went into his room. The smell was stronger there, and she knew immediately what it was. Gathering the clothes from beside his bed, she went back into him, careful to conceal her own growing sense of alarm. She told him to get dressed and then gently shook René, who woke as though from a nightmare, calling out before he saw her leaning over him, a finger to her lips.

'There's a fire,' she whispered. She handed him his pants and jacket and then quickly dressed herself.

René told her he could smell nothing, that she was imagining it, but she remained firm, and waiting until they were all dressed, she opened the outer door and looked into the corridor beyond. The smell was stronger out there, but as yet there was neither smoke nor flame to threaten them. She checked the stairway down to the second floor and that too was clear. She called to them, urging them to follow her, but only her son emerged. Running back, she found René pulling his paintings from the walls and stacking them by the door. He told her to take as many as she could carry, insisting that their son did the same.

Realizing how pointless it would be to argue with him, and because as yet there appeared to be no immediate danger of them being cut off by the flames, she took as many of the canvases as she could carry, gave two to their son, and called again for René to follow them. As she ran she shouted out to warn the others. There were running footsteps above her and she knew that the alarm had already been raised. All that mattered now was to get down and out to safety.

René emerged, but instead of following her to the main staircase, he called for her to go with him towards the centre of the Museum. She asked him why, certain that this was the wrong thing to do, and he told her he had to get to Barnum's office, running on and turning a corner before she could begin to persuade him otherwise. Under his arm, protected by a thick canvas wrapping, he carried only the unfinished portrait of Elizabeth.

Laying down the paintings, Fortuna picked up her son and ran after her husband. She was angry with René for having now endangered them all in this way, but it would have been unthinkable for her to have left him and saved herself and her son, and as she ran she heard him ahead of her, shouting back, urging them to keep close to him.

Turning into the corridor leading to Barnum's office, she saw the flames for the first time, and seeing them she felt a shock pass through her. In her arms, the boy screamed, and she held a hand over his mouth. She saw René kicking at the locked door to the outer office, and when this finally gave way she watched as he ran through towards Barnum's and began kicking at the door to that too. She had never seen him behaving so violently and shouted to ask him what was wrong. She was afraid to follow him in case the flames cut them off, and so she waited by the first doorway and called out to him to hurry, determined that if the flames came too close then she would find the strength to run in and drag him out.

352

She need not have worried. From within Barnum's office there came a splintering sound and then a cheer, and René emerged with the ruined portrait of Charity and Barnum's daughters. He tore at the canvas and then hurled it against the wall, where the frame broke into several pieces. These he picked up and threw into the flames.

'I smashed it over his own stupid head,' René said, exhilarated by what he had done.

'He's *in* there?'

'His bust, his ridiculous bronze bust. I smashed it over his stupid grinning face.' His eyes shone and he laughed as he looked to where the painting was now burning. Retrieving the portrait of Elizabeth, he told her they could now leave and begin their descent.

He stopped again as they ran back past their room and he saw the paintings Fortuna had stacked in the corridor. He tried to gather these up, telling her to put down their son and help him. She refused. Their room was now filled with smoke. She pointed this out to him and her harsh words were as close as she had ever come to striking him. She hesitated, realizing what she had done, but knew that there had been no alternative. René stopped too, caught his breath and looked down at the canvases he held. He told her she was right and threw them to the ground, holding on only to Elizabeth's. Fortuna told him to save that particular one at all cost, and kissed him, relieved that such a fitting compromise had been so swiftly and easily reached.

They ran together to the end of the corridor, but as they began their descent they were forced to reconsider their route by the flames which rose to meet them. Fortuna urged them back up and along to the next staircase. That, too, was alight, and as she opened the door leading to it she was greeted by a rush of scorching air, turning just in time to protect her son, whom she still held, but not quickly enough to prevent her beard from being badly singed. The sudden acrid smell almost choked her as she pushed the door shut and urged them on to find another way down before it was too late.

They heard voices – Henry Butler's and Elizabeth's – but saw no one as they continued to search for a safe descent.

Reaching the second floor, they were confronted by flames at both ends of the gallery they had entered, and Fortuna searched the booths which lined one of its walls for a way through to the rear. She quickly found one and led René along it, arriving in the theatre. The small auditorium was already ablaze. There was a hole in the ceiling and a stuffed zebra sat burning in the stalls, and beside it the charred remains of something already burned beyond recognition.

Forcing a passage through the backdrops and pieces of scenery, Fortuna led them backstage and out into yet another corridor. She heard screams and footsteps ahead of them and knew they had just missed meeting up with someone else fighting to find their way out. She shouted to let whoever it had been know they were right behind them, but no one answered her, the only sound being that of a door slamming in the smoky darkness ahead of them. For the first time she began to fear the worst.

She stopped for a moment to work out exactly where they were and what galleries and corridors now lay around them. She was uncertain about their next move, but was forced forward by an eruption of flame as the stage curtain caught alight. She urged them to turn in the direction she imagined the running footsteps to have come from, pushing René and his painting ahead of her, and holding tightly to her son, his face pressed firmly into her chest as she ran.

*

By the time Vivalla reached Anna Swan's first-floor room she was already unconscious, overcome by the fumes, and a flat cloud of dense smoke hung like a shroud above her bed, descending upon her as he watched.

In the corridor outside, the wall hangings and carpets were ablaze, and having forced open her locked door, he knew that the passageway was no longer open to them as a way back out or down. Around him, a good deal of the flooring had already collapsed and the wreckage burned fiercely in the gutted shell of the ground floor. He knew he had little more than minutes to attempt to wake Anna and then begin searching for a way out for them both, aware also that his chances of achieving either were diminishing with every second the smoke continued to seep into her room.

He ran to the window and threw it open. The glass was hot to the touch and he burned his hands. Sparks and glowing embers blew in from below, but a good deal of the smoke already in the room was also drawn immediately out.

Soaking a cloth in the bowl beside Anna's bed, he threw the remainder of the contents directly into her face. She responded, but only slightly, and the shock failed to revive her. Everything in the room had been blackened by the smoke, and where the water splashed against the walls it turned immediately to steam. He shook her shoulders and tried unsuccessfully to pull her upright. When he released her she slumped back and groaned, and encouraged by this Vivalla began to clear the air around her face with a fan which lay on the cabinet beside her bed. She began to choke and he fanned harder. There was an explosion in the corridor and a further section of the passage floor burned through and collapsed.

Then Vivalla noticed the curtain covering the door to Captain Bates's room, and pulling it aside he ran at the door until it gave way and flew open.

Inside, Bates was on his feet, stumbling through the smoke, choking, his hands covering his face. Vivalla called to him and he responded.

'It's Anna – I can't rouse her!'

'Anna? Anna!' Bates ran towards him, knocking over a table and washstand in his haste. Vivalla rescued the jug and what little remained of its contents and followed him back through into the now clearer air of Anna's room.

Bates continued to call her name. He ran to her bed and pulled her upright.

Vivalla returned and dragged the sheets from Bates's bed, and was about to follow him through when the door and half the wall sagged and erupted into flame. Vivalla beat at the blaze but quickly realized that his efforts were useless. Pulling the door shut behind him, he went back through to Anna.

By then Bates had lifted her from her bed and had swung her feet to the ground.

'We can't use the corridor,' Vivalla told him, already straightening and knotting the sheets as Bates slapped Anna's face, gently at first, but then with increasing urgency as she began to show further signs of coming round. He continued calling to her, and Vivalla gave him the water and a cloth to clean her eyes and mouth.

Anna choked, and black spittle ran from her lips down her chin. A moment later, black tears appeared at her eyes, and she opened them.

'She's coming round!' Bates called to Vivalla, who was then back at the window, leaning through the smouldering woodwork and searching the wall around him.

'Can you get her over here?' he called to Bates.

The cladding of the wall directly beneath the window had already fallen away, but the supports were still intact and as yet little damaged. Mounds of glowing ash and smoking timber lay on the street below, but Vivalla knew that if they could somehow lower Anna into them, she should be able to make her way to safety in the clear space between the building and the watching crowd beyond. The men with the extinguisher were still beneath them, and it was only their efforts which had so far saved the lower supports. Vivalla attracted their attention, and when they and the crowd saw him they let out a cheer and surged forward as far as the heat would allow. If a path could be cleared through the ashes and the hose turned upon anyone who was lowered, then it might still be possible to get them safely and quickly to the ground. Being on the first floor they were only fifteen feet above the street, and even a leap from that height, if broken by the waiting arms or shoulders of someone below, might be attempted with some chance of success.

The men on the extinguisher turned the hose from the Museum entrance and directed it at the window from which Vivalla called down to them. It caught him and refreshed him, splashing into the room behind and spraying both Bates and Anna.

By now Anna was on her feet, supported by Bates. She was still choking and coughing, but she was at least conscious and would soon be fully aware of the urgent need to get out.

Vivalla told Bates of his plan and Bates agreed with him that it stood a good chance of success. But as he spoke, the water from below stopped coming, and returning to the window Vivalla saw that the men beneath were at a loss as to why their supply had so suddenly dried up on them. Seizing their advantage, the flames moved towards him from both sides.

Withdrawing, he told Bates to get Anna to the window. Bates dressed her in her bedjacket and helped her across the room. Vivalla tore a spare sheet in half, soaked it and tied it around her feet. Between them they got her into position, and Vivalla began to fasten a sheet around her chest, Bates holding up her arms so that he might knot it securely and then fasten it to another, by which means she might then be lowered.

The first knot Vivalla tied came immediately loose, as did the second and third. The fourth held, but the sheet itself began to tear.

'I don't think it can be done,' Bates said. 'All we'd do is get her out over the sill and let her drop. If we had something stronger we might be able to hold her and lower her at least part of the way, but with this we'd just drop her into the embers below.'

Vivalla agreed with him, and both looked to Anna, who was

at last able to breathe more easily. She understood what they had been about to attempt and she agreed with their conclusion, ready to do whatever they suggested.

Outside, burning timbers fell into the mounds of ash, and without the water from the hose no one below could clear a path along which any of them might escape should they get safely down.

For almost a minute all three of them were defeated by the apparent impossibility of the situation.

Then Captain Bates spoke: 'You get out,' he told Vivalla. 'You're light enough. You could hang by the sill and drop. Protect your feet with wet cloths and you should make it through to safety.'

Vivalla knew that this was indeed possible, but he shook his head.

Bates and Anna held each other.

'Go on, do it,' Anna told Vivalla. 'Who knows, you might find someone down there with a ladder and you could raise it to the window for us.'

'She's right,' Bates said. 'Go now. You're our only chance. Save yourself. You've done everything possible for us. Without you we might even already be –'

Anna touched a finger to his lips. As she did so part of the floor by the corridor wall rose slightly, erupted into flames and collapsed. Her chest of wedding presents fell with it. Others toppled from their neat piles and their paper and ribbons were quickly set ablaze by these new flames. Anna started across the room to retrieve them, but Bates and Vivalla held her back. More of the floor gave way and the packages fell into the blaze below. Anna began to weep, and Bates held her and covered her face.

'So that's it – you're giving up,' Vivalla said to him.

'I'm not leaving her,' Bates said, stroking Anna's hair.

'Then push her out and jump with her.'

'If she wants to stay then I stay with her.'

Vivalla left them briefly to beat at the burning carpet. Returning to Anna, he pulled her away from Bates and said, 'And what about your house, your beautiful new house? In an hour this place is going to be nothing but a heap of smouldering wreckage. We're all going to be homeless. You two at least have somewhere to go.'

She looked at him for a moment and understood immediately how much more he was saying to her. Turning to Bates, she said, 'He's right.'

Encouraged by this, Vivalla urged them back to the window, where he and Bates pushed out the burning frame, creating a space above the narrow sill through which both Anna and Bates might pass more easily. Upright, they stood only a foot lower than the ceiling, and they were forced to crouch to avoid the new cloud of smoke which had already collected there.

Anna retrieved the knotted sheets and fastened them around her waist. As she climbed into the opening ready to be lowered, the jet of water reappeared from below, and with it another cheer from the crowd.

'Your public awaits,' Vivalla said, paying out the sheets, anchored by Bates as far back in the room as the encroaching flames would now allow him to stand. As the sheets took the strain, both men knew that they would not hold her. Anna crouched on the sill and then manoeuvred herself into a sitting position. Telling her to wait, Vivalla called down to the men below to turn their hose on her, and on any flames from either side which threatened to reach her. He indicated to others what they were about to attempt and for a path to be cleared through the ashes below. Men with shovels ran forward and began digging in the embers, quickly overcome by the heat, their places filled immediately by other volunteers rushing forward from the crowd.

'They're waiting,' Bates told Anna, kissing her and holding her shoulders, knowing now that if she took fright at the last moment, he would release the sheet and push her out. She held out her legs and arms into the jet of water, and when she was ready she closed her eyes, half turned, and let herself fall free of the sill. The sheets took the immediate strain, but it was clear that they would not hold for more than a few seconds.

'Quick!' Vivalla shouted. 'As fast as you dare without letting her drop.'

Bates let the sheets run through his hands, applying only the slightest of braking motions. Vivalla watched Anna go down, and when she was only five or six feet above the ground, the sheets parted and she fell. In the crowd someone screamed, and feeling the sheets go so suddenly slack, Bates shouted, 'No!' and ran to the window to see for himself what had happened.

Beneath them, Anna had fallen into a cleared space among the embers. She rose quickly and was helped out of them by two of the men with shovels.

'She did it!' Bates cried out. 'She's down! She's out!'

The crowd cheered with him, and once clear of the mounds of burning wreckage, Anna turned and waved, then cupped her hands to her mouth and called up to them.

Vivalla searched among those who rushed forward to help her to see if anyone else from the Museum had also made it down to safety. He saw no one, but kept his disappointment from Bates, who was now gathering in the sheets and at the same time trying to push the bed away from the window, the mattress of which was already alight.

'You next,' Bates said, wrapping the sheets beneath Vivalla's arms. Vivalla made no effort to free himself.

'Even if I'd gone down first and found a ladder you'd have smashed it with the first foot you put on it, you oversized oaf,' he said.

'Perhaps,' Bates said. 'Tight enough? You're such a shrimp you could get all the way to the ground without ripping anything.'

'I could jump and land without the slightest effort. I've fallen from stilts higher than this in the past.'

Bates pushed him to the window. 'Best get out of the way because I'll be coming down directly behind you. Stay where you are and you can have the honour of breaking my fall.'

'Only after you'd broken my back first.'

The two men held each other briefly and then parted.

'Don't do anything foolish, you hear,' Vivalla said pulling himself out on to the window ledge.

'Such as?' Bates said, and before Vivalla could answer, he pushed him firmly over the lip, stepping back and steadying himself, taking up the slack as the sheets ran through his hands.

There was considerably less strain this time, and Vivalla was lowered all the way to the ground at the same even, steady pace. When the sheets slackened, Bates looked out to see him free himself and follow Anna through the wreckage to the safety of the watching crowd. A second cheer went up, and Bates waved out to them.

Then, behind him, the floor beneath the bed suddenly gave way and the bed fell through, taking with it what remained of the furniture and the last of the wedding presents. Bates watched as the polished wooden case of his musical orange slid from the cabinet and disappeared.

Seeing this sudden rush of flame behind him, the crowd below began calling for him to get out, to save himself, and the water from the hose was once again aimed into the rapidly disintegrating room.

'We've lost it all,' he said to himself, watching as the entire wall opposite him buckled and then dropped into what had once been the row of booths beneath. The door into his own quarters was torn from its hinges and he saw that the room beyond was now an inferno. Pieces of warm lath and plaster fell from the ceiling, and smoke poured down from above.

In his hands, the sheets themselves caught alight, and he quickly unwrapped them from around his waist, burning his hands and arms in the process.

He turned back to the window and pulled himself out on to the narrow ledge. Every other window on the ground floor was alight and panes of glass shot from them with the sound of bullets. He felt the wall shake beneath his weight. There was nothing now in the room to which he might have attached the sheets and lowered himself even part of the way to the ground.

Beneath him, he could see Vivalla waving for him to stay where he was for as long as possible. He was urging a group of men forward to the spot where Bates would land. They were reluctant to go, not only because of the weight they would have to cushion when Bates jumped, but also because of the burning timbers which were now steadily falling from above.

Bates shouted down for them to get back. He steadied himself and looked down at the crowd and at Anna. All around her people were waving and calling to him, but she herself stood calmly and silently, her arms held across her chest, looking up at him. She stood head and shoulders above them all, and he knew that if he were now to launch himself forward, then he would do so without taking his eyes from hers, and that he would fall and land seeing only her, regardless of whatever else happened to him. He reached out, holding her gaze, the connection between them as strong as any rope down which he might now slide to safety. Upon his back, his nightshirt began to smoulder in the heat.

'Anna,' he said, and pushed himself a few inches further forward. He felt the wall give way beneath him, and kicking back his heels he gained a little leverage and pushed himself forward. The burning wall fell with him and both he and the wreckage dropped in a single burning tangle to the ground.

The men below ran out from beneath it, and then as the timbers crashed around them, they raced back in an attempt to locate him and pull him free.

At the front of the crowd many people had turned away and covered their faces at the impact. Retrieving their hose, the firefighters rushed forward and directed the jet of water where they now believed Bates to lie buried.

Vivalla was the first to arrive at the spot, pulling at the charred and burning timbers and calling out for Bates to let them know where he was.

Anna stood without moving, her eyes closed, praying, her hands together with the tips of her fingers pressed into her lips.

Vivalla was the first to see Bates's arm as it pushed up through the smouldering mound and waved. He told the firefighters where to aim their hose and then he pulled at the arm and shouted until, from beneath his pyre, Bates answered him back. Then Bates's second arm rose, and between them the top of his head pushed free, black and bloody until the jet of water found it and soaked it. Vivalla went on calling to him and Bates went on answering. Vivalla waved back to where Anna stood and prayed, as she finally opened her eyes and stared directly at the mound from which Bates was now being swiftly freed. Tears drove clean white lines down her sooty cheeks, into her mouth.

And then, as Bates finally pushed himself upright and turned himself into the full force of the hose, the loudest cheer yet went up from the crowd. He rose like a statue, grey with ash. He walked towards Anna with little obvious difficulty, and when the hose washed clean his face there was a smile upon it and he was looking directly at her. He called to her and she covered her eyes and thanked God for his safe deliverance.

Vivalla helped him forward, and ahead of them the cheering crowd cleared a path as the two men made their way back to her. Then someone called out for them to run, and as they did so a large part of the burning front of the Museum peeled slowly away from its supports and fell gracefully towards them. They ran and cleared it with seconds to spare, as it sent a rush of hot air, ash and burning embers far into the watching crowd. Only Anna stood her ground, her arms held out to Bates and Vivalla as they continued towards her.

Reaching her, all three of them hugged each other and wept.

Looking back to the Museum, they saw that the fallen front had opened up the first three floors to the street, and that on every level the galleries and corridors were now alight. Floors and walls high above their own rooms were already gone, and even as they watched, the flames, spurred on by this new draught of air, drove into the spaces they had yet to reach and consume.

'We can't be the only ones out, surely,' Vivalla said. 'We can't be.'

Again he searched the crowd around him, but again he saw no one else from the Museum.

The firefighters pulled their extinguisher from the wreckage, and miraculously both the pump and the hose were still working, punctured in several places by the falling embers, but able to play a weakened jet of water upon the main entrance, the only part of the ground floor of the Museum still standing.

'Where are they?' Anna asked Bates. 'Where are they all?' There was no one to be seen through the sheet of flame into which they peered.

The Museum had been revealed to them like a dolls'-house set ablaze by some malicious child. The flames had reached all but the highest rooms and the roof, but there could be no doubt now in the mind of anyone watching that the building would be destroyed completely within the next half an hour at the very most.

Bates couldn't answer her, and so instead he pressed her closer to him and let her weep into his chest.

Looking to the east, he saw the first true rays of the rising sun pierce the sky above the buildings and the river and ocean beyond, and he gave thanks for the miracle of their deliverance.

*

Having left Vivalla, Henry Butler continued to make his way up through the blazing building, forcing open the doors of the living quarters on each floor as he went and calling out in the hope that he might still find someone who had yet to escape. He called out too as he ran between the floors, negotiating burning corridors and stairways, frequently only a few steps ahead of the flames which followed him. He refused to stop trying, but at the same time he also doubted if anyone would hear him above the noise of the fire and the crash of the timbers which now fell all around him.

Both reason and what he had already seen told him to stop and turn back, but something else, something deep inside him told him to go on. His heart pounded in his chest as he ran.

He encountered other birds which had been sprung from their cages by the heat. For most he could do nothing as they flew blindly past him, but some, those like the minahs which could no longer fly on their scorched wings, he was able to put swiftly out of their agony.

Passing the entrance of one of the galleries, he glanced in and saw a running figure stumble and fall, his arms held out, his back, legs and head already alight, and burning with a ferocity which caused Henry Butler to cry out in horror and surprise. He ran into the gallery as the figure fell to its knees and then to the ground, clearly beyond salvation. He called out, uncertain of what he would be able to achieve even if whoever it was was still somehow miraculously alive. He pulled down a heavy drape with which to attempt to smother the flames, but as he threw this over the burning outline, the flames rose immediately through it and the figure beneath collapsed even further under the weight. Then Henry Butler saw the stream of burning liquid wax and realized what it was he'd been trying to save. He almost laughed in his relief and pushed himself away from the liquefied body. He could make no guess as to which of the famous figures had been destroyed, and leaving the rest of the gallery to burn, he ran on.

On the third floor he came across the cabinet of ants, the glass of which had recently shattered, spilling its inhabitants to the ground. Many had died instantly in the flames, and their singed bodies, reduced to ruby beads, gave off a bitter smell as he passed through them, crushing them in their hundreds and leaving a trail of bloody footprints behind him.

Having been forced to a halt by the chasm of the floor-less gallery ahead of him, he turned back and began to make his way to the rear of the building, hoping there to somehow attract Zip's attention and then to be hauled up on to the roof to join him. His last hope now was that the body of the fire might be extinguished before it destroyed the main structural supports of the Museum, and that the skin of the roof might remain suspended by these as the blaze beneath was finally defeated. It was a desperate chance and a feeble hope, but in the absence of any others, and with the stink of the ants and the smell of his own smouldering clothes in his nose, it was the only hope Henry Butler now had.

He left the burned-out gallery, and was about to cross the main corridor of the fourth floor, when he saw moving shapes at the far end through the smoke. There was an unexpected draught and the air around him seemed momentarily clearer. He called out. Someone answered him and he immediately recognized the voice of Bella-Grace Sprague. She was with Isaac, and he rushed forward to join them.

By then, all six of their children had been safely lowered to the alley below, where they had been released from the rope and escorted beyond the reach of the flames by one of the firefighters. Listening to Bella-Grace tell him all this, Henry Butler knew he had been right to persist. She had beaten back the flames in the corridor, and although they again threatened to burst in upon them from the rooms on either side, there was still sufficient clear air for the three of them to make their own escape down the rope.

Leaning out of the window, Henry Butler called up to Zip, who now knelt on the parapet above. He saw the bleeding weals across his arms and chest where the rope had burned him.

'How much longer?' Henry Butler called up to him.

'Not much.' Zip tested the tarred planking on either side of him. Smoke was already rising through it, and drops of molten pitch fell past Henry Butler like the dirty meltwater of thawing icicles.

'Just tell them to keep moving,' Zip shouted down.

Henry Butler pulled in a loop of the rope and started to attach it to Isaac Sprague. To his surprise, Bella-Grace stopped him.

'We're waiting on Herman, Tom and Cherry,' she told him firmly. 'They're still here?'

Bella-Grace explained to him about Herman's attempt to bring Tom and Cherry down from the attic room above. As she spoke, a door half-way along the corridor was blown open by the heat behind it and a tongue of flame swept directly across to the stairs leading up to the attic. Galvanized into action, Bella-Grace let out a loud cry and ran back to do battle, damp cloths wrapped around her forearms. It was vital that the stairway be kept clear if the three men above were to get back down to the rope and their own last chance of escape.

Instructing Isaac to remain at the window, Henry Butler ran to assist her. He told her to get herself and Isaac out, and that he would wait with Zip until Herman, Cherry and Tom appeared. He told her of his plan to go up to Zip, and in return she told him how poor she considered his chances of success to be.

'We get Tom, Cherry and Herman down,' she said. 'Then me, you and Isaac – he's no weight, the two of you could go down as one – can get ourselves down. Then Zip can fasten the rope to something solid up there and shimmy himself to the ground faster than a pedlar's monkey down a greased pole.' She flapped and kicked at the flames as she spoke, and everything she said reassured Henry Butler and allowed him to believe for the first time since rushing into the Museum that all of them might now escape with their lives.

'But you and Isaac could still go now and *I'll* wait for the others to come down,' he said.

Bella-Grace paused only briefly to look with contempt upon his own attempts to hold back the flames. 'And let all four of you fry like chittlins in a pan? No sir. I've got my six children out; now it's someone else's turn. And it's no good trying to get Isaac to agree with you because we're together in this.' She waved to Isaac, who waved back. 'You think I could go down that rope knowing that none of the rest of you might get the chance to follow me? Besides which, I'm the heaviest of the lot of you. If anyone ought to go down last, then it's me.' She turned back to the flames, against which she was evenly matched, and which were once again retreating ahead of her ferocious assault upon them. She pushed shut the open door from which they had sprung and stood for a moment to clear her chest and wipe her face.

'If you still want to do something useful,' she told Henry Butler, 'get up there and hurry that boy and them two niggers along. He's been gone a full ten minutes already.' It had been nearer two or three, but the passage of time had long since lost all meaning in the face of the flames.

Pulling his jacket over his head, Henry Butler ran up the stairs leading to the attic rooms.

'I'll keep it clear down here for you,' Bella-Grace called after him. 'Gets too hot to handle, I'll give you a yell. You hear it, you get yourself out. The niggers are probably overcome already – they don't have our staying power in these situations. Do what you can, but get the boy out. His chest's bad and he could have been out of here and breathing clean air long ago if he hadn't come back up to help us. You get him down safely on that rope and I'll gladly jump out and fly down.'

She heard him open the door and call down to her that there was already smoke up there, but as yet no flames that he could see. She heard him calling for Herman, and then went back to Isaac at the window. She unwound the damp cloths from her arms and rubbed at the scorch marks on her face and hands.

*

In the small attic room there was glass on the floor from the broken window and the rising smoke was making its first tentative curls beneath the door.

'Why they do that?' Tom said, sitting with his legs splayed, having tried to stand but finding himself unable to do so. Blood ran from the cut above his eye into the creases of his puzzled face, defining its ancient folds just as clearly as Cherry's rivers defined their valleys on his map. 'Why they do that?' he repeated.

365

'Accident, Tom. Just an accident, I guess.' Cherry had already smelled the approaching smoke, and having earlier ventured out into the lower corridors, he had also seen the flames far beneath him down the central stairwell. Fires burned upwards, he knew, and he and Tom were at the very top.

Then Herman had arrived to take them down to safety, alarming them both, but especially Tom – who was still confused about how the fire had started and what the crowd outside was waiting for – by describing to them the escape attempt they were about to make. Herman tore bandages from his chest to dress Tom's wound, and it became clear to him as he worked close to Tom's face that he'd been drinking for most of the day and the night and that he was as drunk as he'd ever been. Turning slightly from the smell, his eyes met Cherry's.

'You're perfectly correct in your assumption,' Cherry said. 'Old fool's been pourin' it back like he got a fire right inside of himself. He says we're gonna burn so he'd rather not be here when it happens. Took a slug or two myself. I'd get along to wherever it is he reckons he's goin', but I reckoned one of us had to keep a hold of his senses ready for when the time came to get out – hear that, Tom? – I said one of us got to stay calm and rational for when the time comes for us to get out. Don't want the whole city thinkin' we ain't up to what's expected of us. Not now. Not now the war's so close to wrappin' itself up and puttin' itself down in the history books. No sir, not now.' He spoke with little real conviction, tears in his eyes to match the tears in Tom's.

Tom mumbled his reply. 'Why they do that?' he said again.

'He thinks they're burnin' us out,' Cherry told Herman.

Herman tried again to impress upon them both the need to move swiftly and to get down to where Isaac and Bella-Grace were waiting for them at risk to their own lives.

'They don't like my playing?' Tom held out his hands as though about to start playing. 'Where's that piano?'

'Where it belongs, you old blind fool,' Cherry told him.

Outside, pieces of falling timber clattered against the broken window frame.

'See – they're still throwing!' Tom said, pulling out a bottle and taking a long drink from it.

Cherry watched him. 'You don't think he might have got the right idea, do you?' he asked Herman.

Tying off the bandages on Tom's head, Herman tried to pull

him to his feet. Tom stood, thanked him, and then fell, catching his bottle before it hit the ground ahead of him.

'Smoke,' Cherry said, indicating the vaporous outlines now rising through the gaps between the floorboards beside Tom's face.

'I thought the fighting was all over,' Tom said. 'Or perhaps the war's finally come to take a look at good old New York City before burning it down.'

'It ain't the war, Tom. War's nearly over.' It seemed impossible to Cherry that less than twelve hours had passed since he'd returned to the Museum with the momentous news of the fall of Atlanta.

'I'm bleeding, Hack.'

'Just a scratch, Tom. Just a scratch.'

Tom breathed deeply and said he thought he could smell the fire getting closer, and as Cherry looked down at him, the first slender blades of flame pierced the floorboards.

'Holy Bellacoola!'

'I admire that,' Tom said with a grin.

'What?' Cherry pulled a rug over the flames in an attempt to smother them.

'All this knowledge you're collecting for when the great day comes.'

'Might be here sooner than we think,' Cherry said, noticing with increasing alarm the further sudden spurts of smoke at the door.

'We've got to get him down the stairs,' Herman said, interrupting them. He was having difficulty breathing, and clutched his chest as he spoke.

They dragged Tom by his arms, but only succeeded in moving him a few feet before he fell free of them.

'Save yourselves!' he shouted, caught unawares by the move.

A piece of burning parapet swung down from above, smashing the remainder of the window and showering them all with glass.

Herman was cut on his forehead and both cheeks, and when he wiped his mouth his palm was smeared with blood.

'We're gettin' nowhere fast,' Cherry told him, helping him to pick the larger pieces of glass from his skin.

Above them they heard Zip run across the roof.

'He's checking out what happened,' Herman told them.

'Probably the angels come for me.' Tom smiled up at the ceiling. His lips were bleeding and he blew red bubbles as he spoke.

'Or the devil payin' a house call,' Cherry told him. 'Stand up. Stand up and show some gratitude for all Herman here is trying to do for us, you old fool.'

Herman checked the corridor outside. There was more smoke in it, and flames now showed beneath the doors along the far wall. He pointed these out to Cherry, who immediately made another attempt to get Tom to his feet.

Every breath he took now caused Herman to cry out in pain, and every cry opened wider the cuts on his cheeks.

Cherry's attempts to raise Tom alone were as unsuccessful as their joint efforts had been, and he dropped him with a loud knock back to the floor. He sat beside him and cradled his head in his lap.

'Thing is, Tom, I can't pull you out all by myself, and Herman here's hurtin' so bad he ain't scarcely capable of movin' himself.'

After a long silence, Tom said, 'That fire's coming at us awful fast, Hack. I reckon you and the boy ought to get on down and out of it.'

'Sure,' Cherry said, caressing Tom's bristly white hair. 'Sure, and run smack dab into the arms of that lovin' crowd.'

'Something sure riled them, and that's a fact.' Tom laughed and indicated for Cherry to lift the bottle to his lips.

'You're right – get myself out of here and all I'd become would be the answer to all their problems.'

'Mr Barnum protect you,' Tom said, lifting his lips from the bottle.

'Sure. And Mr Barnum's gonna have this place built bigger and better than it ever was. You see.'

Then Tom pushed him away. 'You ought to go now,' he said. 'This country's going to need clever niggers like you.'

'This country gonna need clever niggers like it always needed clever niggers. Clever niggers the sort that attract rope collars.' Cherry took the bottle from him and drank from it, screwing up his face at the taste. Retrieving it, Tom begin to sing.

'You go,' Cherry then told Herman. 'You can get down the stairs easy enough by yourself. I'll stay up here and keep the old fool company until they get all the flames put out. You can come back in and help us down when it's all over. Nobody's gonna miss us. This particular war might be over, but the next one that comes along will probably put us right back where we started from. Makes perfect sense. You go.'

Before Herman could answer him, there was a noise in the corridor outside, and Henry Butler appeared, calling to them. He ran into the room and told them there was still a way out for them, surprised by their apparent lack of urgency or fear.

'We know,' Cherry said. 'But Herman here's hurtin' real bad and I can't move Tom.'

'Is he injured?' Henry Butler asked, leaning over Tom, who was by now stretched out with his eyes closed.

'Bad enough,' Tom said when Henry Butler's face was only an inch from his own.

Henry Butler smelled the drink on his breath. 'That bad,' he said, sharing a glance with Herman.

'Bad as ever,' Tom said.

Henry Butler pulled Herman to his feet and pushed him through the door. Then he pulled Tom across the room and told Cherry to clear the way ahead of them. He tried lifting Tom up on his shoulders, but the weight was too much for him and the two of them collapsed.

He told Cherry to grab Tom's other foot, and together they dragged him out of the room feet first.

'We're going to do it, aren't we?' Herman said to him as they made their way along the corridor.

'I think so. If the roof holds, if Zip stays up there with his rope, if the alley wall doesn't catch alight and collapse, if the floor doesn't cave in.'

Beneath them they heard the loudest explosion yet, and the floors and the walls around them shook violently and boards sprang loose from their fixings.

'Something big gone,' Henry Butler said, stopping only briefly to ensure that the way ahead remained open to them.

It felt as though the heart had just fallen out of the Museum, and what Henry Butler now feared most was that without it the rest of the building would give up the fight and follow it down.

Beyond the staircase leading down to Bella-Grace Sprague, the end of the attic corridor was already ablaze, and Henry Butler saw with some alarm how secure a hold the flames had already gained on the ceiling directly beneath the roof. He told Herman to go down the stairs ahead of them and let Bella-Grace know they were coming. Herman went down. He called to her and then cheered as she answered him. She urged him to hurry, shouting that the flames had finally beaten her and were already burning at the bottom of the stairs.

Henry Butler and Cherry manoeuvred Tom into the confined space.

'You sure a weight for a blind old nigger,' Cherry told him.

'Then I'll lighten the load some,' Tom said, and taking several bottles from his pockets he laid them gently on the floor as he was hauled along.

Turning him into the staircase and seeing the flames below, the outline of Bella-Grace still beating at them through the smoke, Henry Butler told Tom to wrap his arms around his head.

'What you doin'?' Cherry asked him suspiciously.

'Ready, Tom?'

Without knowing what he was agreeing to, Tom said, 'Ready,' and pulling his knees up into his chest, Henry Butler positioned him at the top of the stairs and pushed him down.

Tom rolled smoothly from top to bottom, where his fall was broken by Bella-Grace Sprague, with whom he collided, sending her sprawling along the corridor.

Herman, Cherry and Henry Butler quickly followed him down. The ceiling to the stairway caved in as they reached the bottom and Henry Butler slammed shut the door to contain the falling wreckage.

Cherry helped Bella-Grace to her feet and she demanded to know why she hadn't been given some warning that a blind old nigger was being thrown down the stairs aimed directly at her.

Henry Butler saw immediately that the situation in the fourth-floor corridor had worsened considerably since he'd left it several minutes earlier. Half of it was now fiercely ablaze and the flames were moving towards the window with increasing vigour, drawn to it by the unavoidable draught it created. The way up and the way down were no longer open to them, and along its full length, right up to where Isaac waited at the window, the floor was already buckling and smoking from the heat of the blaze beneath.

Lifting Tom across his shoulders, he urged them all forward. Seeing the blood on Herman's face and chest, Bella-Grace picked him up and carried him like a child back to the waiting rope.

*

An hour after being woken by the clamour of the passing extinguisher, Barnum himself arrived at the Museum.

It had been his original intention, following the disruptions and disappointments of the previous few days, to stay away until after his daughter's wedding, and thus also prove to Charity that he was not the heartless profiteer she now believed him to have become. He intended spending the day walking around his home making complimentary and flattering remarks about everything he saw and was told. He would polish his speech for the wedding feast and practise his tears for when he finally stood at the altar and handed his daughter over, secretly imagining the glorious day when he was finally rid of all three of them.

That had been his intention, but, as always, the urgency and excitement of the crowd had proved too infectious, and after an hour alone in his room he had dressed and gone down, determined to investigate and to see what advantage might be gained from the fire.

Climbing into his carriage, he instructed the driver to move at only walking pace so that he might carefully compose more of his pamphlet on the blaze and so that the public at large, *his* public, might see him and know that he cared about what happened in the city.

The first few who spotted him cheered and ran alongside him. He thanked them and then urged them to hurry on ahead of him lest they miss out on whatever it was that drew them, and to pass the word that he was coming.

It was definitely a fire, the driver told him, indicating the distant column of smoke rising high and straight into the calm morning air.

Attracting the man's attention, Barnum said. ' "This great city of ours is once again seared to its heart by a vicious and uncontrollable arrow of flame, the very flame which daily threatens to . . . to . . ." '

'Strike fear into the heart of every decent, honest and hard-working citizen,' the driver suggested, quoting lines with which he was already familiar.

'Two "hearts",' Barnum said. 'Questionable grammatically, syntactically unsound.'

'Soul, then,' the driver said. 'Strike fear into the *soul* of every decent –'

'Just drive,' Barnum told him. 'And if we end up anywhere near the Museum, pull up; I'm going to make sure everything gets back on its feet and starts running smoothly again.'

'Into the *very* soul of every decent, honest and hard-working citizen,' the driver suggested and continued with the speech which, in all its essentials, ran parallel to Barnum's own.

Barnum sighed and took a deep breath of the fresh, intoxicating air, barely touched as yet by the fetid aromas off the rivers, but tinged already with the distant smell of burning – nothing overpowering, but something undeniably present and chilling, like a far-off scream on a peaceful day, or like the narrow black border around the clean white card announcing someone's death. Sniffing it, and hearing the ever-growing commotion ahead of them, he felt the hairs on his neck stiffen, as though someone had crept up behind him and whispered something terrible in his ear. He leaned forward and peered over the driver's shoulder.

Around them, the running spectators had thickened. Some were even making their way back from the blaze, their faces already blackened and their clothes scorched. A few stood and watched him drive past. He looked down at one woman and she lowered her head and crossed herself. Another saw him and fell to her knees, causing Barnum to stand and stare at her long after they had passed her by.

'Looks to be awful close to the Museum,' the driver called over his shoulder, and in that instant, his eyes still on the kneeling woman, Barnum knew. His legs gave way beneath him and he fell back into his padded seat and caught his breath. He tried to call out to tell the driver to stop, but the words wouldn't come.

'Cover your mouth with a cloth,' the driver called back, still without turning. Then he too stood in his seat and looked ahead of them over the heads of the crowd through which they were now beginning to pass. 'Holy Jesus!' he shouted and immediately reigned the horses to a halt. He turned to Barnum, his eyes wide and his mouth hanging open.

'The Museum,' Barnum said. He felt cold, then hot, then cold again. He signalled for them to go on, and as they began to move, everything around him disintegrated into an unintelligible kaleidoscope of sound, smell and movement with himself as its pivot. More people called out to him and ran alongside the carriage; others simply stood back and watched him pass, their glazed eyes already having witnessed the terrible calamity he had yet to even imagine.

Approaching where the crowd was at its thickest, the driver called out and the onlookers cleared a wide path to let them through. Then, as they neared the blaze, the horses took fright and tried to turn in their harness, making further progress impossible.

Barnum climbed down and continued forward alone, the crowd still parting ahead of him, everyone turning to watch as his legs turned to feeble stalks and then to lead.

He reached the front of the crowd just in time to see a large part of the cladding of the Museum fall slowly away in a single blazing sheet, and then to hear the solid explosion from within as something at its centre succumbed to the flames and collapsed. The first three letters of his name fell burning from the parapet.

Smoke billowed from almost every window, and steam rose in

plumes where the water from the hose still played upon the entrance. A bird flew from an upper window and glided in flames into the crowd like a failed rocket. Another, a flamingo, emerged and rose almost vertically, trailing smoke and losing feathers as it went, until it too finally lost its battle and plummeted to the ground.

One of the firefighters ran to Barnum and told him to stand back. When Barnum failed to respond, the man shook him until he came to his senses and the world around him stopped spinning, the full weight of its motion finally falling from his shoulders.

'Get back,' the man repeated. They were less than thirty feet from the entrance.

Barnum allowed himself to be pulled away. 'Where are they?' he said.

The firefighter looked at him for a moment and then left him. Barnum shouted out after him and then turned to the spectators standing around him with the same unanswered question. These too looked uncomfortable and began to edge slowly away from him.

Then Barnum heard someone calling his name, and he saw the figures of Bates and Anna Swan pushing through to join him. He called to them and held out his arms. Then he saw Vivalla, and looked beyond them for the others.

Anna was the first to reach him. She held him, his face at her waist, and tried to lead him away from the blaze.

'I thought you'd all perished,' he said. 'But praise God, here you are, alive and safe and —' He stopped speaking at the sight of the burns on Bates's arms, face and chest. Bates assured him they were not serious.

'We got out,' Vivalla said absently, staring into the inferno ahead of them, the flames of which were now high into the attic rooms.

'So where is everyone else? Someone taken them in? Where? Gordon Bennet already buying their stories, is he? Is anyone injured? Get my physician, nothing but the best.'

'We're the only ones,' Anna said.

'Don't let them go to the hospital. Take them to the Astor; I'll look after them there. Don't . . . don't . . .' He pulled free of her and looked up into her eyes. Anna nodded. 'You can't be,' he said. He turned back and looked into the heart of the fire. 'You can't be.'

'It's true,' Bates said, ready to grab him if he attempted to run forward again.

'So far,' Vivalla added. 'We're the only ones out so far. Henry Butler's still in there and Zip's up on the roof.'

'Henry Butler? Zip?' Barnum looked up, but could see nothing. 'How can anyone get out of that?' he said, immediately regretting that the thought had found a voice.

'It looks worse from the front,' Vivalla said, but without any real conviction. 'The rear and the sides may not yet be as bad.'

Barnum continued to stare in stunned disbelief, the world around him threatening to resume its spinning and pitch him into a merciful darkness.

And then, as the four of them stood together and tried to find some comfort in their shared hopelessness, a cheer went up from the crowd around them, and looking up Barnum saw one of the firefighters lead out two of the Sprague children from the alley. Anna and Vivalla ran forward to collect them, eager to hear from them how they had escaped, what was happening inside, who was still alive and what escape routes remained open to them.

A moment later, two more of the children were brought safely out through the falling timbers, and a minute after that the final two. They all clung to Anna and she lifted the four smallest into her arms. They told her of their descent tied to the rope, and for the first time since her own escape she began to have hope, to believe that there was still time for the others to get out, that they had all been fooled by the savagery of the destruction of the front of the Museum, and that elsewhere, further back, there were corridors and passageways along which the flames had yet to reach, along which those others were at that very moment making their own escape.

Urged by her, they moved through the crowd to a position where they might be able to see Zip above the alleyway, and perhaps help him with those being lowered to the ground. But as they approached the narrow entrance a section of high wall, complete with windows and shutters, fell forward and hid the alley from view as it burned, throwing up yet another column of smoke which also denied them any possibility of seeing Zip high above them.

It alarmed Anna that no one else had yet emerged from the alleyway after the appearance of the children.

Unnoticed, Vivalla left them, and moving deftly through the crowd he managed to slip past the firefighters and into the alley beyond, finding a slender gap into which the wreckage had not fallen. There was no one else waiting to be led out to safety, and no hanging rope. He called up, but no one answered him, and the rooftop high above him was obscured by smoke. He ran along the alley to the Ann Street entrance, where he kicked open the door leading to the basement and to the quarters of both Byron and Apollo.

He heard Apollo howling as he ran down the stone steps and into the chamber below. It was not the frantic, terrified howl of an animal with no other alternative but to howl, but rather the long steady howl of an animal participating in the events around him, a howl almost of celebration and joy. And when this ceased, the call was taken up by Byron, whose less spectacular grunting sounded considerably more painful and forced.

Having entered the building, Vivalla was surprised by the relative coolness of the chamber leading to the basement, by the fact that it was as yet untouched by the flames, and that only very little of what was taking place above it could be detected through the solid stone walls of the foundations.

He reached Apollo's room and pulled open the door. Apollo stopped howling immediately, leapt forward and licked him.

'Get out,' Vivalla shouted, but instead of dashing for the exit, Apollo ran to the door of Byron's sty and waited. Vivalla opened that too, and Byron, still in his maroon velvet suit, lurched forward with a squeal of joy. Attaching a rope to his collar, Vivalla gave the other end to Apollo and told him to lead Byron to safety. Hesitating for a moment, and glancing back at the shelves of highly combustible books which lined the walls of his sty, Byron allowed himself to be pulled out.

Seeing them safely away, Vivalla ran to the end of the chamber which led directly into the basement.

He felt the heat before he opened the door, and pulling it ajar only a few inches he saw the flames beyond.

Miraculously, the ground floor of the Museum had not yet collapsed, the flames apparently having raced high beyond it in search of less solidly constructed kindling; but all around the basement floor lay pieces of burning timber and shattered cabinets. The mermaid had burned into an even more grotesque and twisted parody of a living creature, and the glass of all the cabinets had long since shattered.

And through it all, Vivalla saw that the great tank at the centre of the room was still intact. Steam rose from it, and occasionally the scum at its surface bubbled in the heat, but it had as yet suffered no real damage in the blaze. It was cracked in many places and water dripped from it to evaporate in the ashes which surrounded it, but it still stood in one piece and was held together by its supports.

As he watched, the water within it swirled and he saw the

hippopotamus materialize in the gloom and look about him, its nose pressed to the glass. Even if he'd been able to smash one side of the tank completely, there would have been no way the creature could have squeezed itself through the stone arch of the doorway into the chamber beyond or then negotiated the narrow passage leading to the exit Byron and Apollo were now approaching. It rubbed its nose up and down, revealing its gums and its banana-like teeth. It looked straight out at Vivalla and a line of bubbles rose from its mouth.

Behind him, Vivalla heard Apollo barking, insisting that he too should get out of the basement.

As though fully aware of the dilemma with which it now presented Vivalla, the hippopotamus nudged the glass for a final time, closed its eyes and withdrew into the murky water from which it had appeared. Then something fell behind the basement door, slamming it shut in Vivalla's face and sending a solitary disembodied flame into the chamber beyond. Turning, he ran back to where Apollo and Byron were waiting for him.

Back outside, Barnum had passed the Sprague children into the safety of the crowd, and was once again as close as he dared approach to the Museum, his gaze fixed on the entrance to the alley, from which he expected to see the others emerge unhurt at any moment. Bates and Anna stood beside him.

In the adjoining arcade the Siamese elephant began to trumpet as the wind changed direction and the first burning embers were blown in through the unglazed windows. Bates left them and shouted for volunteers to help him lead the animal out to safety. A dozen men ran with him to the arcade.

Barnum was about to clasp his hands and offer up a prayer, when another hand clasped his shoulder and a voice shouted loudly into his ear, chilling him more deeply than his first uncertain smell of the smoke had done. He didn't need to turn to know whose voice he was hearing, whose hard and clutching hand he now felt upon his shoulder.

'Hallelujah!' shouted Jeremiah Bergh, and around him a fanfare of trumpets rose above the noise of the crowd, momentarily silencing it.

Barnum closed his eyes and tried to shake the sound from his head.

'Witness it, Barnum, and witness it well,' Bergh yelled, holding aloft a Bible, which he threatened to bring down upon Barnum's head. 'Witness your walls of Jericho, and see how easily and willingly they come tumbling down in the face of the Lord's wrath. See how they crash to the ground! Witness it, witness it and remember! Witness it and tremble in your boots before the awesome power of the Almighty Himself!'

Barnum looked up to see the final three letters of his own name swing loose from the parapet and then fall.

'Sodom and Gomorrah!' Bergh screamed. 'And the Lord sayeth unto all that was evil, the very fires of hell will find passage to the surface of the earth and will consume there all that is unholy, all that is temptation, and all that shall distract mankind from his righteous path through life. Hell, Barnum! The flames of hell! Hell! Hell! Gaze upon them in awe and confess your sins. Beg forgiveness for your life of fraud and folly before it is too late!'

Barnum looked on, transfixed, mesmerized, speechless. All around him, Bergh's trumpeters continued to blow, pointing their instruments directly at him until every one of their notes pierced him like an arrow. Then Bergh took his hand from Barnum's shoulder and left him, parading into the crowd with his Bible and his prophesying, followed by his legion of trumpeters, determined that everyone should understand the exact and terrible nature of the retribution which was being meted out to Barnum, retribution that he, Jeremiah Bergh, had long since predicted and called down upon him.

Then Barnum was grabbed again from behind, and turning with his hand formed into a fist, he saw Greenwood, who had only just arrived.

'Are they out?' he said.

'Butler's in there,' Barnum said absently. 'They saw him go in.'

'It's madness,' Greenwood said.

Above them, the highest of the flames finally broke through to the roof.

'Zip's still up there,' Anna told Greenwood, pulling his hand from Barnum's shoulder.

'It's absolute madness. We ought to get clear. The whole thing is going to come crashing down at any second!'

Anna knew that he was right, but refused to side with him against Barnum in this, his darkest hour. She reached down and held Barnum's arm.

'He's probably right,' she said.

'He's always right,' Barnum said, still absently. 'But we can't leave now. We can't just walk away without knowing.' He looked up at her imploringly. 'What about Elizabeth? What about Fortuna. What about –'

377

'Elizabeth!' Greenwood shouted. 'Is she still in there?'

'Zip will do what he can,' Anna said, wishing they could see through the flames and the smoke and at least gain some idea of how the rescue attempt was progressing.

'For all we know,' Greenwood said, 'they might all be dead already. Look for yourself. What chance does anyone still stand in that place?' He stopped himself.

Lower down, on the ground and first floors, there were signs that the worst of the blaze had passed. Inside, supports and parts of walls, floors and staircases were black and smouldering, but still relatively intact as the fire continued above them, driven up now by the breeze blowing in off the river.

Everyone looked up as a snake, one of the pythons, threw itself in a rippling, steaming curve from an upper window, tying itself into a knot as it fell to the ground, where it unwound itself and tried to escape, crackling and bubbling in its agonizing death throes. One of the firefighters stepped forward with his axe and chopped at it until each of its quivering pieces was finally still.

Barnum turned away from it, a look of utter revulsion on his face having seen it so soon after both Bergh's and Greenwood's unthinkable predictions.

All three of them were distracted by a further cheer from the crowd as Vivalla, Byron and Apollo emerged unharmed from the clutter of smoking rubble at the entrance to the alley. Someone ran forward to take the rope from Apollo's mouth, and Apollo ran on his hind legs into the crowd, where he was cosseted, petted and fed from a dozen pockets. Byron followed close behind him to seek his own reward.

Vivalla told Anna what he'd seen in the basement, but neither of them mentioned this to Barnum. He then ran to help Bates with the elephant as it emerged from the arcade, the dozen men who held it having difficulty restraining it as it pulled them in its panic into the crowd.

Seeing them, Barnum shouted for it to be released, standing and watching as it raced clumsily and noisily in a straight line along Broadway.

Jeremiah Bergh and his marching trumpeters returned, and hearing them was as much as Barnum could now stand. He clutched at Greenwood's arm and said, 'The devil, all this, the devil. It's a judgment.'

Greenwood glanced at Anna, who shook her head.

Barnum looked up, his face vividly illuminated, his tears like flames themselves as they rolled down his cheeks.

Jeremiah Bergh's trumpeters passed close behind them, deafening them for a moment.

A second writhing serpent launched itself from an upper window and glided sizzling to the ground below, where it too was quickly axed.

'It's a judgment,' Barnum repeated. 'A judgment.'

In the distance, Jeremiah Bergh's trumpeters turned and began to march back towards him, Jeremiah Bergh at their head, still loudly singing the praises of the Lord and still waving his Bible high in the smoky air.

*

Having left Bartola, Maximo and the Albino family as far behind her as she dare, Elizabeth pushed open the third and final door. She opened it slowly, protecting her face, afraid that she might once again be greeted by a rush of flame or blast of searing air. They were on the second floor now, and if this staircase was clear then they might be able to move directly down to the first. It was a long, private staircase, double the length of many of the others, but considerably narrower, allowing only single-file access. She still held the bone with which she had killed the burning parrot, and she raised it ahead of her as the door slowly opened. Behind her the Albino children were crying, and from above and all around them came the sounds of falling timber and shattering glass. By some miracle they appeared to have passed down through the main body of the blaze as it moved upwards, somehow finding the last clear route through it as its separate flaming tentacles now met and joined above them.

A rush of warm air rose from the staircase, but cooler than Elizabeth had anticipated, and looking beyond the door into the poor light below, she saw that their luck was still with them, and that despite patches of smouldering timber and buckled walls where the heat on either side had forced them in, the staircase itself was not ablaze and its distant exit still secure.

Elizabeth offered up a silent prayer. Something heavy fell down the full length of an adjoining staircase, and the sound of its descent as it hit each step reminded her of the drum of distant hoofbeats across an open plain. She patted her chest to reassure herself that she still wore Crazy Horse's pendant.

Waiting until the warm air had risen from the narrow space, she called for the others to join her. Looking down into the same

379

enclosed space, they were afraid of the darkness as much as what might still lie beyond, but she could not allow them to take with them even the smallest torch for fear of igniting the gases which might have collected, or of causing the already overheated air to burst into flame. She formed them into a line, distributing the children among the adults, and signalling to Bartola and Maximo the new responsibility with which they were now entrusted. She ensured also that all their faces were protected by damp cloths. Moving ahead of them, she doubted if they would be as fortunate upon reaching the bottom doorway as they had been at the top of the stairs; she could not believe that what lay beyond had not by then been completely destroyed by the flames. If she had been able to descend alone then she would have done so, knowing that there was every likelihood of the flames beneath leaping up into the confined space once the lower door was opened.

Briefly encouraging them with a few brave words and a flourish of the bone, she led them down, testing each step before committing her full weight to it, and when they were all in a line of descent she called back for the upper door to be closed, plunging them into an even greater darkness, but also reducing the risk of a sudden draught sucking up the flames below.

Half-way down she felt the staircase sway, like a flimsy gangplank supported only at either end, and she guessed that the solid joists beneath it had already collapsed. She called for them to stop moving and went ahead of them. The stairs continued to sway, causing the children to cry out, but they did not appear to Elizabeth to be in any imminent danger of collapse themselves, and she called back for them to resume their descent.

The ceiling of the staircase was little more than a foot above her head, and she could raise her elbows and touch the walls on either side of her. All around her the blistering varnish bubbled and burst with the sound of eggs being dropped.

Two-thirds of the way down there was a further sudden lurch, the staircase dropped, and all of them lost their footing and were thrown down. When the movement ceased and the stairway seemed once again secure, Elizabeth checked to ensure that no one had been injured. There were cuts and bruises, and burns where they had held out their hands to steady themselves, but nothing any more serious.

Above them, a flame appeared beneath the upper door, and it swung open, loosened by the jolt it had received. They all looked up and saw it and turned back to Elizabeth for reassurance. She guessed that more of the joists had fallen from beneath the staircase, and that it was now in effect suspended from above by whatever was still holding it there. It hadn't fallen sharply enough for it now to be resting on the ground floor, and so there must still be something beneath them, she reasoned, which was propping it up.

As she continued down, the stairs rocked from side to side, and she knew that whatever it was which held them from below was not particularly secure, and that it too might collapse at any moment. She kept all this to herself, telling them to follow her as closely as possible, and again silently praying that whatever lay beyond the lower door might still afford them a chance of escape.

By then the top door was fully ablaze, swinging with every movement of the stairs and creating the dangerous draught she had hoped to eliminate. There was little danger of this fire overtaking them, but equally, there was no way now she could prevent or even slow down the rush of flame which might be waiting for them below. Seeing the burning door and the corridor beyond, she was convinced that Henry Butler and everyone else still trapped above them had now perished.

Reaching the lower door, she prodded it with the bone, calling to the others to turn away and cover their faces. The frame was alight, and the wood around it already black and split, but ahead of her there was nothing, only an unfamiliar space, clouded with ash, burning at its edges, and with its floor alight. The corridor at the bottom of the stairs had been completely destroyed, as had the continuation of the staircase at the far side which would have taken them down to street level. The fire, it seemed, had moved around the sealed staircase in which they were now stranded, consuming everything it touched.

She let the door swing open, and edging carefully down to the last step she looked out over the wreckage below. As she'd expected, the staircase was now held from above, and was supported at its lower end by a single charred and smoking upright timber, which looked to Elizabeth as though it might collapse at any moment and pitch them all vertically into the mounds of glowing ash and burning timber above which they were now helplessly suspended.

Then, without warning, the step upon which she was standing suddenly gave way beneath her and she threw herself back to prevent herself from falling. She was grabbed by Bartola and Maximo, who had made their way forward to look out with her over what now confronted them.

Pressing herself almost flat to peer out, Bartola became suddenly excited, tugging at Elizabeth's sleeve and jabbing into the devastated space below. Looking to where she pointed, Elizabeth saw a sudden disruption in a pile of ash, and a burst of steam which scattered embers all around it. Tracing this back, she saw a jet of water curving aimlessly from side to side. She couldn't see through the ash and steam to its source, but she knew that it must be coming from outside, and because it was above the mounds of ash, she guessed that at the other end of it there must be men.

She called out, and for a moment the stream of water faltered in its movement. It rose towards her, but fell away in another cloud of steam before resuming its course. She shouted again, unable to contain her relief and excitement that they had at last made contact with someone else, and that here, against all hope and expectation, a final chance of escape was reaching out to them.

She yelled a third time, this time accompanied by Bartola and Maximo, and beyond the water she saw the outline of a man, his hands covering his head, rush into and then immediately back out of the space below. Her relief and excitement were infectious, and behind her a small desperate cheer went up from the others on the staircase. From below someone called back up to her and she waved everyone to silence: a man's voice.

'Up here! Up here!' she yelled.

In response, the jet of water rose once again towards the hanging doorway, scattering the ash and burning timber beneath and spraying her with a warm grey sludge.

She continued calling, and beneath the line of the jet a second man dashed briefly into the space below and searched around for her, calling down the water upon himself every few seconds. It was another of the firefighters, and when he was directly beneath them he looked up and saw them. He crossed himself and stared in disbelief for a few seconds before calling up to ask her how many others there were with her. This, too, surprised him, and he stood for a few moments longer, unable to bridge the final gap between them, between the hanging door and the Museum entrance behind him.

It was clear to Elizabeth from the look upon his face, and from the burning timbers which continued to fall all around him, that they were still far from safe, and that they had left to them no more than a few minutes in which to get down from the hanging staircase.

Then a larger piece of burning wreckage fell, the jet of water swung wildly to one side, and the man ran back to the entrance. The water returned a few seconds later, but was as yet not powerful enough to reach and douse the staircase, capable only of soaking the ash and wreckage beneath it into sodden mounds, thereby offering some slight protection if the staircase collapsed without warning.

If they could only somehow get to the ground, Elizabeth knew, then there was a good chance that they might also be able to make it through the piles of burning wreckage to the Museum entrance, the doorway of which still appeared to be intact, standing alone and exposed amid the charred and fallen remains of the walls which had once stood around it. She knew that a ladder stood in the flames and propped against the staircase would almost certainly bring the whole structure down and trap them within it, where they would be crushed and then either asphyxiated or burned alive inside their upright coffin.

As she waited for the firefighters to return, there was a noise and then movement in the burning corridor above. The staircase swung violently again, but again stopped short of collapsing, and turning and moving up through the others, Elizabeth heard Fortuna calling out to anyone who might still be able to hear her. With her were René and their son. Elizabeth shouted back to her, warning them to move slowly and carefully down the staircase, calling out again as they came into view through the poor light and gathering smoke.

Their faces were blackened and their clothes smouldering. Fortuna held her son, and René clung to the portrait he had saved. Fortuna's beard and hair were badly singed, and René held a handkerchief to a deep cut on his shoulder, around which the cloth of his jacket had been burned away. They were in a worse state than those already on the stairs and Elizabeth helped them to get forward into the clearer air and spray at the bottom.

Fortuna and René saw immediately what had happened, where they now were, and how close they too had so suddenly and unexpectedly come to getting out. There were tears of relief on Fortuna's cheeks.

Elizabeth told them of the contact she had managed to make with the men outside.

'Then one of us must jump down, take his chances below, and attempt to re-establish contact,' René said. 'A path might be found – *must* be found – and if the water is played over us as we go then we may all yet escape without any further serious injury.'

Elizabeth looked at Fortuna, who nodded in agreement with her husband.

'I'll tell the others,' Elizabeth said, relieved that her burden was at last being shared, but as she turned to signal to them the stairs lurched again, more violently, and unable this time to steady herself in the overcrowded space, she cried out and fell backwards through the open doorway. Seeing her disappear so unexpectedly, Bartola and Maximo both screamed. Acting quickly, René held them back, and clasping Fortuna's hand he leaned forward to see where Elizabeth had fallen, ready to jump himself when he saw her.

She lay on her back in one of the grey mounds below, and at first he feared she may be unconscious and in danger of catching alight. The edge of her skirts lay dangerously close to a small fire beyond the reach of the hose. He called down to her, and then to the two men who ran into her from the entrance. Directed by them, the jet of water sought her out, located her and soaked her, reviving her until she was able to push herself upright and call out for the firefighters to remain where they were. They ignored her, reached her and tried to lead her out to safety, but she pulled free of them and shouted up for Fortuna to throw down her son.

Without hesitation, Fortuna held him over the lip of the stairs by his arms and let him drop before he had time to realize what was happening and perhaps try to struggle free. Elizabeth caught him and passed him to the nearest of the two men. The hose was turned upon them and the second man, upon being handed the child, ran quickly through the wreckage to the entrance.

Beyond this, Elizabeth saw daylight for the first time, and she heard the cheer of the crowd as the man emerged with the child in his arms.

'Another!' she shouted up, seeing also for the first time how close to total collapse the staircase now was, its upper end burning fiercely around the final supports by which it was still precariously held.

The youngest of the Albino children was thrown down to her, followed almost immediately by Fortuna, who landed amid the embers of one of the fires and called for the hose to be turned upon her. She had jumped to lessen the burden on the ever-weakening staircase.

Above them René now stood at the door and moved the others forward, helping them to drop when he saw that those below were ready to catch them and get them out. Fortuna took Elizabeth's place, and Elizabeth joined the two men in a chain reaching to the entrance.

Vivalla and Captain Bates ran in from outside, and both Fortuna and Elizabeth shouted to them and then wept at the simple joy of seeing them alive.

The Albino 'parents' were next down, and they too joined the chain, being soaked and then positioned by the doorway.

The first floor had burned away completely, but above this large parts of the upper floors were still blazing fiercely, threatening to collapse at any moment. When that happened, those below would receive no warning and would without doubt be crushed and killed beneath the wreckage.

Bartola and Maximo were next down, and they ran from Elizabeth to Bates to Vivalla before being led out to the waiting crowd and a further loud cheer. Anna Swan was waiting for them and she took them back with her to where Barnum and Greenwood were watching the proceedings.

Back inside, the firefighters pointed out to Elizabeth that one of the top supports was about to give way, and that when it did the staircase would lose what little stability it possessed and drop to rest at a new angle, twisting the hanging doorway into a diamond shape in which no one would be able to stand.

Elizabeth relayed this news to René, but before she had finished, the support gave and the staircase dropped and swung wildly. One of the remaining Albino children was thrown from it into the wet mound below and was immediately pulled clear by Bates. Then, unable to withstand this violent exertion, the lower support also collapsed, causing the stairs to drop again, this time coming to rest almost vertically and putting a further unbearable strain on the single support which still held them to the blazing floor above.

Fortuna and Elizabeth ran out from beneath the hanging structure. If it fell now then everyone still on the stairs would be trapped inside a narrow funnel, into which burning wreckage would then fall from above, and from which there would be no possibility of escape.

René threw down his portrait, which landed safely beside Elizabeth, and then wedged his legs across the hanging entrance so that the remaining three Albino children would not be thrown out without at least some chance of being caught below.

Elizabeth caught the first and handed him on. But she stumbled with the second, exhausted and dazed and unable to push herself back to her feet. Fortuna dragged her to safety and told Bates to take her outside. Elizabeth fought against this, waiting until she saw the last of the children safely down, and until René alone remained to be saved.

They were all distracted by a loud splintering sound, and everyone looked up to see a wide gap appear in the floor high above, through which a shower of embers rained down upon them. A cabinet crashed through and shattered beside Vivalla, and the glowing skull of one of the dinosaurs dropped like a boulder, only narrowly missing Bates.

Fortuna shouted up for René to jump and save himself, but as he did so, his foot caught where he'd wedged it against the wall, and he hung upside down, unable to reach back up and free himself. Fortuna screamed and held up her hands to him, able just to grasp him and attempt to pull him loose. Bates ran to help her, supporting René's shoulders as he hung suspended. He told Fortuna to stand clear, and clasping René around his chest, he pulled until the obstruction holding his foot finally gave way and the two men fell backwards to the ground. And as René came clear, so finally did the staircase. Glancing up just in time to see it drop, Bates wrapped his legs around René and rolled with him to one side. The staircase fell like a solid trunk, stood upright for a moment and then swayed, threatening to fall in a direct line with the chain of rescuers below, and possibly to smash into one of the main supports, bringing the remainder of the Museum down upon them all.

Urging the others to run, Bates pulled René to his feet and ran with him under his arm to the entrance and the jet of water which continued to play all around them.

Running blindly, they were outside before they even realized it, and only seconds ahead of the falling column, which crashed down behind them, bringing with it not one, but two of the floors above, and sending a rush of flame and smoke high up through the Museum roof.

The crowd cheered again, and the small group stood together for a moment looking back before being led to safety. Bartola and Maximo ran to join Elizabeth and afterwards refused to be parted from her. She was exhausted, but declined all offers of help.

She walked with them past Barnum and told him she was sorry for his loss. He told her he'd been praying for her salvation, and then listed for her those yet to escape. She held out little hope for them, but as she was about to leave him he pointed to the roof, and looking up she saw Zip in a clearing between two columns of smoke, vividly outlined against the brightening sky. She called up to him, but he couldn't possibly have heard her. He ran along the parapet, quickly inspecting which parts of it were still intact and which parts threatened to give way and pull the roof from under him; by then the flames had already reached the parapet above the alley.

Barnum told Elizabeth that the Sprague children were out, that the elephant was free, and that the two chimps had been spotted swinging among the machinery in the offices of the *Herald* behind them. She heard him, but her eyes remained on Zip.

Greenwood joined them and asked her if she'd seen anything of Henry Butler. She looked at him without speaking and then walked past him to where Anna Swan was waiting for her with a blanket. Her eye stung, and around it her hair had been singed back almost to her scalp. Turning away from the blaze she took a deep breath, raised her chin, and with Bartola and Maximo on either side of her, she walked slowly into the waiting crowd.

*

From his precarious vantage point high above everything, Zip looked down on the mass of people below. He saw those who had already escaped from the Museum, and for each one who emerged he gave a prayer of thanks. He knew better than any of them how little time the Museum had left to stand.

The sun had fully risen above the East River and it now shone directly upon him, casting the streets below into deep shade and throwing his own long shadow into the flames which had already pierced the centre of the roof, and which now burned with a new ferocity as the pitch with which it was coated melted and occasionally exploded, throwing burning black pearls in every direction. His exposed arms, back and chest were dotted with burns, but he had neither the time nor the means to do anything about the pain these caused him other than to brush the tar from his skin and endure it.

People were calling up to him, but he could hear little above the rasp and crunch of the flames below. He saw Elizabeth pause and look up at him, just as Anna had turned and looked, and he was grateful to have seen them, for them to be safely away from the fire, and for them to know where he was; he no longer felt alone on the roof.

The blaze now racing up towards him had long since passed high beyond the reach of the men with the extinguisher, and following the dramatic escape of Bates with René, he shouted down in an attempt to get them to direct the jet of water at the entrance to the alleyway. Below, Bates saw him and understood, and he conveyed his meaning to the firefighters, all of whom responded immediately, finally

387

abandoning the Museum entrance, which had resisted the flames for so long, to be at once overcome and destroyed.

Zip alone knew that everyone still trapped in the Museum was waiting at the fourth-floor window, ready to be lowered on his rope, and as he waited for Henry Butler to take charge of the rescue attempt from the corridor, he ran across the roof to determine where it had already been breached, where it was near to collapse, and where it remained sound enough for him to operate from if an alternative lowering point needed to be found. What he didn't know was that the corridor in which Henry Butler, Herman, Bella-Grace, Isaac, Tom and Cherry were now all waiting was their last chance, and that if the roof or parapet directly above the window gave way, then there would be no hope for any of them. The best they might then expect would be a leap into the smoking darkness of the alley, praying as they dropped that their seventy-foot fall might somehow be broken, and that if it were, then a passage into the clearing at the front might still remain open to them. It was an alternative so desperate and with so little chance of success that no one – neither Zip on the roof nor those inside – dared give it voice.

At the front and the south side of the Museum the parapet was already alight in parts and smoking in others, and kicking at several lengths to test them, Zip was alarmed to see them fall so easily away, leaving gaps through which the extent of the fire in the attic rooms beneath was only too obvious. Above the alley, however, the rail still held, and having gained some idea of the condition of the rest of the roof, he ran back to his rope and called down for those below to hurry. He took up the heavy coil and wrapped it once again around his chest and shoulders, still bleeding from where it had cut into him as he'd lowered the children.

Beneath him, he watched Henry Butler help Herman out on to the ledge. It had been impossible, as with the others, to fasten the rope around Herman's chest, and so Henry Butler had devised a sling, in which Herman sat, the rope passing beneath him in a cradle and then up into a loop through which he held his hands. He sat and looked up at Zip as he steadied himself and then began to let the rope pay slowly out over his arm. He tried to call up to him, but his pain was too great and his words choked. Instead, Zip shouted down, telling him to take care of himself at the bottom, to collect as much liquor as possible from the crowd, and to await his own eventual descent.

Positioning himself in the window frame, Henry Butler indicated to Zip that there were moments when he could relieve him of the strain of the rope if it became too great for him. Zip called down that there would be no need, and that all that mattered now was that everyone should be lowered as swiftly as possible. A succession of flames had risen unexpectedly towards the rear of the Museum, attacking the parapet in that quarter. Prior to their appearance, Zip had believed this sheltered side of the building to be relatively sound, but he saw from these new flames that he had been mistaken, and that accordingly his own chances of escape had now been suddenly and drastically reduced.

The rope slackened, and in the alley below Herman released himself and sent up the signal at which the rope was quickly retrieved.

'Bella-Grace next,' Zip called to Henry Butler, pausing only to skim the sweat and blood from his face and arms.

Inside, Bella-Grace refused to go. She pushed Tom forward, saying again that she was too heavy, that she might be too much for the rope, the parapet or Zip to bear, and that those who stood a better chance ought to be given it ahead of her. There was no time for argument, she told Henry Butler, and pulling in a loop of the rope she folded it around Tom, who was still drinking and singing to himself, and who submitted to everything she did to him without dissent. Cherry slapped his face and tried to explain to him what he needed to do upon reaching the ground, but it was clear to them all that Tom was by then too drunk to understand. What was even clearer to them was that if he didn't immediately release himself from the rope then he would jeopardize all their chances.

'You go with him,' Henry Butler told Cherry. 'We fasten him to the rope and you cling to him. It might mean a quicker descent, but you should get down all right.'

Before he could object to be lowered with someone who might be considered a drunken disgrace to his race, Cherry too was pulled to the window by Bella-Grace and his arms were folded around Tom.

'What's happening, Hack?' Tom said as he swung free of the building, and as Cherry let out a loud cry, his eyes firmly closed.

Henry Butler explained to Zip what they were doing, but even as he spoke, Zip began to pay out the rope and the two men dropped quickly into the half-light below, Cherry's cries matched only by Tom's carefree singing.

As he leaned out, Henry Butler felt something wet drip in a line on to his face, and believing it to be molten pitch he wiped it quickly away, only to discover that it was blood. He showed it to Bella-Grace and Isaac and they both shook their heads.

389

'You and him next,' Bella-Grace told her husband. She buttoned his nightgown to the neck. 'Get down there and get out to them children. They're Spragues, and good-looking and healthy; we don't want any of the Irish or Italians trying to adopt them or snatch them off for their factories thinking me and you have perished and gone to meet our Maker in here.' She licked her hand and smoothed back her husband's hair, cleaning the smuts from his cheek with her thumb.

Tom and Cherry reached the alley, Zip called from above, and the slack rope rose quickly back to the window. Then he shouted down for those still inside to wait for a few seconds while he ran to stamp out a small flame which had appeared only a few feet behind him. As he trod it out, he felt the whole area of roof upon which he was working sway beneath him. His hands were slippery with the blood running from his shoulders and he wiped them dry on his hairy pants before returning to the rope. There was a new note of urgency in his voice as he called down again for them to hurry.

Henry Butler was waiting in a sling, Isaac on the ledge ready to hold on to him.

Bella-Grace looked out and called up to Zip. 'You let these fall, pinhead, and I'm up there to throw you off after them with my own bare hands. That man's worth his weight in railroad shares. That might not be saying much – fifty-two pounds ain't everybody's idea of heaven right here on earth – but he's all me and them children have got. So you lower him nice and steady or you start praying for yourself. You hear me?'

Isaac Sprague looked up apologetically and then climbed out into Henry Butler's lap.

'Same goes for you, Mr Butler, sir. You cling to him like he was dear sweet life itself.'

Henry Butler promised he would, and as Zip took the strain and the rope snapped taut, Bella-Grace leaned out, kissed them both, and then turned to peer up at Zip to ensure he'd understood her. But Zip was leaning back from the edge and she couldn't see him; all she could hear was the sound of his laughter above the flames. It alarmed her to see how much of the parapet was now alight, and how it shook as Henry Butler and her husband were lowered. As she looked, a large piece of timber cladding directly above the window suddenly gave way and fell, missing her by inches as it plummeted down towards the two men below. She saw Zip's leg pulled over the edge and heard him cry out as he struggled to brace himself and to hold the rope as the support upon which he'd been standing also gave way. The rope dropped several feet and was then held. She heard Isaac cry out far below her, but knew that enough of the rope had already passed her by then for the two men to be almost at the ground.

Another piece of cladding fell, and as she ducked inside to avoid it she saw the rope swing loose. She immediately reached out and began to haul it back up, calling to Zip that she had it and for him to take care of himself.

Above her, Zip had lost the last stable length of parapet upon which to work. There was nowhere now for him to stand securely, to anchor himself and let out the rope. The flame he had stamped out rose again, much larger this time, and it ran across the roof towards him just as burning liquid might run across warm stone. He brushed at his smouldering pants and saw for the first time that they were soaked and matted from top to bottom with blood.

He called down to Bella-Grace to wait as he decided what to do and she answered him that she was in no hurry, no hurry at all. Her husband and her children were safe and so the two of them had all the time in the world. She too had realized what had happened before the wreckage hit the ground.

'Looks like it's just going to be me and you, monkey-man,' she called up.

Zip came back to the edge and leaned over to look down at her, the roof swaying dangerously beneath his weight.

'You think you can hold me?' she shouted. 'I doubt it. I'd get two inches over the edge and pull us both down.' She turned to look along the alley, and for the first time she saw the sun. 'Looks like a nice day coming up. Tell me, when do you last think Barnum ever had a crowd like this for one of his stunts?' She laughed at a dozen happy memories. Looking down, she imagined she could just make out the tiny skeleton of her husband glowing in the alley below.

Then, behind her, what little remained of the corridor suddenly erupted in a sheet of flame and the rush of hot air almost pushed her out. A length of the floor collapsed beneath her, shaking the window frame, and along the alley the whole side wall of the Museum began to burn. It became immediately clear to Bella-Grace that even if Zip had still been able to lower her, she would be unable now to go directly down from where she sat without being badly burned in the process.

Above her, however, Zip was not so ready to admit defeat, and seeing that she was already fastened to the rope, he searched desperately for some other way of securing his own end of that lifeline so that she might yet be lowered.

At the front corner of the building stood the stump of a flagpole, and this he knew to be firmly attached to one of the main supports. He ran to it and tested it. It seemed solid enough, and unwrapping as much of the rope as he dare from his shoulders he tied it to the pole and raced back to Bella-Grace to explain what he was about to attempt. She would have to let herself fall from the window, take her chances in the flames immediately below, and then swing free until she was directly beneath the pole and overhanging Broadway. The firefighters would be below her at that point, and if the roof and the flagpole held, there should be sufficient time for her to get within reach of their hose and then within a reasonable drop to the ground.

'A reasonable drop!' she shouted up. 'And in full view of all them folk and me only in my nightdress! You're trying to turn me into a laughing stock!'

'That's right!' Zip shouted. 'And when you're down, I'm going to leap straight down after you and claim one of your miserable squawking children as a reward.'

'You leave those children be,' she shouted back. She half turned to try and make him out above her, and as she did so, distracted for a moment from her perch on the window sill, Zip leapt with all his weight on the top of the exposed wall, shaking it and dislodging her. Bella-Grace cried out and fell, and as she disappeared, Zip ran back to the pole and grabbed at the rope, which was already being pulled out. He reached it and held it, and heard Bella-Grace scream as she swung in a wide arc through the alley below. He then saw her briefly as she swung out into the daylight above Broadway and the crowd. A loud gasp went up, then a cheer, and then a second gasp as Bella-Grace, having swung above their heads to the full extent of the rope, hung suspended for a moment and then swung back into the darkness and flames of the alley out of which she had so miraculously appeared.

Having held the rope, Zip braced himself against the almost unbearable strain, and as Bella-Grace swung back he was pulled with great force into the flagpole. He managed to wrap the rope around his arm, but then, as he lost his balance and collided with the pole, there was a loud crack, and in the second it took him to calculate what was happening, he thought the pole had snapped and that both he and it were about to be pulled over the edge with the next full swing Bella-Grace made. And then, after a further second of numbness, he felt a great and searing pain and was unable to prevent himself from screaming out as this rose through him, twisting every

392

bone and muscle in his body. Entwined by the rope against the pole, his arm had been broken above and below the elbow and now hung uselessly by his side, the rope still coiled around it. He struggled desperately to prevent himself from blacking out, and was able with his good arm to wrap more of the rope around the flagpole, slowing Bella-Grace's swinging and reducing her distance from the ground. In her own efforts to reduce the strain on the rope, Bella-Grace had tried to reach out to something to slow her down, but there were only flames to catch hold of. The upturned faces of the crowd below moved with her, few watching Zip as he struggled with both the rope and his efforts to maintain consciousness. He knew that if he passed out now, Bella-Grace would be left hanging, dangling helplessly in the flames which consumed the upper floors, and too high from the ground for her to release herself and drop. With her every uncontrollable movement a further spasm of pain shot through him. He looked down, and far beneath him the ground started to spin. He fought to focus on something and was able to pick out Henry Butler and Isaac being helped through the mounds of burning rubble to where Anna and Captain Bates awaited them.

On the end of the rope, Bella-Grace tried again to steady herself. She alone saw what had happened to Zip, and what he was now fighting against all odds to achieve. She also saw for the first time how almost totally destroyed the Museum now was. She'd guessed that the fire would have been uncontrollable, but not that it would have torn so fiercely or so quickly through the entire building. Looking at the corner against which she swung, she couldn't believe that the remaining upright parts of the structure still possessed sufficient strength to hold her, and she prepared herself for the worst with a prayer as she began to spin, twisting with the rope as it turned her one way and then the other. Above her, where the rope left the pole and ran over the parapet, she saw that its fibres were already alight, and that the flames were beyond both Zip's reach and her own.

She shouted to him, guessing that he was struggling through the darkness and isolation of his pain, and knowing that when it became too great for him to fight, it might simply lead him to the edge and throw him over.

'If I hear just one laugh from down there . . .' she shouted up. 'Just one, and I'll shimmy up this stupid rope and wrap it round your stupid neck until you plead for mercy. You hear me?'

Zip didn't respond and she called again, this time only his

name, repeating it until tears filled her eyes and above her he finally steadied himself and looked down.

'You hurt bad?' she called to him.

He waved his good arm and shook his head. She saw the other dangling beside him bloodsoaked along its full length, both his elbow and hand held out at unnatural angles.

He was now effectively tied to the flagpole by the rope, like a sailor lashed to the mast in a storm, and only by unwrapping himself and standing back from it would he be able to begin to lower her, using the pole as both anchor and brake instead of his useless arm.

The whole of the front parapet had by then fallen away, and the blaze at the centre of the roof was spreading relentlessly towards him. None of the rail above the alley was any longer secure, and as he relayed the rope around the pole even this creaked and juddered and threatened to break. His pants were again smouldering, but he dared not release the rope or delay Bella-Grace's descent to brush at them.

Bella-Grace went down with her eyes closed and her hands together. Isaac stood beneath her and shouted up encouraging remarks. Beside him, a space had been cleared in which, if the burning rope held, she might safely land. The rope, however, burned quickly, and when she could reach them Bella-Grace tried to squeeze out the leading flames between her praying hands. She heard her children calling up to her, and she became determined that she was now going to get herself safely down to them. She had only just resumed her praying, when high above her the flagpole suddenly snapped and the rope around it was pulled out, dropping her to the ground with a lurch. She was by then level with the first floor, and her fall was not a long one. Her landing, too, was considerably less painful than it might have been, coming down as she did on the backs of two of the firefighters standing beside Isaac.

'Lord be praised!' she cried out as the two men who broke her fall collapsed with her. She rose between them, brushed herself down and shouted for Isaac to lead her to safety.

The crowd cheered her, and she acknowledged this with a bow. Her children ran to gather around her and she kissed each of their heads. The two firefighters followed staggering in her wake. She thanked them and raised a cheer for them too. Then she stopped and turned to look up at the roof.

When the flagpole had snapped, Zip had fallen backwards, narrowly missing the pool of molten pitch which spread ahead of the fire. He landed badly, on his shattered arm, and screamed at the pain, as great again as the original break had been.

Beneath the blaze, half of the roof rose, buckled and then collapsed, most of it into the carcass of the Museum, weakening what still stood and throwing up the highest fountain of ember and flame yet seen. As if at a signal, the roof of the adjoining arcade also collapsed and threw up a second vivid shower, forcing the firefighters and their extinguisher away from the alley entrance, above which Zip now lay.

Having dragged himself beyond the reach of the burning pitch, he clung to what remained of the pole. The whole building shook beneath him and he knew that it could not be long before its destruction was complete, that its tremors were now its death-throes and that soon the last of its strength would be gone, just as he felt his own now bleeding away from him. He pulled in the frayed rope and saw that there was insufficient to lower himself to the ground, an impossible manoeuvre anyway with his shattered arm.

He peered over the edge and saw Bella-Grace with Isaac and her children. Blood from his forehead bleared his vision and he tried unsuccessfully to wipe it away. He pressed himself into the last clear space on the roof, and closing his eyes, he saw for a moment the house he had seen on the distant hillside in his dream, and the hill itself, and the river and the woods; and he smelled the grass and the scent of the flowers, and heard the joyful voices of the others all around him.

But the dream, like the Museum, now belonged to another age, both beyond retrieval, both so utterly and completely destroyed. Soon even the memory of them would become unreliable and then painful.

He was jolted from his reverie by the flame which ran forward to burn his feet. He pulled himself clear, but knew that any reprieve, however slight, could now only be temporary. Unfastening the rope, he shook it free of the flagpole and let it drop to the ground. Seeing it fall, the crowd beneath took a step back, and then in a single voice called up to him. Rather than let them believe he had fallen into the inferno below, he raised his arm. He wondered what they now expected him to do, what final superhuman feat they believed him capable of making. Pushing himself up into a sitting position, he looked down at them. He looked too at the purple bruises which had already bloomed on his arms and chest. Blood ran over them, but he dared not wipe at it for fear of the further pain this might trigger off.

Struggling to his feet he stepped out on to the last remaining length of raised parapet, a foot above the roof, eighty above the ground, and only moments away from the flames which raced towards him from every direction, burning with a new and savage rapacity, as though somehow aware of how close they were to complete victory, and to the final act of the fierce and terrible drama they had so far orchestrated, determined now to claim their solitary sacrifice where so many others had escaped them.

*

Far below, Henry Butler looked up and saw Zip outlined against the brightening sky. He saw him balance himself on his unsteady platform, his good arm extended as though calling for silence from those below, his other arm limp and bloody and twisted by his side. He saw him raise his hand in a salute to them all and then tip himself forward in a graceful, unresisted curve to the ground. He saw him wave, perhaps even smile, and then fall backwards into the furnace beneath him. He saw him cover his eyes with his hand as the rising sun caught him full in the face. Henry Butler closed his eyes and saw Zip beckon to him, and a moment later he saw himself up there beside him holding his hand, clenching it tightly and waiting for what was about to befall them both.

Around him, the onlookers were calling for Zip to jump and save himself, oblivious to the self-evident contradiction as their clamour became a chant. This rose in volume and became almost musical, spreading to the outermost reaches of the crowd, and drumming in echo until its eventual release amid the trees and open spaces of the Battery and the water beyond.

'He can't jump,' Henry Butler said to Barnum.

Barnum turned to him, his face expresionless, drained.

'There's still a chance,' Greenwood said immediately, feeling cheated as a result of his own lack of involvement in the proceedings so far, and eager now to reassert himself before it was too late and to make good his advantage for the future.

Neither Barnum nor Henry Butler, anxious though they now were for Zip to be saved, were prepared to accept what Greenwood was suggesting, and even as he began to outline his plan to them, they knew that every last chance of the night had been made and taken, and that anyone who now grasped at anything would feel only the flames between their fingers. The Museum, they knew, had only minutes to survive, perhaps only seconds, and they could not allow themselves to take their eyes from Zip on the parapet, frightened almost to blink in case they missed the true climax of the night's awful journey into day.

But determined to prove himself right and them wrong, Greenwood left them and ran to the firefighters, calling for them to gather round him. The flames were well beyond the reach of the extinguisher and they did as he ordered, partly because there was nothing else they could do, but also because none of them wished to appear to be defeated in the eyes of the crowd when something might still possibly be done to effect this one final rescue and make well-deserved heroes of them all.

Greenwood urged them to follow him to the gutted arcade, and rushing into it alone he emerged a moment later with a rope, attached to which was a heavy tarpaulin, which the men then helped him to pull out and unfold. The sheet was smouldering in places, but still essentially intact, and spread out and held high enough above the ground it would present an easy target into which someone might safely leap, even from as great a height as that at which Zip now stood above them. When the crowd understood what was happening they stopped chanting and raised another cheer, which Greenwood alone paused to acknowledge.

Seeing what he was about to attempt, Henry Butler knew that he and Barnum had been too hasty in their judgment of his chances and motives, and he ran forward to help with the tarpaulin, as did many other men from the crowd.

Fully open, however, the stiff sheet sagged at its centre, touched the ground and became useless, and it was only by reducing it to less than a quarter of its original size that it was possible to hold it high enough to break anyone's fall. Even Greenwood, who had not been entirely convinced of their chances of success in the beginning, saw now that they were likely to be thwarted. He called for more volunteers so that the sheet might be stretched tighter and given a little more elasticity.

Upon being opened, the tarpaulin revealed Barnum's advertisement for the purportedly royal and supposedly white elephant, and seeing this, both Greenwood and Henry Butler realized how improbable and unfitting a rescue net it was likely to make.

397

Bella-Grace Sprague arrived beside Barnum. 'Think they're going to do it?' she asked him.

'I'm praying for it, Bella-Grace, I'm praying for it.'

'He saved all our souls and gave his last opportunity to me. Bust his arm getting me down.' She stood with her palms together and murmured for a moment. 'Tell you what we'll see if they don't get him down,' she said.

'What's that?'

'We'll see him sprout wings and fly direct to heaven, that's what.'

'I hope so, I hope so.' Barnum smiled at the prospect.

'I'm telling you so. You think of anyone else you know who deserves it more than he does after all he's done for us tonight?'

Barnum shook his head, and for a moment he allowed himself to be convinced that what Bella-Grace had suggested might now actually happen. The sky above Zip was of the palest blue, and his ascent would be free, easy and direct, and would be witnessed by everyone below. He would rise on the warmth of their adulation and on the updraught of their cheering voices.

As Barnum watched, a flight of gulls flew in low from the river, barely avoiding the smoke and heat which caught them suddenly unawares, causing them to break their simple formation, scatter and veer off course.

'Just like them birds,' Bella-Grace said. She returned to Isaac and her children, and Elizabeth and Anna came to take her place beside Barnum. They, too, understood Greenwood's true motives in making his rescue attempt, and they watched without comment as he continued to shout his orders and exhort the exhausted firefighters, moving them one way and then another in his attempt to position them directly below Zip and at the same time to dodge the larger pieces of burning timber which continued to fall around them.

The crowd resumed calling for Zip to jump, their increasing repetition of his name like the noise of a giant flywheel as it was started up and began to run smoothly, stopping only when their throats ached and their lungs were empty.

Jeremiah Bergh and his trumpeters continued to parade among them, filling even the briefest silence with their painful music and his own righteous proclamations. Earlier, Anna had restrained Bates from picking Bergh up and pushing him head first through the big drum with which his roving band of fanatics had been joined.

By then the Museum's innards had been almost fully revealed. The fire burned less fiercely now, but only because there was less for it to consume, and because it had risen beyond its source and was pushing further and further out into thin air.

The two corner supports were still upright, and stretched between them like a tightrope between its poles was the single burning beam upon which Zip now stood and looked out over everything and everyone below.

'He's just waiting for it to happen,' Anna said. 'My only prayer is that it comes quick and painless for him.'

Elizabeth accepted the good sense of what she said and agreed with her, withholding for a moment her own last prayer for Zip's salvation.

'There must be something,' Barnum said absently, his eyes still fixed on the parapet. 'Something . . . anything . . .'

'There is,' Anna told him. 'We can watch and we can remember and we can know precisely what's happened here tonight. We can remember what he did and know exactly why he did it. It's nothing glorious, it's nothing done for profit; he did it because of who he was – not what, *who* – and he did it because of what *we* were to him, *all* of us. That's what we've got to remember and never forget.' Tears ran down her face as she spoke. 'Witness,' she said. 'Just bear witness.'

'Even me?' Barnum said, bowing his head.

'Even you. You treated him well enough. You treated us all as well as you knew how.'

Barnum shook his head.

'Look up,' Anna told him. 'That's what he wants us to do – just to look up and watch him and to *know*. Be proud for him. There's nothing else left.'

All three of them lifted their tear-stained faces together.

Henry Butler came back to them, his place at the tarpaulin taken up by ten others.

'Will it work?' Elizabeth asked him.

He looked at her but neither nodded nor shook his head. 'Do you think it stands a better chance of success just because two or three thousand people want it to succeed?'

She took his arm and linked him to them. He, too, had tears in his eyes.

Then someone close by screamed, and above them the high support sagged and snapped at its centre. Zip was thrown from his feet, falling along the beam and clinging to it, waiting until it had finally settled into its new position before once again pushing himself upright. The timber had not broken through completely, but

399

it was now burning both at its centre and at the corner beside the flagpole.

At the heart of the blaze other floors and staircases gave way, and each of these final few inner collapses sent up a rush of flame and embers to threaten Zip from behind.

Back on the ground, Cherry and Tom arrived beside the small group gathered around Barnum, and as they did so there came from within the blaze the sound of someone's hand running roughly along the entire length of a piano keyboard. Tom crossed himself.

'That's the sixth so far,' Cherry told them. 'Tom here's been countin'.'

'Six pianos,' Tom said, his sightless eyes looking directly up at Zip. 'He isn't going to jump,' he said. 'I hope you've all realized at least that much by now.'

Cherry touched his lips. 'Careful, Tom. Mr Greenwood still rushin' about down there hollerin' and shoutin' like ten men tryin' to get him to leap into his ever-lovin' waitin' arms.'

Tom smiled. 'What do you think, Mr Barnum? You think he's going to come flying down?' He flattened his palm and made it swoop like a bird.

'I don't know what to think, Tom, and that's a fact. I feel as though I'm being skinned alive down here, as though I'm the one being flayed and someone else is doing all the suffering.'

'Hallelujah!' Cherry shouted, and the call was unexpectedly echoed by a dozen others as Jeremiah Bergh marched back towards them at the head of his trumpeting spinsters.

'Hallelujah indeed, Barnum! Hallelujah indeed! Nemesis, almighty Nemesis!'

It was clear to them all that Bergh had chosen his moment well to deliver his sanctimonious coup de grâce. His musicians slowed down and then marched on the spot around him. To help counter this attack, Henry Butler, Anna, Elizabeth, Tom and Cherry closed more tightly around Barnum.

'Look at him!' Jeremiah Bergh shouted. 'Look at him and know! Look at him and see how the Lord doth punish a sinner, a sinner as persistent and contemptuous as Mr High and Mighty Barnum has been among us! A sinner who scorns the righteous in their guidance of him, in their pointing out to him the dire and irrevocable error of his ways!'

Tom threw an empty punch towards him.

'Ha! Violence! Violence and scorn! Violence and scorn and a paid-up army of niggers to do his dirty work for him!'

Having restrained Tom, Cherry then threw a punch which knocked Jeremiah Bergh to the ground. Elizabeth took his place ready to throw the next.

Disappointed that there was no blood upon his lips to show the crowd, Jeremiah Bergh rose to his feet, shook his Bible and marched off.

'Did I get him, Hack?' Tom asked.

'You got him, Tom. Fair and square and sent him runnin'.'

Tom cradled his fist and smiled. Barnum took his hand and held it.

A further scream from within the crowd sent all their eyes back up to where Zip still stood.

The support had fallen even further, and to keep himself upright, Zip now had to stand at an angle, leaning into the slope as though into a strong wind.

Beneath him, Greenwood continued to exhort him to jump. He knew that Zip understood what he was attempting because he'd looked directly down at him and watched what he was doing.

The spar now burned to within only a few feet on either side of Zip, and he shifted occasionally to keep himself at the centre of the clear wood.

'Jump!' Greenwood shouted. 'For God's sake jump! We can catch you; it'll hold!' He cursed him beneath his breath.

Zip didn't even acknowledge him; he was looking back out to where Barnum and the others still stood. He could see them all quite clearly, and moving his gaze from one to the other, he recited each of their names, savouring them, and then continuing more rapidly as the tremors beneath his feet rose up into his legs.

Far beneath him the small group was joined by the Albinos and the Aztecs, by Fortuna and René and their son, and by Herman, all of them looking directly up at him.

At the centre of the group, Anna and Elizabeth drew them all together, standing as though they were about to have their photograph taken and they all needed to squeeze within the compass of the exposed plate. They linked arms, and when Anna was certain they were all present, she told them all to say Zip's name. The instruction puzzled some of them, but they did as she asked.

'Just say it,' she instructed them. 'Don't shout it, just say it, nice and peaceful.'

They all said it, falteringly at first, like the first line of a hymn sung in a near empty church, but then with a single voice, harmonious and exact.

Around them the crowd fell silent, as though honouring this prior and more powerful claim on Zip's attention, on his own last few seconds.

'He hears us,' Barnum said, indicating Zip.

They all went on calling, intoning the name, and all around them the silence spread outwards, like crystals of ice over the surface of a shallow pond, until soon the only other voice still raised was that of Greenwood as he continued to shout his orders to the men holding the tarpaulin, many of whom were now close to abandoning it as it too began to burn and fall in tatters from their hands.

High above them flew a second line of gulls, this time unwavering in their course, appearing from below to pass directly through the flames on their way inland.

Then Zip raised both his arms, and a moment later, as though even this simple gesture had been too much for it, the timber upon which he stood broke completely in half, the flames rushing up to meet at its vanished centre until Zip himself was finally caught in them and briefly lost to sight.

Above him the birds altered their course and spun in a slow, close circle above his head.

Below, the spell of reverential silence was at last broken and scream followed scream followed scream.

Zip appeared to hang for a moment where he stood, held up by the flames and suspended above by the circling birds, Icarus-like in the miraculous balance between his fall and his impossible resurrection, then calling out as an even greater fountain of flame rose roaring up from the ground to engulf him.

The screaming finally died with this last exhausted explosion, and after it there came a deep and impenetrable silence, a silence that fell upon everyone as though they had all simultaneously checked their own beating hearts, creating a powerful and all-consuming vacuum into which their every last prayer and hope had been instantly drawn and then extinguished.

Looking up, and shielding his eyes from the growing light of day, only Barnum saw the solitary gull which still circled where Zip had been standing, and after a further minute had passed, he said, 'Amen,', and one by one, as though the word were a baton of release and recognition passed among them, everyone around him said the same.

30

TWELVE MORE HOURS passed before, in the falling dusk of that late summer's day, Barnum was able to cross the divide and wander aimlessly and disconsolately amid the wreckage and the ruins of his crushed and shattered kingdom. He felt as he would have felt at the funeral of everyone he had ever loved, and upon taking his first few steps towards the still smouldering heaps of ash and rubble he wept unashamedly into his handkerchief.

Throughout the day, the crowd on Broadway had increased considerably, and a great many wept with him as he finally broke free of them and walked on alone, guided by the firefighters and kept away from those few parts of the building which were still standing but ready to collapse at any moment. The noise of this other weeping amplified Barnum's own, and upon hearing it he knew that his own grief and sense of loss were far greater than anyone would ever understand.

He looked down upon the revealed hole of the Museum basement and was reminded for a moment of the painting of the mortally wounded Wolfe high on the Plain of Abraham, turning in his own agony and peering down into the still smoking crater of his timely and appropriate grave. Wiping his eyes, he found himself shaking, and stood for a moment until he was able to compose himself and continue.

Zip's broken body had been found and taken out several hours earlier, and when Barnum had gone forward to lift the sheet and look upon him for a final time he'd been stopped by one of the men walking beside the stretcher. Even this small denial seemed to him greater than he would ever now be able to bear.

Anna and Elizabeth had stayed with him throughout the day, and they offered now to accompany him back into the ruins. They had been unable to clean themselves properly, and their dresses and faces bore the marks of their ordeal. Those who had been more seriously burned had been taken to the Hudson Street hospital, treated and then allowed to return. Only Captain Bates had been injured badly enough to warrant the physicians calling for his admission to the hospital overnight, but Bates had refused and they were unable to persuade him to remain. Returning to Broadway, he had waited with the others and looked out with them upon the ruins of their home and their livelihoods, of their past and their present and their future.

Barnum declined Anna and Elizabeth's offer and went forward alone. He was not yet sure of how he might respond to any after-shock of the blaze; he was not yet sure that he wouldn't reach the building, touch its vanished outline and burst immediately into flames himself.

Prayers were offered up, and throughout the day there was a wailing in the crowd like that put up by mourners at a wake.

As he neared the smouldering ruins, he paused and looked around him, at the buildings standing untouched and intact on either side, and then above him at the streaks of scarlet underpinning the evening clouds as the sun rolled slowly down into the west.

Throughout the day, other fire extinguishers had arrived, but all too late to save anything – there only to subdue the steaming wreckage and make it safe, so that he might now enter and wander among it, feeling as though he were the sole survivor of a great cataclysm whereby the surface of the earth had been torn open and destroyed, and he alone had been spared to bear witness to the act. The words of Jeremiah Bergh were ringing in his ears as he made his way into the Museum by the gap where its entrance had once stood and proudly proclaimed its magnificent contents to the passing world.

The bodies of several other, unidentifiable creatures had also been found, and some confusion had arisen as to which of these had been dead before the blaze and which had perished within it.

The ground floor had finally collapsed under the weight of the debris from above, and the basement beneath now lay revealed to him, several feet deep in its grey sludge of saturated ash and embers, and this topped with splinters of shattered glass, which shone in the wet and in the last rays of the sinking sun like dew upon freshly tilled earth.

Ensuring that it was safe to descend the stone steps down into the basement, Barnum made his way to where the aquarium had once stood, surprised as he approached to see his own badly charred desk standing before it. Only the cast iron palm supports of the tank were still in place; the glass had long since shattered, spilling out the water to play its own small part in the final quenching of the flames. He searched for the remains of the hippopotamus, determined to see it before he climbed back out of the building.

Water still dripped from the few warm timbers above him, and passing his desk he saw ahead of him a glint of gold atop a low mound. He forced his way through to this until he came face to face with himself, with the lifeless eyes and cheerful grin of his own shining face. And even as he looked upon this and tried to decide whether or not some small thanks should be offered up for the bust's survival – it might, after all, have melted in the intense heat at the centre of the blaze – more water dripped heavily upon it and washed it clean, streaking its cheeks and scouring its coating of ash into a goatee at its chin.

He was about to reach forward and check if it might be possible for a sling to be lowered and for it to be hoisted up to the street – what, after all, could be more fitting than this shining golden likeness rising grinning through the embers and the smoke to dazzle everyone with its brilliance and suggestion of rebirth and hope for the future? – when he saw for the first time the true nature of the mound upon which the bust now rested.

He looked hard at this, and even when he had satisfied himself as to what it was, he went on looking at it, oblivious to everything else around him and to the noise of the crowd above. For there, a few feet from where it had once floated in its tank, flat on its belly and with its legs splayed beneath it, lay the hippopotamus, its skull smashed flat by the bust which had plummetted down upon it, and which it now wore as a gaudy, mocking crown, its jaws and cheeks buried in the ash, this grotesque new head sitting squarely upon its shoulders as though it were its own.

Barnum stared, unable to draw himself away from it. It must have come down at the same time as his desk, and way down beneath it, the hippopotamus must have just then stepped free of its shattered tank, either to boil or to burn, or perhaps even to find its own unlikely way up out of the conflagration.

The dripping water hit the carcass and turned to steam. The grey skin was drawn taut over the bloated bulk, and along its flanks blisters the size of upturned soup bowls also burst and steamed.

Barnum took off his hat, held it to his chest and said a word of grace for the unfortunate creature, shaken by the shame of having made it the scapegoat for so many of his own recent misfortunes, and shamed too at the way in which it had finally met its end, whether thwarted in its attempts to escape or released at a blow from its own unbearable agonies.

He replaced his hat, and abandoning all thought of raising the bust, he turned from the corpse and made his way to the steps that would lead him back up to the street and away from the crushed and flattened ruins of his temple.

Passing his desk, he stumbled and fell. He didn't injure himself, but as he pushed himself upright, he stumbled again, and this time he came face to face with the slender leering grin of the mechanical cobra, coiled amid a heap of black timber, washed clean and glinting in the last red light of the day, extended and rigid at the furthest point of its strike, its fangs and tongue only inches from his eyes, fixed and immobile where the heated activation of its mechanism had at last abandoned it on this final empty lunge into the flames.